The Student Body

The Student Body

A NOVEL

Jane Harvard

 VILLARD   NEW YORK

Library of Congress Cataloging-in-Publication Data

Harvard, Jane.
    The student body / Jane Harvard.
      p.   cm.
    ISBN 0-679-44858-6 (alk. paper)
    I. Title.
  PS3557.R2659S78   1998
  813'.54—dc21   97-14691

Random House website address: www.randomhouse.com

Printed in the United States of America on acid-free paper

98765432

First Edition

Book design by Caroline Cunningham

For Holly Adiele,
John DeNike,
Elizabeth Fargnoli,
and
Penny Spencer—
teachers who inspire
belief in public education

Indulge yourself. Experience unparalleled pleasure in the form of two Ivy League blondes. Generous gentlemen only.

The ad, which appeared last fall in the now defunct Providence *Eagle,* attracted the attention of a number of not necessarily generous gentlemen in the Providence police force. They had been tipped off by officials of Brown University that some female students were possibly being coerced into performing sex for money. Last week, after a five-month undercover investigation, the police announced two arrests that not only cracked the case but stunned the Brown community, including the administration, alumni and parents.

—*Time*, March 24, 1986

The growing Brown University prostitution scandal sent shock waves through the Ivy League yesterday as investigators disclosed they had seized more than 100 photographs of nude women. . . .

Embarrassed Brown officials were tight-lipped about the latest developments.

Brown vice president Robert Reichley would only say yesterday: "These things occur, and hopefully they don't occur too often."

—*New York Post*, March 13, 1986

The Student Body

1

Toni Isaacs stood in indecision beneath a flashing neon marquee that promised "Live Girls NUDE!" and "Fun, Fun, FUN!" Holding a glove over her nose and mouth to block out the stench of urine and cheap wine, she considered forgetting the whole thing and heading straight home to Cambridge. It was too late for dinner now—all the Harvard dining halls would be closed—but at least she could make a dent in her reading for tomorrow's classes.

As the club's heavy steel door swung open, she took a quick step back. A beefy bouncer in a stained tuxedo shirt exited in a cloud of pulsating music and cigarette smoke. He held the door open, a cigar dangling on his lower lip, and jerked his head sideways, beckoning her inside. Chilled by the icy February wind and mesmerized by the rows of hair plugs that dotted the man's forehead like so many ants invading a picnic, Toni found herself drawn forward. Over his shoulder she could make out a drooping banner that read "College Girl Revue—Every Tuesday!" No doubt about it, this was Boston's legendary Kittycat Klub.

In the foyer, a sullen woman checked IDs and collected the ten-dollar cover charge from behind a thick Plexiglas shield. She waved

Toni through without either; apparently, every night was ladies' night at the Kittycat. Toni pushed aside a beaded curtain and blinked for a moment, her eyes adjusting to the dim red light and flashes of strobe. A long chrome-and-Formica bar bisected the room; metal and vinyl chairs were grouped around high tables. The place reminded her of an airport waiting room—if you could imagine a flight lounge adorned with posters of Marilyn Monroe, cowgirl twins, and other pinup dreams.

Men lined either side of the bar, spaced as evenly as strangers on a subway car and looking every bit as ordinary. One, his hair carefully arranged across his gleaming head in an unconvincing comb-over, reminded Toni of her high school chemistry teacher. A good-looking yuppie in a charcoal-gray suit fanned the edges of a foreign-policy journal; beside him sat a modish leather satchel. As they stirred drinks and sucked on ice cubes, the men kept their eyes glued to the stage at the end of the bar. There, accompanied by a disco version of the *Sesame Street* theme song, a girl—it was hard to think of her as a woman—pedaled in circles on a large tricycle. She was clutching an oversize multicolored lollipop; her bra and cotton underpants were decidedly unsexy.

Though the Kittycat Klub seemed a world away from the ivy-and-brick campus where Toni had spent the last two and a half years, it was only a few minutes by subway from Harvard College to Boston's Combat Zone. It was hard to believe that this concentration of strip joints, porno theaters, sex shops, and adult bookstores was so close to the tony theater district and historic Boston Common. No wonder the city's civic planners and upstanding citizens were embarrassed by the Zone, though Toni could imagine some of them in its darker corners, nursing a whisky and soda while admiring the talents of a bar girl or lap dancer.

The frenzied disco beat continued as the girl dismounted, neatly depositing her lollipop in the trike's white, tasseled basket. Adopting a studied pout, she regarded each of the men in turn and began to move her hips back and forth to the music, pivoting slowly until her back was to the crowd. Then she leaned forward at the waist, showing off her muscled buttocks and shaking them before spinning around. With her hands at her breasts, she tossed back her head in a pantomime of ecstasy, eliciting a chorus of whistles and shouted encouragement from the audience. After pretending to toy with herself a bit, she reached back to unhook her cotton bra and began strutting down the bar. As she passed, men obligingly shoved bills under the elastic of her underpants.

"Hey." A redheaded woman in jeans and a Northeastern sweatshirt nudged Toni. "There you are. You called earlier, right?"

Toni nodded.

"Well, then," the young woman said, beckoning her toward the back, "follow me." As the pair passed the bar, a few men tore their eyes away from the topless schoolgirl writhing on stage long enough to give Toni the once-over.

The redhead pushed through an unmarked door near the men's room and hurried down a long corridor filled with cases of beer and janitorial supplies. Toni followed, and they ended up in a small, square room with an industrial-size sink, a few chairs, and a large mirror propped on a Lucite table against a wall.

Before Toni could protest, she found herself being pulled across the room. "You're pretty," the woman said, gesturing toward the mirror. "That's good." Together, the two regarded their reflections. With her large, slightly tilted eyes and smooth, velvety cocoa skin, Toni was the more attractive. She wore her hair natural and short, the closely cropped curls accentuating her high cheekbones. Her full mouth was generously curved, though slightly marred by a scar she'd gotten falling out of a tree while spying on the neighbors when she was six. That, to hear her mother tell it, was when it all began.

The other woman, in contrast, was thin, pale, and startlingly young-looking. It was hard to imagine her onstage projecting the sexual abandon of a coed stripper. She cast an appraising glance at Toni. "Your figure's nice. Full breasts, high butt. Men love that."

"Really?" Toni smiled weakly. "Thanks."

Her interviewer perched on the edge of a stool and held up her hands, forming a frame through which to view Toni. "The question is how to market you. We've already got an eager cheerleader, a worldly sorority pledge, an icy homecoming queen. But since you're black, I think we should play up—"

"Uh, actually . . ." Toni interrupted, taking a seat across from the woman. She didn't really care to hear what aspect of her race and sex she should play up. "This is moving a little faster than I—"

"That's me." The woman laughed. "I tend to do that. Sorry. Oh, yeah"—she extended a hand—"I'm Karen. From Northeastern."

"And I'm Toni," she said as they shook. "Toni Isaacs." Karen had a strong, businesslike handshake. Reassured by this, Toni plunged right in. "Karen, I have to be honest with you. When I called and said I wanted to talk about the College Girl Revue, I guess I let you think that I wanted to audition."

Karen smiled expectantly.

"But that isn't true." Toni paused briefly, noticing Karen's smile shift almost imperceptibly. "I'm a reporter for my school newspaper, and I'm doing a story on college students who work in the adult entertainment industry." She looked Karen in the eye and delivered her pitch with rapid-fire enthusiasm. "If you have five minutes, I'd love to talk with you about it. I promise not to use your real name. Otherwise, I apologize for wasting your time." Toni held her breath.

After a moment the Northeastern student shrugged. "What do I get if I do?" she asked.

Toni felt a surge of excitement and leaned forward.

"Unfortunately, I'm not authorized to give you anything. It's just a student-run paper, and we can't really afford to compensate our sources"—she turned her palms upward—"much as I'd like to." She suddenly felt a bit ashamed. It wasn't as if Karen was trying to hustle her. Toni rapidly added up the money in her wallet. Two ten-dollar bills, a single, and a handful of change. She had planned on using one of the tens to buy a roll of quarters to do laundry. But she could offer the other. Or both, if absolutely necessary.

Karen shifted in her seat and Toni scrambled to come up with something. "We're trying to perform a service for our readers," she explained. "They're students just like you and me, and they need to know your story."

To Toni's surprise, Karen seemed to buy this. "Sure." She shrugged again. "I'll do it. Just thought I'd check to see if there's any money to be made. Never hurts to ask, right?"

"Right." Toni dug in her bag, dragged out her reporter's pad, and flipped it open, doing her best to block the Harvard seal on the cover. "Thanks, Karen," she said. "I really appreciate this."

"No problem." Karen folded her hands neatly, the perfect attentive interviewee. "I don't mind talking about what I do," she con-fided. "In fact, everybody around here says you can't shut me up."

Toni smiled.

"First of all, I really am a college student. I'm in the co-op program at Northeastern." Toni nodded, and Karen continued. "I try to make sure all the girls in the College Girl Revue are students—truth in ad-vertising, you know? I mean, a lot of them are in beauty school, but that's not stretching it too far, I guess." She and Toni shared a chuckle.

"How did you get started?" Toni asked.

"Well, there's only one reason any of the girls do this, including me, and that's the money. You get paid fifty bucks per show, plus tips. Two shows a night and it adds up. Sometimes as much as five hun-dred dollars."

Out onstage the thumping bass stopped, and was replaced by a roar of male voices: the end of a set. Karen glanced at her watch. "I gotta start getting ready." She crossed to the lighted makeup mirror and started to dab glittery eye shadow on her lids. "Plus there are ex-tras sometimes—you know, like the shower room and the champagne lounge. Or whipped-cream wrestling. And outside work. Since it's all under the table, it's my own private income stream. No one controls it but me."

Toni's pencil flew over the page. "Do you save it?"

Karen laughed. "I wish! No, every dollar goes for expenses. Rent, food, clothes—not that I'm wearing any designer fashions. And tu-ition." She dipped her pinkie into an acrylic pot and spread a layer of sheer gloss across her lower lip. "There's not really any other way to swing it."

She stood up and slipped out of her jeans. She was wearing a G-string. Catching Toni's stare, she said, "Yes, I'm a natural redhead." She shook her head. "Worst part of this job is the bikini wax."

Embarrassed, Toni glanced down at her notes. "Uh, Karen," she faltered, "you said something about 'outside work.' Did you mean ex-tra money from customers? Outside the club?"

Karen stepped into a short cheerleader skirt with crisp blue pleats and gold inserts. "Well, right," she said, pulling it on and zipping up the side. "Extra money from having dates with certain customers. 'Dates' meaning sex."

She yanked off her sweatshirt and wriggled out of her sports bra. Toni had to admit that her breasts were impressive: evenly round, and as pert as Karen herself. She squeezed some adhesive from a tube onto two tasseled pasties and affixed them over her nipples. "Gotta wait for these to dry." She gestured toward the table. "Can you hand me the gold sweater with the blue letter on it?"

"What's it like?" Toni asked, hunting through the clothes piled on the table. "Finding clients, I mean. And spending time with them."

"Finding them isn't hard. I only go with guys from the club. And not the first time I see them." Karen smiled and caught the sweater Toni tossed her. "Though I suppose if Tom Cruise walked in here I'd modify my policy—if he'd modify his."

The sweater muffled her voice as she pulled it over her head. "Sometimes it's kind of fun, looking over the candidates and seeing which ones qualify. Married guys are the best, since they have responsibilities and aren't going to screw with you after they screw you." She ran a brush through her hair. "Sometimes they take off their wedding rings, but you can usually tell by the tan line."

Toni heard tepid applause and a moment later a sweaty dancer wearing a green bikini bottom and Mardi Gras beads hurried in, a load of discarded sequined clothes in her arms. She gave Toni a quick, cool glance.

"Hey, Ruby," Karen said brightly, working her hair into pigtails. "Good crowd out there?"

"Buncha creeps." The woman plopped down in front of the mirror and started slapping at her face with cottonballs smeared in Noxzema.

"Oh, well," Karen answered. "Another day, another dollar."

"And another set of dickheads," Ruby muttered. Toni felt conspicuously overdressed in her wool coat and cable-knit sweater while a stranger sat topless inches away, removing makeup in fierce strokes.

"Ruby, this is Toni," came the belated introduction. "She's writing a story on the place for her school paper." Karen gathered up her blue-and-gold pompoms and bounced toward the bar. "See you, Toni," she called over her shoulder. "Send me a copy of your article." The pounding music segued to the theme song from *Fame,* and with that she was gone.

After a moment Toni turned in her chair to find Ruby checking her out. "A story for your school paper," Ruby finally said. "How cute."

With slow, deliberate movements, Ruby knocked a Lucky Strike out of a crumpled package and lit up. "I won't offer you one, because I'm sure you don't smoke, right?" She jerked her head. "You don't smoke, do coke, or fuck on the first date. A real lady."

Toni kept quiet. It would be stupid to antagonize her.

Ruby blew a smoke ring. "You college girls don't even know what time it is, do you?"

Toni stifled the urge to roll her eyes. So Ruby hated naïve, privileged college girls. Fair enough. If that was what Ruby wanted, that's what she'd get. "I don't know much about, um, exotic dancing," Toni stammered. "Karen was telling me a few things. But I'd really like to hear your perspective."

"Yeah, right," Ruby said. "My perspective. You and Dan Rather."

"Well, sure, Karen's been helpful, but . . ." Toni paused, assessing the older woman. What was it her Nana always said? *Go out on a limb—that's where the fruit is.* She decided to risk it. "Her situation's different from yours."

Ruby bristled as expected. "Got that right," she spat. "Karen's destined for better things. She's just doing her time. This isn't really who she is." She waved away the truisms. "Me, on the other hand, I'm a lifer. Is that it?"

"You tell me."

"I wouldn't tell you my bra size." Ruby turned her back to Toni and took another savage drag on the butt.

"Forty-two double D," Toni guessed, before she could stop herself. "Or did you mean before the surgery?"

Ruby spun slowly around. The smoke seemed to pile up in the thick air as she stared Toni down. Toni held her breath; the cigarette burned unattended in the stripper's hand, a long ash threatening to singe her leg. Ruby finally made a harsh, rusty sound that took Toni a moment to recognize as laughter. "You're all right, kid," she said, nodding. "You see shit and you say it. That takes nerve."

Or a death wish, Toni thought, easing the pent-up breath out the side of her mouth.

"So what do you want to know?" Ruby asked, flicking the ash across the room a nanosecond before it dropped. Her tone now was as close to friendly as Toni guessed it ever got. "I've been doing this for twenty-two years. Worked in thirteen cities." She indicated her tanned, too-perfect globes. "Had three sets of tits."

"Wow." Toni wasn't quite sure how to respond. She leaned forward, her notebook sliding to the floor. "That's impressive. You must know more than a little about dancing."

"Dancing!" Ruby snorted. "This isn't dancing. This is getting naked and shaking your booty for a bunch of losers." She grabbed the trailing corner of a false eyelash and reattached it. "No, I take that back. It's trying to get the waldos into the special rooms, trying to get them to date you up, give you presents, that kind of thing. It's a big tease." She scrutinized her reflection for a second, then began applying fresh eye shadow, shiny copper this time.

Toni tried to keep her expression neutral, but must have failed. The other woman's tone suddenly grew sharper. "Look," she said, "you do what it takes to survive. Yeah, I've worked escort. And maybe I did a few incalls here and there. Don't judge me, Little Miss Harvard. Some of your classmates work in places just like this. Worse."

"What do you mean?" Finding Karen at the Kittycat had been surprising enough; beauty-school dropouts were more what she had expected.

Ruby slapped on a pasty that had slipped. "I *mean* Harvard students working as escorts. Outcalls only, of course." Noting Toni's blank look, she sighed. "Don't you know *jack* about escort services?" She spelled it out: "You run an ad in the paper, saying you'll spend time with lonely businessmen. Incalls mean they come to your place—that's dangerous, you get a lot of cops. Outcalls mean you go to them. Usually their hotel room."

"You place an ad—is that legal?"

"Yeah, it's legal to place the ad," Ruby explained, "and it's legal for them to pay for your time. Whatever arrangements you make on your own are up to you."

"And you know for a fact that actual Harvard students are involved?"

Ruby shrugged. "Why not?" She pulled on a skintight sheath of faux leopardskin. "You hear things. Ask your friends." She took a long puff on her cigarette. "Maybe some of them will turn out to have a little secret."

Now, that would be a scoop. If Toni could actually meet someone, get an interview with a genuine Harvard prostitute—anonymously, of course—it would make her career as a journalist. The story would probably get picked up on the AP wire, and after that, who knows? *The New York Times; The Washington Post; Time; Newsweek.* Adam Steiner would have to give her the best assignments at the *Crimson.* It would almost make up for losing the election for news editor.

Toni pulled herself up short. "Hey, what makes you so sure I go to Harvard?"

"Puh-*lease.*" Ruby hiked up her breasts, arranging them into an impressive display of cleavage. "I may earn my living with my boobs, but I'm no moron. It's on your pad." She pointed to the notebook on the floor. "You know, the coat-of-arms thing. What's it mean?"

Toni picked up the pad. "*Veritas,*" she said, glancing at the cover. " 'Truth,' in Latin."

"Yeah, right. Truth." Ruby laughed. "That, and the fact you talk so fast."

Noticing Toni's crestfallen look, Ruby laughed again, almost kindly this time. "Get going, Veritas. Write your story. Have a nice life." With that, she stood up, dumped her cigarette into a can of Diet Coke, and sauntered back into the lounge.

/ / /

As her classmate shut his eyes and leaned down to kiss her, Tara Sheridan wondered why voluptuous moments like this had been so rare in her Harvard career. Steve Massoudfar was the very definition of Cool Boyfriend. Dark-eyed, handsome, lean—and he didn't try too hard. Here he was on her bed, his chest pressed against her own, the sleeves of his white cotton shirt grazing her bare arms. His five o'clock shadow brushed sharply against her smooth cheek as he nuzzled her ears. He trailed one finger along her rib cage under her silk blouse.

Like any new acquaintance, he glanced around her room, taking it in, checking out the books on her shelves and on the floor next to the bed. "You really like thick ones, don't you, Tara?" he asked, hefting a fat volume she had borrowed from Widener Library.

"That's sweet, Steve," she commented. "How did you get into Harvard, anyway?"

"Not enough rich Persians applied my year." He examined the title. "*Kristin Lavrans*—something. What is this?"

"*Kristin Lavransdatter.*" She sighed. "You should read it. The woman who wrote it won the Nobel Prize."

"What's it about?" he asked, flipping through the book.

"Just your basic girl-meets-fjord story."

Tara had been eating in the dining hall that evening, with only a battered copy of *Don Quixote* for company, when Steve slid his tray in front of hers and took a seat across the table. Although she had developed the habit of eating alone in recent months, she tucked a bookmark in her novel and casually put it aside. They knew each other in the vague, kiss-kiss way that passed for meaningful interaction in Eliot House. He seemed more pleasant than average.

"For a class?" Steve had asked, glancing at the secondhand paperback.

"No," she answered. "Just for fun."

He looked at her dubiously. "You're reading a four-hundred-year-old novel, in Spanish, for fun?"

She shrugged. "Widener was out of Harlequins."

He looked puzzled, briefly—Californians weren't known for appreciating irony—then smiled widely and laughed. "You rule," he said.

Tara felt attracted to him, even though she generally didn't pay much attention to male undergrads. Their attempts to act like grown-ups rarely masked their underlying vapidity. Tara didn't think she was especially smart, but she was appalled at how stupid many of her classmates appeared—almost deliberately so.

Tara hadn't always been a cynic. She'd arrived freshman year as enthusiastic and optimistic as any other high school valedictorian. But, like the boys of Eliot House, Harvard had never measured up to her expectations.

Her conversation with Steve had flowed along in the emptying dining hall. Steve called L.A., his hometown, "Tehran-geles," because so many Iranians lived on the city's west side. Tara liked the play on words. He was charming; his goofiness was sexy. They dawdled an extra hour in the dining hall, then ambled back to her room. After some aimless chatter, they found themselves on her bed. Tara didn't plan to have sex with him—but she wasn't ruling it out, either. She didn't know when such an attractive opportunity would arise again.

Like a raccoon, Steve shifted his attention to something shiny on the floor. He swiped up the thin plastic binder that bound her term paper.

" 'Paul Tillich's Sense of Individual Responsibility,' " he recited. " 'By Tara Sheridan.' "

"Boring," she intoned. "Forget it, Steve."

"No way! I want to check this out." He held the paper out of her reach and inspected it. "You took that Kessler class? 'Ethics and the Modern Man'?"

" 'Ethics and the Modern World,' " she corrected. "And you can drop my little opus back on the floor where it belongs."

He flipped through it. "Hey, you got an A. That's awesome. She's supposed to be really harsh."

"It's just something I wrote one night. Put it down, Steve, or I'm sending you back to finishing school." He laughed and pulled off his shirt.

Tara had lied, of course. The paper wasn't just something she wrote one night. She'd worked damned hard on it.

Though Tara didn't think too much of her fellow students, Professor Kessler was another story. Shulamit Kessler was a real mind, an old-fashioned European intellectual. Her work was sound, well-researched, and serious, her writing a wonder of lucidity. People said that German universities used her translation of Kant because it was clearer than the original. Kessler's was the first Harvard class that hadn't disappointed Tara.

That afternoon, Tara had stopped by the professor's office to pick up her fall term paper from Kessler's secretary. The elderly professor herself had emerged; ushering Tara into her private office, she gestured her toward one of the armchairs and eased herself into the other.

Glancing around the room, Tara noticed a framed photo of Kessler with Aung San Suu Kyi. Next to it, a small snapshot showed a prosperous-looking European couple—Kessler's parents, lost at Mauthausen in the last days of World War II.

"Tara," Kessler began, "your paper was excellent. Your argument was strong and your voice was clear." Tara felt pride wash over her; she knew she was blushing. "Each year," Kessler continued, "there are one or two students who surprise me with their grasp of this material. Of course, I would like it if excellent students such as yourself spoke more in class."

Tara briefly examined her feet.

"But I can understand those who keep their opinions to themselves. Your concentration is Romance languages, yes?"

Tara nodded.

"You find that very interesting, no doubt. But if you have an interest in political philosophy, we would welcome you to the department, and in my graduate seminar this semester."

Tara wasn't sure how to respond. Professors rarely put themselves out this way. If the invitation had come two weeks before . . .

"Niebuhr's theories of moral choice are not your number one concern, perhaps," Kessler said pleasantly.

"Oh, they are. I mean, I do like Niebuhr," Tara began. She couldn't explain to Kessler why her academic career had become irrelevant. "I guess I haven't given much thought to the possibility, Professor Kessler."

"You are very capable, Tara. You would do well in a rigorous area of study." Kessler rose, and Tara followed her example. "At the very least, I am glad finally to know the face behind the paper. If you wish to take up my offer, simply let Jim know so that we can amend your study card. You've only missed one session, so I'm sure you would have no trouble catching up on the reading."

It had been a highly perplexing day altogether. For once, Tara's Harvard experience seemed to justify the years of buildup. Unfortunately, one good day was not enough. Things had been bad for a long time, and they had recently turned worse. Now that she had attracted the attention of Professor Kessler and Steve Massoudfar, her decision would be harder to implement, but she saw no alternative.

Steve was speaking again, with that sexy L.A. rhythm. Staring at his winsome face, she reached up and ran her fingers through his thick black hair, grateful for one final distraction.

/ / /

At 7:20 A.M., Sterling Kwok dropped four lumps of sugar into the delicate cup and stirred. The faint chime of the silver spoon against the Limoges, the rich aroma of the French roast—these barely registered in his consciousness. Even at Harvard, where students and faculty alike were known for their overcommitment, Kwok was an uncommonly busy man: most of his days, and many a night, were spent in University Hall as dean of students. His remaining energies were directed toward Adams House; as house master, he was charged with guarding the health and welfare of the three hundred–plus students who had gotten into one of Harvard's most desirable dorms.

A handsome, elegant man in his early forties, Kwok should have been at the top of his game. Since his divorce, however, he certainly hadn't felt that way. He lifted the cup and took a sip, savoring the coffee's reassuring warmth. Another day of battle over the crumbling towers of academe. Thank God it was Friday.

Kwok smiled wryly. He had not always been so dour; he could still remember a time when his life consisted of something beyond mind-numbing meetings and professional hand-holding. Once, the world had seemed full of possibilities. But that had been nearly twenty years ago, back when he was newly married, full of hope, and practically giddy—after his stuffy Hong Kong upbringing—from breathing Harvard's very air. Since then the world had changed, and Harvard along with it. Now his marriage was over, the private details of his divorce settlement had been splashed across the front page of the *Crimson*, and the institution to which he had dedicated his life appeared to be as venal and self-serving as the students who flocked to it.

The bottom line was that Harvard needed money to thrive. More and more money, all the time. Though the school had the largest endowment of any private university in the world, it wasn't enough. Everyone knew *that*. Faculty wanted smaller classes but wouldn't teach longer hours. Students wanted to unionize all the blue- and pink-collar workers but could not fathom that their tuition might increase as a result. Alumni wanted green lawns and world-class libraries, but at a discount. In short, everybody wanted more, but no one wanted to pay for it.

Six years ago, the university Board of Overseers and the Harvard Corporation had turned over management of Harvard's huge endowment to a new entity: the Harvard Investment Portfolio Committee, now known to all as the Portfolio. The three officers—Gustavus Mims, Philip van Rensselaer, and Lloyd Buckley—were handed the keys to the kingdom and entrusted with the task of making more out of less, in whatever way they saw fit.

Soon after its formation, the Portfolio came up with a clever idea. The university sponsored research; why not sell it? Professors wanted to make money; why not let them? The world was becoming globalized, computerized, rationalized, capitalized. Why shouldn't a leading institution of learning get a piece of the action? In the ensuing entrepreneurial scramble, it seemed that Kwok was the only one who voiced the dangers of such a plan.

Leaning forward, Kwok punched the intercom on his telephone. "Mrs. Hale," he addressed his secretary politely, his accent giving him a courtly air, "would you be so good as to bring in the day's papers?"

A second later a discreet knock sounded on the door, and the formidable Mrs. Hale—another chronic early bird—entered softly. Placing a stack of newspapers and a large padded envelope at his elbow, she quickly scooped up the two letters in his mail tray and beat a soundless retreat.

Kwok glanced at the pile. There were the usual dailies of the well-informed Bostonian—*The New York Times, The Wall Street Journal, The Boston Globe*—plus a few remnants of his Anglophilic Hong Kong upbringing: *The Economist,* the *Manchester Guardian Weekly,* and the *Hong Kong Daily Mail.* At the bottom of the stack sat the *Boston Phoenix* and the *Harvard Crimson,* which he read because they were what students read. Information was the prerequisite to damage control, and damage control was, of course, his primary duty. If anything went wrong, from the football team's losing the Yale game to an explosion in the chemistry labs, Kwok was there in his expensive English tailoring to deflect any questions in his expensive English accent.

His mechanical rifling through the *Crimson* turned up a peculiar story. He skimmed, with more curiosity than usual, a page 3 news item:

TWELVE DANCES A WEEK TO
MAKE ENDS MEET

By Antonia Isaacs

"Susan C.," a student at a private university in the Boston area, took a part-time job last year to keep herself in school: stripping twelve times a week at a club in the Combat

Zone. Her income, which goes to tuition and living expenses, is supplemented by occasional prostitution. "Right now, sex is the most valuable kind of labor I can sell," she said as she donned a cheerleader outfit and prepared for the night's work. "And it's the only way I see to get through college, so I can get where I want to go in life."

What is surprising, or perhaps not surprising at all, is that Susan is not destitute or the victim of abuse. She grew up in a Boston suburb, the eldest daughter of a finance professional and a teacher. But with college expenses in the Boston area exceeding $20,000 per year and loans and grants severely restricted, her family couldn't swing it. So she did, herself.

Susan is not a victim, at least in her own view. The choices of which men to sleep with for money are made with cool calculation, married men being the safest.

The rest of the article detailed the reporter's theories about why someone would become a prostitute, and Kwok soon lost interest. Rooting through the rest of the pile of mail, he came across the padded envelope and hefted it. Instantly all thoughts of the Portfolio and the outside world dissipated. He began to open it, his fingers fumbling at the clasp.

As soon as he touched the videocassette and note inside, Kwok shuddered. He knew at once what was on the tape—though he couldn't be sure who had sent it, or why.

He unfolded the typewritten note and gazed at it. His eyes took a moment to focus:

Your thespian talents have been vastly underrated, Dean Kwok. You may wish to add this exquisite selection to your collection. I know I have.

—A Fan

2

The "teaming" meeting was drawing to a close, and Dora Givens was more than ready for the final handshakes, the ritual erasing of the whiteboards, and the inevitable awkward silences as Biotecnica's researchers and strategists left the hotel conference room and its aura of false camaraderie. Still seated in the folding chair she had occupied for most of the day, Dora checked her watch. She had eight or nine more hours of real work to do; that would take her to three A.M. and allow her to sleep nearly five hours before her Wednesday morning class. Still, she didn't want to miss her workout; perhaps she should work straight through the night, go to the gym, then class, and sleep later. Or perhaps . . .

Dora sighed and stared intently at the ceiling, smoothing her ash-blond hair away from her finely drawn features. Her tailored beige Armani suit still bore a smudge where somebody from Research had grabbed her with pizza-greasy hands during a "trust exercise." She was looking forward to dropping the cleaning bill on Jerry Frost's desk; as CEO of the pharmaceutical start-up, he was the man responsible for dooming them all to this megadose of tedium. Oh, she agreed that Research types probably needed all the management advice they could get—along with some basic grooming tips, a crash course in social skills, and a lifetime supply of Tic Tacs—but these processing workshops were just a waste of time for the Strategy people, who had had enough of them in business school. No amount of time spent determining their Myers-Briggs personality indices would diminish the fundamental distrust between the Rumpelstiltskins who labored long nights in the laboratories and the management types who spun their products into gold.

At the front of the room, the visiting consultants were winding down their chirpy spiel. Groans arose from the restless group as they were invited, one by one, to "sum up, in a word, how you feel about what we've accomplished today." The responses ranged from "Enthusiastic!" from a junior marketing analyst clearly on a suck-up spree to "Um, confused?" from a gangly scientist wearing unsuccessfully tie-dyed jeans.

"Unimpressed" was the summation offered by the bearded, bearish guy opposite Dora. She had to give him credit for integrity. She decided to go with her old standby, "Hopeful." Nobody needed to know exactly what she was hoping for.

Finally the torture ended, and the group shuffled awkwardly to the door, immediately breaking into two discrete camps. As Dora headed toward the bank of phones in the mirrored corridor, a man cleared his throat behind her.

"You're Dora Givens, aren't you?" She turned and saw the bearded guy from her group. His voice had an edge of intensity to it, and Dora recognized a local accent. She nodded silently and waited for him to go on.

"I'm Dave Mantini," he said. "We have a few things in common, I think. Like our alma mater."

"Harvard?" she asked. "Or NYU?" What was his point? All of this information was available in the company directory. The energy didn't feel quite right for a pickup, and God knows Dora was able to recognize those.

"Harvard," Dave said. "Say, I wonder if you have time for a cup of coffee?" He gestured toward the hotel's overpriced coffee shop. "I wanted to ask you a few questions."

Dora looked again at her watch. "I have to get back to work," she began.

"Okay, then," he answered. "We can talk on the way back to the office."

After spending a day learning how to be a giver, not a taker, she couldn't really object, although the last thing she needed was a new friend from Research. As they stepped through the lobby and into Kendall Square, she took his measure: scruffy beard, plastic-rimmed glasses, worn flannel shirt over corduroys. Around them, throngs of scientists, management consultants, software engineers, and graphic designers poured out of the area's new high-rises to grab microbrews before heading home to their condos in Back Bay.

"You've been with the company awhile," Dave announced.

"Three years," she answered. That made her pretty senior in a start-up like Biotecnica.

"You know how much things have changed, then." He sounded slightly antagonistic. "When I first came to BT," he continued, "it seemed like a place where you could really do science. It wasn't like school, but still, everyone believed in the science. Mark Tansen would meet with us once a week for beer and Buffalo wings and talk about what was happening in the company, his plans for the future, stuff like that. People joked a lot and helped each other figure stuff out."

His words tumbled out more quickly, his anger and frustration plain. "Then, when the board invited Jerry Frost in, things became different, practically overnight. Now business is the only important thing. It's all about the bottom line." He managed to make the last two words sound obscene.

"Why are you telling me this?" Dora asked. She had nothing to fear from Mantini, yet she heard a quaver in her voice.

He ignored her question, and continued his tirade. "Where's the science now? Why is everything kept so secret?" The two of them had slowed to a stop, and Mantini took a step toward her. "If you want to know what's really going on, you have to find out for yourself. Fortunately, I'm a research scientist. Finding things out is what I do best."

Bonding time was over. "Look, Dave," she said, "I'm sorry if you miss the old days, but I don't see what this has to do with me. I'm just another colleague, and I have a lot of work to do tonight."

"I wouldn't say that," he challenged. "I hear you're a big equity holder. Seems to me I practically work for you."

"All the salaried employees have stock options," Dora answered tersely. So that's what this was about. Everybody wanted a big equity stake, but not everybody deserved one.

"True," Mantini agreed. "Though some of us who've been in the field for years get a pittance, while others waltz in with a few management buzzwords and end up being vice president for strategic development." His tone turned sharper. "How did that happen, I wonder? Do you have connections back at our alma mater? I hear there's a crimson edge on some of Biotecnica's stock."

She wasn't going to tell him whether Harvard, or anyone else, owned part of the company. And until the IPO—the initial public offering—was launched, the number of stock options each member of management had would remain confidential. It simply wasn't relevant to Dave's reality.

"I'm sure our compensation is far more similar than different," she said.

"Yeah, right," he answered. "I'm on to you, you know." He folded his arms and stared at her.

"I don't know what your problem is," Dora retorted. "And I don't want to know. I'm going to work now. Alone. And I don't expect to have any more of these little encounters—or I call Security." She drew her coat more tightly around herself. "Got it?" She strode away, her angry steps ringing on the icy sidewalk.

"We'll see about that!" Dave shouted after her. "Because I've been watching you, and I know what you and your friends are up to!"

/   /   /

The white-coated doctor ushered the woman into the examination room. With a knowing smile, he unbuckled his belt and slid his pants down to his ankles. He stretched out on the blue daybed and urged his patient to begin her therapy.

Eager to comply, she inched forward, her mouth open wide. He leaned back, hands behind his neck, watching her every move.

"I read that her secret was aspirin," a woman announced in a stage whisper. "I mean, she *gargled* with aspirin, so she was able to do these unbelievable things—and she didn't gag at all! I tried it once, but—" The woman's neighbors shushed her angrily.

The doctor closed his eyes in ecstasy as he slid his hips back and forth. His low moan seemed almost dragged from his lips; he put a hand out and stroked the woman's back. Her pace was growing increasingly feverish when suddenly a garbled whine filled the air, and the screen in the Science Center B auditorium went black.

Immediately the room erupted in boos and catcalls. "Oh, no!" a smart-ass shouted from the back of the room. "This gives a whole new meaning to coitus interruptus!" A few students across the aisle giggled; others began imitating the lusty sighs they had just heard on the soundtrack.

Toni bent over her seat and checked her watch in the footlights illuminating the stairs: 8:30 P.M. *Deep Throat* still had at least an hour to run. A chant began from the back of the auditorium. "Pull the plug on porn! Porn speech is not free speech!" She sat up and craned her neck to see, in the dim light, a group of women advancing toward the podium. Flipping open her reporter's notebook, she waited. The screening itself was unusual—after all, it wasn't every Thursday night that Harvard University screened a pornographic movie for academic credit—but a group of women storming the projection booth and forcibly stopping the film? That made the event downright news-worthy.

Toni watched intently, trying to make out the faces of the pro-testers as they passed. She would definitely have something to write about for tomorrow's *Crimson*. And what timing, following on the heels of her Kittycat Klub story.

The cluster of demonstrators reached the stage. "Someone get the lights!" one woman shouted. As the auditorium grew brighter, mem-bers of the audience blinked, still too taken aback to realize what was happening. The women unfurled a large banner urging their fellow students to END THE OPPRESSION! BAN PORNOGRAPHY! and braced themselves against the boos, hisses, and paper airplanes now being di-rected at them from the awakening audience.

A handsome man in his mid-thirties rose from a row of chairs on the side of the auditorium and headed toward the protesters. Profes-sor Dayton Moore had scheduled the screening as part of his course "Sexuality and Social Institutions." He had also organized a panel discussion to follow, with Shulamit Kessler, the elderly professor of political philosophy; Chandra Chandrashekaran, a young professor at the law school; and himself. The two women smiled uncertainly and followed Moore's lead.

The first demonstrator, a young woman with a clump of disheveled hair, reached the stage, stumbling over a microphone cord. "Walk much?" someone in the audience jeered. She flushed and consulted the crumpled piece of yellow paper clutched in her hand. "We are here to speak out against the *exploitation* of women that films like this represent," she began. Too close to the microphone, she set off a howl of feedback that interrupted her reading. "Sorry," she muttered, and went on. "We are *shocked* and *saddened* that a faculty member has chosen to show such a film—"

"Yeah, well, *we're* shocked and saddened by your hairdo!" someone shouted from the back of the room. "You don't see us staging a protest."

"Uh, excuse me," a second person interjected. "I believe that the correct term in this case is a hair-*don't.*" Snickers spread through the audience.

"C'mon now, folks," A deep voice commanded. "Let the woman have her say." Toni turned around to see Horace Glover standing in the aisle a few rows behind her, his hand raised for silence. She was a bit surprised; helping young white girls find their voices seemed more the work of Ed. School guru Carol Gilligan than the president of the Black Students Association. Horace acknowledged her bemusement with a grave nod before taking his seat. With a few halfhearted grumbles, the heckling subsided.

The demonstrator continued. "We are *appalled* that other professors—*female* professors and role models—have condoned this action by taking part in tonight's panel discussion. And we are *angered* that our fellow students have come to *gape* at these women's degradation and humiliation."

The protester looked up for a second and blinked. Students were absorbed in private conversations, trading munchies, walking up and down the aisles of the crowded Science Center auditorium. Very few were paying any attention to the demonstration.

Toni noticed another group organizing its signs and banners on the opposite side of the auditorium. She recognized several campus conservatives—staffers from the monthly *Right Thinking* and members of Christian organizations.

Noting the speaker's exasperation, Dayton Moore stepped up to the podium and offered some conciliatory words. The young woman made a gesture of annoyance and surrendered the mike. Moore addressed the now attentive audience.

"Thank you for your patience during these recent unexpected developments." His tone was smooth and masculine, as if nothing could faze him. "Rather than continue the screening, perhaps we should just start the discussion now. I think we have a good sense of what the film is about." With an air traffic controller–like wave, he indicated the left and right aisles. "Microphones have been set up on both sides of the room. Please go ahead—there's no reason for us to speak first."

First in line was a nervous freshman in a baseball cap. "Yes, go ahead, young man," Moore encouraged him.

"I think, um, that, like, the First Amendment guarantees the right to, you know, free speech." There was a moment of silence as the panel waited for him to go on, but he stepped away from the microphone, red-faced, and returned to his seat.

"Well, thank you for those thoughts." Moore signaled to the other microphone. "Yes, you, please."

The inarticulate freshman was replaced by an equally inarticulate member of the Spartacist Youth League, who was in turn replaced by an overly articulate male debater eager to outfeminist the feminists. Toni sighed and settled in to wait. If only Harvard students weren't so damned convinced of their own capacity for original thought. The next speaker, a bearded man in an oversize parka, looked to be in his late twenties. His appearance was unkempt, though in this setting it was difficult to tell whether he was an exceptionally disheveled graduate student or an unusually well-groomed homeless person.

"I have a bone to pick with you, Professor Moore!" he declared. He clutched a sheaf of tattered, slightly grimy papers, on which Toni could make out masses of complex drawings in various colors of ink. They looked almost like molecular diagrams, but he seemed to refer to them as he spoke.

"Who are you—who is anyone in this room—to feel superior to the people on this screen? All they have sold is their bodies." He paused dramatically. "What about your souls?"

Students in the audience began to giggle. "What about your

souls?" someone whispered in a melodramatic parody. Cambridge was full of oddballs and eccentrics. They turned up at campus receptions for the free wine and cheese, and you could pretty much count on any high-profile event being interrupted by one.

"Thank you," Moore said blandly. "I'm sure you've given us a lot to think about. Any other comments?"

"Hey, I'm not—" The man started to protest, but a woman in a pink cardigan sweater with a protruding starched collar shoved him aside.

"Could we please call an end to this charade?" she demanded. "This 'discussion' is an absurdity, an embarrassment to the very idea of learning." Toni jotted down, "Betty Jo Orten, president of the Conservative Club." Rumor had it that her father was a prominent televangelist in Indiana. "This film is trash, pure and simple," Betty Jo continued. "And this seminar is a joke. The demented lifestyles portrayed in this film—"

"Could you clarify what you mean by 'demented lifestyles'?" Professor Chandrashekaran interrupted sharply. Murmurs traveled across the audience.

"Things that I find deeply offensive," Betty Jo trumpeted. "Oh, I know that's not p.c. to say here at Harvard, but there's a role for tradition in society; there's a reason why some things are normal and others aren't."

"While respecting your freedom to speak as you wish," Professor Chandrashekaran responded, "I must say that I find your comments disturbing. Not because I am a lesbian, but because I am a libertarian."

"Betty Jo!" a jock bellowed from the back of the auditorium. "Don't let her bully you!" His friends erupted into raucous laughter.

Meanwhile, the original group of antipornography protesters seemed to have reconvened. "Pull the plug on porn!" they chanted from the back of the auditorium. "Porn speech is not free speech!"

"There's no need to silence any one viewpoint," Moore stated without effect. Professor Kessler nodded gravely, looking wise and slightly pained, as usual.

"Oh, so what about my feelings?" Betty Jo complained. "Conservatives are the victims on this campus, if you want my honest opinion."

"Uh, don't believe we do," someone quipped from the front row. A group of students bellowing "U.S.A.! U.S.A.!" competed for attention against the antipornographers' chant. Giving up, the trio of professors leaned toward one another and conferred.

"Seems like if you don't sign on with the gays and lesbians, you're un-American nowadays," Betty Jo went on. Her remark was met by an explosion of applause from her faction in the back, which was immediately followed by hissing from every other part of the auditorium. Both were soon drowned out by the excited buzz that greeted a new outbreak of protest.

A few rows back in the auditorium, a handsome man had climbed onto a chair. Toni brightened at seeing her friend Nguyen Van Minh. She tucked her pencil away and waited. Even among the hipper-than-thou residents of Adams House, Van was a standout, as famous for his wit and good nature as for his perfect cheekbones. Though it was evening, he looked as if he'd just gotten out of bed. Given his habits, this was entirely possible. His spiked black hair was adorably tousled, and his famous bedroom eyes looked even sleepier than usual.

Van panned the auditorium with a languid smile. Then he stretched and, in the same motion, began tugging at his black ribbed-cotton T-shirt. He raised it over his head, exposing first his golden stomach with its flat abs and delicate navel ring, then his tight pectoral muscles, and finally his toned lats, biceps, and triceps. Squinting, Toni imagined she could make out the outline of a few tattooed twigs and leaves of bamboo peeking up from his tender hip bone. There was a collective intake of breath, and Toni felt her ears burn and her stomach go soft; she hadn't realized just how attractive her friend was. With studied nonchalance, Van dropped the shirt to the floor beside him.

A young woman on the aisle was the first to break the silence. "Woooo!" she screamed, like one of the girls at the airport when the Beatles first came to America. "Take it off, Van! Wooooo!" The crowd went wild, encouraging whistles and catcalls resounding. Startled, Betty Jo spun from her position at the mike.

"Hey there, Betty Jo!" Van said and made a smooching noise. He began to unfasten the silver buckle of his thick black belt.

"And I suppose you're part of this whole act?" Betty Jo accused, her face a mottled shade of purple.

"I *am* the act," Van corrected. It didn't sound arrogant; he was simply stating the truth.

Professor Kessler spoke up from her microphone. "May I ask the young gentleman to please take his seat or to continue his performance somewhere else?"

"Oh, I'm sorry not to have explained, Professor," Van apologized politely as he kicked off his shoes. "This *is* my statement."

"Your statement, Mr. Nguyen?" The question came from Professor Moore. Apparently Van's reputation had preceded him.

"Yes," he said, unzipping his jeans. "I'm having a be-in. Or perhaps 'bi-in' would be the more accurate term." He flipped Betty Jo an insolent grin. "You'd think that in this day and age, bisexuality would have more vocal sponsors. Don't you agree, Betty Jo?" He stepped out of his jeans, revealing a sexy pair of light blue cotton boxers.

With a glower at Van that could have made a small building implode, Betty Jo abandoned the mike and went to rejoin her faction. Toni saw a twitch of triumph at the corner of Van's mouth.

"Hey, Van, can I join your be-in, too?" A woman with asymmetrical blond hair, a pierced eyebrow, and entirely black clothes pulled off her T-shirt and began unfastening her bra. She was Aimee Milvain, a mainstay of the Adams House in crowd and Van's biggest follower. A hippie-ish guy next to her joined in the stripdown. "U.S.A.! U.S.A.!" the jocks screamed. The two other sets of protesters resumed their chants.

Suddenly the room fell silent. All eyes were on Van, who had his fingers on the waistband of his boxers.

"Under the circumstances," Professor Moore intoned, glancing at his two colleagues for confirmation, "I think it best to consider this seminar concluded."

"Oh, well, in that case," Van said, "I guess I'm done too." He leaned down to pick up his clothes as acquaintances rushed over to bask in his glory.

Toni got up to leave and noticed Horace Glover motioning to her from the door at the back of the auditorium. "Just a sec," she mouthed.

"Nice story, Toni," Aimee Milvain called from across the aisle, where she was collecting the scattered pieces of her Adams House uniform.

"Thanks, Aimee. Nice stripping."

"You know," Aimee persisted, "the one about the coed hooker. It was cool. I was all over it."

You would be, Toni thought wryly. Aimee was quintessential Adams House—shallow, trendy, and self-dramatizing. In addition, she had a nasty tongue. She did, however, consider Toni a friend, and she could be amusing on occasion. "Thanks," Toni answered again, more warmly this time, before heading up the aisle.

She found her way blocked by the homeless guy. He seemed much less scary close up; he was probably just a grad student who'd lived in Somerville too long. He stood regarding her a moment. "You're Antonia Isaacs?" he finally asked.

"Um, maybe," she hedged. "Listen, I'm kinda in a hurry. Deadline and all. Sorry." She edged her way up the aisle.

"Hey," he barked. "I was just asking a simple question! I read the article, too. *Jeez!*"

"Hi, Horace," she said when she got to the back of the room, safely out of reach of her fan. "Boy, am I glad to see you."

"Good to see you too, Sister Toni," he replied. Horace had a gravelly, stern voice, the definition of sober. Rumor had it he was the youngest ordained minister in the country. He nodded and gave her hand a strong squeeze. "How's it going? We've missed you at BSA."

Instantly recognizing Horace's intention to give her the Talk, Toni regretted approaching him. The Talk was an extension of what she and her best friend, Valerie, had dubbed the Freshman Week Racial Identity Assessment period. During Freshman Week members of minority groups closely monitored one another for proper group affiliation. Any indication of traitorous leanings, such as missing group meetings, sitting in the dining hall with nongroup roommates, or interracial dating, was reported to the group's self-appointed enforcers. Offenders were then taken aside and rebuked for insufficiently clear commitment to the Cause. Valerie in particular resented the Blacker-Than-Thou Police, as she called them. "You know they're the only black family in their nice suburban neighborhood and the only black kid in their five-figure prep school," she ranted. "Now suddenly they're here, and they think they're Malcolm. How they gonna get all up in my face and teach *me,* born and raised in Harlem, how to be black!"

Toni always laughed at Val's outrage. For herself, the issue was simply that she didn't like folks knowing her business. But given her visibility on the *Crimson,* it was becoming increasingly difficult to maintain a low profile. Someone must have noted and reported her sporadic attendance at meetings of the Black Students Association.

"Uh, yeah, Horace," she faltered. "I've really been meaning to check what's happening at BSA these days. It's just, with the paper and everything . . ."

Horace nodded sagely. "We just have to *make* the time, don't we?" He switched out of preacher mode and got down to business. "But that's not why I wanted to talk to you. I read your article—"

"Thanks!" Toni responded automatically.

He leaned forward and spoke quietly. "If you don't mind a word of advice from a friend, you might want to show a little more leadership in the future." He lowered his voice even further. "Be careful about doing cheap, exploitative stories. A young sister in your position—you could give people the wrong idea."

She turned and shot him a look of controlled disdain. The Talk would have been preferable to this self-righteous crap. "Thanks for the advice, Horace. I'll give it all the thought it deserves." She disengaged her arm and kept walking. "I've got to head over to the *Crimson* now. I'll catch you later, okay?"

"All right, Sister," Horace said jovially enough, though something about the set of his mouth gave Toni pause. "We all have to do what we have to do."

Toni raced out of the auditorium, swearing to herself. What was he, the spokesman for Black Harvard? What sort of "news" should she focus on—the school play and the PTA bake sale? Dammit, she'd write about what she wanted to.

/ / /

Chelo Santana stood in the doorway of Tara Sheridan's dorm room and regarded the shambles before her in dismay. She and her friend had planned to get together for coffee after their Friday afternoon classes, but apparently the plan was off. Clothes covered every surface of the common room—strewn across the polished hardwood floors, draped over the leather sofa and chairs, piled atop the radiators. A matched set of Hartmann travel bags sat in the foyer, half filled with a jumble of books, sweaters, and pantyhose. The Velvet Underground blared out of the sound system, while endless footage of figure skating flickered across the television set. Every light in the place was on.

Chelo stepped into the room. Though she was a junior, this was actually her first visit to Eliot House. Besides Tara, whom she hadn't known all that long, her only other acquaintances in Eliot were Latin American aristocrats. She knew them well enough to say hi on the rare occasions when she attended the Latino students' parties, but they didn't exactly travel in the same circles.

Harvard College had a unique housing system. Every spring, freshmen entered a lottery to determine where they would live during their sophomore, junior, and senior years. Each "house," as the thirteen residences were called, had its own administrators, library, and facilities, as well as its own distinct character. Of all the houses, Eliot was the most enduringly traditional. One of the coveted river houses fronting the Charles, Eliot had been home to preppies, WASPs, and legacy kids for generations. Weekly dinners in the impressive dining hall were still formal, and social events tended toward sherry hours rather than the beer-swilling dance fests held at other houses.

Chelo surveyed her surroundings. Though it was just a few blocks from Adams House, where she and Toni Isaacs shared a suite, Eliot seemed miles away. Not so long ago, all of Harvard had seemed as far from East L.A. as the moon, and even less familiar. Sometimes it still felt like a dream. One day she had been living in a tiny apartment with her mother and taking the bus to the graffiti-covered halls of Southgate High School, and the next she was furnishing a wood-paneled dorm room previously occupied by two vice presidents and one Hollywood star.

Chelo smiled, remembering the day she had walked into her freshman suite in Weld Hall and found her roommate, an outgoing, pretty girl with an endless supply of energy, scattering her things haphazardly about the place. Toni had been a slob then, and three years of living with Chelo's meticulously organized systems hadn't changed her one bit. Luckily, Toni had other charms—one being her generosity with the trail of belongings she continually left behind her, and another her sheer guts. Chelo was always hoping some of that audacity might rub off on her.

A noise in Tara's bedroom brought Chelo back to the present. Quickly crossing to the open door, she poked her head inside. Tara was standing next to the bed, bent over her nightstand. Her fine blond hair fell in a curtain over her face as she thumbed through a little address book. With an exasperated sigh, she tossed the book into a beat-up army duffel bag and swept the contents of the table in after.

"Tara," Chelo called out. "What's going on?"

Tara jumped, her cheeks high with color. Seeing Chelo, she relaxed a bit and gave a self-conscious laugh. "Nothing," she answered. "Just packing up some things. How did you get in, anyway?"

"What?" Chelo blinked and tried to think. "The door was open, so I just—" She strode into the room and peered closely at Tara, who continued flinging items into the bag. "What in the world is going on, Tara? What's wrong?"

"Nothing," Tara declared brightly, tossing her hair. She pulled the duffel shut and tossed it onto the bed before disappearing into the closet. "I've decided to get away for a while," she explained, kneeling over a rack of shoes. Her voice sounded strange and muffled. "I'm burned out. I need a change of scenery."

"Burned out." It was the classic Harvard student complaint, used to excuse everything from a late paper to a failed romance to a criminal spree. Given the general reading load and the number of hours the average student spent immersed in extracurricular activities, it was a hard claim to dispute, banal though it was.

"What do you mean, 'a while'?" Chelo asked. "If you're going away for the weekend, why do you need all this stuff?"

"I'm not sure how long I'm going for," Tara said, suddenly losing interest in her shoes and beginning to rifle through her lingerie drawer.

"But the semester only started last week, Tara. You can't just take off."

Tara stopped abruptly and swung around to look at Chelo. She smiled. "Well, that's where you and I differ. You're responsible. You wouldn't just take off in the middle of school. I, on the other hand"—

she led the way back to the common room and punched off the power on the television and stereo—"have no difficulty running away. In fact, it's my forte." She plopped herself down in front of her open luggage.

Chelo couldn't agree. During the few months she and Tara had been acquainted, Chelo had come to understand her friend's fundamentally serious nature. She knelt next to Tara and picked up one of her sweaters, a delicate blend of cashmere and lambswool. "That's bullshit, Tara."

"No," Tara said, her green eyes holding Chelo's. "You just don't know me. It's the truth."

For a moment they folded clothes together silently. Without the music and television commentary, the sudden stillness in the room was oppressive.

"Wanna talk about it?" Chelo finally inquired.

Tara ducked her head. "Not really," she said. "It's nothing. I'm just heading home to Darien for a few days."

"Okay then," Chelo said briskly. "We won't talk about it." She stood up and grabbed a heap of sweaters from the chair. Dropping them onto a suitcase, she began folding in quick, expert motions.

"Thanks." Tara placed a thin hand on Chelo's arm and squeezed. "You're a good friend." A sudden thought occurred to her. "Oh, my God—coffee! I completely forgot. Chelo, I am so sorry." She looked chagrined.

Chelo waved aside the apology. "Don't worry about it, Tara. You had other things on your mind." She wedged in the last of the sweaters and snapped the case shut. "The point was to spend some time together, and that's what we're doing. So tell me about Darien." Chelo had never been to Connecticut, but she envisioned it as very pretty, with curving lanes and stately mansions and vast lawns.

"It's very *Who's Afraid of Virginia Woolf*," Tara answered. "Moms on lithium, dads making their nightly martinis in the den." She tossed Chelo several mesh bags filled with silk lingerie. "I'm being pretty weird, aren't I?" Tara asked, stuffing her shoes with cloth trees and sliding them into matching flannel shoe envelopes. "Figures. I can't remember anymore why I'm even here, why this is supposed to make me happy." She shut the final suitcase and spun the tiny gold combination lock. "It's just that . . . I feel like my entire life I've jumped through these hoops to get here, and now I wonder what for. You know what I mean?"

Chelo nodded. In truth, however, she didn't know what Tara meant. Chelo could still remember every emotional high and low of the roller-coaster college admissions process. She had spent months writing her application essays, weeks proofreading them. On April 15, she was called to the principal's office during lunch hour. Startled, afraid that she was considered so fragile that the principal himself had to tell her she had been rejected from Harvard and every other university, she'd crept nervously to his office—only to find a surprise party organized by her teachers and her counselor. Somehow they had managed to find out directly from Harvard that their Consuelo Santana had been admitted. Chelo hadn't been the only one who cried that day.

Surely it had been no surprise to Tara Sheridan when she got her news on that same day in April. Up until today, Chelo would have imagined that Tara had everything going for her. But maybe Tara was right; maybe Chelo really didn't know her at all.

/ / /

"And then he took his shirt off," Aimee announced with her usual flair for drama. "Two words, you guys. Only two words do justice to his physique. *Total washboard.*"

"Am I missing something?" Toni asked with a smile as she joined her friends at their usual table in the smoking section of the dining hall. Chelo flashed her a look of relief.

"Trust me, no one missed anything at that screening." As she spoke, Aimee scanned the crowd, searching out strange new gossip that would boldly go where no gossip had gone before. "I mean, I knew that washboard stomachs existed. I had just never seen one on anyone outside a Calvin Klein ad, you know what I mean?"

Toni noticed Van strolling over outside Aimee's peripheral vision. "Danger, Will Robinson," she warned, flapping her arms like the robot on *Lost in Space.*

Aimee ignored her. "And the boxers! My, they grow 'em big in Texas." She arched her eyebrows significantly.

"Well," Van said in his teasing rich baritone, "I do aim to please, Aim." He sat down.

Aimee jumped, reddening slightly. "Any advance tix for the next performance, Van?" she teased, recovering her customary aplomb. "Hey, Toni," she said, "why not turn your writing talents to Adams House? There are a thousand stories in the naked city, and most of them are right here, in your own backyard."

Toni smiled thinly. Everyone on campus seemed to have read her story and have an opinion about it. It was great to be so widely read, but . . .

Now that Van had joined them, the table would quickly fill to capacity. His energy was intoxicating. Though he was leagues beyond Toni and Chelo in popularity, he seemed to enjoy hanging out with them, at least in the dining hall. Toni suspected it was because Chelo actually listened to what people said, rather than spending every moment trying to think of clever quips to bat back.

"How did you find that girl, anyway?" Ravi Singh asked. Ravi, a freshman *Crimson* wannabe who seemed to consider himself Toni's personal Sancho Panza, had stopped into Adams for a quick dinner before going back to the paper next door. "I mean, was she for real?"

"Sorry, I have to protect my sources," Toni responded. "But, yes, she's a real student, at a real college."

"Did you ask her if she used drugs?" Ravi asked. "A lot of prostitutes are drug users, you know. I mean, that's what I've heard."

"Ravi, she didn't do her research by watching *Klute*," Aimee retorted.

"What's *Klute*?" Ravi and Van asked simultaneously.

"A movie with Jane Fonda playing a prostitute," Toni explained. "Post–*Barbarella*, pre–*On Golden Pond*."

"Post–Roger Vadim, pre–Ted Turner," Aimee added.

"Oh, thanks," Ravi said with an exasperated sigh. "That helps a lot."

Toni stabbed one of her Tater Tots with a fork. She held it out to him, a peace offering. Ravi beamed.

One of the house tutors, a misplaced chemistry grad student named Carl Christianson, spoke up. "If there's so much student prostitution, why don't we hear anything about it?"

"You do hear about it," Van said. "Haven't you ever seen those ads in the *Phoenix*? 'Randy the Harvard Freshman' and 'Sabrina the Cambridge Coed'?"

"Those can't be real," Chelo said. "It's just marketing."

"I'm sure," Van said wryly. "Randy's been a freshman my whole three years!" The table laughed. "But there must be something sexy about the Harvard name."

"My parents think so," Aimee confirmed. "The day I got in I could hear them screwing the whole night."

"Ugh." Chelo was appalled. "You can *hear* your parents?"

"Hey, it's Manhattan. We don't have a lot of rooms."

"I just don't think that there's a big moral component to having sex for money," a normally shy sophomore chimed in. "It's not selling your body; it's actually more like renting it."

"No one should have to do that," Chelo said.

"But the woman Toni wrote about didn't have to do it," the sophomore pointed out. "She chose to."

"Exactly," Aimee agreed. "I mean, if someone takes me to Maison Robert, I'm not going to send him home with just a goodnight kiss."

"You guys," Chelo admonished, flicking her long, dark braid over her shoulder. "You're so detached from everything. I think it's terrible to have sex with all those pudgy middle-aged men!"

"Oh, come on," Van joked. "Lots of people are slutty—pudgy middle-aged men don't have all the fun, you know."

"Yeah," Aimee echoed. "The whole concept is so brutally ironic. Our sad little generation forced to sexually service aging baby boomers just to pay for college so we can get the jobs they got just for waking up in the morning. Our collective destiny."

"Well, I don't know about that," answered Chelo. She inspected a forkful of broccoli-cheese pasta dubiously. "It's a pretty defeatist attitude."

Toni checked her watch. "Yikes!" She jumped up and started piling her dishes onto her tray. "I'm already twelve minutes late for my meeting with Adam." This was no way to start her pitch to the *Crimson*'s managing editor.

Waving good-bye to the assembled crowd, she dumped her tray at the clean-up window and raced out through the lobby. She headed up Plympton Street at a run. When she reached the familiar red door of the student paper, she yanked it open and nearly crashed into a tall, good-looking man with almond skin and perfect teeth. "Oh, hey,

Lucius," she said. "Sorry I can't talk—Adam's waiting for me up-stairs."

"Always in a rush," he teased.

"A girl's gotta keep moving, right?" she joked awkwardly.

Four months after she had parted ways with Lucius Cornell, Toni still found it hard to talk to him. Unable to articulate exactly why she wanted to end their two-year relationship, she had claimed that the differences between them were too vast. She wanted to right the wrongs of the world; he, in contrast, planned to attend business school, return to the South, and enjoy the social standing maintained by his family. Firmly established members of the black bourgeoisie, the Cornells joined the exclusive Jack and Jill social clubs in high school, and in college headed straight for the oldest black sororities and fraternities. When Lucius had pressed Toni, she added that she had little respect for his chosen major—networking, with a minor in administration ass-kissing. As class marshal and treasurer of the Undergraduate Council, he seemed to live in suits and ties; Dean Kwok, of all people, was one of his mentors. Toni told herself that Lucius was too shallow, though she suspected the real problem with their relationship was simply that he hadn't helped her become the person she wanted to be.

At the beginning of the term, in one of those ironic twists of fate that Nana no doubt would interpret as "the Lord's way of helping us build character," Lucius had been elected business manager of the *Crimson.* His office was now across the hall from her desk in the news-room.

"Listen," he said, flashing that politician's grin of his, "we should have coffee sometime."

"Sure," she said, nervous at being so close to him. "Fine. Just not this second."

"Give me a call, then."

"I'll do that," she agreed. "'Bye." She rushed past the editors, re-porters, and general hangers-on who populated the headquarters of the student newspaper at all times, threw her bookbag and coat into a chair at the desk she shared with one of the sports editors, and jogged up the stairs to the second-floor meeting room.

Adam Steiner was sitting at one of the battered desks, drinking a mug of coffee and watching a *M*A*S*H* rerun. He waved a casual greeting while Toni caught her breath. "Got your memo," he began.

"What do you think?" Toni asked.

Adam flicked the remote control, and Radar O'Reilly shrank to a tiny white dot. "Do you really think the paper should do a whole series on prostitution?" he asked. "Isn't that a bit sensationalistic?"

"Not necessarily, not the way I'm seeing it." Toni took a deep breath. "This is big! Check it out—parents send their kids to college to live out the American dream, but it turns out to be a fantasy. Students prostitute themselves to get through school, before graduating to prostitute themselves for high-paying corporate jobs." She spread her hands. "What do you think?"

"Well, the job part's a little excessive. And as for the rest, you've already written about it."

"Yes, but there's been a huge response to Karen's story." Toni leaned over the table. "I could follow it up. What's it really like for this student, and others like her? I've wondered myself, What would it take for me to be in a similar situation?"

Adam grimaced and rubbed the back of his neck. "It's just not relevant to us here, Toni. Let's face it, people like to read about their own reality. And if we're just peering down into the experience of some student at a third-tier school, it'll seem exploitative."

Toni took a moment to reassess. That certainly was not what she was suggesting; in fact, just the opposite. She decided to play her trump card and worry about nuances later.

"But it's not just other schools, Adam." She cocked her head. "My contact said there are students at Harvard doing it, too."

Instantly she had his attention. "Really?" he asked.

She grinned, giving him a single, quick nod. "There's your relevance."

"Now, *that* would be a story." Adam warmed to his subject. "'Finding the Ivy League Prostitute.' 'What I Never Wrote on My Application Essay.' 'The Harvard Escorts.' Letting the readership know that they're not so insulated from the seamier side of life after all. It'll be great—if it's true, I mean."

Toni suddenly felt a little off-balance. She wanted a big story, yes, but Adam was making it sound like a tabloid nightmare.

"Toni, don't you see it?" Adam put his feet up on the table and folded his hands behind his head. "This could be your big break here. Can you imagine the reaction of the administration if something like this came out?"

"Yes, but what's the point exactly?"

"The point? Exposing the truth. 'Veritas,' isn't that Harvard's motto? Who knows, perhaps you'd end up helping some sex worker move on to less risky employment." Adam leaned back, lost in day-dreams. "The most important thing is that this could give you a lock on the news editorship position for next year. The election'll be as tough this year as it was last year. It's so hard to distinguish yourself from everyone else. But this could do it."

Lord knew, at Harvard the competition never ended. It wasn't for grades, but to show that you were exciting and with it and ready to make your mark on the world. Toni had run for news editor as a sophomore and lost. She had imagined herself the model of cool effi-ciency, a cross between Brenda Starr and Charlayne Hunter-Gault. Her loss was a disappointment but not unexpected; sophomores rarely won. And at least no one could sing the refrain that her victory was some affirmative-action scam.

"Okay," Toni said with more brightness than she felt. "I'm gonna go for it."

3

Ten minutes into the session, it became clear to Toni that she was just not going to get her money's worth from the man sprawled across the gold-and-avocado bedspread of her motel room. She scrambled to come up with a Plan B. It had been a long shot, after all, to think that hiring "Randy the Harvard Freshman" would bring her any closer to discovering the elusive Harvard prostitute. After perusing the adult section of the *Phoenix*, Boston's tepid answer to *The Village Voice,* and studying the dozens of phone-sex and escort ads featuring tacky photos of lascivious women with large breasts and overmuscled men with hairless chests, she had figured what the hell. A good reporter followed any potential lead. She dialed the number and asked to speak with Randy.

Toni's phone queries about Randy's official academic status met a brick wall. The dispatcher had assured her that Randy was "every inch a Harvard boy" and asked when she wanted to "schedule a date." The implication was clear. Before she knew it, she was arranging an afternoon rendezvous with Randy. When the dispatcher asked for a location, the Travelers' Inn sprang instantly to mind. Once a year a recruiter for the Ivy League issue of *Playboy* came to town and set up shop at the hotel. And each year Toni was amazed to watch the stream of female students from Harvard and nearby colleges make the trek to his room. In addition to offering the cheapest lodging in Harvard Square, the Inn seemed relatively safe for the business of meeting with a strange male prostitute. Its proximity to campus and squat seventies architecture were somehow comforting, particularly after the seediness of the Combat Zone.

Once inside the room, Toni checked the location of the emergency exits. She decided to stay near the door, so that if anything went wrong, she could escape—or at least scream for help. Making these preparations, she felt a little like her childhood heroine, Christie Love. But when the knock on the door came at last, her heart began to race and she felt more like a scared teenager than a kung-fu-fighting blaxploitation queen. Taking a breath to steady herself, she opened the door.

A red-faced blond man stood in the hallway dressed in a pink oxford-cloth shirt and chinos, topped by the ubiquitous vintage wool overcoat. Despite the cold, he wore loafers without socks; a crimson Harvard backpack hung over one shoulder. He looked about thirty. His eyes flickered upon seeing her, though his face betrayed nothing. Without missing a beat, he extended his hand and pumped hers with all the vigor of a Young Republican at a recruitment drive.

"How do you do?" he said. "I'm Randy. You must be Karen. It's really great to meet you." Toni flushed and nodded. Karen had been the first name that popped into her head. She opened the door wider, and Randy charged inside as if she were giving out free samples.

His mood shifted abruptly after Toni closed the door. "So," he said, casting an experienced eye around the room. "You a cop?" She blinked. "You know you're required to answer if you are." At her silence he turned to look closely at her, one hand on the top button of his shirt. *"Well?"*

"No," she answered. "I'm not a cop."

Suddenly he was all smiles again, ducking his head shyly and busying himself once more with his buttons. "Sorry," he mumbled. "I guess exams have me on edge."

What exams? she wondered. The semester was barely two weeks old.

"How about you, Randy?" she asked, regaining her composure. "Time to come clean. Were you ever really a Harvard freshman?"

Randy peeled off his shirt, revealing a decently toned chest with a sprinkling of sandy hair. "Sure," he said cheerfully, tossing the shirt on the chair and throwing himself across the bed. "Why don't you come over here and take a look at my résumé?" He grabbed his crotch and squeezed. "Ten inches of pure dangling Ivy."

"Well," she said, leaning back against the door. "I'd actually like to talk a bit. About Harvard."

"Didn't get in, huh?" Randy guessed. "Don't take it so hard." He sat up and flexed a bit. Whoever he was, he had certainly mastered the Harvard arrogance. "There are cheaper ways to buy happiness."

He launched into a story about his life in prep school, getting perfect SATs and grades, rowing crew. His tale was riddled with clichés and only halfway plausible. Toni surveyed the slightly creased skin, the clothes that were almost a caricature of a Harvard student's. When he described his freshman roommate as someone who had been home-schooled—"He never went to school before; his parents kept him at home and taught him with the goats or something"—her suspicions were confirmed. Everyone knew the goat-boy had a single in Canaday his freshman year.

"Listen, Randy," she said with a sigh, "no offense, but I'm looking for a real Harvard student."

"Hey," he objected. "I can be a real Harvard student. That's what I do."

"No, you don't understand," Toni said. "I'm doing a newspaper story on college students and sex, and I heard that there was a real Harvard prostitute working the area."

Randy shot her a glare that would have melted the tar off an Alabama road. He reached for his shirt.

"Of course, I'll pay you for your time," Toni rushed to explain. "I wasn't trying to trick you or anything. I just thought you might be a lead, and I couldn't ask over the phone."

"Well, that certainly explains it." He shrugged the shirt onto his shoulders.

"What do you mean?"

"Well, I don't usually get customers like you."

Toni bristled. "What, you don't *do* black women?"

Randy grinned. "I don't usually do *women.*"

"Oh." She felt foolish.

He smiled, and she warmed to him. He was much nicer when he wasn't imitating a Harvard freshman on hyperdrive. "So," he asked, buttoning up, "are you serious about wanting to talk?"

She nodded and placed three crisp twenty-dollar bills on the table.

His smile spread. "What do you want to know?"

Toni flipped open her pad and thumbed to a clean page. "Why the 'Randy the Harvard Freshman' thing?"

He laughed. "It's my act; it's who I become. All the best entertainers and illusionists have stage names. I look real young, so I get dressed all clean-cut, very preppy. Then I put on a backpack, and I'm Randy the Harvard Freshman. I'm all tentative and virginal—the old guys just eat it up. Believe me, it's easy to fake being a Harvard student. And profitable, if you play it right."

"Yeah." Toni sighed. "I figured it was just a marketing thing."

She heard a faint *click-click-click* and looked up to find Randy reclining on the bed, trimming his fingernails. Little shards of nail ricocheted around the room.

"You ever run across any Harvard students in the business?" she asked.

"Hmm." Randy stopped to think, the nail clipper poised in midair. "Not personally, though I've been with a couple of guys who claim to have hired Harvard dates. One old geezer took me to some fancy tea party at a professor's house on campus. Everyone was all dressed up, talking about philosophy and eating cucumber sandwiches and drinking cold tea. Anyway, he got all coy and said that there was another rent boy in the room. One of the students. He wouldn't tell me who."

"Really!" In spite of herself, Toni let her enthusiasm show. "Any idea who it might have been, or how he got connected?"

Randy's eyes shifted imperceptibly. "Oh," he said vaguely, "there were a lot of people there. A lot."

Toni laid another bill on the table.

Randy stood up. "Okay," he said, his tone businesslike. "I don't know who it was, but I'll tell you this: It's not a question of *if* there's a Harvard hooker; it's just a matter of who." He jammed his feet into his loafers and shouldered his backpack. "Because if someone with money wants a taste of the Ivy, he's gonna get it. That's market reality." He snatched up the cash and tucked it into his back pocket, along with the nail clipper. "It's the only reality."

He strode to the door and Toni stepped aside to let him out. "The key is the johns," he advised her, putting his hand on the knob, "the Harvard johns. I'd talk to them."

/ / /

"Classified Advertising," a teenager answered, audibly stifling a yawn.

"I'd like to place a personal ad—a professional services ad, I mean." Toni's mouth was suddenly dry. It occurred to her that she hadn't really thought this plan through.

"You mean like for an escort service, right? Not for a dating service."

"Right."

"I'll put you through to the 'Entre Nous' section," the young woman said.

The phone clicked as her call was transferred. "*Boston Phoenix,* 'Entre Nous' desk. Naomi speaking." The voice sounded the same.

"Hey, didn't I just talk to you?"

"Yeah," Naomi explained, bored as ever, "but we're supposed to make it sound like there's a whole bunch of us here. How can I help you?"

"I'd like to place an ad for professional services," Toni repeated.

"Seventy-five dollars for a two-column ad," Naomi quoted. "Hundred fifty for four columns. Visa or Amex?"

"Visa."

"Just goes on the card as a normal charge," Naomi assured her. "Nobody needs to know what it's for."

Toni took careful notes, keeping her voice down since Chelo was still sleeping in the next room. Naomi explained the process: a phone-drop service would answer her calls, take clients' numbers, and allow Toni to get back to them without revealing her home number. Naomi went on to enlighten Toni about services she could use to bill her future clients. Toni didn't listen too closely to that, since she never intended to provide anything anyone wanted to pay for.

"What kind of ad do you want?" Naomi asked.

"What do you mean?"

"Incalls? Outcalls? TVs, TSes, pre-ops, or just regular women and guys?"

"Um, outcalls only," Toni said. "And regular men and women, please."

"Okay," Naomi said. "Straight and gay, right?"

"Yes."

"You're not allowed to use the word 'bisexual,' you know. Company policy. Anyway, what do you want the ad to say?"

Toni recited from memory the text she had composed during her sleepless night. Naomi promised that the ad would appear next Thursday.

/ / /

The seventy-odd hours between Toni's Monday morning conversation with Naomi and the Thursday publication of the *Phoenix* merged into an ordinary blur of classes, extended dining hall lunches, and *Crimson* deadlines, peppered with vivid memories of her encounters with Karen and Ruby and Randy. By Wednesday she could barely sit through her two o'clock class, "Form and Function in Twentieth-Century Film."

A woman was giving an oral report on Ingmar Bergman. "We see here some problems of the auteur in the postmodern moment," droned the woman in a high-pitched Long Island accent. "Poised in this moment, part of the ongoing dialogue between the self and the other, Bergman expresses the alienating effect of alterity—ironically enough, in the very medium most implicated in late capitalism: the film." The woman shuffled her papers together and looked around the dozing seminar room. She might as well have been speaking Martian. Two literature majors were surreptitiously opening a pack of Gitanes; at the front of the classroom, Professor Lou Hrabosky was gazing blankly out the window. It was clear to Toni that he had heard not one syllable of her classmate's presentation. What an utter waste of time this hour had been. Hrabosky, at least, was earning a salary, but the rest of them were actually paying for this tedium.

Professor Hrabosky cleared his throat. "Thank you for your report, Miss Barker. Does anyone have any questions?"

Jerzy Zaleski raised his hand and Toni felt the entire room tense up. Jerzy had a single ambition in life: to become a Rhodes Scholar. He had even taken last year off from Harvard to improve his chances, an increasingly common phenomenon among Rhodes-hounds. On his résumé, he claimed to have spent the time living in refugee camps along the Thai-Cambodian border, but according to Aimee Milvain he had actually been in Bangkok, hanging around massage parlors.

Jerzy cleared his throat in that particularly irritating way of his and let loose. "I think what Willa may be overlooking—I almost missed it myself—is the highly *manufactured* quality of the Bergman-ian image. In a way, I think that the true artist of the postmodern is Visconti, a true *bricoleur*, or tinkerer, if you will. . . ."

As Jerzy's stream of unconsciousness poured forth, undammed by any internal sense of restraint, Toni studied the grain on the seminar table. Hrabosky gave a hoarse cough and looked at his watch. "Well, thank you, Mr. Zaleski," he said. "I am sure you have given us some-thing to ponder." The professor then launched into a nearly incom-prehensible story, the point of which seemed to be that he had once had lunch with Visconti and Rossellini and both of them had told him that he understood their movies better than they themselves did. Toni wasn't really listening, though, and she doubted that her class-mates were either; after all, it wouldn't be on the final.

/ / /

Later that afternoon, still unable to focus on anything but killing time until Thursday, Toni stepped into a tiny alcove and pulled open the door of the Custom Barber Shop. A bell tinkled and Louie, her barber, greeted her with his usual bright smile from his post at the chair nearest the cash register. "Hey there, Toni. How's my favorite reporter doing?" Louie had an uncanny ability to relate to all his cus-tomers, discussing politics with former governor Michael Dukakis—a regular client and fellow Greek—one moment, swapping hockey scores with local teens the next.

Toni smiled and climbed into the red leather chair. Louie fastened a paper collar around her neck and clipped on a fresh white towel. He stepped back and held out his hand: "Earrings." He put the gold hoops on the counter as Toni looked around. Postcards from satisfied clients around the world adorned the mirror, along with photos of

Louie's two little girls. A sign on the wall urged: "If you like our work, tell a friend."

After he made his usual inquiries about the health of Toni's parents and the state of her classwork, and after she inquired about his daughters, they subsided into companionable silence. Toni's head started to droop, and she was wakened by Louie's touch on her temple. "Working too hard, hey?" He laughed.

"Oh, you know, Lois Lane stuff," she answered drowsily. Louie's big black comb moved expertly over her head. Toni could see his scissors, razors, and thinning shears laid out with precision on the counter, next to bottles of discontinued hair tonics and new styling gels. She had a thought. "Hey, Louie," she said, awake now. "You know all the dirt. You ever heard rumors of Harvard students working as prostitutes?"

Louie grinned. "So *that's* what's got you going."

"No, not really," she protested. "I'm just sort of curious, you know." She could see Louie's amused expression behind her in the mirror and added, "You have to admit that if it's true, it would be a pretty major story."

"Well, it's one of those rumors that gets started every year. You know, there's a brothel upstairs at the Hong Kong restaurant, wild orgies in that swimming pool you got over in, er—"

"Adams House," she supplied.

"Exactly." He shook his head and laughed and Toni joined in halfheartedly. She wondered if she had staked her entire journalism career on a silly urban myth, the collegiate equivalent of child star Mikey's tragic death from mixing Pop Rocks and soda.

Louie continued. "I betcha, though: if it's true, the school knows all about it."

"You think so?" she asked dubiously. She was never one for conspiracy theories.

He shifted positions, picking up a small pair of scissors. "Think about it. Harvard's been around for three hundred and fifty years, and you don't last that long without learning a thing or two. They know everything that's going on."

"What do you mean?" Toni asked.

The barber bent over the nape of her neck, scissors flying. "Oh, there's been a lot of funny things over the years. Nothing as bad as that Tufts professor who murdered his hooker girlfriend, but stuff they wouldn't want your parents to hear. For instance, why do they have bulletproof glass in the windows of University Hall?"

"They do?"

"Sure, the guy who put it in comes here all the time. Then there was that professor who was fired for hiring his girlfriend as his secretary and then not giving her any work to do. Tenured, too."

Toni was intrigued. "So what do *you* think about the idea of a student prostitute trading on the Harvard name? You know, 'only the best,' that kind of thing?"

Louie shrugged. "Hey, we all have to trade on something." He palmed her face in his hand and cleaned the nape of her neck. Toni felt tingly where the clippers danced over her skin. He held a large, square mirror behind her, and Toni turned her head from side to side.

She smiled. "Perfect—as always." Louie nodded graciously. Loosening the towel and collar, he ran a soft shaving brush lightly across her face and neck, dusting away the bits of hair. Toni closed her eyes. When he was done, she slid out of the chair.

"You *do* know everything, Louie," she said, extracting a ten-dollar bill from her bag and handing it to him. "I've got to come here more often."

He thanked her soberly and crossed his arms, surveying her critically as she made for the exit. "I really wish you'd let me try something new next time." Toni wrinkled her nose. "Aw, c'mon," he begged. "I've been studying *Essence*. There's lots of exciting new styles for black women." Toni grinned and pushed open the door. Just before the heavy glass door jingled shut, she heard his final pitch: "I've got big plans for you!"

/ / /

Eighty percent of success in life was just showing up—and nowhere was this truer than at Harvard Business School.

As luck would have it, a seat was available on the skydeck, the last curved row in the well-appointed B-school classroom, and Dora Givens nailed it ahead of a student creeping in from the other entryway. Sitting up here, Dora had an unobstructed view of the entire room, but wasn't in anyone else's line of sight. She surveyed the high,

vaulted ceilings, the glistening windows designed in an artful sun-
burst, the elaborate cream-colored moldings. It was an unexpected
coup, all the more because she'd been at work for the past thirty-six
hours and hadn't prepared for class.

She set down her plastic "Charity Challenge" commuter mug of
latte with an extra shot of espresso and pulled the day's discussion
case, her name card, a stack of mail, and a copy of the paper from her
sleek leather briefcase. As the professor industriously arranged student comments on the sliding triple blackboard, Dora unfolded the
ad-choked *Phoenix* and scanned the art and film reviews.

"What was Pepsi's strategic intent?" Professor Swenson barked,
scrawling "strategic intent" on the board as if that elucidated things.
"What was the point of the Pepsi Challenge?"

"To win more market share," a former marine called out from the
right side of the front row. *Duh,* Dora mouthed to herself. Typical
wormdeck comment.

The professor hit a button on the podium control panel, and a
blank section of the blackboard scrolled down. "And what made them
think they could win more market share?" He glanced down at the
class roster. "Ms. Benson!"

A bespectacled woman with blotchy skin, one of a handful of
women in class, turned pale. "Building on Jake's point," she stalled,
"I'd say that consumers had insufficient brand recognition, so this
was a way of breaking past consumer indifference."

The professor nodded and turned back to the blackboard. Dora
tuned out and flipped to the *Phoenix* personals. They were always
good for a kick.

"Has anyone quantified the value to Pepsi for each point in market share?" The professor lobbed the question into the room. "Ball-
park estimate." Everyone scrambled for their HP12C calculators.
"What kind of range do we have?"

Dora absently placed a hand on her calculator and continued
reading.

"Ms. Givens," the professor demanded. "A valuation?" He stood
poised with his chalk.

Dora looked up in annoyance. Normally women couldn't get the
time of day in this class. Now Swenson was calling on two in a row.
What was this—Women's History Week?

She leaned her elbow over the newspaper, examined the numbers written so far on the board, found the highest, and divided it by two. "Three point five," she guessed.

The professor nodded seriously. "So you're at the lower end of the range. Why?"

"Diminishing returns," Dora bluffed. "They've already approached the limit of the cost/quality frontier." The students around her raced pens across paper to record her every word. She shook her head. Couldn't they tell she was making this up?

Having spoken once, she knew she wouldn't be called on again. She picked up the paper—and was startled by an ad that straddled the professional-sex and personal-love sections. Automatically, she checked the paper's masthead to make sure this really was the *Phoenix*, not some *Harvard Lampoon* publication spoof. Having established that the issue was indeed authentic, she studied the ad with interest:

Find out what makes Harvard #1
Harvard coeds and studs eager to meet generous patrons who
demand both brains and beauty. Call the Crimson Escort
Service . . . and experience the unparalleled stimulation that
only the Ivy League can offer.

"Check it out," Dora whispered to herself, shaking her head. She cast an eye about the room, but the rest of the students were all staring down at Swenson, enraptured—or terrified—by his ramblings.

Pushing the paper aside, she turned her attention to her mail, mainly bills, magazines, and mail-order catalogs. She took out her checkbook and paid her long-distance, cellular, cable, Amex, and Barneys bills. Then she checked her balance. Good, and getting better all the time. She wrote out a hundred-dollar donation to Transition House, an underground shelter for battered women. That accomplished, she rifled through the Sharper Image and Williams-Sonoma catalogs, affixing Post-It notes to pages of interest. Her movements were smooth and efficient. Why waste time? She knew what she liked, and she got what she wanted.

/   /   /

Finding Chelo settled in for a night of physics homework, Toni returned to the *Crimson* building and cased it quickly for hangers-on. Two or three reporters sat at their desks, intent on finishing their stories before the weekend. They weren't likely to notice her or what she was doing. A couple of the sports guys were playing cards near the comment book, a six-pack of Carling's Black Label at their feet. Closing the door at the foot of the stairs, she headed up in search of a phone and seclusion.

She settled herself into a chair and, hands trembling slightly, opened the *Phoenix* again to the dog-eared page. Sure enough, just as Naomi had promised, her ad occupied a prominent spot, providing the bridge between "Entre Nous" and "People Meeting People." The "Entre Nous" section came after the ads placed by people selling their used Stratocaster guitars, after the help wanteds (mostly commission jobs for Greenpeace and MassPIRG), and after the "People Meeting People" ads. The difference between "Entre Nous" and "People Meeting People" was that "Entre Nous" was frankly a section of sex ads, whereas "People" were "Meeting People," at least in theory, for a variety of activities of which sex would be just one. Walks on the beach seemed to be a favorite hobby of the people who wanted to meet people. Toni smiled, thinking how crowded Massachusetts beaches must be with aimless singles pacing up and down, looking for "new friends . . . and possibly more."

As she dialed the phone-drop number, she felt a familiar lurch in her stomach and tried to identify it. From her childhood—yes, it was like the moment when a roller coaster's wheels bounce on the track before it starts its first descent. Or like the second before you know a man is going to kiss you, and everything seems to stop dead. A voice answered. "Hello?"

"Hi, I'm Crimson Escort Service and I'm calling for my messages." Toni gave her code number and the person on the other end put her briefly on hold. She pulled out pencil and paper, ready to take the information down.

"Crimson!" the dispatcher's voice sang out. "It's a big night for you guys." Toni had gotten eight calls and five messages—including two from New York.

"Is that a lot?" Toni asked. She wondered how someone from New York had already gotten a copy of the *Phoenix*.

"Sure is. Lotta people don't go for new ads. They like a sense of security, I guess. And most don't leave messages."

"I see."

"So here you are. The first one is from Dan." She gave a number. "You should call him between eleven and eleven-thirty." She rattled off the rest of the details of the day's callers and suggested that Toni check again later.

After hanging up, Toni flipped her reporter's notebook to a new page. Then she decided to get some more pens and pencils. Feeling suddenly thirsty for a Diet Coke, she went off in search of a couple of cans. Finally, having run out of reasons to procrastinate, she dialed the first number. It was a hotel room.

Once the call was transferred, he answered on the first ring. "Hello, Dan?" she began. "I'm calling from Crimson Escort Service."

"Oh, hello," he said. His tone was friendly.

There was a silence that seemed to last forever as Toni racked her brain to think of what to say next. "Um, you know we do outcalls only? And only regular men and women?"

"Okay," he said. "A regular woman is all I want." He laughed.

"Well, then," said Toni, "when would you like to schedule your date? And, um, by the way—have you used any of our competitors' services? Recently?"

"No," Dan admitted. "I'm from out of town. I've never used an escort before in Boston. You're my first." He laughed again.

Well, this was a strikeout, apparently. But he was the first potential john she'd ever talked to. Maybe there was more to find out. "Tell me about yourself, Dan," Toni said. "Are you in town on business?" She wondered if he was telling the truth about never using a Boston escort. Maybe she could string him along for a while. This seemed as good a time as any to learn the tricks, so to speak, of her new trade.

"Yes, I'm here on business," he said. "I'm a salesman."

He sounded youngish, a little like Robert De Niro. Why did he need an escort, anyway?

"How about you?" he asked. "Why don't you tell me about yourself?"

"Okay," Toni said tentatively. "My name is Karen. I'm a student at Harvard. Working my way through."

"I'm impressed," Dan said. "Hard work, that's a good quality. I always thought Harvard students had a lot of money."

"Yeah, well, you know," Toni answered indifferently. "With the cost of college these days, a girl's gotta be creative. So," she asked, turning the focus back to him, "what kind of woman are you looking for?" She checked a list she had jotted down while browsing the competition. "Girl-next-door, dominatrix, career woman, nurse, athlete . . ."

He whistled. "You've got a full selection there! I'm a pretty simple guy compared to most callers, I guess. Me, I'm happy with just the girl next door. Probably someone like you."

"Well, thanks for the compliment, Dan," she replied. He seemed nice enough, if you overlooked the fact that he wanted to have sex with a stranger—and a young one at that.

"Let me see what I have here." She pretended to flip over index cards. "No, busy tonight. Hmm . . . already assigned. Out with her boyfriend. Here's one—oops, Dan, Jennifer here has chicken pox. I wonder why she's still in this pile. You know, Dan, let me do you a little favor. I'm going to give you the numbers of a couple of agencies I know of personally that I'm sure can help you out tonight."

"Oh," he answered, disappointed. "I thought *you* wanted to go out with me."

"Dan, I really wish I could." The anonymity of the phone lines gave her a sense of security. It also allowed her to construct a moderately cute image of Dan.

After reading him the other numbers, Toni hung up the phone and smiled. Maybe this wouldn't be so difficult, after all.

/ / /

Most of the callers seemed pretty ordinary. What they shared was an unwillingness to say much over the phone and a desire for action rather than talk. The first New York number was a no-go; the caller talked to her by speakerphone while simultaneously shouting at his late-night support staff. When she told him that she couldn't guarantee two girls to meet him at the Delta Shuttle next Friday night to spend the weekend with him at his place in Vermont, he cursed at her and hung up.

After taking a break to get two slices at Tommy's Pizza around the corner, she dutifully dialed the second of the two Manhattan numbers.

"Yes," a quiet male voice answered. Toni could hear papers shuffling lightly in the background.

"Hi, I'm calling for David. I had a message he called me."

"Who's this?" the man asked.

"Karen," she replied. "From Crimson Escorts."

"Karen, hold on a sec." She heard him close the door and settle back into his chair.

"Late night at the office?" Toni asked.

"Tell me about it," he answered with a soft laugh.

"Um, David, you realize that we're just a Boston-area service, don't you? We can't really—"

"Right, I know, the ad. I picked up the paper at the airport just before flying back here. I'm actually just calling to ask a question or two, if you don't mind. About Crimson Escorts."

"Go ahead," she answered cautiously.

"See, this is the first time I've called this service, at least under this name; maybe you guys use other names. I go to Boston pretty frequently on business, and—"

At least under this name. Toni's mind raced. She heard every syllable he spoke but she had trouble understanding what he was saying.

"—hard as hell to get appointments but I understood why—once I finally hooked up. It was pretty fantastic. Seriously. It was great."

"You're a satisfied customer," she said.

"So it is the same outfit?" he asked intently.

"Maybe yes, maybe no. What outfit did you use before, David?" she asked, holding back her excitement.

"It was Harvard-specific," he answered. "I think it was called Class Ring or something."

"Do you consider that a Harvard-specific name?" she asked herself as much as him.

"Not really," he admitted. "But it was the real thing. I could tell."

"How did you know that?" she asked. "What would make you sure that your date was a Harvard student?"

"Because she brought *The Peloponnesian Wars* with her. I had to read that when I was in college." He laughed, savoring the irony. "Plus, all the condoms said 'Veritas' on them. That was cute. Unfor-

tunately, starting a couple months ago I couldn't get my calls returned anymore. Thought I'd fallen off the A list."

"Well, you've found us out, David," Toni said. She listened to
herself for a second; she sounded seductive. It hadn't been a conscious decision. "There's been a reorganization of sorts. But we're
mostly the same."

"This is great. So I won't have a problem getting an appointment
next week? I'm coming up Thursday for meetings."

"Not at all . . . provided you answer some of my questions," she
teased.

"Quid pro quo, that's fair. Doing market research?"

"You're a smart one. Just a quality verification process," she improvised. "First, some demographics. How old—"

"Twenty-eight. Five-ten. One-sixty. White male. Professional. In-
come level low six figures. Full head of hair." He chuckled. "Thought
I'd save you some trouble—I'm a marketing consultant. This is what
I do."

Twenty-eight? Why was a man like this hiring prostitutes?

"Do you have a regular girlfriend?" she asked out of the blue.

"Girlfriend, no," he said a bit wistfully. "Wife, yes. And one child,
eighteen months." She put her pen down. What was wrong with his
marriage—or rather, what was wrong with *him*—that he would hire a
prostitute?

"How many times have you used Class Ring?" she asked.

"Just twice. Apparently I never attained the status of a regular
customer. I got in late."

"Why do you say that?" she asked. "We're not supposed to play
favorites. Have you heard that there are regular customers?"

"Friend of mine, Brett—God, he'd kill me if he knew I'd just said
his name like this—Brett was up there every week for several months.
He was like an addict. He said it was the best sex he ever had, didn't
think twice about shelling out four hundred dollars a pop. He's the
one who gave me the number. He said the clients were as exclusive as
the escorts."

"Did he mention a particular girl?" Toni asked.

David chuckled. "No, the last thing he wanted was to be stuck
with one woman. It's the story of his life, but that's another conversation. I got the impression he was on good terms with the dis-

patcher—your predecessor, I guess. She always chatted with him about his experiences. Very accommodating—apparently she made sure he had variety. But he said it was always the same: they were gorgeous, they knew sex, and they were young."

"And that was your experience as well, David?" she asked.

"I did it twice with the same girl. I guess I should say 'woman,' but she wasn't like that."

"What do you mean?" Toni asked.

"I mean, it was innocent. She was a girl and I was a boy. She said I was cute, she tousled my hair. I guess I was pretty nervous. See, my wife was my first girlfriend, practically. Mona and I got married just out of college, and it's been pretty good, by and large. I'd never mess it up by having an affair or anything. But sometimes you just wake up in the morning and realize how little of life you've seen. Daphne—the girl they sent me—she seemed to understand all that. She told me to pretend I was a senior and she was a freshman. I spent so much of my life just studying hard, working hard, getting ahead. . . . I know it sounds selfish, but I feel like I finally have the time to make up for all the great experiences I've missed."

Toni kept silent as he spoke, not sure how she felt about his confession.

"So you liked it enough to request Daphne the second time?" she asked finally.

"Definitely. I couldn't stop thinking about her. She made me feel . . . *secure*. All the more so because of the condom policy."

"You were in favor of that?" she asked.

"Absolutely. Hey, I've got to be around to support my family. The fact that they were so insistent on using condoms made the whole experience less scary. It almost made it more exciting. It might seem weird, but once she put it on me, the thrill went up another notch."

It was surreal to sit deep in the *Crimson* at night, talking to a New York yuppie still immersed in his work about his most personal feelings and sexual feats. Toni heard a knock on David's door and a woman giving some instruction in business-speak. The door closed again.

"So there you have it," he concluded. "I guess I need to go."

"I appreciate the call, David," Toni said. "This will be very helpful for our—"

"Listen, it's gonna be all set for next Thursday," he asked eagerly, "right?"

"Absolutely," she replied.

"I'm counting on you, Karen!" he stressed. "Check you next week."

Toni set down the receiver and spun around in the swivel chair several times. If she could trust David's story, then she had found much more than a single Harvard prostitute. There was—or had been until very recently—an actual Harvard prostitution ring.

She gripped the arms of the chair and tried to concentrate. There was no point in getting excited until she had proof. Not some shrouded-in-mystery figure like Woodward and Bernstein's Deep Throat. Real proof.

/ / /

Back in his room, Van tossed his leather jacket and black scarf on the bed and tugged off his sweater. He splashed cold water on his face and ran his wet fingers through his hair to try to get rid of some of the cigarette smell. One in the morning and he was already beat. A year ago, this was when he'd have been getting *ready* to go out.

There were better ways of enjoying an evening than seeing the Marlo Thomas remake of *It's a Wonderful Life* at the Brattle and spending two hours swilling beer at the Boathouse Bar. The worst torture was not the movie itself, but listening to a hundred and fifty self-proclaimed arbiters of wit and taste trying to top one another in unclever asides. He wished he had stayed home reading, but Gabriela, an Argentine sophomore in the house, had caught him at a vulnerable moment—shortly after he had been stood up at the last minute by a certain someone.

He pressed the PLAY button on his answering machine and settled back on the bed to listen. Aimee Milvain. Aimee Milvain. Baby Watanabe. His econometrics T.A. Aimee Milvain again. An unfamiliar voice: "Hi, Van, we really haven't met, but, um, I was standing next to my friend Tom at Lamont when you two were talking, and . . ." At least once a day he got a call from someone he'd never even heard of. A couple more messages. He used to return calls, but had found it didn't matter; people just called again, with the same conversations. All except for the person who was *supposed* to call, having had *all night* to think of what constituted appropriate behavior and all.

He lay back on his pillow and flipped open a copy of *Lysistrata*.

Half an hour later he'd only gotten to the fourth page. Okay, he would be a doormat. He picked up the phone and dialed, giddiness flooding him as soon as the call went through. "Yeah, it's me. Listen"—he swallowed his pride—"I was wondering . . . Well, I know that. Look, I'm sorry for giving you a hard time, okay? The things I said were out of line." He held the phone away from his ear and half listened. Apologizing wouldn't be such a chore if everyone else wasn't always so happy to hear you say you were wrong.

"Well, anyway, what are you doing now? Mm-hmm, I thought so. They say that no one should go to bed angry. So I think I should come over. Okay? I'll be there in fifteen minutes."

Elated, he threw on his jacket and ran down the stairs.

4

Somewhere near MIT, a few feet from the Charles River, Dave Mantini waited. His two-hour vigil on a park bench had done little for his state of mind; each jogger made him increasingly certain that someone from work would spot him.

Finally, a few minutes before eight, he sighted a spry blond man on cross-country skis. Dave jumped to his feet and called out, but the man paid no heed. He maneuvered past with a sharp swishing noise. Dave stretched out a hand. "Hey, hold up, Mark! It's me, Dave Mantini." He jogged heavily alongside the skier, his boots destroying the elegant symmetry of the ski tracks. The man looked at him in incomprehension. "Dave Mantini, from the Floor. I used to be in Dr. Waxman's lab."

That worked. The skier gradually brought himself to a halt. Gracefully he twisted his torso and pointed his skis at Dave. He nodded with an abashed smile.

"Sorry about that," he said. It was the same reassuring tenor Dave remembered from the good old days. "I didn't hear you. I keep myself pretty focused when I'm training." He nodded again. "How'd you know I'd be here?"

Dave ducked his head and smirked. "I'm a researcher, remember?"

Company lore had it that Biotecnica founder Mark Tansen skied any day there was snow and sailed any day there was sun. The older he got, the more he behaved like a happy kid, thrilled to spend his life outdoors. Of course, the baby-faced M.D.–Ph.D. from Johns Hopkins could spend his time as he saw fit. He *was* Biotecnica.

Tansen laughed. "Good to see you. How are things?"

"Great," Dave said automatically. "Terrible, I mean." He got right to the point. "Did you get the fax I sent to your home? About the irregularities in the protocols? I assume you got it, but since there wasn't any answer, I thought I should try to talk to you in person."

Tansen looked blank; then his youthful features morphed into a mask of responsible concern. "Oh, yes. The protocols. That's really not my area any more, Dave. Perhaps you should raise these issues with Jerry—"

"Jerry won't do anything, Mark!" Dave exclaimed. "He's part of the problem. Dora Givens couldn't do these things without his approval."

"Well," Mark drawled, tucking his ski poles under one arm, "I'm sure Jerry has reasons for his decisions. Things always look simple from the outside, right?"

This made no sense. Mark Tansen had every reason to hate Jerry Frost; that was why Dave was risking this meeting. Tansen had hired Frost during the company's bad period, a year and a half before, when the venture-capital group bankrolling the start-up pressured him to find management they could trust their money with. Within six months, Frost had forced Tansen out and gotten himself appointed CEO. Worse, Frost knew nothing about biotech; his previous job had been managing the snack-chip division of a large tobacco conglomerate.

Mark Tansen had built Biotecnica, and seeing him treated so badly had made Dave yearn to be back in his lab at Harvard. But Harvard wasn't the same, either, ever since Dr. Waxman . . . Dave wanted to shake Tansen. "Listen, Mark, everything's crazy at BT. You must have heard. And like I said, I've figured out who's responsible. Please, you've got to do something about it."

Tansen rubbed his hands together rapidly, as if they were a Rubik's Cube. Finally he looked up. "I'm afraid that doesn't make much sense to me, Dave. Why would Strategy have anything to do with testing? Anyway, it just wouldn't be right for me to invade Jerry's turf at this point."

"Listen, I'm not saying this to get at anyone; I'm saying it because I always believed in . . ." His voice trailed off. "You don't believe me, do you?"

Tansen sighed. "We've all had unexpected setbacks in our careers, Dave. Sometimes we can take personal conflicts and blow them out of proportion." He clapped Dave on the shoulder and smiled. "Listen, why not try to reason things out with Dana Gibbons, or even talk to Jerry during one of the Wednesday afternoon milk-and-cookie sessions? Jerry can be simpatico, when you catch him in the mood."

Impossible. He would lose his job if he brought this up with Jerry Frost. Not to mention the fact that he hadn't figured out how everything fit together; he might just end up looking foolish.

Tansen didn't see Dave shake his head. "Change is good, don't you think, Dave?" The founder bent his knees slightly and gave a deft thrust with his poles. "Change keeps us young and healthy." He didn't wait for a reply as he started to sail forward.

/   /   /

Toni stayed late at the *Crimson* on Tuesday evening to check back in with her service. Someone named Bill had left several impatient messages. "Said he didn't care how late you called," the operator said.

A man answered on the first ring. "Hello, I'm calling for Bill," Toni began, confident and collected.

"This is Bill," he replied quickly. "Are you from Crimson?"

"Yes, I am. I'm Karen. I'd like to ask you a couple of questions first, if you don't mind." She took his silence as acquiescence and started right in. "Are you a first-time client, Bill, or have you used escorts from Harvard before?"

"Oh, I've had my share of Harvard girls before," he said.

"Really?" she asked. "What agency did you use?"

"Whoa, honey!" he replied. "You're a curious one. Why don't you tell me what you like, Karen?"

"Walking on the beach," Toni improvised. "Nothing beats a good walk on the beach."

"No, I mean in bed, Karen. What do you like to do? What would you like"—he cleared his throat—"me to do to you?"

Boy, this one really got right to the point. "I'm just the dispatcher, Bill."

He laughed nervously. "And I'm just a healthy, red-blooded American male, heh, heh."

"You certainly sound that way," Toni said. "So what about those Harvard girls?"

Bill ignored her question. "I like my ladies—I mean, I like a lady to be active in bed, but, you know, real feminine. I guess I'm just a traditionalist. Panties, those lacy things like from that catalog. I just love those. And high heels."

He was silent for a moment. "You got those, right?" he inquired.

"Of course, of course," she answered, stifling a yawn. "Our women—our girls—are very traditional. They love to wear ruffles and silky things."

"No, I mean *you,* hon," he barked. "You wearin' any of those panties now, Karen? Bet your cute ass really sticks out behind you when you wear high heels."

Toni said nothing.

"Hey! What's going on there?" Bill said, his voice insistent.

She tried to laugh in a sophisticated way. "Yes, I'm still here, Bill. Of course I love my high heels and, um, teddies and such. I'm a regular girl, too. But you do realize I'm the dispatcher, right?"

"Sure you are," Bill said, laughing, his voice once again average and unthreatening. He paused again. "But I'll bet your pussy likes a good piece of meat now and then, huh?"

Toni remained silent, the receiver growing slippery with sweat.

"You still there, Karen?" he barked. "Hey, sorry about that." The first Bill was back. "I'm just kidding around. Look, I can tell you want something from me. This some sort of marketing project? You want to find out more about those Harvard girls? Or are you just new on the job? Either way, I seem to know more about this kind of stuff than you, honey. I'm a friendly guy. You cut me some slack, I'll answer your questions." He paused. "All of them."

Toni sat back in her chair. It was just a role. Karen did it, Randy did it, Daphne did it. "All right, Bill, go ahead."

"I knew you'd see it my way, Karen," Bill said. "A much more . . .

ladylike attitude." His irregular breathing made it hard to understand all his words. "So there we are, on the beach. Tired of walking. We find a nice private spot, and you're all over me before I know what's hit me. Yeah, before I know it, you're cramming my dick up your hot, tight pussy. Yeah, I'll bet you'd like that, Karen. Sure you would. Right? . . . Answer me, Karen!"

"What's not to like?" Toni replied.

"I haven't had any complaints," Bill said jovially. His breath was still audible. "You like to be on top, Karen? On top's best."

"Yeah, Bill, it's always best to be on top of things," she said.

"Riding my thick cock," he urged. "Say it, Karen."

"No, I *won't* say it." She heard a distant tinny clinking, like a belt buckle repeatedly hitting something, a chair arm perhaps. Of course—he was masturbating. This was ridiculous; the jerk didn't know anything.

She shuddered, shaking off her paralysis. "Fuck off, you pathetic pervert," she snarled, slamming down the receiver.

She banged the phone two more times. A loud after-ring sounded and she jumped, convinced that Bill had somehow managed to trace her. She sat with her hand trembling over the receiver. Once her legs felt steady enough, she bolted from the room.

/ / /

"Oh, *fuck* Thucydides," sighed Chelo, slamming down the well-worn paperback copy of *The Peloponnesian Wars* onto her desk. *Why* had this tedious book been assigned in yet another Core course? Chelo's friends, who sometimes found her a bit uptight, would have been surprised by the expletive, but of course no one was in the room to hear. Toni was off investigating, as usual; and according to a report from Aimee Milvain, Tara had left school—at least for the semester and perhaps for good.

Standing up from her desk, Chelo pulled another Diet Coke from the battered mini-fridge; after a moment of hesitation, she unwrapped a peanut-topped brownie scavenged from the dining hall. She wolfed down the slightly disgusting treat and instantly felt fat.

She glanced sideways at her reflection in the mirror on the bathroom door and inspected the slightly distorted picture. God, her posture was atrocious—better get to work on that. Her features were okay, she supposed, even vaguely dramatic. Skin tone good; that was a plus. And her beautiful long black hair, which her high school boyfriend Johnny Espinosa had loved to stroke . . . was done up in a goddamned *braid.* She suddenly realized that the person she most resembled was the fake Native American woman on the T.V. commercial for Mazola Oil. "This is corn," she said aloud. "My people call it maize."

Enough moping for one evening. Maybe the best thing was to go work at her employer's office; it would be easier to concentrate there. Her job in the sociology department had an important fringe benefit: Professor Moore let her use his state-of-the-art Macintosh whenever she wanted. She might not need the computer time this evening, but she would certainly appreciate fewer distractions.

She trudged through Harvard Square and across the Yard. The sociology department was housed in William James Hall, a tall white building near the north end of campus.

Chelo entered the lobby, waving her ID at the security guard, a grad student whose polyester check pants and velour shirt identified him as either a retro seventies hipster or a recent arrival from the People's Republic of China. "Off to loot and pillage," she told him pleasantly, stepping into the open elevator.

"Mmph," he responded, his eyes never once leaving his biochemistry text.

Once up on the sixth floor, Chelo entered Moore's dark office, tracking in snow with her duck boots. She snapped on the desk lamp, sat down in the huge leather chair, and watched snowflakes careening against the window. The moonlight cast an eerie blue glow, and shadows played across the floor-to-ceiling stacks of books along three walls. There were hundreds of volumes from all disciplines and in several languages. It was the sort of office the young Consuelo Santana might have imagined as the haunt of an Ivy League professor. But she would have portrayed the office's inhabitant as a crotchety fellow with a red forehead and unkempt white hair, not a striking young genius who might, in fact, make excellent husband material.

Chelo laughed, embarrassed by her own fantasies. But actually, Moore wasn't so much older than she; though tenured, he couldn't be much past thirty-five.

Toying with little items on Moore's desk, she wondered what he was *really* like. She glanced at the few pictures on the wall and desk.

A younger-looking Moore with college friends; a framed picture of a couple with two kids, probably his sister's or brother's family; a fairly recent picture of Moore with some woman, in front of the Taj Mahal. Rumor had it that the professor had a girlfriend who was a senior staffer in the White House. Chelo disapproved. As they said in Spanish, "Amor de lejos, amor de pendejos"—"Long-distance love is for assholes."

She noted the envelopes neatly stacked on the desk blotter. Lots of bills. She picked up a hand-addressed letter from someone in New Haven and pondered the ethics of opening Moore's mail. That was a no-brainer. On the other hand, perhaps reading the letter would help her understand Moore better and make her a more effective assistant. Quickly, before she changed her mind, she slid the note out of the neatly sliced envelope and unfolded it.

"How goes it, Dayton?" she read. "Peg and I had an *incredibly* interesting time on our research grant in Cologne this summer . . ." It was an *incredibly* dull update from a colleague. Chelo carefully returned the letter to its original position. Then she opened another.

Twenty minutes later, she wondered if she had fallen down some slippery slope to criminality. Her snooping had taken her to shoeboxes of old correspondence under the desk, and then to Moore's file cabinets, where she found course outlines, research proposals, grant applications, letters of recommendation for students. "While Roger is an effective learner, he lacks the intellectual discipline of the true scholar." *Ouch,* she thought in sympathy for the unknown Roger. She would have to be careful when applying to medical school.

She had reached the third file cabinet and was browsing through the top drawer. More of the same. No love letters or family pictures here.

He's about as fascinating as I am, Chelo mused. In the fourth drawer she found some more personal correspondence, but the files only went halfway back. Behind the divider, though, she noticed some large yellow interoffice envelopes, the kind that fasten shut with a little red string around a cardboard circle. There were three or four of these, stuffed with documents.

She set the envelopes on the carpeted floor, her heart beating fast. Unwinding one of the strings from its clasp, she pulled out a sheaf of papers. There were fifteen or twenty documents of various thicknesses. Some were typed, others handwritten. All were photo-copied. The first one looked like a girl's handwriting; the lettering was large and round, with frequent underlinings and circles over the *i*'s:

2/5   My life is generally quite dull, so I hope this course perks it up somewhat.

2/10   I had a totally weird dream last night. In this dream, Brad, the guy across the hall, came up to me and touched my cheek. He said, "Are you still working on that English paper?" I was confused because I'm majoring in bio and I'm not taking any English classes. Then I somehow realized in that weird dream way that he was talking about the fact that I hadn't had sex since I broke up with Dennis in December. Before I knew what was happening, Brad reached out and touched my breasts, which for some reason were exposed through my robe. Then I woke up.

With a start, Chelo realized what she was reading. These had to be the journals students were required to keep for the "Sexuality and Social Institutions" class Moore taught. But they were supposed to be strictly confidential. The course, in fact, had an elaborate system by which section leaders monitored only whether students turned in written materials. No names were attached; no grades were assigned. Even so, how could you ethically make a photocopy of someone's private journal?

But Chelo couldn't stop reading. This particular girl, it seemed, was all talk and no action. Leafing through the stack of photocopies, she noticed that some bore marginal comments in Moore's handwriting. One read "transference"; another, "child's need for approval." She read on. "Unresolved Elektra fixation." "Bipolar illness." "Latent homosexuality." "Parental expectations." "Borderline personality disorder."

Chelo hoisted a particularly thick journal with marks throughout. Here was someone who was having fun.

2/10   While I feel this class is completely bogus, I welcome the chance to express to the world a more innovative view of sexuality. Are you turned on yet, section leader?

2/12   Went to Dada last night. It's getting tired; they're letting in too many ugly straight people and grad students. Met this art history grad student, Janet something. Cute hair, not much personality. Went to her condo on Mass. Ave.; I think her parents are rich. She was totally into oral sex, especially receiving. I remembered I had an hourly this morning, so I went back to Adams.

2/15   This blond-haired jock from McLean, Virginia, flirted with me in Lamont Library near the reserve-book checkout. He filled his jeans nicely, but then he mentioned he was an East Asian Studies major; that burst the bubble. He's certainly entitled to his preferences, but I've had enough conversations about "the wonder and mystery of the Orient" for one lifetime. Much as I hate the term "rice queen," it has a certain applicability. Later that night, Aimee happened by my room in her slut pajamas, allegedly to borrow the aforementioned reserve reading (from this course, in fact). She's cute, and I find a certain satisfaction in her shallowness, but frankly it's much more stimulating to tease her than to do her.

Aimee? Was this Aimee Milvain from down the hall? Surely there were few others with that contrived spelling. And if the author was male, bisexual, Asian, and lived in Adams House, he must be Van.

3/3   Sylvia called from Simmons. I said come over, it had been a while. She's kind of into a leather thing now, wanted to be blindfolded. I said, "Aren't you concerned with being objectified? I'm more of a feminist than you!" She said, "Okay, we'll both be blindfolded." So we were. It was totally awesome sex. She's definitely precocious, sexual peak–wise. I started counting the number of thrusts but lost count after about 140. Felt kind of sticky afterward, though.

3/10   Course and life strangely connect! I actually talked to our esteemed professor, dear section leader. I know you totally have the hots for him. Anyway, he's smart. In like five minutes he asked me if my grandparents were from Hanoi or Saigon, figured out the thing with the French blood, and correctly deduced I'm traumatized on some level by adolescent rejection from the stupid Vietnamese community in Dallas. Too bad he's straight. Maybe this course isn't *totally* bogus.

3/13　Serge Abudu of the tennis team came on to me after practice. That was kind of a surprise. We went to his room in Kirkland House—my first time there, so it was like a field trip. He offered me coke—I declined, of course—and was totally into illicit same-sex sex but didn't want to use a condom. Asshole. Hope he's alive in 10 years, but I didn't care to seal my fate with his. I left him coked-out and masturbating to U2.

Chelo had never read anything like this. She was leafing through the rest of Van's diary when she heard the elevator door open. She froze. But it was only two graduate students talking about some psych experiment. The moment rattled her, however, and she told herself she would read just one more entry.

4/1　Betty Jo Orten, the goon, came up to me when I was slumming in Winthrop House. She said, in her subtle way, "So, Van, are you bisexual or what?" The girl has some cheek. I said, "Why do you want to know, do you want to be converted?" She has that wide-eyed fanatic look of those Koreans from Mather House who used to invite me to Bible study all the time, before they got scared when I actually showed up. Anyway, then I said, "No, Betty Jo, I don't really have any sexual preference. Not everyone does, you know." She looked really horrified and ran away, clippety-clop. . . .

5/3　I have launched an affair with the most incredible hunk of all time. We're talking warm, funny, smart, good clothes, doesn't wear too much cologne, older but charmingly innocent. I had to explain to him the principles of fellatio. Kind of scary that I actually like someone. I'm being surprisingly discreet. Really, I'm quite amazed at myself.

The graduate students were making more noise in the hallway, and Chelo felt jittery. She replaced the journals in their oversize manila envelopes and was about to return them to the file cabinet when she was struck by a thought. Tara had taken Moore's class last spring. If her diary was in the file, it might offer a clue to her sudden departure from campus. Where Tara had gone, Chelo wasn't sure. She was never home when Chelo called her in Darien. Maybe the diary would offer an explanation.

Chelo knew this was dubious reasoning at best, but she didn't care to examine her motives in great detail. She grabbed as many of the envelopes as would fit in her knapsack, swearing to herself that she'd return them as soon as her research was done. Quickly gathering up her books, she flicked off the light and sprinted for the elevator.

/   /   /

Several more nights, many more callers. Toni got better at playing her role: the respondents to the ad were just men, some nice, others not so nice. She was growing into the job, she supposed.

Unfortunately, as she mastered this particular skill, the returns diminished. No more Bills, but no more Davids, either.

Then her luck changed.

/   /   /

Alone in her room, nearly a week after her ad appeared, Toni punched in a number from the night's list. A machine picked up on the fourth ring. To her surprise, the voice that crisply recited the phone number and instructed callers to leave a message was female. "If you want a real person, try after eleven." John Coltrane played in the background.

"Hi," Toni began. "This is Crimson returning your call. I'll try again after eleven."

She attempted to study for the next two hours but ended up doodling, the pulse of anticipation building. If the woman was an actual escort who had been attracted to Toni's ad because of its Harvard theme, she might have scored a big break.

Eleven o'clock came. Before touching the black phone on her desk, Toni counted to one hundred, as slowly as she could stand.

She dialed again, her pounding heart defying the command of her brain to keep cool. The phone rang twice.

"Hey," a woman answered, emotionlessly, as if she were glancing through mail.

"This is Karen," Toni said. She was surprised to hear her voice several tones higher than normal. "I'm from Crimson Escorts. I had a message that someone called."

"Right. Thanks for returning my call, Karen." The woman said "Karen" as if in quotes, her tone both intimate and condescending.

"You called regarding our ad?" Toni asked.

"I did," the woman said. "What's up?"

"The usual," Toni replied, settling back in the regulation Harvard dorm chair. In front of her was a jar of quarters that Chelo had labeled "Laundry Money." "Are you interested in an escort experience?"

"An escort experience?" the woman answered, idly. "Perhaps sometime. Not now. I'm more interested in—"

"In joining up?" Toni interrupted. "We're always looking for qualified escorts."

"Well, that *is* convenient, because I'm always looking for competent organizations." This woman wasn't used to being interrupted.

"Do you have any relevant work experience?" Toni asked. "I'm sorry, I didn't get your name."

"I didn't give it, babe," the other woman replied. "You know, I appreciate your inquisitiveness, but I have a few questions myself, a few things I'd like answered before I give any personal details to strangers."

"Ask away," Toni said. She didn't mind. She'd thought this through.

"Why do you call yourself Crimson Escorts?"

"It's Harvard's school color. And its mascot, too."

"Amazingly enough, I did know that. But why do you use that particular name?"

"Because our escorts offer the best, just as Harvard is the best in—"

"So it's just a metaphor?" the woman pressed. She was smarter than Toni had anticipated.

"Our clients want real Harvard students," Toni explained. "They want the best. And we aim to give it to them."

Silence.

"Do you find that hard to believe?" Toni asked after a moment.

"That people want to fuck the Harvard name?" the woman asked. "Not at all. That you can supply it? Yes."

"Seeing is believing, I suppose."

"You've got that right," the woman answered. "Tell you what, Karen. Let's get together. And if we're both satisfied the other is real, maybe we can form a business relationship. I'm looking for new venues."

"I'm game," Toni answered, her neck stiff, her grip tight. "Where, Harvard Square? One of the cafés?"

"No. That party at the graduate school of design, next week."

She must be referring to the Mardi Gras costume ball. It was a wild event, but few outside Harvard knew about it.

"Who are you?" Toni blurted.

"You'll find out later, Karen. And I'll find out something about your résumé, too. Midnight, in the design cubicles."

"Which one?" There were scores of cubicles in the open, lofty spaces of Gund Hall, where architecture students spent endless hours putting together models of buildings and landscape designs.

"Number sixty-nine, of course," the woman replied. "I'm sure you can find it—if you know which end is up."

5

Like everything else at the Austen Riggs Sanatorium, the meeting room was discreetly lavish. Nothing but the finest would do for the troubled children of the privileged classes, a group in which Tara Sheridan was included, courtesy of her father's health insurance plan.

She recognized some of the women from her hall and greeted them with a nod as they took their seats. The clock hands clicked to three, and a middle-aged woman with frizzy auburn hair bounced into the room.

"Hi," she announced blithely. "I see we have some new members today." She checked her clipboard. "Jeanne, Susan, and Tara. Are all three of you here?" Tara raised her hand self-consciously and noticed two other women doing the same. One of them was just a girl, a waiflike teenager in a Concord Academy sweatshirt; the other was a plumpish woman in her thirties wearing a navy blue cardigan, a pleated flannel skirt, and pearls. They exchanged glances, shy in the new setting. The other group members settled into their chairs with a comfortable smugness.

"I'm Linda," the frizzy-haired woman went on. "I'll be facilitating the eating disorders group. I'm a licensed social worker with over fifteen years of experience in helping people come to terms with their relationships with food and with themselves. I'm here for you." Tara saw looks of boredom cross the faces of her fellow patients and realized they must have heard this speech many times before. Linda went on to describe some of the clinical features of anorexia and bulimia, and Tara found her attention wandering.

She snapped back into focus when she heard Linda saying, "And so I'd like to ask Jeanne, Susan, and Tara to begin today's session by telling us a little bit about why they're here."

Susan, the preppie anorexic, began her story. It seemed to Tara that she had heard it before, or maybe she had watched it on a made-for-TV movie. It was a classic tale: girl gets body fat; girl loses body fat; girl keeps on losing. The only unique aspect of Susan's story was the particularly weird calorie-free meal that had been her exclusive diet for years: sugar-free orange Jell-O and water chestnuts. Tara felt a little ill, thinking about it.

Jeanne went next. Tara listened intently; as she had suspected, Jeanne was a bulimic. Interestingly enough, she was a nurse. The clinic where she worked had insisted on her going into treatment when she was discovered stealing hospital-strength ipecac from the pharmacy.

"It induces vomiting," Jeanne explained. "It's mostly used in cases of accidental poisoning." Tara saw a few of the other bulimics exchange knowing nods. These women really were sick.

Then it was her turn. She had expected this moment for several days, but she still wasn't sure what she was going to say. It had been a simple task to convince her parents that she had an eating disorder. She was thin and distant; they were as ready as anyone else to buy into stereotypes about young WASP women. But around her were authentically ill experts.

In a low voice, careful not to look at any of the other patients, Tara began to tell a story. Not her story, but a story she thought would pass muster: young woman in college, away from home for the first time, worrying desperately about everything, and deciding to worry most about her weight. Obsessive exercising, solitary chocolate cakes followed by hours of sit-ups; Tara was surprised at how easy it was to turn the average American woman's neuroses about food into a genuine psychopathology. "I just couldn't stop," she confessed.

Then the laxatives. The enemas. The vomiting. Sleepless nights and dizzy spells. It was a familiar tale.

"Yes," Tara concluded, encouraged by the smiles and assenting murmurs of the others. "I felt that I had lost control." To her own surprise, she could hear her voice breaking into a sob. "I thought I was in charge, but I wasn't. And I couldn't stand that." She felt the heat and sting of tears on her face, and couldn't go on.

Linda reached over and patted her arm. "Thank you, Tara. I think we all know what you're going through."

I wish you did, Tara thought. *I wish it were that simple.*

/ / /

"You really look fantastic, Toni," her date said admiringly as she stepped out of the limousine he had rented for the Mardi Gras ball. "Though I wouldn't have known it was you."

"Maybe it's the mask," she suggested, referring to the white satin covering she had added at the last minute. She had dressed as Cleopatra in an off-the-shoulder white tunic of shimmering, fluted silk tied at the waist with a sash of gold brocade. Her dark, flowing wig was woven with cowrie shells; gold bangles adorned her upper arms and ankles.

Didi Carón inspected her from head to toe. "No, it's not just the mask. It's something else. You look different."

She smiled and they headed for the entrance to Gund Hall, home of the graduate school of design. Maybe she was becoming a different person.

Toni had met Didi in Professor Santoprieto's "Modern Media" seminar earlier that year. Throughout the term, the two had dated a bit, just a few movies and good-night kisses; since the breakup of her two-year thing with Lucius, casual dating was more appealing than the idea of having a boyfriend. Didi was the scion of a wealthy Cuban-American publishing empire based in Miami. The Caróns were rumored to contribute to various right-wing causes, mostly associated with failed attempts to overthrow Castro, but Didi himself had always seemed eminently reasonable. In class, he listened to Professor Santoprieto with unfailing respect and attention. He wasn't universally popular; Van had made a face when Toni mentioned she'd be attending the event with Didi. He wouldn't explain, though she got the impression he considered Didi a big homophobe. On balance, though, she liked him—and face it: going out with someone so good-looking felt like a major score. When dressed in black tie, as he was tonight, Didi was resplendent. His thick, glossy hair was stylishly gelled, and he had the exquisite grooming of the South American elite. His only bit of costuming, aside from his tuxedo, was a French opera mask on a stick.

Didi and Toni entered an explosive swirl of colors and sounds. Several bands and DJs appeared to be playing near top volume, but the music was drowned out by laughter and shrieks from the costumed crowd. The main area on the ground floor had been partitioned into sections; steamed-up glass doors led to the student loft areas, where a few hardy design students continued their labors. The air was filled with the odors of champagne, sweat, and perfume. All of Harvard's beautiful people, such as they were, had turned out for the event.

Didi pointed toward a group of architecture students in elaborate models of various Harvard buildings. One tall, pale man was dressed as William James Hall, in absolutely accurate detail, down to the tiny winking red light on top of his head. Behind them, Yasir Arafat stood telling jokes to Marilyn Monroe. The Grim Reaper was getting punch for a group of friends who included a giant condom, Divine, Raggedy Ann, and Al Sharpton.

A Latin beat pounded out of the speakers, and Didi swept Toni onto the floor in an expert salsa move. She spotted some friends on the other side of the room, laughing and joking with a thin girl who seemed to be dressed as a member of the cast of *Les Misérables*. Toni recognized her as "the Quad Refugee," so nicknamed for her haunted displaced-person look—though that effect might have been a function of her all-black attire and white lipstick. She *was* one of the several hundred unfortunate students who lived in Radcliffe Quad, a mile north of Harvard Yard.

Sidestepping a huge papier-mâché head resembling the controversial Harvard lawyer Alan Dershowitz, the couple ended their dance and went in search of drinks. The walls of one room had been covered entirely in black velvet, and people were swaying gently as a ska band played soulful reggae versions of Elvis tunes. Toni covertly checked her watch. Fifty minutes before the appointed hour.

Following the trail of glow-in-the-dark planets and stars, Toni and Didi pushed their way downstairs and emerged into the blue-lit basement. Humming aquariums filled with exotic fish covered every surface, and lava lamps undulated slowly. "Tainted Love" by Soft Cell was playing on the stereo; the tinny, synthesized homage to the Supremes seemed appropriate underwater. A buffet table was spread with sushi and seaweed crackers.

Toni fell into a chair near a group of Adams House people on the sidelines. Aimee Milvain and Refugee were huddled in a corner, pointing at various people on the dance floor and giggling evilly, probably about figure flaws. Toni spotted Van in the distance, surrounded by his usual throng of admirers. He wore only a pair of dark green dance tights; hundreds of dabs of body paint covered his bare torso. He set aside the unwieldy picture frame that accented his outfit and began to dance by himself. His first halting moves became more and more energetic; sweat smudged some of the painted dots on his body and created transparent patches on his tights. He danced, in his own world, for a good fifteen minutes as others watched from a respectful distance. Finally, he put his hands on his knees and breathed deeply. Then, spotting Toni and Didi, who were back on the dance floor after a brief rest, he flashed a smile and walked over to say hello. The floor was so crowded and the music so loud that the trio had to press close together to hear one another. Toni was startled to see that Van's eyes looked unfocused and almost afraid.

"Great costume, Van!" she exclaimed, wondering what was up.

"Yeah, it is," agreed Didi. "But what is it, exactly?"

"It's a cross between *Number One* by Jackson Pollock and *Jeune Homme Nu* by Flandrin," he explained. " 'A Portrait of the Artist as a Young Postmodernist.' " Then, as if this effort at small talk was too taxing, he said, somewhat plaintively, "This scene really sucks, don't you think?"

Neither Toni nor Didi could hear him clearly. They moved to the sidelines and Van leaned over to whisper to Toni. "We should get together sometime. Just to talk."

"Sure!" she answered quickly, flattered by the attention.

Van glanced at Didi. "Yeah, whatever. We can have lunch or something. Gotta run. 'Bye, hon." He kissed her cheek, a drop of sweat falling on her. "See ya, Didi."

She and Didi were silent for a minute. The tone of the evening had changed, somehow. She checked her watch; it was nearly midnight.

"Didi, I have to go talk to someone," she said. "Can I just meet you down here in a few?"

"Sure," he answered unsteadily. "No problem. I'll be around."

Toni hurried toward the exit that led up to the sealed-off artists' space. The doors closed behind her and the cacophony of the dance floor faded to a dull echo. She clutched the fabric of her dress and ran up the stairs; she wanted to get to the designated cubicle before the other woman did.

The workspace was cavernous: huge concrete steps, as wide as a highway lane, were covered with hundreds of drafting tables. In a few thousand years, it would make a great ruin. She found Cubicle 72, then 73, 74 . . . 69 must be behind her. She turned around.

The other woman had arrived first.

"Hello," Toni said evenly.

The woman in front of her closed a slim mobile phone and looked at Toni with large hazel eyes. She was dressed in black leather as Catwoman—more Julie Newmar than Eartha Kitt—and a mask covered her face. Her costume fit her slim body snugly, showing off round, firm breasts and narrow hips; a desk light cast her shadow along the wall formed by the next giant step. She had straight, shoulder-length hair that looked light brown or blond in the half-darkness, and a thinnish face with a pointed chin. She stood the same height as Toni.

"You're on time," the other woman said. "That's good."

"As are you," Toni answered. "What's your name?"

"Desirée. You like it? Feel free to use it."

"I'm Karen," Toni replied.

"Right, I know. Why don't you tell me about your work?"

Toni took a step toward her. She felt slightly intoxicated, though she hadn't drunk any alcohol. It was as if she already knew Desirée's scent.

"At Crimson Escorts," she recited, "we try to give people what they want. Our experience is that they want the Harvard name."

"What else?" Desirée asked.

Toni inched closer. "Harvard is a big fantasy. We sell it to people who never came here."

"And to the ones who didn't get lucky while they were here," Desirée said. "But now can afford the best."

Toni nodded, silently. Any closer and Toni would rub up against her, but Desirée seemed not to notice.

"So they call from their law offices or their medical suites or their hotel rooms," Desirée continued, staring at some point in the distance, "ready to have some fun."

"To do what they could never do before," Toni said, "when they were too busy studying for the MCAT or the LSAT—"

"—or too nerdy, or too poor."

"They're successes now, and they're ready to enjoy it," Toni concluded. She knew she was on target; the two women were part of the same rhythm.

"Sounds like you've got real experience," Desirée said, relaxing her posture. "You'll have to forgive my skepticism. Not everyone has what it takes to get ahead. But you seem to understand—it's not just about sex. It's about power and imagination."

"I couldn't have said it better myself," Toni said, relaxing her own posture. "Why don't you tell me where you've worked before?"

"Let's just say I have highly impressive credentials," Desirée replied casually. "Why don't you tell me what *you've* done before?"

"You first," Toni responded.

"Look, babe, I'm the one who's out on a limb here."

"Excuse me?" Toni said. "It's my ad, it's my school—"

"There seems to be a little trust barrier between us," Desirée observed.

"What a surprise," Toni muttered.

"Tell you what, then. We'll go fifty-fifty."

What did that mean? Toni wished she could just ask as a reporter would, without the costuming and manufactured identity. But she didn't want to take off the mask just yet.

"We'll do a scene together," Desirée went on. "You can see if I'm all talk and no action, and I'll have the same opportunity. How about it, Crimson?"

A scene? Call girls did scenes. Reporters didn't. "I'm not sure that's a good idea," Toni said.

"Well, it's the only idea, as far as I'm concerned. Either you're legit or you're not." Desirée stepped around Toni and started toward the roaring party. "*Ciao,* babe, and let's not do it again sometime."

"Wait, Desirée—" Toni called after her.

"I don't wait for anyone," Desirée said, but she hesitated on the stairs.

"We're on," Toni said impulsively. "Tell me when and where."

Desirée laughed. "I'll let you know." She graced Toni with an unexpectedly intense smile and disappeared into the maze of cubicles.

/ / /

Returning to the hot, humid dance floor, Toni wound her way in and out of the dancers, reviewing the details of her meeting while looking for her date. She'd made a breakthrough and it felt good. Mostly. She passed a be-fezzed Shriner in a polyester leisure suit, a giant tampon, *Love Story*'s Ali McGraw and Ryan O'Neal, a can of Spam, and a woman dressed entirely in black with an index card reading "Angst" pinned to her shoulder. She saw her ex, Lucius Cornell, dancing nearby and finally made out Didi's graceful form at the edge of the dance floor.

"Hey, sorry about that," she said, as she grabbed his warm hand. He grinned broadly at her. He really had wonderful teeth.

"I think I need a drink," she said.

"Be back in a sec," he said instantly. True to his word, he returned a moment later with two glasses. Toni tossed her head back and laughed as they interlocked their arms to drink. She drained her vodka punch and gladly accepted Didi's as a replacement.

"I'm going to regret this," she said.

"No regrets tonight," he said. "You're looking really beautiful." A flush spread down her body. The dance floor became more crowded, and she fell into Didi's arms, laughing. Her nipples hardened as they brushed against the fine wool of his exquisite tux.

Half an hour later, they were in Didi's limo, gliding toward his final club. A bastion of Harvard tradition, final clubs were a more exclusive version of fraternities—the school's answer to Delta Sigma Phi and Alpha Epsilon Pi. He uncorked a fresh bottle of Veuve Clicquot and poured two glasses. *"Salud!"* They toasted in a burst of giggles. Toni's body felt warm and liquid. Didi definitely seemed to be "the answer," as Aimee called the most desirable men.

They entered the club through a discreet white door almost unnoticeable from Mount Auburn Street. Didi ushered her into the main suite, a series of large, paneled rooms with the decorative moldings, green leather chairs, and oriental rugs that seemed to furnish every Harvard building, and introduced her to several couples. After a few minutes of pleasantries Toni scanned the crowded room. Assorted overdressed, elaborately made-up women she had never seen before stood awkwardly in stiff slipper-satin dresses, their arms in front of them. Wellesley women. Their dates, engaged in lively conversation involving a great deal of laughter and backslapping, seemed utterly oblivious to them. Every so often one of the women would flash a vacant smile at no one in particular. They did not even speak to each other.

She turned impatiently to Didi. He had been staring at her and, upon being caught, blushed. Emboldened, she hooked a finger under his bow tie. "So, are there billiards in your little clubhouse? Or are girls not allowed?"

Didi grinned, nodding toward a door across the room. "Back there." On an impulse, she leaned over and kissed him, pressing her warm mouth hard against his beautiful lips, and then pulled back. Didi seemed startled, but after a moment he laughed and leaned closer. Toni could feel the hairs on the back of her neck standing on end.

Didi led her downstairs to the pool room and then went to the side bar for a bottle of champagne. The stereo was on, and the sensual sounds of "Smooth Operator" eased into the room. Didi set the bottle on a chair, frowning. "They appear to be out of glasses. I'll go upstairs to look for some."

Toni handed him a cue stick. "I think we can make do without glasses, don't you, Didi?"

Taking the stick, he smiled. "Are you sure?"

"Just shoot." Toni hoisted herself up onto the wide wooden ledge of the billiard table, and Didi watched intently. As he leaned over to make his shot, she kicked off her sandal and touched his calf with her stockinged foot. Didi flashed a look around the room, but her foot was hidden from view. A couple of boys were busy downing mixed drinks and placing bets on who would or wouldn't score with the "Wellesley heifers," as they called them. Didi relaxed and shot, but missed the ball entirely. Toni laughed. "Aren't you the 'smooth operator'?" She hummed a few bars of the music.

Didi straightened up and stood directly in front of Toni. She pulled him closer to her. "I'd say that you're the smooth one in this particular instance," he replied.

"Hmm," Toni murmured, drinking in his rich scent. "The jury's still out on *that.*" She nuzzled her way up his neck, taking small nips at his smooth skin; he closed his eyes. As she looked up at him again, he placed both his hands directly on her cheeks and lifted her face toward his. He kissed her slowly, first her upper lip, then her lower one. Her hands would have been shaking had they not been clasped around his waist. She gave him a long, deep kiss and slid off the table, pressing the length of her body against his. Pulsing hot and cold waves spread down her legs, making her toes curl with pleasure.

Toni craned her neck to scan the room, but the two pimply, tuxedoed boys stared vacantly into space, clearly drunk. "It's okay," Didi murmured impatiently, his fingers traveling up the sides of her torso. As his hands approached her breasts, a warm flush began at the base of her spine and moved upward. Toni's head began to swim with desire. "I think we should go back to Adams," she whispered.

/ / /

Didi kissed Toni wildly, pushing his hard tongue into her eager mouth. Glancing at the interior door to Chelo's room to make sure it was firmly closed, Toni returned the kiss and allowed her hands to roam down his body to his rounded buttocks and firm legs. As he caressed the inside of her thigh, she dropped her hand to his crotch and brushed his erection through his wool trousers. Didi moaned softly and reached inside her lacy underpants, his fingers sliding into her and stroking her with urgency.

Toni choked back a gasp, shocked that so much sexual power could be evoked from her so fast. She heard him unzip his trousers and a moment later heard the rip of a condom wrapper. He fumbled with it and gradually pushed her down onto her bed, the cool, lubricated latex pressing against her abdomen.

/   /   /

When she awoke two or three hours later, they were curled up like spoons on the single bed. The luminous digital clock read 4:28 A.M. Toni's comforter had fallen off them and Didi had replaced it. "Toni," Didi whispered, "I can't really sleep." Passion didn't always extend to an ability to sleep with a new person in a single bed.

"It's okay, you should go to your own room if you want," she answered groggily. Didi dressed quietly, kissed Toni on the cheek, and slipped into the hall. He felt haggard but wide awake at the same time.

He closed the door quietly behind him and straightened up. He felt like such a heel for being so happy that Toni had released him. But most guys would admit that freedom from intimacy was almost as pleasurable as intimacy itself.

As he clipped down the circular staircase, Didi noticed someone trudging up the stairs. It looked like Van Nguyen. Slowing his descent, he felt his heart begin to pound and his leg muscles tighten up.

Van noticed him from a floor below and leveled a derisive stare. They passed each other on the steps, and Van eyed him clinically, almost contemptuously. Didi felt the pain as acutely as a slap in the face.

Two steps above him, Van turned and looked down. Didi stood rooted to the marble steps, knowing that his open mouth and wide eyes revealed everything. Letting down his guard for even a moment would be disastrous, but he found that he couldn't move his legs.

After what seemed like an eternity, Van spoke. "You know what you want," he said in a voice so quiet it seemed to come from inside Didi's head. "Why don't you just take it?"

The statement felt like an accusation, yet Didi found himself riveted by the sight of Van's muscled chest and legs. He glanced up at Van's handsome face, his own eyes filling with tears.

Van moved down a step. "It's okay, Didi," he assured him in that seductive whisper. "There's nothing to be afraid of with me."

Didi raised a tentative hand but quickly lowered it when it trembled. Van turned slightly as if to leave. Didi raised his hand again and this time reached across to touch Van's waist. Before he could make contact, Van grabbed him and pulled him into an alcove off the stairwell. Pressed against the deep bay window, they embraced roughly. Didi felt he might explode; his penis was already painfully erect. He told himself that embracing would be enough, that he could stop at will, but he couldn't keep his hands from reaching down Van's legs and stroking his thighs, couldn't stop his mouth from nuzzling Van's neck and face. As he ran his teeth over Van's smooth shoulder, the images that had drifted through his mind hours earlier with Toni sprang to life.

They kissed again and again. As he clung to Van, the forces Didi had successfully kept in check for so many years flooded over him. It was terrifying and wonderful at the same time.

Not quite sure what he was doing, he sank to his knees, plunging his tongue into Van's navel and teasing the tiny gold ring. He followed the delicate bamboo tattoo on Van's hip. Impatient, he grabbed the waistband of Van's tights with both hands and pulled it down over the bulge that had mesmerized him all evening. Van's warm organ sprang out of its confinement: the sweet-sour aroma of Van's body mixed with the faded musk of Didi's cologne.

"Watch your teeth," Van whispered, pulling the thick damask curtains of the window box around them. An old girlfriend had once told Didi that tongue was everything in oral sex. He glided his across the width of Van's member and heard a pleased moan. The sensation of having this warm, throbbing muscle fill his mouth, pulsing with urgent desire, was surprisingly enjoyable. Didi continued the motion, occasionally glancing up to check on Van. Eyes closed, Van twisted his fingers through Didi's hair, sparking electricity across his scalp.

After a while, Van drew him up by his shoulders and kissed him tenderly. He looked sad and strangely fragile. Pulling up his tights, he turned his back and sank deeper into the shadowy recesses of the alcove, resting his palms against the wall. He guided Didi with one hand. "On me, not in me, right?"

Didi nodded, not entirely sure what that meant. Raising his knee up to the window seat, he thrust passionately against the scratchy fabric barrier, feeling Van's firm buttocks against him. Van turned his head to meet him with an open-mouthed kiss. As their tongues entwined, Didi saw tears in Van's eyes.

"Will you do one thing for me, Didi?" Van whispered. Thrilled to hear his name in Van's mouth—this time with such tenderness—he nodded forcefully. "Tell me that you love me." Van's voice cracked. "Say you will love me before all others. Okay? I want to hear someone say those words to me tonight."

"I will love you before all others," Didi murmured, eager to be whoever Van needed at that moment. Van smiled. Moving his hips in sync with Didi's frantic pumping against his costumed body, he pulled his own swollen cock back out of his tights and began to work it in front of him.

"I'll never leave you, *querido,*" Didi continued, his excitement mounting. *"Tu eres mi vida, mi amor. Sin tí, no soy nada."* He ground himself harder and harder, faster and faster, against Van. *"Ay querido."* His heart was throbbing so fast, it seemed to have stopped. He felt a tremor rising from deep within him and feared he was becoming paralyzed. A second later he doubled over and groaned as spasm after spasm overtook him. He grabbed at Van and felt powerful spurts coursing out of him at the same time. They kissed, clinging to each other.

After a few moments, careful not to break the spell, Didi took out a monogrammed handkerchief and tenderly wiped them both off. They rested, slumped against the wall, their breathing audible.

When they could no longer ignore the light streaming into the alcove, Van turned around and helped Didi pull his clothes together. Face to face, they stood exactly the same height.

"You're a good guy, Didi," Van said. "I think you can find someone really nice."

Didi nodded, committing the words to memory as if they carried great wisdom. He stepped forward and hugged Van hard. For a moment Van held him in a tight, masculine embrace; then, putting both hands on Didi's waist, he steered him to face the stairs.

Didi brushed his lips again and started down the stairway. Halfway to the landing below, he stopped and looked up. "Thank you, Van," he said, and was rewarded by a tired smile.

Didi took the stairs two at a time; once he reached bottom, he was fairly galloping. As he swung open the heavy wooden door, the first rays of morning sun struck him, easing the winter chill. Exhaust from the waiting limo plumed the air. He waved the driver on. It was a glorious morning; he should take advantage of it, perhaps with a walk by the Charles. He should, in fact, begin to take full advantage of his life.

6

Sterling Kwok returned from lunch at the faculty club—risotto primavera and a very pleasant Chardonnay—only to be informed by an uncharacteristically agitated Mrs. Hale that a group of students had burst into the outer office demanding to see him. Now they refused to leave and were sitting in a circle singing "Kumbaya." The dean's handsome features twisted in a scowl, but by the time he opened the door to his office, they had rearranged themselves into a blandly inquisitive smile.

"I understand that you wished to speak with me," he greeted the group. "How may I be of assistance?"

"Tomorrow's Ad Board meeting," said one surly type. "We know you're talking about David Fox, and we all know it's a crock. How can you accuse him of taking money from 'Hip-hop Against Homelessness'?" he demanded.

"You know very well that I cannot discuss the college's Administrative Board or any of its proceedings." Sterling swung open the polished oak door. "I believe this meeting is at an end. In future, please make an appointment with my assistant."

"I don't think we're finished, Dean Kwok." A crew-cut woman

with a slight German accent spoke firmly. "We are your paying customers, and we're not happy with how our money is being spent. I think you owe us a few minutes of your time."

Sterling drew a deep breath. "As you all know, there are excellent reasons why the college does not discuss the administrative . . . problems students may encounter. I respect your opinions, and your right to hold and express them, but I must preserve the privacy of other students."

"Don't you have better things to do than play policeman?" the first man asked aggressively. "Or is it just a control trip for you, a little power game?"

Sterling relished the irony. How little these students knew about the inner workings of the university! The whole business of student discipline was a tiresome chore. Much more was at stake than whether Jimmy would have to take a semester off, or whether Linda's roommate should pay for the damage to her car.

"What's wrong with you, anyway?" The speaker was a law school student well known as a campus radical, and as the son of a seventies sitcom star. His scruffy counterculture appearance was light-years away from his mother's aproned, squeaky-clean TV image, and that was fine with him. Sterling could hardly resist a gesture of distaste at the man's posing.

"Are you for real?" the student continued. "Or are you just some android dean they dug up somewhere? You're the token here, don't you know that? Spin doctor for the WASP oligarchy who really run this place. Wake up and smell the java, my friend. You're going to run a Native American off campus and let the preppie no-necks continue to terrorize women!" He advanced threateningly on Sterling. "So, were you born like this, or did you take a special course in how to be an Uncle Tom?"

How dare this overprivileged pseudo-revolutionary criticize him? Sterling had been on the front lines with SDS; he had stormed the administration building, heart pounding with fear as he remembered the demonstrators killed at Kent State. He knew what it was like to spend all day struggling to end a war, and all night dreaming about what he could have done differently. He had no time for these armchair radicals whining about handicapped bathrooms and dolphin-safe tuna. It was a tough world, and action was what counted.

Maybe he could explain to them that the issues weren't so clear anymore. As always, he tried to take action for what he believed in, but the world had changed, and he had new responsibilities. "I—I don't—" But as he stared at the hostile, expectant faces, the words caught in his throat. It was no use.

"I don't believe that you meant to be offensive, Mr. Carter," Sterling said with more charity than he felt. "But it is clear to me that we cannot conduct a civilized conversation under these circumstances. I'm afraid I'll have to ask you all to leave."

The students stared at each other, clearly trying to assess the possible effectiveness of a renewed attack. Muttering under his breath, Carter got up and trooped sullenly out. The others followed. Sterling closed the door behind them with a grateful sigh.

/ / /

Self-confident, fit, in control—Dora Givens was all of these, and it was usually obvious. This afternoon, though, things felt different. She caught a glimpse of her reflection in the windows outside the B-School gym and frowned. Her hair was tied back in a decidedly unglamorous ponytail, and she looked preoccupied. This kind of image wouldn't carry her very far. She paused for a moment and rearranged her features into a mask of assurance. Immediately she felt better. There were no problems, she reminded herself as she pulled open the door to the gym, only opportunities.

Inside the locker room, Dora stripped quickly to workout gear, shoving her sweater, jeans, and coat into a locker along with her athletic bag. She unzipped the bag, yanked out a water bottle and a crisp copy of the day's *Financial Times,* then hesitated a moment before pulling out a slim cell phone as well. Bundling these into a towel, she headed for the workout area, nodding to a few regulars as she entered the bright room. She walked past the well-maintained Nautilus and Cybex machines to her favorite treadmill and arranged her workout accessories on the reading stand. Programming a vigorous workout, she stepped onto the machine and began trotting in place.

Thoughts crowded into her mind. It hadn't been difficult to find out who Antonia Isaacs was and where she lived. Dora had simply followed her mystery date after the Mardi Gras Ball. It had been very helpful to her mission that "Karen" dated a man who expressed his masculinity through the size of his limo. That car was as hard to miss as the *Queen Elizabeth II*. She'd trailed the two of them to some childish social club and then right back to Adams House. The next day a House facebook made it easy to match Cleopatra with her student bio. Toni's name seemed familiar, and after a few hours Dora realized why: her byline had headed that *Crimson* story on student prostitution. Dora had walked right into that one. Trouble was, she still wasn't sure what she was going to do about it.

As intended, the exercise began to help Dora concentrate, the endorphins turning her anxiety into clear, focused energy. She had told a reporter about the "side venture," as she liked to call it, the little experiment in personal services. That wasn't good, but the chance that this woman could find out enough to make any criminal charges possible was tiny. After all, the Mayflower Madam had gotten off practically scot-free.

That wasn't the real problem, though. She wasn't afraid of facing prosecution on some crummy procuring charge. Big deal! The issue was publicity. Negative publicity at the wrong time would ruin everything she had worked so hard to put together.

More than that, she was angry. She was angry at herself for being careless enough to talk to the woman in the first place. A competitor had appeared out of nowhere, and she had let her curiosity affect her judgment. Of course, she wasn't the only one at fault—where was her so-called partner when she needed him? He was supposed to know these Harvard kids better than she.

Dora flipped the cell phone open and punched in a familiar number. As soon as she heard an answer, she began to talk in a low, rapid voice. She'd figure out how best to deal with Toni Isaacs. And *he* would be responsible for preventing any further screwups. It was time for him to add some value to this operation.

Call finished, she folded up the receiver. Then she took a swig of Evian and set the treadmill to "Incline."

/   /   /

Dayton Moore strode through the drafty concrete corridor of William James Hall, heading briskly toward his office. He gathered up a handful of letters from the mailbox outside his door, then went inside.

Four students were seated in his office chairs, one on the floor. Dayton greeted them and took his place behind the desk. "What can I do for you?" he asked. "It must be pretty important for you to come all the way up here."

One young woman cleared her throat. "It's about David Fox," she began. "You're hearing his case tomorrow at Ad Board."

Dayton tried to smile politely. "I'm sorry, but I can't discuss the administrative proceedings of the college with other students. That wouldn't be fair."

There was a murmur of protest from the students. "I told you," a man whispered angrily. "It's Kwok all over again." Several voices tried to shush him.

Dayton's eyes flickered. "I take it you've been to see the illustrious Dean Kwok?"

"Yeah," the man snorted. "Earlier this afternoon. He threw us out of his office."

"Really?" Dayton arched a brow. "Well, Dean Kwok can be a little . . ." He paused, a conspiratorial smile teasing the corners of his mouth. "Let's just say that he's not the most *flexible* of administrators."

The students snickered and exchanged glances. One piped up. "That's why we came to you, Professor Moore. Everybody knows how supportive you are. Not like the Great Kwok, who just—"

Dayton raised a hand. "Now, now, let's be charitable. This has not exactly been an *easy* year for him." The students chuckled at this reminder of the humiliating divorce papers that the *Crimson* had managed somehow to obtain.

Dayton continued. "I'm interested in hearing your thoughts about Mr. Fox." He leaned back in his chair and brought his hands together to form a steeple. "If I ever have to make any decisions about David's future, I'll take your opinion into account."

An intense-looking Korean man, dressed in tie-dyed T-shirt and battered fatigues, jumped in eagerly. "We just think David deserves a chance to tell his story. He's had a difficult time here, and people are too quick to judge him."

"He's being railroaded," added a woman who looked and sounded like Eva Braun. "And I don't think it's a coincidence that he's Native American."

Dayton looked from one student to another, amused at their righteous enthusiasm, and a little envious of it. "What would you like me to do?" he asked. "That is, if there were anything I *could* do." His tone left no doubt that he was mocking the rules that governed his position as part of the powerful, semisecret Administrative Board.

"Just speak up for David," the first woman said. "He's already been punished enough. He needs another chance." Her friends nodded vigorously.

"That seems reasonable enough," Dayton said, panning the room with an easy smile. The students beamed in response. "I'll do what I can. Well," he said briskly, standing up and crossing to the door. "Thank you for coming to see me." They filed out of his office, and he shook each student's hand. "I respect your commitment to helping your friend." As he closed the door, he could hear a buzz of excited conversation from the hall.

/ / /

By the time the Administrative Board began filing into the soundproofed room in University Hall, Dean Kwok had recovered his equanimity. He nodded to the secretary who was arranging coffee, tea, and cold drinks on the shining sideboard; she took her cue to slip out the door. Nobody but the administrators and faculty members who took part in the board's deliberations was allowed in. From time to time, students protested the closed-door policy, but the university was adamant. This was partly to protect the rights of the undergraduates accused of violating college rules; after all, everyone was innocent until proven guilty. But also—and to a greater extent than most Ad Board members would have liked to admit—secrecy was ingrained in the university culture. Not everything said in private would reflect well on the Harvard name if it were made public. Closed doors were closed for a reason.

Coffee poured, papers stacked and shuffled, ties loosened and throats cleared, the Ad Board began its deliberations. Andrew Onderdyck, the wizened patrician who had presided over the Ad Board for as long as anyone could remember, laid out the agenda for the day.

"As for the matter of the gentlemen from one of our less abstemious final clubs," said Onderdyck, "I am glad to say that the lads concerned have chosen to take a semester's vacation. All charges will be dropped, unless any of you has an objection."

Kwok looked around the table, careful to keep his face expressionless. The old-boy network had triumphed as usual, and no one in the room would speak out against it. He saw the shadow of a scowl on the face of one woman, the senior tutor of one of the concrete-and-glass houses in the former Radcliffe Quad. Kwok watched her open her mouth to speak, then saw her set her lips in a tight line as she thought better of it. He understood the feeling very well.

Onderdyck rattled through a number of routine cases, from roommate conflicts to plagiarism. Nearly all the students' fates were decided by a unanimous and perfunctory vote. From where he sat, Kwok could see two university vice presidents playing hangman. Others, their indifference barely hidden, were checking their electronic calendars.

"Our last case, ladies and gentlemen," Onderdyck said, "concerns Mr. David Fox." As his reedy voice pronounced the syllables, the assembled colleagues sat up and took notice. The case was extremely controversial. It wasn't exactly clear whether Fox had been criminal or just careless with the charity concert proceeds when he allowed his friends to use the money to buy stereo equipment; certainly, his accuser held a long-standing grudge against him.

A few years earlier, the whole matter would have been settled quietly. After all, the charity had ultimately received all the funds, and an outside firm had audited the books to everyone's satisfaction. Kwok got the uncomfortable feeling, however, that Fox was about to become an example. Too many cases of financial malfeasance by Harvard students had made the papers and the national news lately. The university needed to show that it had zero tolerance for undergraduates who dipped into the cookie jar. It was Fox's bad luck that he was going to be Exhibit A.

"Would anyone else like to say a word on Mr. Fox's behalf?" Kwok realized with a start that he had missed a quite impassioned speech from Fox's thesis adviser. The senior tutor who sat across from him was blinking hard to hold back tears; there were other expressions of concern around the table, but—Kwok tallied quickly—not quite enough. With a slight sinking feeling, the dean cleared his throat.

"I know this body is very concerned with making it clear that the college, and the university, expect the highest standards of behavior from every student." Except for the sons and daughters of wealthy alumni, he thought, who were given many chances to make things right with Mother Harvard. Rumor had it that some important works of modern art hung in campus galleries thanks to dismissed drunk-driving charges and conveniently lost term papers. "However, I think that in this case, given the profound ambiguity of the circumstances, it would be best for us to reserve judgment. No harm has been done, after all. And Mr. Fox's record as a student is impeccable." He looked at Onderdyck, whose weathered features betrayed no emotion.

"Thank you, Sterling," the older man said with a wintry smile. "Would anyone else like to say anything?"

Kwok glanced around the table, trying to read his colleagues' moods. The popular young professor Dayton Moore glanced up from wrestling with a paper clip. They stared at each other, and for a moment Sterling felt sure that the other man was trying to tell him something. He nodded encouragement, but Moore looked away.

"Professor Moore," Sterling pressed. "Did you have anything you wanted to say?"

The entire table waited.

"Ah." Moore smiled, the curve of his lip slightly mocking. When he spoke, however, his tone was smooth and innocuous. "Not that I can think of, but thank you for asking, Dean Kwok." He returned to his paper clip project.

Sterling had never much liked the slick young professor, who had made a big name for himself with his flash-in-the-pan scholarship. In the old days, Moore would never have been tenured. He sighed and surveyed the room once more. The vice presidents wore twin expressions of self-righteousness. The faces of the others, except the senior tutor, were guarded and blank. David Fox was out of luck.

/ / /

"Your son and daughter are here," said Mrs. Hale, greeting Dean Kwok with an exasperated look and gesturing toward the army surplus backpack and Louis Vuitton overnighter piled on a chair. Kwok raised his eyebrows at her as he opened the door to the inner office.

His daughter, sleek and carefully blasé as only a pampered

thirteen-year-old could be, greeted him without looking up from her French *Vogue.* His son quickly wrapped up a phone conversation with someone named Razor and hailed him with a cheerful "Hey, Dad."

"What a nice surprise," Kwok said, feeling like a bad impersonation of Ward Cleaver.

His daughter snorted delicately. "I told you he'd forget, Trevor."

"Give him a little credit, Princess," said her brother. "Don't you remember, Dad? Mom went to Grand Cayman with Harold, and we're staying with you for the weekend."

"*Char*ming, I'm sure," the girl muttered as she tore out a perfume sample and tossed it to the floor.

Kwok picked up his appointment book. Sure enough, "Trevor and Arianne" was penciled in. He felt a wave of guilt. "I'm sorry, kids," he said, hating his own fake joviality. "Let me make it up to you. I'll take you out to dinner, anywhere you like." *And give in to your every whim and buy you expensive gifts. Just another day in the life of the divorced dad.*

"Dad, I've only got an hour," Arianne said, smoothing her glossy hair. "I'm going to Olivia's to work on Balinese shadow puppets for the school talent show."

"Yeah, I'll need a rain check too," said his son. "There's a film noir marathon on Bravo tonight, and I'm going to catch it over at Razor's. His mom will bring me back to Adams around ten-thirty."

"I'll get a cab from Olivia's around nine," his daughter added. "I have ballet in the morning, but I can get the bus to Brookline."

"All right, then." Kwok had a strong sense of his own redundancy. He could hardly believe that these were the babies he had once held and marveled at. But then, a lot had changed. His ex-wife, Joan, for example, snorkeling in the Caribbean with a stockbroker ten years her junior. He watched his children head off for the evening with hardly a backward glance at their dad.

Sterling Kwok stood alone in his office, his shoulders slumped with exhaustion. Sometimes he was just so very tired.

/ / /

Four hours after settling down to work in Lamont Library, Chelo still hadn't finished tonight's installment in the seemingly endless stream of physics problem sets. She leaned back in the wooden chair and rubbed her eyes. Her back was stiff. She knew she wasn't dumb—her grades attested to that—but physics sure made her feel that way. It made organic chemistry, the time-honored nemesis of pre-meds, seem easy.

She picked a Supremes tape from the collection stacked in front of her and put it into her Walkman. As Diana Ross's bubbly voice sounded, she rolled her head around in a circle to loosen her neck and shoulders. She reached into her backpack for a highlighter and grazed the manila sheaves that she'd taken from Professor Moore's office. What had possessed her to walk off with them? They were just pornography, really—stories without plots, images without context. She should take them back.

Chelo glanced down at the paltry evidence of the day's careful labors. Surely it was time for a little treat, a few more tantalizing morsels from the diaries before she returned them all. She scanned the library for faces she knew; confident she wouldn't be disturbed, she pulled the manila envelopes out of her bag. If only she had some potato chips, she thought, everything would be perfect. She opened one folder at random, pulled out its contents, and began reading entries written in an aggressive male hand.

> Feb. 1   Hello, diary, and section leader who's grading it. It's
> rather unnerving writing down these thoughts knowing someone is
> going to read them. There's no minimum amount we're supposed
> to write, is there? I suppose I should ask you that in section, since
> these are anonymously graded (ha!) but now I can't, since you'll
> know who I am anyway. Well, that's enough for now. Yes, I know
> this is lame but what do you expect?

Chelo could certainly identify with this writer's sentiments. She'd heard two or three of Moore's lectures and found them interesting, but she didn't really want to take his class. People made enough judgments about you already; there was no reason to provide them with extra ammunition by chronicling your innermost thoughts.

> Feb. 7   Hi again, section leader. It's been a while. I see no need
> for the pretense that this so-called journal is in any way a personal

exploration. I was talking to some friends at dinner—I live in Mather, so now you can narrow me down to 12 or so people in the class—and the pre-law tutor said there's no way these could be graded according to content or the prof. would have hell to pay if any of us complained. So fuck it, I'll write what I think, and what I think is this: first of all, I, for one, am no great fan of the strangely popular Professor Moore. Oh, I know, boo hoo hoo. The man is a quack! Wake up, people! Second, it's not necessarily healthy to think out all your sexual "issues" ad nauseam. People spend far too much time beating these issues into the ground. Just do it, kids! Physical masturbation is natural, mental masturbation is not!

This person didn't seem very nice at all.

Noticing the absence of marginalia on the copy, she hoped that Professor Moore hadn't happened to read this entry, though she supposed he had become accustomed to professional backbiting and jealousy in his time. People would do anything to malign you when you were successful.

She selected another journal and opened it in the middle.

12 Mar.   The readings on dream analysis were pretty correct; now that I've started writing things down, I remember everything much more vividly. It's kinda scary, but I'm excited. Maybe I'll discover some past lives! (Just kidding, I'm not like that.)

22 Mar.   I had the most incredible experience yesterday—I'm serious, this really happened. It was like this: yesterday I was at Gnomon Copy, trying to photocopy my résumé on the self-service machines. Everything was screwing up royally and I was about to cry, I was so frustrated. As I'm trying to fix the paper jam I hear someone say in a slight foreign accent, "I think you need to fan the paper first." I turned around and saw the repair guy in his cute gray coverall and was awestruck. He wasn't extremely handsome or anything but he had beautiful eyes and he was *just so sexy*. Like he was oozing testosterone or something. I swear—I've never once in my entire life actually picked someone up. But oddly enough, I had just read the essay "Building Our Own Prisons" for class the

night before and it really struck a chord—I mean, it's true, I never
have actually *asked* for what I wanted sexually or romantically. I
just hoped that guys would infer it somehow. So I kept talking to
Firoz, that's his name, and I didn't feel scared at all, or even
nervous, and when he asked me if I would join him that night for
drinks I said yes, without hesitation. The rest of the afternoon, I
was just on a cloud.

Anyway, we met at the Boathouse and he had changed into
neatly pressed chinos and a white shirt, against which his skin
looked dazzling. We talked for a while (he's from Morocco and is
sort of studying engineering in Boston—I wasn't too clear on that),
and then he was stroking my hand on the tabletop

Chelo paused for a moment to fix this exciting picture in her
mind. She hoped the evening would go well; she practically had a
stake in this unknown woman's date.

and then he said, so softly, "Please, may I kiss you?"

Of course, that's what I'd been wishing he would do, but I was
flustered so I laughed and said, "Here? But you don't even know
me." "I don't know you?" he said. "What does this mean, to know
someone? That I know you are drinking your morning coffee with
milk and no sugar? That I know what kind of shampoo you use?"
(He pronounced it like "champoo," which seemed incredibly sexy
to me.) "Holding your hand I know you better than some
husbands know their wives after years of marriage."

Of course, I knew this was all b.s. but in a way it wasn't. You
know? So one thing led to another and (I swear I have *never* done
this before) he came back to my single with me. And that's when
the really memorable stuff happened. See, we were making out
and we'd progressed to the point where neither of us had any
clothes on and he wanted to penetrate me but I wasn't really
ready, and for a split second I thought to myself, oh, this is like all
the other guys (well, all three or four I've ever been with) and
suddenly I said, "No, not that. Not yet. I want something else."

"What do you want, then?" He nuzzled my neck and said this
quite solicitously. I was too embarrassed to say it at first. "Tell me
what you want me to do," he repeated. I looked at him and saw

that his eyes were flashing, in excitement. So I took the leap and said, "I want you to, um, go down on me. . . ."

Right away, he sort of slid his tongue down my body, licking my nipples, my rib cage, my belly, the edges of the lips of my vagina. "Like this?" he whispered in this sort of gruntish way. "You want me to do more of this?"

The part of me that wasn't incredibly excited was just amazed. *You mean it's this easy?* "Yes," I said, "this is what I want, so keep on doing it." And then, "Now put your tongue inside me, taste me." He was so incredibly eager to please. He just went on and on and eventually he made me come and—get this—he was so into it that he masturbated himself as he did *me*. In other words, there wasn't even any "fucking" per se, and it was the most fantastic thing.

Well, for me, this was a huge breakthrough. Huge! I mean, I won't be surprised if I don't see him again and perhaps next time he'd want me to go down on *him* (which I've never been into) but let me just say again, this practically makes up for all the lame sexual experiences I've had.

Chelo's palms were damp with sweat, and her mouth was dry. She wondered what she would have done in the crucial moment at the Boathouse Bar.

7

Toni shifted from foot to foot as she waited outside the Cromwell Hotel. The high heels were already pinching, and she felt as if everyone was staring at her. Acting on Desirée's advice to be "sexy but not too obvious" for the evening, Toni had borrowed a burgundy velvet minidress and pumps from the former Miss Black Alabama who lived in E-Entry. The beauty queen had been thrilled to share her pageant finery when Toni had mentioned her hot date; now Toni felt overdressed and a little guilty.

Desirée had assured her that this was what they called a scene—no actual sex, just role-playing. Toni wouldn't even have to take off all her clothes, "just down to the undies." Toni had headed for the Victoria's Secret downtown; her usual cotton bikinis wouldn't make it in this setting.

And then there was the makeup. Miss Black Alabama had advised "contouring," but that was way beyond Toni. Eyeshadow, lipstick, and mascara would have to suffice. With the big pearl-and-gold earrings her aunt Winnie had given her, the look was complete. As Toni gazed at her reflection in the lobby window, she realized that she looked like somebody in a soap opera—or a TV anchorwoman. She hoped she didn't run into any of her friends.

The Mardi Gras Ball had already become a distant, slightly unreliable memory in her mind, like a favorite childhood birthday party. Two days after the event—the precise length of time that polite, self-assured single people waited, she imagined—Didi had telephoned. Although she was home, she hadn't picked up the receiver to talk to him; she wasn't entirely sure why. Perhaps her life was too complicated for a relationship. Or perhaps, notwithstanding their night of passion, a certain spark was absent. Anyway, she questioned whether a lover as smooth as Didi Carón would be satisfied with one woman. She would wait a few days, see how she felt, then call him back.

The wind whipped at Toni's coat. Desirée was already ten minutes late, and this whole plan was seeming like a worse and worse idea. Toni reminded herself that Desirée's invitation to get in on her action was a stroke of good luck. Now was not the time to mess things up.

Somebody tapped her on the shoulder, and she turned quickly, expecting to see Desirée. A leering, white-coated man—obviously one of the hotel's kitchen staff—was speaking to her in Spanish.

"No habla español," she said. This guy was definitely not asking whether Pablo was in the garden, or if her mother's cousin had traveled often in foreign lands. Her Spanish didn't encompass the polite, or not-so-polite, refusal of an invitation to go to bed with a strange busboy.

Just then, Desirée showed up. "Fuck off, *pendejo,*" she said, grabbing Toni by the arm. "My friend and I have bigger fish to fry." She yanked the startled Toni toward the Cromwell's ornate bronze doors. "Sorry I'm late," she continued. "Phone call just as I was leaving the house. You know how that is."

Toni nodded.

They walked into the hotel lobby, and Desirée breezed past the concierge with a smile. She certainly stood out in the lobby—it was full of overdressed middle-aged couples—but not because she looked like a prostitute. Her straight, ash-blond hair streamed over a quilted silk coat. With a multicolored eight-foot muffler wrapped around her throat and a flowing Gypsy skirt peeking out from under the coat, she looked like a Deadhead dressed for a wedding. "They pretend not to recognize me, but they never stop me," she confided.

"Yeah," Toni agreed. "And the room service isn't bad here, either."

In the elevator, Desirée leaned close. "So what are you wearing?" Toni opened her coat. "You look great. What's your name, anyway? I assume you don't give the johns your real name, do you, Karen?"

"No, of course not," Toni answered, staring down at her velvet dress. "It's . . . Sherry."

"Fifteenth floor—suckers with money to burn!" Desirée said brightly as the elevator doors slid open. "Let's see, our friend Rodney is in"—she consulted a slip of paper—"Room 1509."

It was really happening. Toni felt a flash of excitement through the fear, as if she were kayaking over the biggest rapids of her life.

One light tap and the door sprang open. "I've been expecting you ladies," a man's voice said. "Come on in." They walked into a narrow entranceway, and the door swung shut behind them.

They were in a smallish suite, decorated in Muted Early Colonial Hotel. Living room with table, couch, and chairs; bedroom and bathroom beyond. Nothing special, but Toni knew the Cromwell charged the highest prices for even these relatively ordinary accommodations. Rodney must be pretty prosperous to afford this evening.

"Hello, Rodney," Desirée simpered.

"Yes, hi," Toni said. Okay, she wanted to laugh out loud. And then she wanted to run out of the room. But it wasn't that kind of party.

"Hello, there," said the john. Toni took a good look at him: average middle-aged white man, late forties, thinning hair, glasses. She could make out a little potbelly under the silk robe and pajamas. Real Hugh Hefner stuff, slippers and all.

"What would you ladies like to drink?" he asked, ushering them into the living room. He opened the minibar proudly. "I've got some bourbon I think is pretty special; or you could have a beer. . . . Only the best for the ladies from Class Ring."

"Any organic wine?" Desirée asked. "They have a pretty good Oregon chardonnay here, I think." Rodney rummaged in the minibar and found a bottle.

"And for you, Brown Sugar?"

Toni froze. *Brown Sugar?* "Sherry," she said firmly. "I mean, my name's Sherry. I'd like a glass of Perrier to drink."

Desirée laughed. "Hey, that's pretty funny."

Rodney chuckled as he handed her the sparkling water and settled onto the couch near Desirée. "Sherry, I can tell that you and I are going to get along just fine. I bet we'll be seeing each other a lot after tonight—or should I say we'll be seeing a lot of each other?"

Not if I see you first, you racist asshole, Toni thought. She took the glass from him and sipped.

"Soooo, Rodney Dangerfield," Desirée said coyly, toying with the lapels of his robe. "What's first on your agenda for the evening?"

He cleared his throat. "Well, maybe we can all get a little more comfortable, and then you and I can, uh, spend some time together."

"Sounds good," she purred. "Okay with you, Sherry?"

"Sure, fine," Toni said. Whatever was over the quickest got her vote.

Desirée really seemed to be getting into it, though. She was all preening, head-tossing, and little lingering touches. It certainly had an effect on Rodney, who was clearly thinking that he was a hell of a guy. Toni sipped stolidly at her Perrier, willing the time to pass.

Desirée uncurled herself from the arm of the couch, where she had been fondling the few strands of hair left on top of Rodney's head. "Let's get started," she said, motioning to Toni. Toni joined her where she stood in front of the couch, facing Rodney, and once again felt the urge to giggle.

"Sherry, let's listen to some music, okay?" Desirée said, in a strange, thin voice. She was acting, Toni realized. The scene had started.

"Uh, sure," Toni said. Desirée took a cassette out of her pocketbook, walked over to the stereo console in the corner, and popped the tape into the player. The sounds of Jimi Hendrix—at a discreetly low volume—filled the room.

"My folks are away," Desirée continued, "so we have the whole house to ourselves. We can do anything we want."

"Great," said Toni halfheartedly. What was with this, anyway?

Desirée danced to the strains of "Crosstown Traffic" for a few moments, gesturing for Toni to do the same. She shuffled her feet in the borrowed pumps, trying to look anywhere but at Rodney, who was leaning forward on the couch, lips parted, his breathing growing heavier.

"Hey, Sherry," Desirée said in an ultra-cheerful voice, "let's take off our clothes and pretend we're go-go girls. It'll be a kick."

"Great!" Toni answered. "I love pretending." She definitely needed help with her dialogue.

Desirée peeled out of her Gypsy blouse and skirt in no time. Her breasts bobbed to the rhythm as she danced in just her panties, stockings, and heels. After a little trouble with her zipper, Toni extricated herself from the velvet and set it carefully over the arm of a chair. She felt really stupid dancing in bra and panties in front of a complete stranger—who, she realized, reminded her of Mr. Wilkinson, her driver's ed instructor, down to the bald-spot-camouflage hairdo and the terrible breath—but she couldn't turn back now. And there was something exciting about this, in a really sick way.

"I hope nobody sees us, Sherry," Desirée went on. "That would be so embarrassing."

"Yeah," said Toni. "It would."

"Especially not that cute guy next door." Desirée giggled.

"Right. Especially not him." Toni was getting the picture now. And Rodney was getting turned on. Maybe he and Desirée would get on to the next phase of the fantasy soon, and Toni could get out of there.

"Hey, girls." Rodney stood up. "What are you doing?"

Desirée shrieked with laughter. Toni joined in, glad the hysterics fit her role.

"Nothing, Rodney," said Desirée. "Go away, or you'll get in trouble."

"Hey, no way, man" was Rodney's brilliant riposte. Toni wondered if something like this had once happened to him, or if he had just seen too many late-night cable TV movies. "Don't you want me to join you?"

"Oh, Rodney," Desirée tittered.

"Come on, I know your folks are away. Let's go talk in private, okay?" Rodney inclined his head toward the bedroom.

"Well . . ." Desirée hesitated, her finger in her mouth. "If it's okay with Sherry . . ."

"Yes! Sure! Fine!" Toni almost shouted. "Uh, don't do anything I wouldn't do, you guys." That sounded adolescent enough.

"Hey, guess that leaves just about everything," Rodney joked. Toni managed a weak smile. He put his arm across Desirée's shoulders and led her toward the bedroom.

"Look what I've got for you, Rodney," Desirée cooed, seductively waving a shiny crimson packet in front of his face. Toni realized it was a condom and was surprised at Rodney's apparent eagerness to make use of it.

"Wait here," Desirée mouthed silently as she followed the john through the door. Toni nodded her head, although she had no intention of spending one more minute in the room than was absolutely necessary. She heard the door close behind them, and the sound of Desirée's muted giggles. Okay, that was over with. No harm done.

Just then a deafening noise erupted on the outer suite door. It sounded like someone trying to break in.

"Cambridge police!" a voice announced from out in the hall. "Open up in there!" The banging continued—heavy, incessant, unbearably loud; the door quaked beneath its force. "Police!" the voice repeated. "Open up or we break it down!"

Toni cast a wild-eyed look at the reverberating door. Her heart was hammering against her rib cage, but she couldn't get her legs to move.

The bedroom door burst open, and Rodney ran out, clutching his robe about his jiggling middle. "Just a second!" he called in the direction of the outer door. "I'm coming." He motioned Toni frantically toward the bedroom.

"C'mon," the cops shouted from the other side of the door. "Open up!" The single, ear-splitting crack of a nightstick against wood punctuated the order.

Toni grabbed her dress and dashed into the inner room, expecting to find a half-clad Desirée. To her surprise, the room was empty. She must be hiding out in the bathroom; after all, she was an old pro at this. Toni closed the bedroom door and slumped against it. Now everything depended on Rodney. Maybe he would be cool enough to convince the cops to go away.

Toni put her ear to the door. "What's the trouble, officers?" Rodney was asking.

"Sir, we have a report that you're entertaining a prostitute in your room. I'm sure you're aware that's a crime in this state."

"A prostitute? You must be kidding, officer." Rodney wasn't too convincing. "Do I look like the kind of guy who'd have to go to a prostitute?"

Actually, you do, Toni thought. *Page one of the textbook: "A Field Guide to the North American John."*

"Can we come in to discuss this, sir?"

She heard footsteps. Rodney must have nodded. *Let's just settle this among us guys,* his look would tell them.

"Do you have any company here, sir?" asked one of the police officers.

"As a matter of fact, I do." Weak laugh. "My secretary and I were just having a little drink. You know how it is." Ten points for effort, but a big fat zero for results. The cops weren't buying it.

"Could you tell us the name of your—your secretary, sir?"

This was it. Toni would have to hide somewhere. Anywhere. She looked around the room for a closet, but the decor ran to big cupboards instead of built-in closets. Cupboards big enough for clothes, but not for people.

The bathroom, then. She ran to the door and tried to turn the knob. No dice.

"Mind if we take a look around?" she could hear one of the policemen saying, a lot closer to the door. She tried the bathroom again, without success. "Desirée, let me in!" she hissed. "Desirée!" She didn't dare raise her voice. She shook the knob, her sweaty hands slipping on the metal. "Desirée, let me in there!" Getting no response, she stepped into her dress and tugged at the zipper, which would not budge.

The bedroom door opened, and two burly figures loomed over her. Rodney was right behind them.

"Excuse me, miss, but could I see some ID?" Toni closed her eyes for a minute. This was the single worst moment of her entire life. Here she was, a young black woman in bra and panties, discovered by cops in the hotel room of a middle-aged white businessman. No ID in the world was going to convince them that she was anything other than a cheap hooker. Besides, she had made a point of leaving her

Harvard student ID back at Adams House. Which, she realized, was probably for the best.

"Gee, I don't have any on me. Why do you ask?"

The two policemen exchanged a knowing look. "Just wanted to know who we were talking to, that's all."

"Where's your warrant?" she demanded.

"No, no," said Rodney, oblivious to her question. "This is some kind of mistake. She's my secretary. She just—um—spilled a drink on her dress, and was trying to wash it out. . . ." His words trailed off as the cops exchanged amused glances.

"Okay, mister," said one of them. "What's her name?"

"Her name? Uh, Susan . . . no, Sharon . . . Sherry!" *Brilliant, Rodney.* Toni could hear the cell door slamming in her face.

"He doesn't know her name," one of the cops said to the other.

"Must be a temp." They snickered; then the older of the two cops came over to Toni. "Look, sister, let's go down to the station."

"Am I being arrested?"

"No," the policeman said with exaggerated politeness, "we'd like you to type a few memos for us. It's not often that we meet somebody with such"—his eyes raked her breasts—"outstanding secretarial skills."

"Where's your warrant?" she demanded again. She glanced to her side. This time, Rodney seemed intrigued.

"Don't need one," came the reply. *"He,"* the cop continued, pointing at a now-confused Rodney, "invited us in. Doesn't have to be an engraved invitation. A single yes suffices."

A muffled snort came from his companion. Toni hoped Desirée was getting an earful from the safety of the bathroom. She was tempted to tell the cops about her "co-worker," but what would be the point of them both getting arrested?

"You can't take me in without reading me my rights," Toni said. "And you haven't even arrested me." That was about all she remembered from TV.

"Hey, she must be a *legal* secretary," the younger cop said. "Okay, miss, you're under arrest for criminal solicitation. You have the right to remain silent. Anything you do say . . ." Toni felt a chill of fear wash over her as he droned the familiar litany. She had heard this a million times, from *CHiPs* to *Starsky and Hutch* to *Columbo,* but now it was happening to *her.*

"Come on, let's go." The older cop was prodding her.

"At least let me get dressed." She smoothed the velvet dress into some kind of order and, after a couple of fierce yanks, finally managed to get the zipper closed. With the white-haired cop's oniony breath on her neck, she grabbed her coat from the couch and pulled it on. Picking up her bag, she turned and faced the pair defiantly. "I'm ready."

"Well, you look just lovely," said the younger man. "Very professional."

"You're a laugh riot, aren't you?" muttered Toni, as the older cop escorted her out the door. His companion remained behind. "Hey!" Toni delivered the parting shot over her shoulder. "Here's an idea— why don't you go after a john for once?"

"Will do, Ms. Steinem," the cop replied, giving her a salute. She could hear his laughter all the way down the corridor.

"I'm not going to put cuffs on you," the cop announced as they waited for the elevator. "You seem like a smart girl. You know the best thing is just to come down to the station."

"Mmmm," Toni answered. Her mind was racing. This guy was at least fifty-five, and his waistline showed that he was no stranger to the doughnut shop. Besides, he had the kind of red Irish face that makes a heart surgeon order a new Porsche. She could easily outrun him.

They didn't know her real name; if she could just get away . . . She thought furiously during the elevator ride down. They walked together through the lobby, Toni feeling that at any moment she might die of shame. She was sure that everyone was looking at them, though her rational mind told her that the wedding guests and visiting French businessmen couldn't have cared less about any of this. She fixed a bright smile on her face to hide her distress.

Maybe she could lose him in the revolving door. But when they approached the exit, he gestured toward the handicapped entrance, through which two people could easily go at once. Damn.

Out in the hotel's brick plaza, the cop glanced around for a second before spotting the police cruiser, blue light flashing, pulled up on the sidewalk. "Over there," he instructed, giving her a little push.

"Ow," Toni said, pretending to stumble over one of the shallow steps. He leaned over to help her up, and she pulled on his out-stretched hand. He overbalanced and fell to the bricks, cursing loudly. Toni tore into the street, running her fastest, wobbling in the borrowed heels.

She sprinted over to John F. Kennedy Street, pushing startled pedestrians aside as she ran. Once on the main street, she lost herself in the crowd, walking quickly but trying not to look suspicious. The pavement was full of cops on Saturday night, patrolling the area around the more popular student bars. She tried to make herself look like just another happy partygoer.

From behind her, Toni could hear the shouts of her would-be captor. She picked up her pace to a trot, forcing herself not to turn her head. "'Scuse me, sorry, pardon me," she chanted as she jostled through the masses of drunken business-school students who thronged the sidewalks. Her heart was thumping, and she felt dizzy. Almost home. She fixed her eyes on the ground, willing herself not to collapse.

"'Scuse me," she said to the feet of a man blocking her way. "Pardon me. Hey, can you get out of my way?" She looked up angrily to see the face of one of Cambridge's finest. The man gripped her arms, and before she knew it, he'd snapped handcuffs around her wrists. Then he began marching her back down the street to the Cromwell, calling in his triumph on his walkie-talkie as they went.

8

"Goddamned motherfucking pigs! Goddamned—!"

Midway into a stream of shouted obscenities, the woman next to Toni suddenly doubled over and began to vomit. The liquid spewed out in a greenish cascade, hitting the linoleum and splattering up just inches from Toni's feet. Toni winced and moved her leg. The odor brought her back to the time in second grade when Kenny Johnson hadn't made it to the bathroom after eating a tuna sandwich that had been out in the playground sun too long. She hadn't been able to eat tuna since.

"Oh, hell." The officer who had been processing the woman slammed her fist down and pushed back from the desk in disgust. "Not again!"

"I told ya," the woman wailed, squatting with her head between her knees. "I'm sick. I need my medicine."

"Yeah, I bet," the policewoman said, coming around from behind the desk. "What kinda medicine they giving junkies nowadays?" She yanked the woman out of the chair. "C'mon, let's go." She shook her head. "You're lucky I don't make you clean up this mess."

Toni watched as the officer led the protesting woman back to a cell. The prisoner could barely stand; she sagged against the police-woman's grip, a thread of spittle working down her chin. Though the body beneath the cheap clothes looked young and muscular, the coffee-colored skin was dull and lined. Her straightened hair was drawn back tight, revealing gaunt, masculine features. Toni had never seen a junkie close up, but she could imagine that this was how one might look.

She turned back to the cop sitting across from her. "Shouldn't she see a doctor? What if she's really sick?"

He looked up from the keyboard. "Good point," he said. "And what if you're really a Harvard student?"

Toni closed her eyes and balled her hands into fists. The metal of the handcuffs cut into her tender wrists. "I am," she said evenly, but by now she herself was almost beginning to doubt it. For the past half hour she had been chanting her student status like a Hail Mary, but the Cambridge police seemed to be agnostics. It was like one of those movies where the detective goes undercover in order to expose abuses in a mental hospital, only to be discovered and held captive by the corrupt warden's henchmen. The more you claim not to be crazy, the crazier you appear to be.

"Let's go, Harvard," the policeman said, finishing the arrest report and getting up from the desk.

He guided her around the pool congealing on the floor. Nearby a young skinhead gave a bark of laughter. "Heil, Harvard!" he taunted. He grabbed his crotch with his shackled hands and leered at her. "Come over here, honey, if you're so interested in playing with the white boys. I'll teach you something new!"

The cop turned a bored eye in the youth's direction and kept walking.

She hadn't resisted as they hauled her out of the backseat and into the noisy station; she was docile as they photographed her holding a board bearing her name and arrest number, and silent as they inked her fingers and rolled them onto a fingerprint form. But now she felt the urge to cry. Not here; not in front of all these jerks. She concentrated on the fact that as soon as they learned who she was, she was out of here.

Instead of leading her toward the bank of pay telephones on the far wall, the policeman approached the holding cells and grabbed the heavy metal door. Toni realized what he was up to and gave a low, throaty wail of alarm. Momentarily caught off guard, he loosened his grip on her arm, and she threw herself against a glass door opposite the cells.

"What the—?" He yanked her back, scowling at the cut on her temple. "Are you crazy? You trying to get me in trouble for brutality?"

"I can't go in there," she moaned, a bit disoriented by the dull ache spreading across her forehead. "I'm not a criminal. I didn't do anything wrong."

"And I'm Cardinal Law," he said wearily. "Now, come on. I don't have all night."

"Wait!" She struggled in his grasp. "You never asked what I was doing at the hotel. And what about my phone call? I know I get a phone call!"

"For Christ's sake—"

Just then the glass door opened and a man in shirtsleeves peered out. Quickly, his dark, mournful eyes took in Toni's rumpled hair and clothes, the bleeding cut on her head, the tears filling the corner of her eyes. He turned to the policeman. "Dobbs," he asked easily, with just the hint of an accent, "what's going on here?"

Dobbs shook his head. "Nothing, Detective. Just one of the ladies making a little noise."

"Are you in charge here?" Toni pounced on the newcomer. "Because I'm supposed to get a phone call, and this sorry excuse for a *policeman*"—she gave her captor a withering look, though her lip was quivering—"is violating my rights!"

The detective regarded her with some amusement before addressing the uniformed policeman. "One of the ladies? She's been in before?"

Dobbs snorted. "Not this one. No, she's definitely a virgin. Claims to be a *Hahvahd* student."

"*Is* a Harvard student," Toni interjected.

"Right. And I suppose you dress like this and hang out in men's hotel rooms on your way to the library."

"I've told you a hundred times already—I work for the newspaper. I was meeting a source."

The detective listened quietly to this exchange, and his attentiveness gave Toni the impression that he was sympathetic. He looked to be in his late thirties, with black hair and dark olive skin. He wore pleated pants, a blue cotton shirt, and a haphazardly knotted knit tie that was a bit too skinny; Toni noticed that he had forgotten to button down his collar tabs.

"Who was the source you were meeting, Miss, er . . . ?"

"Isaacs. Toni Isaacs. And I can't reveal the name of my source."

Dobbs snorted, but the detective simply looked amused. "Well," he inquired politely, "could you at least tell me what it was about?"

She glanced around the station, her eyes coming finally to rest on Dobbs. "Uh, sure, I guess," she said.

Noting her reluctance, the detective turned briskly to the uniformed man. "Tell you what, Dobbs," he said with a smile. "It won't hurt to call the college and check on her story. She can wait in my office. We need to get that cut fixed, anyway."

Dobbs regarded the two of them, his eyes flickering back and forth between Toni and his superior. The insinuation in his gaze was almost palpable, and for the first time that night Toni actually felt like a hooker. "Yeah, sure," he grumbled. "I'll get right on it."

The detective watched Dobbs go, an affable smile still on his face. When he turned to open the glass door for Toni, however, she saw anger in his dark eyes.

"Thank you," she blurted out, feeling suddenly shy.

He looked down at her sternly. "Don't thank me. Turning tricks is still turning tricks, Harvard or no."

"I wasn't turning tricks!" Her voice shook. "I swear I wasn't." For just a second he looked relieved. Then he became businesslike. "We'll have to discuss that further."

He opened a door with "Detective C. G. Rivera" stenciled on it and ushered Toni in. The tiny office was done up in old-fashioned government style: wooden desk, metal file cabinets, faded posters extolling the virtues of community policing. "The Cambridge Police," one read, "a Tradition of Pride." It was precisely that tradition of pride Toni feared. "We're Here for You," another one crowed. Where had Dobbs been during the big love-in? The office was surprisingly neat, compared with the general disorder of the receiving area outside. "Have a seat," Rivera said from the doorway, indicating a metal armchair. Toni sat on the edge of the chair and tried to exude more poise and self-assurance than she felt.

"Feel free to make that constitutionally protected call of yours," Rivera said with a grin before heading into the hall. "I'll be back soon with a bandage."

/ / /

By the time the detective returned with a mug of lukewarm tea and a rusty metal first-aid kit, Toni was much calmer. She had had a moment of panic at not finding Chelo home, but she had managed to track down Cabot Winthrop, who promised to locate her roommate as soon as possible. The nightmare would be over soon.

The detective noted the change as he handed her the mug. "Feeling better?" he asked. Toni nodded and took a deep gulp of tea. "Good." He settled into the wooden swivel chair behind the desk and found a letter opener to pry open the first-aid kit. He regarded the contents somewhat dubiously. "Lean forward," he said, tearing open a packet of cotton wool and dousing it with disinfectant. "And why don't you tell me what's really going on?"

Toni was sorely tempted. It would be such a relief to get everything off her mind, and perhaps he could even help. But her journalist's instinct warned her never to reveal all, no matter what. She felt an icy sting on her brow and gasped.

"Sorry," Rivera muttered, dabbing tentatively at the cut. "Does that hurt?" He kept his eyes trained on her forehead, a flush creeping over his cheeks.

"Uh, no, I mean, it's okay, I'm fine." Toni realized she was holding her breath and tried to let it out unobtrusively, little by little, while she told him about her work at the *Crimson* and her search for a prostitution story. She tried not to think about the touch of his fingers, but it was hard to concentrate on anything else. She left out the information about Desirée, making it appear as if she had received an anonymous tip about a source at the Cromwell Hotel. Rivera worked steadily, cleaning and bandaging her wound, silent but for an occasional grunt.

He finished and looked about to say something, when a sharp rap sounded on the door. "Open," he barked, and a woman stuck her head into the room.

"Hey, Carlos," she greeted him. "Visitor for her." She jerked her head at Toni.

Rivera raised a brow. "Looks like the cavalry has arrived, Miss Isaacs," he said. He waved a hand toward the door.

Rivera deposited her in the waiting room, and Toni looked around for Chelo. To her surprise, Cabot Winthrop himself was standing near the water cooler, shoulders hunched. As always, he looked handsome—all cheekbones and easy blond athleticism, like someone in a Bruce Weber photo—and intense. He was dressed as usual in a drab sweatshirt and mechanic's pants, with a baseball cap jammed backward over a spray of golden hair. The only piece of his wardrobe that indicated his status as Harvard student and Boston Brahmin was a pair of tiny, round glasses that gave him a thoughtful look.

Seeing Toni, he returned her smile somewhat uncertainly and loped forward. "Hey, Toni. How are you holding up?" He looked concerned.

"Oh, Cabot, thank you so much for coming! I'm fine. I just wanna get out of here." She looked around. "Were you able to find Chelo?"

Cabot shook his head. "I didn't bother looking. I wanted to get here as soon as possible, so I just hopped in the van."

Toni was touched. She and Cabot didn't really know each other all that well, but she had immediately thought of him when Chelo hadn't answered the phone. As president of the Phillips Brooks House Association, Harvard's social service program and the largest student organization at the school, Cabot was a successful activist leader both on and off campus. He knew how to handle trouble.

Seeing him here now, Toni realized that she hadn't really wanted to call a close friend. Apart from her best friend, Valerie, who was off in Senegal for the year, and Van, who was God knew where for the night, everyone she knew was bound to be disapproving, no matter how supportive. She had no desire to add the censure of Lucius Cornell—or God forbid, Horace Glover—to the night's traumas. Cabot, she was sure, wouldn't judge her.

"That's so sweet of you, Cabot."

He regarded her curiously, for the first time taking in her outfit and makeup. "What happened?"

Toni felt self-conscious. She had just started to explain when a commotion at the front desk caught her attention. She turned to watch, straining to make out the brusque tones of Sergeant Dobbs and the softer rhythms of Carlos Rivera. Both seemed to be reasoning with a third man—and *his* voice, cultured and controlled, was unmistakable. Toni's heart sank. Just what she needed right now: Sterling Kwok, the dean of students and master of Adams House.

Of all the college officials Dobbs could have called! Toni groaned. She turned back to Cabot, ready to suggest that they bolt—but he was gone. Stunned, she spun around, searching the room for his trademark shock of hair. He was nowhere to be found. When Rivera came to collect her, she was still looking for Cabot, though he was long gone, vanished as if he had never been there in the first place.

/ / /

Dean Kwok was livid. He maneuvered the car through the back streets of Cambridge with a cold efficiency that left Toni dizzy and disoriented. It was a short ride back to Adams House, ten minutes at most, but to Toni it was an eternity in purgatory. In the police station Kwok had been his usual self, all icy civility and reserve, but once they reached the dim privacy of his BMW, he really let Toni have it. Her contacts with him had always been brief, though he was, in theory, doubly responsible for her well-being. She had certainly never seen him visibly angry at anyone.

"You appear to have lost all judgment and sense of decorum." Kwok shook his head, thoroughly disgusted. "You are lucky indeed, young lady, that I convinced the police not to press charges." Toni's ears pricked up. Was this a bluff? The real danger, as far as Toni was concerned, was how this would affect her student status. She couldn't afford to be put on probation; that would mean the curtailment of all extracurricular activities like the *Crimson,* and possibly the end of her Harvard career. Plus, her parents would be bound to find out.

"You're on your own now," Kwok was saying. He slid the long dark car up to the curb in front of Adams House and threw it into Park. Staring straight ahead, he said, wearily, "I won't call your parents yet, but you will have to explain your actions to the Administrative Board."

After a few seconds during which Toni's heart thudded so rapidly she could hear ringing in her ears, she managed to gasp out a question. "When?"

Kwok turned to face her. "At the next meeting, which will occur in four weeks," he said coldly and clearly.

The news was like a slap in Toni's face. Her flesh stinging, she groped for the door handle, trying to get out. "I need to go. I'm not feeling well."

Kwok hit a button; with a click the lock sprang up. Toni opened the door and staggered out. She was vaguely aware of Aimee Milvain and some other students milling about on the sidewalk, their mouths open, but she couldn't worry about that now. They seemed far away, like the backdrop to a movie set. She turned back to the open car door and managed to thank Dean Kwok for taking the trouble to come get her. "I'm sorry. I know it was inconvenient," she finished, stumbling over the words.

Kwok listened impassively, nodding twice. As Toni prepared to shut the door, he held up a hand. "Remember, Miss Isaacs," he said, having regained his normal reserve, "you have one month to demonstrate your worthiness to remain a member of this community. I'd advise you to spend that time wisely."

/ / /

The morning after her visit to the Cromwell, Dora closed the conference room door and surveyed the assembled men triumphantly. They were all waiting for her. She narrowed her eyes and savored the moment. To a man, they returned her look. The excitement in the air was palpable. She extended a languid arm in the direction of her assistant and said, "Chad is passing out the reports as I speak, so you can verify my figures."

One of the vice presidents, a casually dressed man named Bob, chuckled at the word "figures," wagging his eyebrow at his neighbor, who joined in nervously. Dora decided to ignore them. Nothing was going to ruin this day for her.

Smoothing her skirt, she strode calmly to the front of the boardroom, giving the entire executive committee of Biotecnica the same view that had Bob giggling and making innuendoes like a schoolboy. She wore small tortoiseshell spectacles and a tight-fitting suit of shimmering raw Thai silk; her hair was swept back and pinned up in the Bardot look. Her heels clicked purposefully on the polished wood floor. Gone was the hippie prostitute of last night; in Desirée's place stood a controlled, no-nonsense businesswoman.

Approaching the overhead screen, she switched on the laser pointer in her hand and directed the small red beam at a series of graphs hovering above her head. "As you can see, gentlemen," she began in a loud, clear voice, "our hard work is about to pay off. It's time to go public." She spun around and faced her audience with a grin.

The room erupted in applause and whistles. This was it, then. God knows it had been touch-and-go for a while, but everything was finally under control. The product was consistently yielding the desired results; that creep Mantini was leaving her alone; and she had taken care of the nosy Harvard reporter. The past was behind her. Dora nodded and stepped to the podium, where she rapidly manipulated the keys on a laptop computer. Immediately another series of graphics and charts appeared on the overhead screen. "All right, gentlemen. Let's talk product, shall we?"

9

Toni was tempted to spend the rest of her life in bed. There was certainly no reason to get up. She had just lived through the worst night of her life. She was weeks behind in her classes, her investigation was a mess, and now, to top it all off, in four weeks she would probably be kicked out of school, which would destroy her entire future and her parents. The only thing she had managed to do right was not turn the cops on to Desirée. That's what they wanted you to do—to turn on each other.

She burrowed under the covers and sobbed quietly until she fell into another fitful sleep. Around noon Chelo knocked a couple of times to see if she was okay, but Toni didn't feel up to explaining about last night, and Chelo eventually gave up in favor of the library. Once she heard the heavy click of the suite door closing behind her roommate, Toni sat up and rubbed her eyes. She felt better after her cry. Perhaps all she needed was a shower and some food and something productive to do. Chelo had the right idea: work, work, work.

/ / /

Toni set off at a brisk pace for the Square, her breath forming clouds in the frosty air. She would spend a few minutes at the newsstands, browsing the competition. That always got her in the mood to work. Maybe they had a copy of her hometown paper, the *Seattle Post-Intelligencer.*

Pushing open the door of Out-of-Town News, Toni took a deep breath of musty newsprint. People pored over the well-stocked plywood shelves in search of familiar mastheads and tidings from afar. Four Brazilian men were looking excitedly at the latest soccer results; next to them, a white-haired dowager delicately extracted the last copy of the *Vineyard Gazette.* Toni was scanning the *Post-Intelligencer* headlines when she heard a familiar voice behind her.

"Sad, huh?"

It was Van, standing at her elbow.

"Those businessmen, I mean," he went on, indicating a group of besuited young and middle-aged men, whose greedy eyes scanned magazines with titles like *Juggs* and *Chinese Delight.* "If they had any guts, they'd just buy them." He raised an eyebrow.

She wondered if this was a veiled reference to her arrest, but it couldn't be. "Well, they wouldn't want to take that kind of thing home. What if the little woman were to find it?"

Van picked up the theme with every appearance of solemnity. "Yes, and you can't take them to the office, either. After all, the secretary might come across them in your desk drawer. *That* wouldn't look good. So what's a poor guy to do?" He shook his head. "I guess it's best to do your reading here." He strode to a shelf, picked up a magazine, and took it over to join the intent group.

After a few seconds, Toni realized that the magazine Van was reading, with exaggerated licking of lips and rolling of eyes, was *Modern Bride.* She laughed out loud as the others in the group became aware of his parody, then, one by one, set their selections down and went back out to join the respectable world.

"That's the real pornography," Van said as he rejoined her. "All that hearts-and-flowers stuff. Give me *Motorcycle Mamas* any day. Or *Leatherboys*—I'm versatile."

"I haven't seen you in ages," she said. "Where've you been hiding? You're going to lose your title as King of the Scene if you don't look out."

Van's handsome face twisted in a mock scowl. "What's a man to do? They've been showing some very important episodes of *Bewitched* the last few weeks." He leaned over and whispered, "I'm comparing and contrasting the psychological profiles of Darrin Number One and Darrin Number Two." Straightening up, he put his finger to his lips. "I don't want this turning up on the front page of the *Crimson,* now. Not until my research is complete."

"Are you ever serious, Van?" asked Toni, laughing.

"As rarely as possible." He placed a hand on her arm and lowered his voice. "And I'd advise the same for you over the next few days."

Startled by his suddenly grave tone, she glanced up. Van was staring at her intently. She realized that he knew all about last night.

Van shook his head and then leaned over to give her a quick peck on the cheek. "Screw them," he whispered in her ear. He leaned back, straightened his jacket, and tucked his scarf inside. "Okay, I'm off. Be cool, stay in school." With a quick wave of his hand, he was out the door. Heads turned to watch his progress.

/   /   /

Still bleary-eyed at two in the afternoon, Toni sank into her chair at the *Crimson* and dropped her head in her hands. Coming to work as though nothing had happened had been a decidedly bad idea. She felt like shit, and people were acting strange. She was probably just paranoid after last night, but it seemed that every conversation in the dining hall or in the paper's corridors had stopped when she passed.

Sitting up and surveying her desk, she grimaced. Someone had seen fit to festoon it with condoms—a lovely little arrangement, worthy of June Cleaver, with a centerpiece Trojan impaled on a copy spike. She had a good idea who the decorator was. Milt Bach really picked the worst possible times to play his little harassment games. Toni jumped up and grabbed the spike. *I'd like to impale him,* she thought, striding out into the hallway. "Where's Milt?" she barked at a comper. The would-be *Crimson* staffer shrugged.

Toni headed for the business offices. As she rounded the corner she heard Milt's unmistakable nasal murmur from the other side of the wall. "Well, at least we know how the Happy Hooker gets all those tasty assignments!" He laughed, confident of his audience.

"Here I was blaming affirmative action when it was good ol' on-your-back action."

A woman laughed. "Milt, you're terrible! What about poor Lucius? I mean, he used to date her or something. How humiliating!"

Toni stopped short, the blood flooding her face. That sinking feeling of being ridiculed, dormant since junior high, came rushing back. She had just decided to retreat and save her energy when she heard Adam Steiner join the conversation. "Come on, you guys," he said in that low-key, designed-never-to-offend way of his, "let's try to be cool."

Milt saw an opening and charged through. "Hey, Adam, I'm not about judging anyone. It's just that I don't think she should be working here." He raised his voice a notch as if someone else had entered the room. "We have to consider our reputation, after all."

The unfamiliar female voice concurred. "We're not unsympathetic to her plight. I'm sure she's had a hard life and had to overcome a lot. It's not easy to leave, uh, certain learned social responses behind when faced with the pressure of a place like Harvard."

Toni had to restrain herself from leaping around the corner and slapping the girl. She clenched her fists and waited to hear what Adam would say. *Overcome my ass,* she muttered to herself.

"Oh, c'mon now," Adam chided. "I'm sure it's nothing like that. Keep in mind that we don't know the facts here. Toni has been putting out a lot of good *Crimson* stories. And we don't even know that anything illegal actually happened."

Milt pressed ahead. "Exactly! We can't verify illegal activity at this point, but if we can, we—I mean, you, Adam—have a duty to act. Something like this could jeopardize the *Crimson*'s legal standing with the college. You wouldn't want to be responsible for that."

Bastard. Adam would see through this in a minute.

"No," Adam agreed reluctantly. "But I don't really think it will come to that, Milt."

"Perhaps not." Milt could now afford to be generous. "You want to think the best of everyone on your staff. I understand that. But now's the time to think about what's best for the paper. This is the time for *real* leadership." He paused, letting the effect of quoting Adam's campaign slogan sink in.

The three moved down the hall in the opposite direction, leaving Toni in the shadows. She grabbed the doorjamb to steady herself.

/ / /

"Toni, *c'mon*!" Chelo knocked harder this time on the bathroom door. "Open up! Your mother's on the phone." She waited a few seconds and then beat again on the door. "Toni!"

"Tell her I'm out, please," Toni finally answered.

Chelo sighed and dropped her hand. "No. I've been covering for you all day, but I don't lie to parents." She rapped the receiver against the door. "Tell her yourself." She stood back and waited.

Toni cracked the door and peered out. Her eyes were red and swollen, and she looked a mess. "Sorry, Chelo," she mumbled.

Chelo shrugged and handed her the phone. "Let's talk after you're off the phone. I'll make some tea."

Toni nodded and retreated with the phone to her bed. She plopped down on the comforter and faked a smile. "Places, everyone," she told herself in her best Ricardo Montalban accent, giving a regal sweep of her arm. "Welcome to Fantasy Island!" She punched the mute button. "Hi, Mom!" she said brightly. "Sorry for the delay."

"Toni?" Matilda Isaacs sounded suspicious—or was it just her lilting Barbados accent, always putting the emphasis on the last syllable? "What's going on there? Are you all right?"

"Yeah, Mom, I'm fine. It was just a little mix-up. . . . Chelo thought I was out. Nothing to worry about."

"Hmmm." Noncommittal, her mother rolled the syllable around in her mouth. Island women and their "hmmm"s! No one could convey skepticism or disapproval as vividly as a Bajan mother, or with fewer words. The sound hummed between them. It was as if Matilda were picking up vibrations over the phone, assessing the very air and electrical currents to determine whether Toni was telling the truth. When she had been younger, Toni had inevitably caved, convinced that if her mother stared at her hard enough and muttered the magic "hmmm" long enough, she could actually read her mind. She held her breath.

Finally Matilda seemed satisfied—at least for now. "Really?" she asked.

"Yeah, really," Toni said weakly. What if Kwok had lied about not calling her parents? "What makes you think anything's wrong?" she asked.

"*Should* I think anything's wrong?" her mother countered.

"No."

"Good."

This contest of wills was nerve-racking. "I don't understand why you always assume the worst!" Toni blurted.

"Who says I'm assuming anything?" Matilda sounded exasperated.

"Oh, never mind."

"Girl, you're downright peevish today!" Her mother's voice softened. "Are you sure you're all right, pumpkin?"

Hearing her childhood pet name, Toni nearly burst into tears. What a relief it would be to tell her mother everything. For a moment, she regretted insisting that her parents treat her like an adult. But even if she wanted to tell them, there was no way they would ever understand her actions.

"I'm sure, Mom," she gulped. She cast about for one of the standard student excuses. "I just have a lot of work, and I haven't been getting enough sleep. How are you and Dad?"

Her mother paused for a moment, presumably weighing Toni's response. Finally she replied: "We're both fine. There's talk of a possible corporate merger and some downsizing at Boeing, so that's got your father all in a state, but I tell him he's got nothing to worry about."

"What do you mean?" Toni asked, wondering if she should be alarmed. "Dad could get laid off?" It was hard to imagine her father "in a state." In his climb to become the first black vice president at Boeing Industries, Harlan Isaacs had somehow managed to remain sweet and even-tempered.

"Don't get yourself all vexed, pumpkin. I doubt it could happen. Your father's very highly thought of. And if it ever did come to that, I'm doing well enough at SPU." Matilda Isaacs taught nursing at Seattle Pacific University. She continued: "Don't worry about a thing. Your job is to be a student. Just do well and make us proud."

Her parents wanted only two things from her: to do well and

make them proud. So far, she was 0 for 2. "How are you, Mom?" Toni asked.

"I'm fine, baby. Looks like your Nana's hip isn't healing right, and your father wants to bring her from Chicago to stay with us. She, of course, is fighting it—wants to be independent and such!" Matilda gave a low snort. In Barbados, as she constantly reminded Toni and Harlan, family stuck together. Folks didn't live scattered all over the country, hardly ever calling or seeing one another. It just wasn't natural!

"Is Nana okay?" Toni resolved to remember to call her grandmother once things had settled down a bit, and this time she meant it. Funny, she'd never really realized that her parents had worries of their own. They always made their lives look so easy—being married, holding down demanding jobs, raising a child, maintaining a house, supporting relatives back in Chicago and Barbados who weren't as comfortable.

"Your Nana will outlive us all." Matilda chuckled. "Now, are you eating right? Could you and Chelo use some of my world-famous coconut bread?"

In spite of everything, Toni felt a smile cross her face. It didn't change anything, and it wasn't the same as being able to crawl into her mother's lap and make the world go away, but coconut bread was a pretty good start.

After chatting briefly with her father about his latest fishing trip to the San Juan Islands, Toni hung up and went out into the common room to give her roommate a hug. Chelo hugged her back and handed her a mug of tea.

"I guess I have some 'splaining to do," Toni said.

Chelo nodded calmly and asked if the rumors were true: Had she been picked up the night before for solicitation at the Cromwell? Somehow the news had leaked out; everyone was talking about it. No wonder Toni had been so interested in doing a story on sex on campus, people were saying. Toni sighed. She explained the whole chain of events. It was a relief finally to be able to tell someone the truth without having to decide how much to keep back.

Whatever shock Chelo might have been feeling was overshadowed by her concern for Toni. "I can't believe that Milt Bach," she marveled. "After everything you've done to make the *Crimson* look good, when all he's done is cause trouble!"

Toni shrugged. "That's business, I guess."

"And Kwok," Chelo said reprovingly. "Imagine going to get you after such a traumatic experience, and then just making it worse by blaming and threatening you. He's been such a jerk ever since his wife left him. I wonder if he thinks you're responsible for those *Crimson* stories on his divorce."

"Probably," Toni agreed, "even though I had nothing to do with them. He always was a pompous ass, but I don't remember him being this nasty."

Chelo fell silent a moment. "Couldn't you just tell your parents the truth? You seem to have such a good relationship, and they seem so cool."

Toni shook her head. "No way. They've got their own problems. And besides, you know how it is."

"Yeah," Chelo agreed reluctantly. "My mama can't hear that 'La Harvard' is anything less than a dream come true for me."

"They just don't get it," Toni complained. "I guess college was less complicated when they were going."

"Hmm," Chelo said, and Toni remembered that not everyone's parents had gone to college—or even high school.

"Sorry. Do I sound like a middle-class brat?"

"Absolutely!" They both laughed.

Toni was reminded of something she had forgotten in all the excitement last night. "Chelo, what do you think about Cabot disappearing at the police station? Isn't that weird? I mean, he takes the time to rush down there as soon as he gets my call, we're in the middle of a conversation, and then—poof!—he vanishes without a word."

"Well, maybe he figured you were okay. Dean Kwok was there by then, right?"

Toni thought a minute. "I think so."

"Well, that's probably it, then. He saw the dean, and he assumed everything was under control."

Just then the phone rang, and Chelo reached for the receiver. *But why didn't Cabot at least say good-bye?* Toni mused. For now there were more pressing issues to attend to. "Just a minute," Chelo told the person on the other line. "I'll check." She punched the mute button, and

Toni looked questioningly at her. "It's a Detective Carlos Rivera," Chelo announced. "He says you probably won't want to talk to him, but it's nothing bad."

She took the phone gingerly and cleared her throat. "Hello?" she said tentatively.

"Miss Isaacs?"

He was so formal. She said, a little more boldly, "Yes, this is Toni."

"Detective Rivera of the Cambridge Police Department. You may remember me from last night." He paused.

"Yes, of course I remember you."

"Good." He coughed. "How are you doing?"

"Fine, I guess."

"I'm sure you must be pretty upset after last night's experience. How's your head?"

"My head?" Toni touched the bandage above her eye. She had forgotten all about it. The cut throbbed faintly, and she recalled the cool touch of his fingers as he bandaged her up. "It's okay. Thanks."

"I didn't want to alarm you by calling," he explained, "but I was just wondering how you were doing."

"Oh, that's nice of you." This couldn't be standard procedure.

"You had quite a scare," he said. She could hear his chair squeak; he must be fidgeting. He cleared his throat. "I apologize for not believing your story initially—especially when you said you went to the Cromwell on a tip."

Toni was puzzled. "Why do you say that?" she asked.

"Because *we* responded to a tip that someone called in."

"Someone called it in?"

"Yes." His voice tapered off, and Toni could hear the rustle of papers. "Let's see—twelve minutes before we hit the hotel, we got a telephone call from a young woman. From the Caller ID, looks like a cell phone."

Toni nearly dropped the phone. It took everything she had to convince Detective Rivera that she was all right and get off the phone before she started screaming. *Desirée!* Desirée was definitely a young woman—with a cell phone. She must have slipped into the bathroom and called the cops. And ten minutes later they started banging on the door. She'd been set up.

How could Toni have been so stupid as actually to cover for her? With this final bit of news, a thought that had been developing clicked into place. There was only one way she could fight all this— the loss of her reputation, the Ad Board charges against her, the trouble at the *Crimson,* whatever "Desirée" was up to: she had to go ahead with her investigation. No more lying in bed feeling sorry for herself; she had to act swiftly and decisively. The only way to redeem herself was to write and publish the truth. Until last night, journalistic integrity had demanded that. Now it was a matter of her own survival.

10

"Hey, girlfriend, how's tricks?" Van called out from the entrance of the café.

From the table, Dora nodded slightly in acknowledgment. He'd better make his charm work overtime.

He was late, of course. As always, he seemed to think he could live by his own rules. That would catch up with him someday. Or maybe not—Van Nguyen had a way of getting away with things that other people couldn't.

Dora was no fan of Café Pamplona, where she'd been sitting at a rickety black table for a good twenty minutes. It was no more than a smoky little room in the basement of a red wooden house at the intersection of Bow and Arrow streets, with low ceilings, overpriced coffee, and underwhelming service. The clientele ranged from scruffy chain-smoking undergrads who eavesdropped openly on one another's self-important conversations, to crazed Cambridge types who staked out tables for hours at a time, scribbling poetry about a master race of women with three nipples. All the waiters were tall prettyboys who spent more time fluffing their up-to-the-minute haircuts than making or serving coffee. In a just world, all these people would be working in a factory somewhere.

It wasn't her scene.

"Am I to be punished?" Van inquired in his silky baritone, dropping a schoolbag on the ground. He was the only man she knew who could be catty and masculine at the same time. It pissed her off that it was hard to stay angry at him.

"Wishful thinking, dude," she answered, closing her copy of *Us*.

As Van scanned the menu, Dora glanced around the room. Every pair of eyes had turned to check out who was sitting with whom. Dora felt a flush of excitement at being seen publicly with the guy, a feeling she immediately quelled. This wasn't New York, for God's sake.

All the cigarette smoke was giving her a buzz. She eyed the beat-up furniture and the rough, undecorated walls. Thank God it was only a matter of time before the Californiazation of America was complete and smoking was banned everywhere. After a while, one of two boys chatting in the back room poked his head out and surveyed the café. He spotted Dora and Van, but apparently they were not in his section.

A few minutes later, the second waiter, his skinny black necktie tucked in below the second button of his shirt, emerged from the back room and headed over to their table.

"Double decaf cappuccino, nonfat milk," Dora commanded. The boy noted her order dutifully.

"What's orzata soda?" Van asked.

The waiter stood with his head cocked to one side and stroked his ponytail. "Almond, okay?" he answered. He seemed nervous.

"Just bring me something green, then."

"Green?" the waiter asked, baffled. "What kind of order is that?"

It was fun to see Van go after people. So long as the victim wasn't her.

"Just, you know, green. Mint, or kiwi, or green tea. Whatever."

The waiter stood indecisively for a few seconds. "Oh, all right."

"You're such a freak," Dora commented.

"Well, thank you. That's the nicest thing anybody's said to me all day. But let's talk about you."

"Why start now?" she parried.

"I just had a few questions I could use some answers on. Related to certain extracurricular activities."

"Off limits," she replied, crossing her arms.

"Who do you report to?"

Dora did not answer. This boy had no sense of boundaries.

"Someone you know well, right? At the university?"

"How 'bout them Mets?" she asked.

"Let me see, how to ask this delicately—"

"See, that's the thing, Van." She leaned in toward him. "You don't ask, and I don't tell. Not that I have the slightest idea what you're talking about."

The waiter was back with the drinks. "And a glass of water—when you have a chance," Van requested. The waiter gave a curt nod.

Dora sipped her coffee noisily. "So you want to know who pulls my strings, right? Who the puppet master is?"

"That might be it," he answered.

"Well, if you even have to ask, you don't know me at all. You just go back to your little pre-med courses and leave the thinking to us grown-ups, okay?" She started pulling some bills out of her wallet.

"I'm not pre-med, you big racist. And who do you mean by 'us'"? He took a sip of his green thing.

Not much of a comeback, Dora thought with satisfaction.

He stood up as she did and placed a hand on her forearm. "Dora, don't go yet. There's something I really want to ask you."

"And there are lots of things I really don't want to tell you." She shook off his hand. "Tell me, though, what you would give me for the information that you seem to think I have."

"My undying respect?"

"I'm thinking of something a little more concrete. More physical, as it were."

He laughed, broadly, for the first time. "Well, sorry, Dora. I'm not for sale."

"Everyone's for sale. It's simply a question of the price."

"I'll be your best friend," he whined.

"I have enough friends," she replied, glad to be on top in this exchange. "Too many, in fact. And they all call me about their bad relationships. It's some weird national trend. So bug off, baby." Dora threw on her coat and headed toward the door. Just before leaving, she paused in the doorway to the kitchen and called out to the waiter, who was engaged in a conversation on the phone. "You can drop the attitude, buster," she informed him. " 'Cause in case you haven't noticed, you work in a café."

/ / /

The redbrick and marble façades of the business school came into view as Toni walked down JFK Street. She felt a chill of apprehension. Desirée had upped the ante. And now Toni was going to get the bitch, whatever it took.

Toni marched on. From across the river, the stateliness of the buildings was menacing. Harvard's campus was aesthetically impressive by any standard, but the business school, which to the average Harvard undergrad seemed impossibly rich and far away, was stunning. Lucius alleged that the business school gym was stocked daily with fresh flowers. Too bad that beauty was wasted on all those selfish B-school types.

Since Desirée seemed older than Toni, and more together than the average Ph.D. student, Toni had guessed that she attended either law school or business school. Indeed, it hadn't taken long to confirm "Desirée's" identity. Among the "G"s in a B-school face book she'd borrowed from a tutor was one Dora Givens, a second-year student whose interests were "biking, sea kayaking, and travel"—the same as those of at least a dozen other students in the book's first ten pages. Despite the pictured woman's smooth chignon and perfect lipstick, Toni was certain that she was the erstwhile New Age hooker "Desirée."

Feeling like an impostor, Toni crossed Storrow Drive onto the business school campus. A couple of men dressed in college sweatshirts were playing hackeysack on the frozen ground in front of one of the dorms, their sports-dude act not particularly convincing given their pale skin, receding hairlines, and sagging midsections.

"Sweet!" one of the men bellowed as the other dove into the mud to kick up the tiny striped ball.

Toni asked them how to find the Office of Career Services and was directed to a spacious room in one of the main buildings. No basement digs for this career center; it—and access to the occasional business guru—were the two reasons M.B.A. candidates paid the ungodly tuition. Inside, several students were absorbed in planning their brilliant private-sector careers; despite Toni's fear of being carded, no one so much as looked up. Roughly half the people in the room were dressed in casual clothes. They carried on breezy conversations as they leafed through large black binders filled with job descriptions. The other students were men whose sharp suits outlined their muscles effectively, and gaunt women swathed in Ann Taylor and Jones New York, with power jewelry and picture-perfect makeup and hair. One woman, her hair pulled back tightly enough to simulate a facelift, stared intently at a photo on the wall, practicing for an interview in a loud whisper. She even mimicked laughing at a joke told by her invisible interviewer.

In the center of a large mahogany table were several huge plastic binders labeled "Class Résumés." This was the prize Toni had come for. Excited, she slipped into a seat and began flipping through the résumés, each a picture-perfect one-page tribute to achievement, leadership ability, and the wonders of desktop publishing. Out of curiosity, she tried to read a few, but they tended to blur together; every bullet-pointed description of past accomplishments contained the words "international," "creative," and "spearheaded."

She turned another page and felt as if she'd won the lottery. There, in a nutshell, was the life of Dora Givens—and with a larger, clearer photo. Yes, Dora was her mysterious nemesis. Toni laughed aloud. The woman speaking to the invisible interviewer turned around and smiled nervously at her.

Toni read quickly through Dora's life on paper. She had graduated four years earlier from NYU, where she was active on the committee to help the homeless and in something called the Media Center. Then she spent two years as a production assistant and assistant producer for some MTV entity. A career switch took her to Cambridge, where she worked for a firm called Biotecnica, "a medium-size pharmaceutical start-up." From there she'd landed at HBS.

Toni searched in her bag for a pen to write all this down. No—too slow. After a quick glance around the room, she cleared her throat loudly, ripped out the résumé, and slammed the binder shut. Then she fled, hoping she wouldn't get arrested for stealing valuable human software.

Outside, the cold air smacking against her face was a relief. Toni sat down on the stone step and pulled out the résumé, covering it like someone reading *Hustler* on an airplane. Her eyes were drawn again to the section on work experience: the entry on Biotecnica listed the dates as "to present." So Dora was still connected to that company. Despite the rigors of the M.B.A. program, she'd kept her day job.

Toni smiled broadly. Mission accomplished. Dora had something to lose: her professional reputation. And Toni was going to let her know it.

/ / /

Dressed in the closest approximation of a power suit she could contrive—short skirt, tan wool jacket, black hose, black pumps—Toni walked quickly up the subway station escalator and past the glossy hotel. Kendall Square lacked the self-imposed squalor of Harvard Square—no middle-class high school kids from Winchester or Woburn posing as skinheads or hippies; no Peruvian musicians; no smelly street philosophers. Instead, it was all glass and young urban professionals, expensive-looking briefcases and espresso stands. Checking the directions to Biotecnica once more , Toni felt supremely out of place.

The wind whipped between her legs as she headed down Main Street past various MIT science facilities. This career-woman thing would never work for her if outfits like this were the price of admission. She'd get pneumonia before she could master quality circles.

Finally she located One Technology Plaza. There it was, Biotecnica, right next to Infomatrix Strategy Group, just as the receptionist had said.

Toni gave her name to the woman at the front desk, and after depositing her Harvard I.D. card was issued an orange guest pass to pin on her jacket. She sat down on a pastel-blue couch in front of a chrome-and-glass coffee table and picked up a copy of *The Wall Street Journal.* Across from her a yuppie in a pinstriped suit sat mumbling into his cell phone, a briefcase popped open in front of him and a ticket for the Delta Shuttle in his jacket pocket. After a few moments, a longhaired man in his early forties who wore a T-shirt and faded jeans came out and introduced himself to the yuppie. "Walt Stevens, New Product Development." In Walt's friendly grin, Toni detected a slight smirk—the condescension of someone who doesn't have to wear a uniform, talking to someone who does.

A pert woman in a bright red suit strode out of the same door. Her hair was done up in a tight, shiny bun, and she wore a large pin in the shape of an alligator on her lapel. She looked over to the receptionist, who inclined her head toward Toni. The woman in the Adolfo getup affixed a large smile to her face and marched over.

Toni stood and offered her hand, which the other woman grasped firmly enough to cut off circulation to her arm. Her father would love a handshake like that. "Antonia, hi. I'm Melanie Bradford, from Human Resources?" She handed Toni a thick plastic folder filled with shiny pamphlets and papers. "Welcome to Biotecnica. We're really glad you could make it in today? I've put together a dossier for your visit?" Melanie raised her voice at the end of every sentence, as if asking a question. "Why don't we just sit down here for a minute?" Melanie carefully arranged herself on the sectional sofa and opened the folder in front of them, like a first-grade teacher reading a story aloud and making sure that everyone in her class saw the pictures.

The center page was Biotecnica letterhead with "Visit of Antonia Isaacs (*Harvard Crimson*) to Biotecnica" printed in large bold letters. Several appointments were listed underneath, the first with Melanie Bradford, "Human Resources Specialist," from 9:30 to 9:40 A.M. Five or six others followed, and Melanie issued informational squibs about each of them.

Well, checking out Biotecnica was going to be a cinch! Toni had never realized what authority she had merely as a reporter for the *Crimson,* even using the absurd pretext of writing a story about career options for this year's grads. It had taken her all of eight minutes to contact the VP of human resources—Melanie's boss, apparently—and schedule a morning of "informational interviews" with various departments. Desperate as college seniors were for entry-level jobs, companies seemed to be equally desperate for bright young things to do whatever one did at a place like Biotecnica. It was a wonder everyone didn't live happily ever after.

Melanie checked her watch and popped up instantly on her Etienne Aigner heels. "I'd love to read whatever article you write. Of course, we pull things down on-line, but it takes forever to circulate, if you know what I mean?" Toni nodded vaguely.

Melanie waved an ID card in front of a red sensor light and held the door for Toni. They passed into a hallway; one side was still unfinished and had been recently plastered. The other side, painted a soothing light green, was covered with a series of quilt sections. Melanie beamed. "That's our antique quilt collection. They're from Appalachia and the Midwest, mainly? There is also a collection of old quilts by African-American artists that is kept in a boardroom, which unfortunately is in use today."

"They're beautiful," Toni said.

"It makes for a more friendly workplace, don't you think? Most corporate work offices are filled with those cold, abstract pieces that no one really understands. They aren't very good, but they tend to be favored by the men making the decisions. I studied art history in my previous incarnation."

"No kidding?"

Melanie started walking again. "Three years of grad school. But I saw the writing on the wall; there aren't many jobs. One day I had to admit to myself that I just wasn't going to make it big in the field."

"Aren't you—" Toni was going to say "overqualified for this kind of work" but stopped herself.

"Lucky to have this job? I know I am. It's not easy to reestablish yourself, and HR is so competitive. But we're growing like gangbusters and always looking for new people. That's why we were so tickled to get your call."

"It must be a good environment for women, then," Toni said. "I have a friend who works here. Dora Givens." She clocked Melanie for a reaction.

Melanie shook her head blankly. "I don't know her, but I haven't been here that long. Anyway, it's a big company." She entered a warren of cubicles, half of which seemed empty and unlit. A blond guy with preppie glasses and a polo shirt appeared to be talking to himself. Melanie knocked on the cubicle partition and he spun around and waved. Toni saw that he was wearing a telephone headset, the kind worn by Madonna and Time-Life operators.

Melanie made the introductions—the man turned out to be

Jerome-who-worked-in-Marketing—and said she'd be back in twenty minutes to escort Toni to her next appointment.

/ / /

For the next three hours, Toni played the happy recipient of friendly wisdom on jobs, academia, and life; she dutifully wrote down the maxims offered by Jerome, Sandeep, Lucy, a different Sandeep, Yevgeny, and Max. All the interviewees were stiff, businesslike, and uncommunicative for about three minutes. Then, as soon as they figured out that Toni wasn't actually looking for a job, they launched into revelations about office politics, career frustrations, problems with their parents, girlfriends, or boyfriends, how much they hated the person in the next cubicle, how they got screwed on stock options, how they were going to jump ship as soon as they could cash out, the advantages of living in Boston instead of Cambridge, how important it was in this life to be "really centered," the difficulties of being vegetarian, and whether it would be a trifle "too much" to buy a Miata.

Toni did learn a few things of value. For example, Biotecnica hadn't actually made any money yet, though no one seemed worried about that. Sandeep II told her that three years earlier, the company had staked its hopes on an antidepressant shake for dieters called Grinfast, which, unfortunately, had been supplanted almost immediately by a better-selling strawberry-flavored competitor. Biotecnica was larger than she had realized, with more than a hundred and fifty professionals. Unfortunately, Toni didn't learn much about Dora Givens, only that she worked in "Strategy," a department disdained by Lucy and Yevgeny, researchers who worked on "the Floor."

A bearded scientist who had wandered by during this session snorted in agreement. "How do you know Dora?" he had asked, stepping into the cubicle. "Just friends of friends," she replied. "Why do you ask?"

"You look familiar, is all," he said.

Melanie arrived punctually at one, as Toni was finishing up her final session. She chatted gaily, though Toni was too exhausted from faking interest in the world of Biotecnica career prospects to take part.

On the way out, she asked for the restroom. Melanie sent her down the quilt-lined hallway and told her to take two right turns. Ex-iting the washroom, she was startled by someone waiting just outside.

"You're not really writing about career options, are you?" he asked. It was the scientist who had wandered into her meeting with Lucy and Yevgeny. "I recognize you, you know. You were at that film screening at the Science Center a couple weeks ago. *Deep Throat.* I've been following your stories. They're pretty good."

Upon closer inspection, she remembered: he'd tried to strike up a conversation with her at the *Deep Throat* screening. In an actual work environment, he looked less like a homeless person.

"Well, yes, I was there, but I am, in fact, writing about career op-tions. It's that time of year." Toni started walking down the hall to get away from him.

He followed her, whispering. "You're undercover, aren't you? I'll bet you're not even friends with Dora, are you? You're going the wrong way, by the way. The exit is the other direction."

Toni stopped short, took a deep breath, and turned around. "What makes you think that?"

He didn't answer the question. "Writing about recruiting isn't re-ally your style, is it? Not after that big piece on the college-student prostitute. You're more the investigative type, I think." His face wrin-kled in thought.

"Have you been following me?" Toni was worried, but only for a second. There was serious security here.

"So why would you be asking about Dora now?" he continued. "I bet she wouldn't want a newspaper reporter looking into *her* various activities."

She heard the security door open in the hall behind them. Melanie might be looking for her.

"Maybe we should talk more about this later," Toni suggested.

"About what?" he asked.

She looked him straight in the eyes. "About Dora. About what she's up to. Let's pool information." She tore off a piece of paper from her Biotecnica dossier, pulled a pen from her bag, and scribbled her number. "Call me."

He took the piece of paper and stared at it.

"I'd thought you'd gotten yourself lost!" Melanie said, suddenly on the scene. She looked at the scientist a little suspiciously, but he closed his hand over the paper.

"I did get lost!" Toni laughed. "I wandered off in the wrong direction entirely—then I ran into this gentleman, who set me right." She pretended to check her watch. "Oh, my God, I've probably got you entirely off schedule, Melanie." She waved at the scientist. "Thanks again for pointing me in the right direction."

/ / /

"It's your phone pal again," Dave Mantini said into the receiver. The mouthpiece felt warm and he held it away from his face. He didn't like public telephones, but he wasn't about to make this call from work.

The voice at the other end was irritable. "How long do you plan to keep up this little game, Dave?"

"I'm not playing," he answered.

The man at the other end emitted a condescending sigh. "We've gone over this a thousand times, Dave. I don't know any more than you do. Anyway"—the voice was mocking—"I hear research is what you do best."

"You can treat me like a paranoiac if you need to," Dave said calmly. "I don't care, because you have no appreciation for the rigors of science. But you might want to know that I'm not the only one who wonders what you're doing in Biotecnica and why you're so intimate with Dora."

There was silence.

"The Fifth Estate," Dave sputtered. "The press. I'm thinking of going public."

"Is this another scare tactic, Mr. Teenyman?"

Dave hated how the man made fun of his name, the way kids in Revere used to. "The interesting thing," he continued, "is that I didn't seek her out myself. No, this reporter came up to me on her own. She's going to check out Dora—and I don't have any doubt she'll discover your business relationship with her. If I were you, I'd start planning how to undo everything you've done, before your name is all over the front page of the *Crimson*. And then everywhere else."

Silence again. "Why don't we get together and talk this over?"

the voice said. "In person." Dave heard a hint of anxiety in the normally supercilious tone. The other man was surprised, no doubt, that there were other people as smart as he.

Dave hung up.

Mark Tansen hadn't been willing or able to help, not if Dave wanted anything besides pointers on outdoor sports. His old hero was a figurehead now, as out of the loop as the night cleaning staff. That didn't matter, because Dave was going to take control of things himself, with the assistance of Toni Isaacs. She wasn't an ally—but then, she didn't need to be. Their interests were the same. Her work would benefit his.

11

From a pay phone outside the language lab in the basement of Boylston Hall, Van heard his own voice instructing callers to leave lots of messages on his answering machine. One by one, with a hopefulness that struck him as detestable and pathetic, he listened to the chatty greetings left by the people who called him. Like he really expected to get the call he needed. He slammed down the receiver and scowled; his worn German text toppled to the ground.

God, he hated to be in this position. It was so ridiculous to be powerless, so pathetic to have handed over his personal allotment of happiness to someone else for safekeeping, someone who basically didn't give a shit about him. Or so it seemed, sometimes.

He wasn't used to being scared. Maybe that was worse: knowing that he wasn't really up to facing the future alone.

Cursing his inability to be more stoic, he fished out another coin from the front pocket of his black jeans and pumped it into the metal slot. He dialed a number that he'd long since memorized. Two rings and then the predictable machine. A beep sounded, announcing his chance to seem weak and self-loathing and naïve.

"Listen," he said to the machine and whoever might be monitor-

ing the recording. "We're going to talk about this, okay?" He took a
breath and continued. "We're not going to dwell on how things got
to be this way, okay? We'll just figure out how to fix it. This isn't
some crash-and-burn that I'm just going to walk away from. You got
that?"

He hung up the phone, grabbed his German book, and shouldered his knapsack. Fuck it all.

/ / /

Toni crossed through a little park and passed a bakery and conve-
nience store, checking house numbers against the address Dave Mantini had given her. She paused for a moment in front of a dilapidated
Art Deco pharmacy that featured a large window display of prosthetics. It was a particularly forlorn sight.

She'd been pumped with excitement since midnight, when Chelo
told her that some guy wanted to talk to her on the phone. The guy
turned out to be Dave Mantini.

For all the drama Toni felt at having her first inside source on the
line, it was weirdly difficult to connect with Dave on any level. After
identifying himself, he fell silent. From the Biotecnica materials, she
knew he had spent several years at Harvard as a grad student in biochemistry before opting for the rewards of the private sector. But that
didn't seem a fruitful topic of conversation. He might know nothing
about Dora and the escort service. Or he might be in cahoots with
her, although she doubted it. They didn't seem to travel in the same
circles. "Mr. Mantini, you said Dora wouldn't want a reporter looking into her activities. What did you mean?"

"No one calls me Mr. Mantini," he said.

"Okay, Dave. I need to be up-front about something. I am not a
friend of Dora Givens, your colleague. Quite the contrary. I've had—"

"Dora Givens isn't my *colleague*," he interrupted. He sounded annoyed. Good.

"What do you mean?" she asked lightly.

"I'm a biochemist, okay? I work on the Floor. Dora Givens"—he
nearly spat out the syllables—"works in 'Strategy.' Whatever *that's*
supposed to mean."

"So you've never had occasion to work with Dora." She'd go in
the direction he'd established. "Is that right?"

He was silent. Toni heard the sounds of people talking behind him. After the pedestrians moved on, he spoke again without answering her question. "Hey, what do you really know about Dora, anyway? I'm not sure it's such a great idea for me to talk to you. This could be a big risk for me."

She had to bring him in before he changed his mind. "I know that Dora has engaged in illegal acts. Maybe she does the same thing at Biotecnica. I got burned by her—and whoever she's connected with—because I was unprepared. You don't have to do the same thing. You don't have to trust me, but you can trust the power of the press."

She forced herself to count to ten slowly. She'd hit eight when he finally spoke.

"Okay," he said. "But not now. And not on the phone. Come to my house tomorrow night. I'll show you some things." He gave her an address in Somerville and then hung up.

/ / /

Dave's building, directly across from a white frame house bearing the proud sign "Portuguese-American Social Club," was three stories of brown shingles, a little run-down. A concrete birdbath sat in the middle of its tiny lawn. The water in the bath had frozen.

The rusted mailboxes in front indicated that Dave's apartment was on the first floor. Toni stepped into the small entryway and pressed the buzzer. No answer. After a few seconds she buzzed again.

Half an hour later she was still waiting, her patience gone and her excitement deadened. The temperature had dropped dramatically after sunset, which in midwinter came before five P.M. Toni was chilled and tired of ignoring the suspicious looks of passersby. Whatever his reasons might be, Dave had stood her up. She was getting up from the stoop, brushing dirt and ice off her jeans, when she heard a clatter inside the building. Two wiry brown kids burst out of the inner door, giggling as they lunged wildly from side to side, barely balancing on their in-line skates. They rattled down the peeling wooden stairs that joined the stoop to the sidewalk. In a flash, Toni was up. She grabbed the outer door before it closed and lunged toward the knob of the inner door, reaching it just before it slammed shut. Stopping for a second to steady herself, she held the inner door and then closed it quietly behind her.

The building seemed to have been partially renovated. There were three apartments on the first floor; the hallway was well lit and seemed clean. But the wooden staircase going up to the second and third floors wasn't in such great shape. Two or three of the balusters were missing. The brown wood was streaked with black, the accumulation of years of shoe leather and dirt, and each step was noticeably recessed in the middle.

Mantini's apartment was in back. Toni rapped on the door half-heartedly, then tried the knob: locked but slightly loose. There were two or three keyholes above, dating from different generations of tenancy; she wondered if any were still in use.

She dropped her leather schoolbag between her legs and rummaged for her American Express card. Despite the loose knob, the door was too tightly closed for the card to slip in. Toni rocked back on her heels and inspected the door frame. It jutted out slightly to the right; the pins on the left were slightly misaligned. The building must have settled over the years, until the door no longer quite fit its frame.

Toni put the Amex card between her teeth and, checking the pins again, grasped the knob securely. Bracing herself against the wall, she pulled up and back at the same time. The door definitely moved, if just a fraction of an inch. She braced herself and pulled again. This time when the door shifted she pulled the charge card out of her mouth and pushed it into the crack that had opened up. It went in halfway.

She jiggled the card. It was clearly pressing against the lock, but the plastic was no match for metal. She grunted in frustration. She took a deep breath and then, in one movement, yanked up on the door handle and pushed the card into the metalwork.

And then she felt a rush as the card penetrated the lock mechanism with a sharp click, and the knob turned in her hand. Her body a rigid slab of tension, she opened the door carefully so as not to explode into the room.

After a moment, her eyes began to distinguish forms within the field of black. A coatrack stood next to a worn-out futon slumped over against the wall. The centerpiece of the room was a 1950s yellow Formica kitchen table with three unmatched chairs. Toni's fear was replaced by curiosity. It was exciting to explore someone else's private world, however pedestrian that world was.

A blue light shone in the next room. Toni took a quick step forward and heard herself yelp loudly even before she felt pain sear her leg. She had bumped into the edge of a low table with mounds of newspapers stacked on top. Tears formed in her eyes, but she limped over to the next room, ignoring the pain in her leg. There were books everywhere, and stacks of newspapers at various places on the floor. She picked up one paper and instantly sneezed; it was covered with dust. She couldn't make out anything on the page.

On the computer emitting the blue light, a screen saver endlessly repeated geometric patterns. Toni leaned over the desk and moved the mouse. The machine made a quiet chugging noise as the screen-saver image vanished.

And then she saw it. Amid the icons for the various drives and applications was one for the floppy disk inserted in the side drive, called "Givens."

Her hand trembling slightly, she double-clicked on the icon. The computer again made its spinning sound, and then a message with two arrows going in opposite directions appeared. "Insert disk into drive," it commanded.

Toni fumbled across the desk, but there were no floppies. She moved the cursor to "File" and scrolled down to the "Eject" function but received the same message as before. She felt for the drive slot and prodded the opening. Nothing.

Dave had a whole file on Dora Givens that he had been checking out the last time he was at this machine. She had to find him. He knew something—perhaps too much to tell her.

/ / /

It was well after midnight on Saturday when Chelo stuck her head into the hot dryer. She sighed, though it was hard to say whether from exhaustion, boredom, or self-pity. How could socks simply vanish between the washer and dryer?

Chelo started another load of laundry and wandered over to the soda machines. Both were out of order. Jingling the change in her hand, she went in search of a working machine and found one in the weight room. After a moment's deliberation, she bought just one can of liquid caffeine. If she drank two she might end up staying awake all night, and she needed to get up early Sunday morning to stay on schedule.

As she popped open the can, she thought she heard a sound farther down the tunnel. A second later there came the diminishing echo of footsteps and the distant slam of a door. She didn't think anyone else was down here, but she couldn't really know for sure. The tunnels under Adams House featured all kinds of hangout spaces, created by artistically inclined students who seemed to have a lot of time on their hands.

She wiped her forehead. Her skin felt too warm. She took a swig of Diet Coke. The can clicked against her teeth and the metallic taste overpowered any pleasure provided by the aspartame.

There *was* someone nearby. It was an eerie feeling. She padded over to the edge of the tunnel.

Again she heard a human sound—a sigh, actually. It appeared to be coming from an alcove near the tunnel leading to the pool.

Chelo crept forward and peered ahead. Leaning against the rough, stained walls of the tunnel was a lone male figure, his head cradled in his arms. Chelo stood transfixed. The guy's posture was defeated; his shoulders quivered as if he were crying. The image was beautiful and almost obscene at the same time. Just as she was about to step forward and ask if she could help, he moved his arm and revealed his profile. She froze, staring in disbelief. The tear-streaked face that stared blindly ahead belonged to Van.

With a gradual accumulation of energy, Van straightened up. Chelo shrank back along the corridor, embarrassed. She felt shy about letting Van know what she had witnessed; she wasn't on intimate terms with him.

She held her breath, her heart pounding. Van hadn't seen her. He gave his head a careless toss and seemed to grow taller, his back straighter, his shoulders broader. He wiped away the tears with the back of a hand. Chelo watched as his features seemed to rearrange themselves into a pale, impenetrable mask. The firm cheekbones. The slightly mocking mouth. But for a flicker in his eyes, his beautiful face was empty of emotion. With a brush of his sleeve, all traces of tears were gone.

Throwing back his smooth shoulders, Van set off in the direction of the pool. He moved fast, hurling himself along the tunnel. Chelo followed, wondering how he could have changed moods so quickly and where he was going. The air grew warmer and more humid as they approached the underground pool. Chelo could hear muted shouts and splashes coming from within. She hung back, afraid of being spotted.

Adams was the only house to have its own private swimming pool. House residents knew they had a good thing going; they jealously guarded their aquatic sanctum, with its lovely wooden details and cavelike intimacy.

Van flung open the heavy door. For a brief moment Chelo heard laughter, splashing water, and the cry of voices. A thick cloud of vapor billowed out into the corridor. Then, just as quickly, the noise stopped and Van disappeared inside, the door clicking shut behind him with finality. Chelo sneaked forward and, raising herself up on her toes, peered through the diamond-shaped window in the door. Through the fogged glass, she saw huge shadows flickering over the walls. At first the figures inside seemed to be playing an elaborate game in slow motion—throwing their arms around each other and falling to the ground in a pantomime of touch football; turning this way and that, limbs interwoven, as if caught in an early morning game of Twister.

Her eyes widened. So the rumors were true, after all. Chelo was no jet-setter, but she considered herself fairly sophisticated, even liberated. Yet she was speechless. Witnessing an orgy was a first for her.

Van! Chelo scanned the room through the window. There he was, striding jerkily through the crowd, head thrown back at an odd angle. He had stripped off his clothes; his muscled body rippled in the murky light. He moved toward some woman with long hair who was on her hands and knees in the corner with a man who was clearly not a student. Chelo cracked the door and strained to hear the muted conversations.

"Hey, babe." The woman glanced up at Van, her bored look dissolving instantly. "Where have you been?"

Flushed, the gray-haired man, considerably older than the woman, looked up from his task and grinned. "I am in de 'ecstasy,' as you say!" he announced in a German accent. The woman rolled her eyes.

"Why don't you stick around, Van?" she whispered with a hungry look.

Van's lip curled. "Thanks, but I don't think so . . ." he said, wandering off in mid-sentence. He moved toward a noisy group near the pool, where Chelo was repulsed to see Toto Hartounian reclining naked on his back. Toto was an annoying artistic type who claimed to be an actor but spent most of his time smoking in cafés, tossing his long, asymmetrically cut hair.

One of the Solokov sisters leaned over Toto, caressing his shoulders. The other sister was wearing a pair of swimming goggles and snapping Polaroid pictures of herself. Her laughter echoed in the cavernous room.

"Hey, Van!" she shouted. "Photo opportunity!"

The other sister immediately adopted a glamour pose, sucking in her cheeks, putting her hand behind her head, cocking her chin haughtily. With the other hand she grabbed Van. "Perfect!" her sister shouted, snapping the photo.

Van stopped in his tracks, looking wild-eyed and lost. He put up his hand as if to shield himself from the light. After a minute he began to laugh jaggedly. "Why not?" he cried, grinding the woman's face into his groin.

Fascinated but embarrassed, Chelo looked away. She cast her eye around the rest of the room and was shocked to see Adelaide Stephens, the aristocratic British music tutor, sitting on the edge of the pool. Toni had given Chelo the skinny on Adelaide a few weeks back. A brilliant composer younger than many of the undergraduates she taught, Adelaide was desired by male and female students alike, a fact of which she was only too aware. She enjoyed teasing both sexes and hotly pursued students, only to hold back at the very end. She would then explain that she was celibate. Or that she was a devout Catholic. Or that she'd had a tragic love affair. Or that her upper-class parents disapproved of lowly Americans. But here she was, wearing nothing but a pleased expression.

As Chelo watched, Martina, a diminutive and flamboyant Filipina who was the loudest person she had ever met, beckoned to Adelaide from the shallow end of the pool. Tossing aside her usual reserve, Adelaide lowered herself into the water and grasped the other woman's head, burying her hands in her lush hair. The two kissed fiercely. Grabbing a breast in each hand, Martina eagerly began sucking on a hard nipple. Adelaide's back arched and a faint pink flush began to spread across the white skin of her chest. Her head dropped to one shoulder, her eyes closing in delight; she gasped little cries of desire. The water lapped wildly against the side of the pool as they churned.

The whole thing would have been too ludicrous, too absurd, if only Chelo weren't so worried about Van. Where had he gone? The only people left around the pool were Baby Watanabe and Refugee, who lay naked on deck chairs, watching the others from a distance. Baby, a glamorous Japanese-American woman with a dramatic haircut, was usually inseparable from her crowd of five black men. The men would perform street dances in Harvard Square while she stood, as still as a mannequin, with their boom box on her shoulder. They wore urban street gear, while she was always in elaborate costumes that accentuated her delicate features.

Baby held a mirror in her lap; she seemed to be cutting lines of coke with a razor blade. She looked bored and a little amused. From the glassy-eyed expression on the Quad Refugee's face, she was clearly high. Chelo was surprised to see how white Refugee's body was, even without the contrast of her usual black clothing. One hand moved between her legs while the other toyed with her taut nipples. Rolling her head from side to side, she gave a low moan. This was really too much.

Catching Van's eye as he walked by, Baby motioned toward her clean lines of powder, but he shook his head and dove into the pool. There he turned over on his back and casually stroked back and forth, oblivious to the bacchanal around him.

Breathing hard, Chelo gently closed the door and headed for her laundry. The prospect of searching for missing socks seemed suddenly appealing.

/ / /

By her second visit, Toni found herself quite familiar with Dave Mantini's neighborhood. Although she was uneasy at the possibility that someone had witnessed her break-in—didn't criminals always return to the scene of the crime?—or that Dave himself had detected something wrong and filed a police report, she felt surprisingly calm. Dave knew something about the prostitution ring and about Dora's role in it. Armed with this information, perhaps she could tease from him the other details he seemed so reluctant to give over the phone. She was directed and in control.

She rounded the corner of the prosthetics shop and nearly ran into the two skaters she'd seen the night before. They didn't seem to recognize her. A few men congregating around a tavern checked her out in a purely licentious way but then went back to their bull session. Dave's house was farther up the block. She expected him to be home, for the very reason that they had not made an appointment.

Ahead, a cop was lounging outside his car, talking into the radio. Another police officer came out of the entryway of one of the triple-deckers. Toni's chest tightened and her legs froze. The building the police were coming out of was Dave Mantini's.

It would be too obvious if she suddenly turned around and ran the other way. She should just continue her walk and calmly turn the corner on the next intersection. She had every right to be on this block, she was looking for an inexpensive sublet, she had her Harvard I.D. with her, she . . .

And then she was there, stopped in front of the squad car. The cop with the walkie-talkie looked at her expectantly.

"Evening, officer. Mind if I ask what's going on?" Her own voice spoke as if it had no connection to her will.

The policeman all but ignored her. "Police matter. Just go about your business, miss."

"I'm with *The Harvard Crimson*." Toni pulled out her wallet and flashed her tattered press ID at him. "Of course, I could check the police blotter later, but it sure would save me some time to just find things out on this end. What kind of crime was committed?"

"No crime," the other officer said, coming down the sidewalk. He was a decade or so older and more relaxed than the rookie. "Missing-person report. Just a routine investigation."

"And the name of the missing person?" Toni asked, cocking her pen. *Missing?* "David Mantini, right?"

The senior partner looked at her suspiciously for a second, but then continued. "His mom called. Hadn't heard from him in three days. Lives in Revere, saw him all the time. She's sure something happened. Turns out his employer's looking for him, too—they say he ran off with some confidential data. How'd you hear about this?"

"Inside tip," Toni lied. "Dave Mantini used to be a grad student at Harvard. His mom must have told you that already." She added hurriedly, "Do you think he's in any danger?"

"Nah. My bet is he turns up in a day or two and patches it up with the boss. Wouldn't be surprised if they give him a raise to keep him happy. Happens more often than you think with these Einstein types."

Toni thanked them for their time, turned, and walked steadily down the sidewalk, forcing herself not to look back.

12

Dora leaned closer to the man in the leather chair. "Okay, Doug," she whispered in his ear, giving his lobe a little nip. "You know the deal." She ran her tongue down his neck below his beard, and the man moaned. A bit impatient, she tightened her hold on his rigid, quivering penis. "So," she demanded, "let's talk."

Doug opened his eyes and stared around the room for a moment. The lenses of his round spectacles were fogged up, and two bright circles of red highlighted his cheeks. "Oh, come on, baby," he finally managed to blurt. "Can't you just do me first?"

"I don't think so." Dora stepped back and abruptly released her grasp.

Doug snatched at her hand and slid it back into the fly of his chinos. "Okay, okay. I'll talk." He squeezed her hand repeatedly. "Just don't stop."

"Sure, Doug," Dora purred, resuming her stroking. "It's up to you. The sooner you talk, the sooner I'll be down on my knees, sucking you dry."

"What do you want to know?" Doug shuddered and rubbed harder against her.

Dora couldn't prevent herself from rolling her eyes. As if she hadn't said it three million times already. How in the hell this pencil-pricked geek ever got to be senior VP of a multimillion-dollar operation was beyond her. But Doug was the undisputed center of the office information flow—and a staunch believer in the barter system.

She forced the anxiety out of her throat before she spoke. This was all about damage control. "Dave Mantini," she reminded him. "What happened to him? What has he said?"

"I—thought," he gasped, his words echoing the rhythm she had set, "you—couldn't—stand him."

"Whatever. What do you know?"

She slowed down, drawing out the strokes, changing the direction of the motion.

Doug started whispering in thick, urgent tones. "No one's really sure—and no one wants to talk about it. Yeah, that's good. People are saying he just lost it and ran off. That he had lots of personal problems."

"And what is Jerry saying?" If Dave had managed to talk to the CEO, things might start to unravel. Jerry would get cold feet at the thought of bad publicity.

"He told me the police don't know anything. Harder, baby. Jerry swears he's baffled. Even hired a private investigator, but there's no sign of Mantini."

"So why the P.I.?" Dora demanded in alarm.

"It's standard." Doug started sucking his cheeks in and out as his breathing intensified. "In case of any stolen trade secrets."

Dora furrowed her brow as she pumped away on Doug. Her plan made no allowance for a conspiracy-freak co-worker. Her partner had said he would take care of Mantini—she didn't want to know how—and it looked as if he might have fixed things before Mantini had a chance to blab. But she would have to see to it that Mantini stayed away. No more screwups.

Her mind flashed to the *Crimson* reporter. Getting her arrested hadn't seemed to work. Toni Isaacs was still snooping around, meddling in matters she couldn't possibly understand; she had even been spotted in Mantini's neighborhood in Somerville.

Doug pawed impatiently at her limp wrist and rubbed against her. "Hey, baby," he whined. "Don't forget about me."

"Don't call me baby," she snapped.

"Okay, okay. Whatever you say. I'm just saying that I sang for you. Now it's your turn to, uh, play my instrument."

"Oh yeah?" Dora threw him a snide look from beneath her lashes. Doug smiled broadly and reached for her breast. He thought she was being sultry. Honestly! Intercepting his hand, she guided it downward and slapped it onto his straining penis.

"Here," Dora said, giving his hand a squeeze and stepping back. "Do what you do best. I've got a business to save." She spun on her heel and headed for the darkened exit.

/ / /

Jerry Frost arrived in his spacious, minimalist office at seven the next morning to find Dora Givens waiting. As they headed for the coffee station down the hall, he read the press release she had prepared the night before. After pouring two cups of Coffee Connection's special start-up blend and handing one to Dora—Biotecnica was the kind of firm where the CEO poured coffee for his troops—Jerry scanned the release again.

It was pretty self-explanatory. A top scientist who had access to nearly all of Biotecnica's intellectual capital had unaccountably flown the coop. The company was making every effort to cooperate with the authorities to prevent the loss of valuable trade secrets.

Dora took a sip of strong black coffee and waited for her superior to speak. Things would proceed more smoothly if Jerry imagined that everything was his idea.

"Knowledge is invisible, so we can't really prove that Mantini stole anything," Jerry mused as they walked slowly to his office. "On the other hand, by the time we *can* prove something—say Progenera comes out with the same product—it'll be too late."

Dora nodded.

"Still, if Mantini really wants to, he can come forward and clear his name. That seems fair," he concluded, handing the crisp sheet back to her with an approving nod. "Thanks for being one step ahead."

"I'll have it sent out," Dora said.

It was a sexy enough story—deranged local scientist tries to defraud high-tech start-up. It didn't matter *what* he was really up to. After the papers and television stations chewed it up, Dave Mantini wouldn't have a job anywhere.

/ / /

"Excuse me, Dean Kwok." Mrs. Hale stood in the doorway to Sterling's office, wearing rubber duck boots and a puffy down coat. Behind her, the shades of the outer office had been drawn and the lights dimmed. Almost everyone had left University Hall hours ago, and a hush had settled over the stately building. Kwok swiveled around— he had been staring out his window at the picturesque snow in the Yard—and regarded his secretary.

"Oh, are you still here, Mrs. Hale?" he inquired politely. Much as she loved to leave at five, she loved even more to play the martyr. "What can I do for you?"

"Well, you said that you didn't want to be disturbed, Dean Kwok," she began, "but I need to be going, and I wanted to let you know that the files you requested from the Cambridge police arrived by special messenger an hour ago."

Kwok managed to suppress a sigh, along with his vexation. "An hour ago?"

"Indeed." Mrs. Hale pursed her lips almost imperceptibly. "I would have been only too happy to notify you immediately, but you left instructions that you weren't to be disturbed under *any* circumstances." The disapproval in her voice would have been evident only to the most discerning listener.

"I see." Kwok was just such a listener. Thirty years spent navigating the land mines of WASP etiquette had developed his ear. It was almost like being able to hear the upper ranges of a dog whistle. He was never quite sure, however, whether the excessive touchiness he encountered was just par for the course of uptight New England life or whether it was garden-variety racism. Did other deans have to treat their employees with kid gloves? Or were they allowed at times to be oblivious—or even gruff?

"The mistake was mine, Mrs. Hale," he apologized smoothly. "I should have been more precise." This was the problem with hiring executive assistants who were overqualified. What in the world was a forty-year-old woman with a Ph.D. doing working as a secretary?

Mrs. Hale nodded curtly. "It's all right, Dean Kwok." Her innocence reestablished, she relented a bit. "Would you care to see the delivery?"

"Indeed I would."

Once Mrs. Hale had tucked her bob into a knit beret and departed, Sterling ripped open the packet. A stack of computer printouts spilled onto the desk. He switched on the green-shaded desk light and bent over the documents. They were separated into two batches; someone had written "Tara Sheridan" at the top of one, "Antonia Isaacs" on the other. He leafed through the pages, a luxuriously satisfied feeling flowing through him. At least his connections had *some* value. The listed items appeared to date back three months. He chose a page in the second stack and ran his finger across a column listing, by date and location, the telephone numbers called this month from Antonia Isaacs's dorm room. He was going to find out exactly how far this little journalistic crusade had taken Ms. Isaacs.

/ / /

Toni sat in the passenger seat of the Phillips Brooks House van, waiting for Cabot Winthrop and rereading an article in *The Boston Globe* about Biotecnica's accusations against David Mantini. Though the Saturday morning was bright and clear, she felt nervous and frustrated; there seemed to be dozens of different stories she was trying to track, and the one about Mantini was slipping away. He'd disappeared three days ago, and she still had no idea what had happened to him.

Just then Cabot climbed into the driver's seat and leaned over, the sleeve of his sweatshirt brushing against Toni's chest. Her breath caught in her throat. Immediately he sat back, a deep flush spreading over his face. "Sorry about that," he said, starting the engine and pulling out into traffic. "There's a map in there," he said, waving his hand toward the passenger side of the van. "Maybe you can reach it—sorry about the clutter."

Toni gladly busied herself in the glove compartment. It was as messy as the floor of the van, which was piled high with empty

McDonald's containers, cereal boxes from the dining hall, and dog-eared paperbacks. The crowded compartment was stuffed with worn copies of Malcolm X's autobiography, Angela Davis's *Women, Race and Class, Pedagogy of the Oppressed* by Paulo Freire, and a book by someone whose name she didn't recognize, *Inside the Third World.* "Are these for a class?" she asked.

Cabot shook his head, waving the shock of blond hair that stuck out from under his baseball cap. "Nope. Just stuff I was reading."

Toni was impressed; then again, Cabot was full of surprises. Spending time with him was like being on a perpetual first date, with flashes of electricity deadened by frequent miscommunication. Sometimes Toni felt that the two of them shared a special closeness, but she knew at least half a dozen people who claimed to be his best friend. At other times, simple questions could shut him down, turn him as closed and blank as the portraits of his ancestors that lined many a campus wall.

Toni found a map of the Greater Boston area. Now, where was Revere? Got it. She took her trusty reporter's notebook from her bag and read the address aloud. "Can you find it?"

Cabot nodded. "I think so. We visit some Cambodian families out on Beach Street," he said, referring to the activities of the Phillips Brooks House refugee committee, "so I know I can get you that far. Do you think you can navigate us to Mrs. Mantini's from there?"

"Affirmative, Captain Kirk," she said, bending her head to study the maze of streets in her lap.

The van wound in and out of the Harvard Square weekend traffic, and Toni took the opportunity to sneak a glance at Cabot. His eternal sweatshirt and chinos were quite wrinkled, as if he had slept in them. He hadn't shaved in a day or two, and the late-morning sun glinted off his small, gold-rimmed glasses, highlighting the slight creases around his eyes. Somehow he still managed to look attractive. When Cabot caught her look, his smile sparkled.

"I really appreciate you offering to drive me in the PBH van," she said, "especially on a Saturday."

PBH kept the vans to transport student volunteers to service sites, bring kids on campus for tutoring sessions, and take community members on field trips. PBH members weren't supposed to use them for personal business, though the vans could frequently be spotted late at night at the twenty-four-hour Star Market in Porter Square, or crammed with student belongings on moving day. Saturday morning was prime official van time, as hordes of groggy, hung-over Harvard student volunteers spread out into the housing projects and neighborhoods of Cambridge and Boston, eager to enrich the lives of the underprivileged. Leading the troops was Cabot, who had been elected president of the thousand-member organization at the end of the fall term.

"No problem," Cabot said with that wide smile of his. "It's the least I can do after that mix-up the other day."

Toni was still mystified about why he had abandoned her at the Cambridge police station—did he actually think, as he'd told her, that Kwok was going to take care of everything and that he'd just be in the way? She had just about decided never to forgive him when he called to apologize and see if there was anything he could do for her. As it happened, there was: he could drive her to meet Blanche Mantini in Revere.

"Besides," he added, interrupting her thoughts, "Revere's not a place you'd want to go on your own."

On target again, she observed. Unlike most of Toni's white classmates, Cabot had noticed that there were places in Boston where black people couldn't count on being safe. This point was omitted from Freshman Orientation, when the orange-shirted Freshman Task Force waxed eloquent about how Boston's myriad neighborhoods afforded culinary adventure, historical charm, and cultural diversity.

The van rolled along a two-lane highway, passing rows and rows of identical vinyl-sided houses. The address matched a small pink house with an even smaller manicured yard. Dominating the lawn was a plastic figure of the Madonna standing in a structure that looked like a miniature pink bathtub. Cabot pulled up to the curb, and Toni got out to take a better look. A sign on the lamppost read "The Mantini's."

Toni walked up to the front door and pressed the bell. The place looked deserted. There was no car in the cement driveway, just several trash cans and a couple of shopping bags filled with papers. The door was shut tight and the shades were drawn. She could hear the bell echoing in the empty house; a dog was barking in the backyard. Looking around for some neighbors to ask, she saw the venetian blinds in the house next door snap shut. She wondered if the neighbor was dialing the Revere police as she stood there. Their trip appeared to have been a waste of time.

As she walked back down to the curb to make her apologies to Cabot, an elderly but well-maintained Chevy Impala pulled into the driveway. A middle-aged white woman with tightly permed hair got out of the driver's seat, followed by a small girl and boy. The children—Toni was surprised to see that they had Southeast Asian features with hazel eyes and straight, almost blond hair—ran ahead into the house. The woman toiled up the flagstone path, two grocery bags in each hand. As she paused on her front doorstep, Toni approached.

"Mrs. Mantini?" she asked, attempting a tentative smile.

The woman looked her up and down and then took in Cabot sitting in the van. Her eyes narrowed suspiciously. "I'm Blanche Mantini."

"I'm a reporter for—"

Mrs. Mantini shifted her load to her hip. "Not again," she said angrily. "My David is a good boy. I want him home with me, not in the headlines. I'm tired of you people trying to make him out to be some kind of high-tech criminal. Seems like everybody just wants to hear the worst nowadays." She hefted the bags up and turned toward the house. "Whatever sells papers."

Toni stepped in front of her, shoving her reporter's pad into her bag and holding her arms out to help with the heavy groceries. "That's exactly why I'm here, Mrs. Mantini," she began nervously. "I think your son is innocent of any wrongdoing, and that he's in hiding from the real criminals who've set him up. I want to make sure the true story—*his* story—gets out."

The older woman paused, still holding on to the bags, and regarded Toni suspiciously. "*Globe* or *Herald*?" she finally asked, looking over Toni's shoulder at Cabot. "Or is that your cameraman?"

"Neither. I'm a reporter for the *Crimson*. That's the daily paper at Harvard." She gently took one of the sagging bags from the woman's arms.

Mrs. Mantini's eyes flickered. She gave a brisk nod, as if deciding something, and nudged the screen door open with her knee. "All right, then," she said, "come on in."

The inside of the little bubble-gum-colored house was just as neat and well-maintained as the outside. Plastic runners covered the carpet in the hallway, while crocheted doilies protected the well-oiled furniture from the countless knickknacks. Two framed black-paper silhouettes of a boy and girl hung facing each other over the mantelpiece, above a Christ statue with a glowing sacred heart. The small girl and boy sat on the living room floor, their faces inches away from the television set. A floppy cocker spaniel sprawled at their feet, sighing loudly. "You kids get back from that TV," Mrs. Mantini scolded. "I've told you a million times."

"Aw, Grams," they protested in unison, inching back imperceptibly, their eyes still glued to the set. With a jolt, it occurred to Toni that they might be Dave's children.

"More." They retreated another inch.

"You can leave the groceries in the kitchen," Mrs. Mantini told Toni, following her to the back of the house. Toni deposited the bag on the counter and looked around at the dark wood paneling and yellow ruffled curtains. "Thanks," Mrs. Mantini said. "Can I get you a soda?"

Toni was about to say that a glass of water would be just fine when it occurred to her that Mrs. Mantini might be insulted if she refused her hospitality. "A soda would be great. Thank you."

By the time she handed Toni the glass of Coke, Mrs. Mantini seemed to have forgotten that she had ever distrusted her visitor. "Here you go, dear," she said. "Would you like to see David's room?"

They doubled back toward the front of the house, passing Mrs. Mantini's grandchildren, who had resumed their original positions in front of the television, and a statue of St. Francis of Assisi with eyes that followed them down the hall.

Mrs. Mantini opened the door to a dim bedroom. It was spookily reminiscent of a shrine. Trophies for Little League, debate team, and Paperboy of the Year covered the shelves. Toni slowly took in framed clippings from the *Revere Transcript* that charted Dave Mantini's illustrious academic career from Revere High valedictorian to

Boston College scholarship recipient to Harvard University graduate student. She wondered how long it had been since Dave had lived here. It was hard to connect this eternal Boy Scout to the disheveled, slightly manic person she had spoken with at Biotecnica and on the phone.

"Can you tell me about your son's experience at Harvard?" Toni asked, gesturing to the crimson "H" on the wall.

"He didn't finish his doctor's degree," Blanche Mantini said. "Just the master's. He says they didn't understand him there; only his adviser, and when she was gone, there was nobody he wanted to work with." She cleared her throat. "Maybe there was nobody who wanted to work with him. Dave is—I don't know, he seems strange, maybe, until you get to know him. Not everybody wants to take the time."

"And then he got the job at Biotecnica," Toni prompted.

"Yes, a good job, too. He was lucky to get it, or so we thought. I know he hasn't done anything wrong, no matter what they say. They told me they were going to press charges if he didn't give them back the computer files or whatever it is they want from him. Dave wouldn't have taken anything that didn't belong to him." She spoke anxiously, words flooding from her. "I know what people think—poor Italian family from Revere. Like he's some master criminal, stealing computer files for the Godfather. That's a laugh. He just, I don't know—" The stream of words dried suddenly as Blanche fought back tears.

"Asked the wrong questions?" suggested Toni.

Mrs. Mantini fingered some of the memorabilia, her eyes carefully averted from Toni's. "Dave's always been too smart for his own good," she said. "He's always had to figure everything out, whether or not it was his business."

Toni absorbed this information. "Dave contacted me before he disappeared. Do you know what he was concerned about, Mrs. Mantini?" She wasn't sure if she should bring up the prostitution ring. For all she knew, Dave had been a client. "We were supposed to meet on Wednesday, but when I went to his apartment, he wasn't there. Do you have any idea what he might have known?"

Mrs. Mantini's eyes shuttered, and for the first time since she had invited Toni into the house, she looked guarded. Finally she sighed and shrugged. "He's been worried for a long time. He came and stayed here for about a week, working late nights in his room with one of those portable computers. Said he didn't feel safe at home. He went back to Somerville for a few days—then, *poof!* he disappeared."

She turned to Toni. "Are you going to use my boy's photograph in your story?" she asked, her pale blue eyes watering. "No one else even showed his face."

"Uh, sure," Toni answered. It was a small thing to ask. To the rest of the world he was a faceless failed honor student accused of stealing valuable research data. "In fact, I was hoping you'd have a good photo you could lend me."

"Let me get you one." Mrs. Mantini began rifling through one of the dresser drawers and Toni took a closer look around the room. Right above the desk was a constellation of tiny pinholes, as if papers had been tacked to the wall and removed. She glanced in the wastebasket near the door. It was empty except for the pages from yesterday's *Herald* that lined it. The room had been cleaned recently; perhaps there were things Mrs. Mantini didn't want anyone to see. Toni remembered the shopping bags of paper she had seen in the driveway, next to the trash barrels.

"It must be very difficult for you right now, Mrs. Mantini," Toni apologized. "I don't mean to pry."

"That's okay, dear." Mrs. Mantini lifted a scrapbook from the dresser and flicked off the overhead light. "Why don't we move into the parlor?" she said, crowding Toni toward the door. Once out in the living room, she selected a photograph from the scrapbook and handed it to Toni. It showed Dave as valedictorian of his high school. He had long hair and wore a shiny blue graduation cap and gown. "If you could just make sure to mention that he was Revere High's Boy of the Year," she said. "He was always a model student."

The doorbell rang. Mrs. Mantini got up to answer it, the plastic covering of the couch slowly inflating with a sigh. Toni thought of her West Indian relatives, who also swathed every last inch of their furniture in protective plastic.

"Excuse me, ma'am," Cabot said to Mrs. Mantini, pulling off his baseball cap and stuffing it into his pocket. "I hate to disturb you." Mrs. Mantini looked impressed. He looked over at Toni. "I'm sorry to rush you, Toni, but I have an appointment at noon back in Cambridge."

"That's okay," Toni answered. "We were just finishing up." She jumped up from the sofa and crossed over to the door. "I need to get one of my cards from the van," she improvised, pulling Cabot into the room. "Please excuse me for a moment, Mrs. Mantini—I'll be right back." She shut the door behind her and sprinted down the porch steps and over to the driveway, hoping Cabot would keep Blanche Mantini occupied. Glancing about, she knelt by the trash and hefted a shopping bag in each hand. The street was still empty, and Mrs. Mantini's shades were down. Unfortunately, there was a good chance the busybody from next door was watching; Toni hoped Mrs. Mantini and her neighbors weren't on speaking terms. Her heart racing, she tossed the bags into the van and fumbled in her bag for a business card.

When she got back to the house, Cabot and Mrs. Mantini were sitting next to each other on the plastic-covered couch with the photo album between them, discussing interracial dating.

"Well, you never know these days," Mrs. Mantini was saying. "I mean, look at the kiddies." She gestured at her grandchildren, whose noses would have to be surgically removed from the World Wrestling Federation if they got any closer to the TV. "My daughter never liked her own kind. I told her, 'Mary Ann, this is Revere. We may not like it, but that's the way things are.' But did she listen? No." Her voice dropped to a whisper. "Now she's living with some guy over in Charlestown who don't want 'em."

Cabot nodded, his round glasses giving him an owlish look. When he noticed Toni in the doorway, he jumped up, upsetting the album. He knelt down immediately to pick it up, apologizing profusely. Toni smiled at Mrs. Mantini and stuck out her hand. "We have to get going now. Thank you so much for everything. I really appreciate your taking the time." She proffered her card. "Here's my number, if there's anything I can do—"

Mrs. Mantini took her hand, and the card, with an odd, piercing look. Toni wondered if she knew what had just happened to her garbage bags. The woman was intelligent, there was no denying that, and Toni liked her. But she had to find out what Dave Mantini knew about the prostitution ring, whether or not his mother wanted to tell her. "I'll be watching for your article," Mrs. Mantini said, ushering Toni and Cabot to the door.

Toni could barely wait for Cabot to start up the van and pull away from the curb. He smiled as she fidgeted in her seat. "Oh, my God, Cabot," she burst out as soon as the little house was out of sight. "Thanks so much for covering for me back there. You won't believe what's going on! Just before her son disappeared, he called me. I think he knew about some kind of scandal and wanted me to do an exposé. Then, when I got to his apartment, he was gone. Now he's on the run. His company says he stole data, but his mother doesn't think he did anything wrong." She paused for a breath and patted the shopping bags at her feet. "Anyway, she didn't want to talk about it, except to say that he was good at figuring things out that weren't his business, but I managed to get some stuff from his room. Maybe there's some kind of clue."

Cabot stared at the shopping bags, noticing them for the first time. His face was expressionless. "You took those bags?" he asked finally. "You *stole* them?"

Toni flushed. "Well, yes . . . but they're just garbage. I mean, I'm sure Dave wouldn't mind. He wants this story to come out. He contacted me to tell me about it!"

Cabot's mouth curved in distaste.

"What?" she demanded.

"Anything for a story," Cabot replied, his eyes averted.

"That's not fair," Toni protested.

"Don't talk to me about fair!"

Toni was stunned. She was certainly not going to be lectured by Cabot Winthrop III of Beacon Hill and Phillips Exeter Academy about how unfair life was, but she didn't want to fight with him, either. They had seemed so close all morning. She couldn't understand what had gone wrong.

During the rest of the ride back they were both silent; Toni got out in front of Adams House with an awkward thank-you and a wave good-bye. She stood on the brick sidewalk for a moment, a shopping bag in each hand, and watched the van chug away. She felt a little ashamed, and at the same time angry with herself for letting Cabot's opinion matter so much. She gathered together the bags of papers and took them up to her room.

She wanted him to be on her side, but if he wasn't, so be it. She'd figure out what Dave Mantini had wanted to tell her. And she'd deal with it. Alone.

13

Toni upended the bags of trash, letting papers, envelopes, and magazines fan out across her bed, along with broken pencils, paper clips, and dusty Post-It Notes. She sat cross-legged on her pillow, sorting through the detritus of Dave's late-night work sessions. A number of the papers were memoranda from Biotecnica; Dora's name appeared on some of the distribution lists. One was a memo about the company golf tournament—Dave must have saved everything, no matter how insignificant. Toni put all the Biotecnica materials in a careful stack; she would review them later.

A Filene's Basement bag held newspaper clippings. Toni unfolded the already yellowing newsprint, its margins covered with scrawled notes, and tried to make some kind of mental connection among the stories. A wealthy businessman had suffered a heart attack while traveling in Boston on business; a major auto manufacturer had recalled several hundred thousand trucks and vans; the Harvard Club of New York had hosted an evening seminar on personal finance and investing; a new book had been published on men's crises in middle age—Dave had written "PROSTATE" in big letters at the top of this clipping; one of Biotecnica's competitors had gone public, selling its stock for huge sums.

Dave seemed to think he was Ralph Nader or somebody. Maybe even a little more paranoid than that. He'd clipped articles on all the latest scandals, from toxic waste dumps in upstate New York to racism in the FBI. There was no way to determine from this collection what it was that Dave had wanted to tell her.

As the afternoon light weakened into an early dusk, Toni continued searching, not knowing what she hoped to find. Finally she came across a plain business envelope sealed with tape. She carefully peeled back the tape, her heart racing when she saw her own byline on the newsprint. On top of her "Deep Throat" article, Dave had scrawled "I WAS THERE!!!" Her article on Karen's work at the Kittycat Klub was also included.

She quickly rooted through the rest of the pile and spotted another business-size envelope, this one held shut with two large paper clips. She pulled it out; it contained a stack of photographs. Flipping through them with a shaky hand, Toni examined them: attractive young women and men, each in a pose of studied casualness. She turned over the first photo in the stack. On the back was written "Phoebe."

Despite the makeup and evening wear, Phoebe didn't look much older than Toni herself. Toni didn't know who Phoebe was, but she had a pretty good guess what she did for a living.

/ / /

Professor Dayton Moore noticed a familiar figure standing in front of the refrigerated shelves at the Science Center Café. Consuelo Santana, his research assistant, picked up a plastic container of yogurt and examined the label. In her other hand was a package of miniature chocolate doughnuts. She frowned as she looked at one and then the other, weighing pleasure against duty. Finally, after turning sideways and glancing at her reflection in the unflattering mirrored panel that separated the refrigerator doors, she put the doughnuts back in their cardboard stand.

He couldn't stand to see such a surrender to virtue.

"Hello, Consuelo," he said, striding up to stand in line behind her.

"Oh, hi, Professor Moore." She touched her hair.

"So you're not going for the doughnuts?"

She laughed airily—a mannerism not entirely convincing. "Oh, no. They're totally unhealthy. Unhealthful, I mean. Loaded with fat."

"Check out my choice." He pointed to his bagel, well slathered with cream cheese. "It's another forty minutes on the StairMaster. But for the time I eat it, it makes me truly happy."

"I'd probably just feel guilty," she said, in the refrain that women seemed predestined to repeat throughout history.

He reached over and grabbed the doughnuts. "How about we share them? Please, let me," he said, waving away the money she was hurriedly pulling from her pocket. "And two cappuccinos."

She smiled gratefully. He'd forgotten how much joy there could be in saving a couple of bucks.

Consuelo reminded Dayton of a lot of things, good things about himself and people he used to know. Her capacity to evoke the optimistic and confident side of him was one of the reasons he'd hired her for the work-study job a year and half before. She had not been a very good interview; her simple, slightly embarrassed answers to his softball questions about her courses and past work experience contrasted markedly with those of the other applicants. *They* were typical upper-middle-class undergrads with a practiced air of self-promotion; their ready replies invariably included not-so-subtle statements about their admiration for the professor's work. In contrast, Consuelo seemed uncomfortable in his presence. She kept her lumpy parka on throughout the interview and spoke in an almost inaudible voice, with a slightly singsong, mildly irritating accent.

"Is there any special reason you want to work for me?" he had finally asked.

She nodded briskly. "I don't want to do dorm crew again," she said.

As soon as she spoke, a look of horror—what a ditsy, unprofessional remark!—came over her face. But when she saw the glint in his eyes, she started laughing. So did he. And within the confines of their roles, they'd become friends.

"I'm stealing a break from an endless seminar," he said, pointing to a pile of books he had set on the table to stake his claim to the space. Among the stack were copies of Moore's own treatises: *Shame, Shame, Shame,* his latest book (which Consuelo had helped him type); *On Doing the Nasty* (which had been short-listed for the National Book Award); and *Beaux and Eros,* his first book. "Are you still toiling away? Shouldn't you be outside enjoying your youth?"

"If I enjoy my youth, I might not be able to enjoy the rest of my life," Consuelo answered, deadpan. Something was bothering her, Dayton realized. He couldn't ask her directly, though. Although they were as close as professor and student were likely to get, there was a certain formality in their relationship.

They drank the foam off their respective cappuccinos.

She gazed at him intently. "Professor Moore, do you get the impression that a lot of people here are totally stressed out?"

"Are you kidding?" he asked.

"No, I'm not." She flicked back her hair nervously.

"Consuelo, Harvard has the highest per capita production of stress outside of Wall Street."

"Do you mean the students?"

He gestured expansively. "Students, faculty, administration—you name it. There are more mentally ill people here than you might think, some resting quite comfortably in the seats of power. And that's not counting the Prozac poppers. From time to time you may hear about newsworthy disasters—suicides and the like. But those exceptional cases obscure the daily freaked-out state of a lot of ordinary Harvard types."

"Oh," Chelo responded.

"Are you experiencing a lot of stress lately?" He was concerned, but thought best not to show it.

"Not really." She was already polishing off the last mini doughnut. "Not more than usual, I mean. Maybe I'm becoming sort of disillusioned. Well, not disillusioned. Just tired." She glanced at her watch and stood up. "I'd better go get a good seat for Statistics. It fills up pretty quickly. Thanks again for the coffee."

He wondered what she had meant to say, if anything. She did look tired. He would give it another shot.

"Don't get disillusioned, Consuelo. It's better not to be cynical. Trust me on that one."

She neither agreed nor disagreed. She just thanked him again and hurried off to her class.

/   /   /

Toni stood hesitantly in the empty office in Mallinckrodt Hall. She didn't expect the biochemistry department to be abuzz on Monday night, but she did have an appointment, and she had arrived on time. The smell of formaldehyde was strong in the air. Stacks of papers, weighed down by big jars of murky liquids, covered the metal tables. A cheap tape deck blared REM.

Hearing voices down the hall, she followed the sounds until she saw a man and a woman in a lab four doors away. Both in their early thirties, they were clad in jeans, T-shirts, and hiking boots, and were drinking coffee out of paper cups. They appeared to be having an argument about sectioning and microtomes, whatever those were.

"Hi," Toni called out from the doorway. The two turned toward her. "I'm supposed to meet Morgan Lee here. Does either of you know where she might be?"

"That's Morgan," the man said, gesturing to his colleague. "I'm Phil."

"Hey," the woman said, running her fingers through long, stringy hair. "You called about David Mantini, right?" She looked back at her colleague. "She's from the *Crimson*—they're doing a story about Dave's disappearance."

The man began humming the theme from *The Twilight Zone.* Toni waited for him to finish, not sure of the etiquette in this situation. Suddenly he stopped his performance and whispered "Teeny Man!," widening his eyes for effect.

"I take it you know him," Toni said.

"We all started together eight years ago," Morgan explained.

"Only he sold out," the guy added. "Went into corporate biotech."

"Are you familiar with the charges his company has made?" Toni asked. "They've accused him of stealing trade secrets."

Phil snorted. "That's a laugh. Those firms steal everything from the research universities in the first place. I'm surprised Dave's not accusing *them.*"

"Why did he leave the program?" Toni asked. "Was he having problems?"

"No, he was doing well," Morgan said. "Until Waxman died, that is. His adviser. After that, he went a little over the edge. None of the other professors wanted to sponsor him. Then, when he got that job offer, he just left."

"Could you tell me more about his adviser?" Toni said, her pen poised over her notebook.

"Moira Waxman," Morgan said. "She won the Morton Prize in '83. Groundbreaking hormone researcher, but kinda weird. Reclusive. Dave was her pet student. He was really broken up when she died. He said there was a conspiracy to cover up her death."

"Typical Teeny Man stuff," Phil said.

"How did she die?"

The two scientists exchanged an awkward look.

"Bike accident," the woman explained. "She was coming home late at night, and the driver of the car swore he didn't see her. She probably wasn't looking where she was going—I think her bike light was burned out. Dave didn't buy it, though. He kept pressing for a criminal investigation. Actually, it was kind of embarrassing for all of us."

Toni was disappointed to hear about the banality of Waxman's death and immediately felt ashamed at her own callousness. "What kind of research was Waxman doing?" she asked.

"Hold on," Morgan said. "I'll show you." She disappeared into the corridor. Muffled thumps sounded from a few rooms away.

"I wasn't surprised to read he was having problems," Phil said in a confidential tone. "I always thought he was a little, you know, off. He wasn't very aware of how he appeared to other people."

Toni nodded, taking in the man's stained T-shirt and low-hanging jeans. This guy was scruffy, and his friend could use a haircut and some Lady Speed Stick as well. They certainly weren't ahead of Dave on the fashion front.

A few moments later, Morgan Lee reappeared, dusty but triumphant, a slim red volume in her hand.

"They did a memorial volume when Waxman died. A bunch of her articles. You can keep it." She handed the book to Toni. "I only took it to be polite. Not my area."

Toni thanked her. It wasn't her area, either, but maybe Chelo could make sense of it.

/   /   /

Toni burst into her room, nearly sending Chelo out of her skin. "Hey, Chelo," she said, leaning in the doorway. "*¿Que pasa?*"

Chelo, who had been staring intently at Toni's desk, started violently and slid something under a stack of papers. "Toni!" she stammered, a flush spreading across her face. "I didn't hear you come in the front door. I, uh . . ." She indicated the object in her other hand and smiled apologetically. "I really needed my calculator back for my orgo homework and I didn't think you'd mind."

"Oops." Toni winced as she stepped into the room. "Sorry, Chelo, I really meant to return it this time. You're much too good to me." She tossed her bag in the general direction of the bed and headed toward the bathroom. Apparently, Toni hadn't noticed Chelo rifling through her things, or she wasn't going to mention it.

Chelo watched the bookbag glance off the unmade bed and hit the floor, landing atop a half-empty package of Little Debbie snack cakes and a tangle of silk lingerie. She resisted the urge to pick up the bag and lay it neatly on the bed. Instead, she retrieved the object of her speculation from beneath the papers on Toni's desk and followed Toni out. She stationed herself outside the open bathroom door and stared at the photograph she had filched from her roommate's desk. Though the name written on the back of the Polaroid was unfamiliar, she definitely knew the face. Chelo rehearsed what she was going to say.

"Uh, Toni?"

"Yeah?"

Chelo plunged ahead. "Uh, well, I didn't mean to be snooping or anything . . . but when I was looking for my calculator, I kind of noticed that you have this picture of a friend of mine—"

"Your friend?" Toni leaned forward, pushing the bathroom door farther ajar. "What do you mean? Which picture?"

Chelo held up the photo of a young blond woman, heavily made-up, wearing a silk dress.

Toni's eyes widened. "You know who that is?"

Chelo nodded.

"Oh, boy," Toni breathed. "Okay, hold on. I'll be right out." She washed her hands and joined her roommate. "Chelo, this is an incredible break."

Chelo smiled uncertainly. She didn't understand why Toni had this strange photo to begin with, or why it was labeled "Phoebe." "There's nothing to tell, really," she said. "It's just I noticed you had this picture of my friend Tara." Toni looked blank. "Tara Sheridan," Chelo explained. "She lives—well, she used to live—in Eliot House."

"So she *is* a student! I knew it!" Toni burst out.

"Why is that important?"

Toni rubbed her cheek. "No reason. I mean, it's not. I just had this stupid theory about—" She stopped mid-sentence. "Chelo, what do you mean, she *used* to live in Eliot? Did she graduate already?"

Chelo bit her lip. "No. She's taking some time off right now." She already regretted bringing this up. Whenever she'd called Tara's house in Connecticut, Mrs. Sheridan told her Tara wasn't home or wasn't taking calls. Chelo had been hurt, not knowing whether this reflected parental overprotectiveness or a snub by Tara herself. Well, she'd *thought* they were friends. . . .

"Hmm," Toni said aloud, half to herself. "I wonder if she's pregnant—or if something else, even worse, happened. Some kind of breakdown, maybe."

Chelo gaped at her roommate, who was jotting rapidly in her notebook, as if interviewing a Mob informer. What was she talking about? Toni didn't even know Tara. She surveyed Toni's desk, the other photos covering the surface. What was she doing with all those pictures, anyway?

Toni's eyes met hers and softened. "Chelo," she said gently, "we have to talk. I think your friend is a prostitute."

14

With its pristine, manicured lawn and main hall of ivy-covered brick, the Austen Riggs Sanitorium looked exactly like an elite private school for girls—except for the two ambulances stationed in front. Toni swung the white subcompact rental car into the parking lot, and she and Chelo climbed out. They stretched their legs, cramped from the three-hour ride from Boston, and took deep breaths of the fresh country air. "At least it's good to get out of the city," Toni said with false cheer. Silent, Chelo got their gift out of the trunk.

Secluded in the Berkshires of western Massachusetts, Austen Riggs, an exclusive institution that treated the psychiatric disorders of the well-bred, had an alumnae roster almost as impressive as Radcliffe's. According to Aimee Milvain, who made it her business to know such things, behind these discreet walls the rich and famous had long sought refuge from the strains of being rich and famous. Edie Sedgwick, for one, had lived for months in a private frame house located on the huge grounds.

Chelo contemplated the irony: Tara Sheridan had trained all her life at schools that looked just like this, in order to assume her rightful place at Harvard . . . which had driven her here.

The two roommates surveyed the imposing building. After she had processed what Toni was saying about Tara, Chelo had agreed to get in touch with her Eliot House friend. Impelled by a new sense of urgency, she had managed to determine through a series of phone calls that Tara wasn't at home in Connecticut at all. Her parents had sent her away for treatment shortly after she left school—though bulimia hardly seemed to be her major problem.

After signing their names at the front desk and depositing their bags with an attendant, they were directed to Tara's room. Chelo had half expected to see her lying strapped to a gurney in the middle of a cold, sterile cell. Instead, the luxurious bed was empty, and the room, decorated with subdued flowered wallpaper and antique furniture, looked more like an upscale European hotel than a clinic.

"Tara?" she called. "We've come to visit!"

"Wow," Toni mouthed. They stepped inside and looked around. The suite consisted of a bedroom, sitting area, and private bath with old-fashioned porcelain fixtures. Oriental carpets covered the floor, while vases of fresh-cut flowers adorned the marble-topped bureau and French writing desk.

"Hey, Chelo," a voice said. Tara, smiling faintly, stood in the doorway of the sitting room. She wore a thick, monogrammed robe and seemed to take up very little space in the room. Behind her, a neat pile of books lay on a cushioned windowseat overlooking the garden. Though she was somewhat pale and tired, this was the Tara whom Chelo remembered, no longer the sophisticated siren in the photograph.

"Tara!" Chelo hurried forward to embrace her. "It's so great to see you. I really, really apologize for barging in here uninvited—but we were a little afraid to call first." She indicated Toni standing in the doorway. "This is my roommate, Toni Isaacs. She came because"— Chelo searched for a believable lie—"she has a driver's license and I don't."

Toni and Tara exchanged greetings and Tara invited them to sit down. Settling down on the window seat, Tara regarded Toni with a steady gaze.

"So, Tara," Chelo asked. "How are you doing?"

"Fine," Tara answered brightly. "I think I really needed a break from school."

"Don't we all!" Chelo beamed as sincerely as she could and put the pot of African violets down on the windowsill near Tara. "These are for you. I wasn't quite sure what you could use. But we'd be glad to get anything you need. Books, magazines, Godiva choc—" She caught herself and stopped awkwardly.

Her faux pas went unnoticed. Tara's gaze slid over the plant and then toward the window, her social energy already depleted.

Chelo shot Toni a desperate look; small talk didn't seem to be working. Toni grabbed the chair from the desk, pulled it over to the window, and sat down facing Tara. "Tara," she began, "I hate to bother you with questions, but they may be important."

"Toni!" Chelo was worried. "I don't think you should be—"

Toni ignored her. "Tara," she pressed, "I work for the *Crimson*. I've been writing a series about—"

"I've read your articles, Toni," Tara said unexpectedly, assessing her again with that cool gaze.

"You have?"

Tara nodded.

"I need to know about Phoebe—" Toni began.

Tara interrupted her. "Got any smokes?"

Momentarily startled, Toni hurriedly dug in her bag and pulled out a crumpled pack of Newports. Avoiding Chelo's reproving stare, she lit up a butt for Tara and another one for herself.

Tara took a deep drag and leaned into the experience, closing her eyes. After a few private moments she opened her eyes and gave a wry grin. "Thanks; I was going nuts. We're in a 'nonsmoking environment,' you know.

"So," she continued briskly. "You want to know about the Class Ring?" She pronounced the name ironically.

"Yeah," Toni answered eagerly. "Everything you know." Chelo, too, felt a jolt of excitement.

"Well," Tara replied, "I don't know much. We were kept pretty much in the dark, and now that I've taken early retirement"—she arched a brow and brought the cigarette to her lips—"it's not like there's a newsletter to keep us up-to-date."

Chelo, frowning, examined the pile on the carpet at their feet. Why was Tara even willing to talk about this? Tara's transformation from exhausted patient to cocky Harvard undergrad was unsettling.

"Do you know who ran everything?" Toni asked. Her voice skipped up on the last syllable. Chelo didn't understand why Toni was so nervous. *She* hadn't been a prostitute.

Tara shook her head, her face obscured by a cloud of smoke.

"I didn't think to ask, really. I got calls, I met people. The money was great and the people were just swell." She sounded like Jennifer Jason Leigh at an Amway convention.

"But how did you get calls? How did you know where to go?"

Tara frowned as if trying to remember a verb conjugation for French class. "A woman named Dominique. That was her nom de guerre, I suppose. Straight dark-blond hair, a little older than us. She interviewed me and set me up with clients who called the number."

Chelo's heart skipped a beat as she recalled what Toni had told her about her own "interview." Desirée—Dominique—Dora. They sure sounded like the same woman. "You think she could have been the leader?" Toni asked.

Tara looked dubious. She ground out the cigarette butt on the iron radiator, slowly, as if doing so helped her think. "She debriefed me after the sessions sometimes, and she collected the money, but she seemed . . ." She looked up. "I'll tell you who she reminded me of. You know the kind of student who claims to be vice president of the *Political Review* or a contributing editor to *Padan Aram*? You just know they're padding their résumés, trying to impress the world with publications that barely come out once a year. That's the impression Dominique gave me. Caught up in her own drama."

Toni scribbled on her pad. "How did you first meet Dominique? For the interview, I mean?"

Fascinated in spite of herself, Chelo listened as Tara described a phone call from Dominique in the fall—she was a friend of a friend, she'd told Tara, and had seemed to know all about her. That first meeting at the Pasha Bar, the Cromwell Hotel's Turkish-themed lounge . . . the decision to call herself Phoebe Hilton—it seemed witty at the time, a joke name invented on the walk over from her dorm—the condom requirement . . .

Toni asked for elaboration.

"They were really strict about safer sex," Tara explained. "They insisted on condoms for everything. I thought it would turn the clients off, but actually it seemed to be our 'comparative advantage.'

Clients loved it—we were the safe fantasy alternative, apparently."
She laughed self-consciously. "The service had its own brand, and we
were supposed to use it for name recognition. Veritas."

"Weren't you scared?" Chelo asked.

"Compared to what?" Tara answered. She leaned in close to
Chelo. "The first time, yes, I was terrified. But then I saw what the
clients looked like—picture our classmates in ten or twenty years—"

"Why did you leave?" Toni interrupted. "Sorry," she added.

"The interesting question is why I started, don't you think?"
Tara's voice trembled slightly on the last words. "But I can't really
help you on that one." Her chin quivered and suddenly she covered
her face with her hands.

"What is it?" Chelo asked, rising quickly. "What's wrong?"

"What the hell did I think I was doing?" Tears streamed down
Tara's cheeks. "I messed up." She closed her eyes tightly. "I left after
one of my clients had a heart attack. While we were having sex."

Chelo put an arm around her. "It's okay," she whispered, "you
don't have to say any more."

"Till then, it was just a big game for me," Tara said. "You see, I
thought this made me special—that I was good at something unimag-
inable to anyone who knew me. My secret play life—all my own."

"When EMS came, I had to say I was his girlfriend," Tara continued in jagged bursts. "Everything turned out okay in the end, but,
God, the way they looked at me—" She shuddered. "The worst part
is, until then I actually liked it. I liked the control. I felt I was doing
things my way—ironic, isn't it? I liked who I was. And I don't have
the slightest goddamned idea why."

Chelo hushed her, giving Toni a look that required no interpreta-
tion. Toni developed a sudden interest in examining her notes.

Chelo found a washcloth in the bathroom and started bathing
Tara's face. She pulled her chair closer and launched into a torrent of
small talk, describing the exams that loomed ahead, a concert of the
Bach Society she had attended the week before, and the recent
Chuck Wagon night in the campus dining halls. Kindness worked;
the color slowly returned to Tara's cheeks. In a shaky voice but with
the wit Chelo remembered, Tara joined in the repartee, describing her
fellow patients and their even more wacked-out families.

Toni seemed to be only half listening; Chelo positioned herself to block her from making eye contact with Tara.

Finally, Chelo hugged Tara good-bye. When Toni didn't stand, Chelo addressed her icily. "It's time for us to go."

"Tara, please," Toni pleaded. "I only have one more question. Did you ever meet Dave Mantini?"

Tara shook her head. It was clear she had no idea who he was.

"You didn't give him your photograph?" Toni asked uncertainly.

"My photograph?" Tara was surprised. She pondered a moment. "Dominique took a picture to show clients. Are you saying some man has it? That he could blackmail me?"

Tara looked ashen.

"No," Toni answered, "not at all."

"We're leaving now, Tara," Chelo said. "Call me if you need anything." She pulled Toni out of the room with her, suspecting Tara knew far more than she had disclosed, but not at all sure it would do them any good to find out.

15

The delicate china thimble of hot sake plummeted through the mug of icy Kirin, leaving a trail of amber bubbles. As soon as the tiny cup hit the bottom of the beer, Van thumped his hand on the glass-topped table and cried out: "Now!"

Toni hoisted the glass and started chugging. The lager poured down her throat, paving the way for the kicker—a shot of warm rice liquor. She drained the glass, bringing her teeth together just in time to stop the sake cup from sliding onto her tongue. Snatching the cup from between her teeth, she shook her head to clear the effects of the shot. The black walls and gleaming chrome of the Newbury Street restaurant swirled before her eyes.

Partying with Van was like being on the run; he had a penchant for out-of-the-way restaurants, and underground clubs that changed location and name weekly. Toni didn't quite understand this mania for finding new hangouts in which to hide out—wherever Van went, people seemed to know who he was anyway—but she reveled in his taste.

"So," he asked, "are we celebrating, or drowning our sorrows?"

Toni sighed heavily and twisted her lips. "A little of both, I guess."

She picked at the label on the beer bottle. "I mean, I got the four-one-one this afternoon on the legendary Harvard prostitution ring." She described her visit with "a student" at Austen Riggs.

"Hey." Van clinked his glass to the bottle in her hand. "Way to go! Sounds like a cause for celebration to me."

"And yet," Toni continued, "today I officially became a journalistic jackass."

"*Another* milestone to celebrate," Van declared, a cocky grin lighting his handsome features. He tilted the mug to avoid making a head, and poured Toni another beer.

"Join me?" she invited.

He shook his head. "I only enable." Keeping his eyes on his task, he lowered his voice a notch. "But seriously, Toni, it seems to me that you just did what you had to, like all of us."

Troubled by her memory of grilling Tara, Toni was not convinced. "But what if what I have to do hurts someone else?"

"*Please.*" Van was impatient. "You didn't create the situation. This girl knew the risks."

"That's pretty cold. Besides, I'm not sure she did. I think that up to now her life has been very sheltered."

"Hmm." Van smiled wistfully. "Wouldn't that be nice?" he murmured, almost to himself. Her look of inquiry broke his reverie. "Sorry, childhood flashback."

Toni held her breath, afraid to break the spell. "Wanna talk about it?" she finally suggested, hoping she sounded casual.

Van wrinkled his nose. "No biggie. You know, the trauma of the immigrant, and all that."

"No," Toni answered. "I don't know that one." It was hard to believe that Van had ever felt like an outsider. Stories proliferated about his phoenixlike rise from poor, non-English-speaking refugee to tennis star, first Asian homecoming king in his Texas town, and Harvard scholarship student. Unlike Toni's best friend, Valerie, who felt beaten down by a faculty and student body that didn't quite know how to handle someone from Harlem who had a domestic for a mother, Van reigned from the heights of the Adams House social whirl. Perhaps Harvard required its so-called success stories to discard their pasts.

Toni was so preoccupied, thinking about Valerie's decision to leave Harvard for a year, that it took her a moment to realize Van had started talking. He was telling her about how his parents had chosen to settle him and his four younger siblings in Highland Park, a suburb of Dallas. Somehow, though Toni hadn't noticed exactly when, their friendship had turned a corner.

"Of course, they couldn't afford it." Van shrugged. "But that's the way Vietnamese parents are. They find the cheapest house in the least affluent neighborhood in the best school district possible." He described how America-bound families in refugee camps from Malaysia to Hong Kong, even back in Saigon, had memorized the names of America's most desirable public school districts and whispered them like mantras: Shaker Heights, Irvine, Brookline; McLean, Evanston, Los Gatos.

Toni laughed. "Sounds like my Nana—'Study your books, work hard, the most important thing for a black person is—' "

" '—a good education'!" Van finished, joining her laughter. "Yeah, well—did you have the homework factory?"

"The *what*?"

"I thought not." He made a great show of flexing his arms and cracking his knuckles. "Believe me," he advised, "you can't be a properly obsessive Vietnamese parent until you assign supplemental homework over Christmas vacation and terrorize your children into starting their own homework factory!"

"You're kidding."

Van adopted an angelic look and held up two fingers. "Scout's honor. The Nguyen household always had two kinds of homework: regular and 'extra.' "

"So you really took charge of your siblings," Toni said.

Van shrugged. "I was the eldest. Until my brother Andy and my sisters got up to speed, I was the only one who spoke English. I translated documents from school; I did my parents' taxes; I took them to the INS and arranged their naturalization; I kept the files on the mortgage." He took a sip of seltzer. "No big deal."

Toni shook her head. "Are you kidding? That's huge." When Toni was fifteen, her biggest responsibilities had been remembering to practice the violin and managing not to lose her retainer again. Van, in contrast, had abandoned his homeland and already lived an entire lifetime.

Van filled her sake cup and lifted it delicately between his thumb and middle finger. "Enough talk. No more tragic pasts, no more coed scandals." He positioned the cup over the glass and lobbed it down into a sea of beer.

That reminded her. "Apart from the woman I spoke with, I wonder how many other students were involved in this thing. Do you think—"

"Shh." Van waved away Toni's words and handed her the foaming glass. "You know I hate details, much as I do appreciate the sordid."

"But—"

"Hush." He put a finger to his chiseled lips. "You are here but for one reason and one reason alone—oblivion." He signaled the waitress and then turned back to Toni. "Drink—then on to our next port of call."

With a shrug, Toni did as she was told.

"Three bombs and we're outta here," laughed Van, and Toni, her spirits soaring, found it hard to argue.

/   /   /

Huddled over her wooden desk, Chelo gazed dubiously at the slim red memorial volume of Waxman's writings. Did Toni have any idea how esoteric this stuff was? Chelo'd take sex diaries over this turgid publication any day.

Chelo had been perplexed when Toni first thrust the book at her.

"This woman was Dave Mantini's thesis adviser," Toni explained. "She died three years ago. Maybe his disappearance and her death are related."

Well, it was an interesting notion, if rather sensational. Chelo had scanned the introduction, which told her that Dr. Waxman had died in a tragic bike accident, then thumbed through to the article co-authored by Waxman and Dave Mantini. " 'On Variant Models of Androstenol Reception,' " she read aloud.

"That's great, Chelo, I'm sure you'll figure something out," Toni exclaimed before dashing off.

The article was heavy going; Chelo understood maybe five percent of it. Still, she'd deduced a few things. Androstenol, a metabolite of a male hormone, could possibly be used for treating prostate cancer. There seemed to be other, unnamed commercial implications.

The rest of the articles in the book were about female-hormone research; the introduction reminded the reader that Waxman's findings were important in developing a treatment for ovarian cancer. Perhaps she had been trying to do the same kind of work for men.

Glancing back over the equations that decorated the perplexing text, Chelo experienced a stab of familiar fear—fear that she would never make it as a doctor. That she would never make it, period.

At Southgate High, Chelo had been a big star, the school's first student to go to Harvard—or any elite private university, for that matter. The attendance office still displayed a framed photo with a copper plaque that read: "Consuelo Santana: Student of the Year & Harvard University Acceptee." And her U.S. history teacher, Mrs. Claborne, still started each year's class with a motivational speech on a certain former student who had "really applied herself" and thus went off to "America's finest university."

Back home in L.A., everyone thought Chelo was smart, though they didn't always agree that being smart was a virtue. Her cousin Lupe had always called her Poinsy, short for Poindexter, the dorky guy with glasses in Felix the Cat cartoons. As a girl Chelo had shrugged it off, but maybe Lupe Gutierrez would have the last laugh. After all, it was no longer possible for Chelo to get the highest grade on every test. No matter how hard she worked, someone always scored higher. She wasn't going to solve a big mystery with her scientific brilliance; she'd be lucky if she got into a third-rate medical school. A wave of sadness slowly engulfed her.

Chelo walked over to Toni's desk and picked up the phone. A few seconds later she heard her mother's voice. *"¿Bueno?"*

"Hola, mamá. Soy yo, Consuelo."

"¿Cómo estás, mi amor? Is everything okay there? *¿Está todo bien allí?"*

Chelo assured her that she was fine. Beatriz Santana tended to shout into the receiver, as if the miracle of long distance depended solely on the strength of her lungs. "It's Saturday night! Why aren't you out having a good time *con tus amigos*?" she bellowed.

"Tengo mucho que hacer. I have a lot of work to catch up on this weekend—"

"Is it snowing?" her mother asked.

"Yes, *mamá,* it snowed last night. And the temperature is about twenty degrees."

"*¡Híjole! ¡Imagínate!*—twenty degrees! So, are you going to mass tomorrow?"

"No, *mamá,*" Chelo answered patiently. She decided on a different tack. "I'm helping my roommate with some research. *Una investigación científica.*"

"*Ay, chiquita.* You were always so thoughtful. But you need to take it easy, too."

Chelo sighed and felt a lump growing in her throat. She sat down hard on her desk chair. Outside, she could hear the occasional hollow sound of a lone set of footsteps hurrying across the pavement. At that moment she could feel the great distance between her and her mother, and it was more than the three thousand miles between Massachusetts and California.

Beatriz Santana launched into various stories about her relatives and neighbors. It seemed that Chelo's cousin Lydia had gotten pregnant—just weeks before her fifteenth birthday—and all the preparations for her *quinceñera* coming-out party had to be canceled. "Imagine, your *tía* Trini had already bought the dress—beautiful white lace with oceans and oceans of ruffles—and ordered *such* a cake, one of those nice pink ones that *los chinitos* make, *Díos mío.*"

Chelo felt a vague sense of relief at being so far from home. "*Mamá,*" she said, "I should go. It's three hours later here, you know, and I have to get to the library before it closes."

"Okay, *ten cuidado,* Chelo," her mother said. "Be careful."

Chelo knew what her mother really meant: Don't get pregnant. She sighed. "I'll be careful, *mamá,* I promise." Under the circumstances, that was a promise she would have no difficulty keeping.

/   /   /

Near midnight, Toni slipped her keys from her bag with clumsy fingers. Chelo hadn't responded to her knock—she must have gone to the law library—and Toni's first attempts to find the keyhole were unsuccessful. After the sake bombs, she and Van had ended up at a karaoke bar dominated by transvestites. "Asian Theme Night," Van had christened their travels, prior to giving her a kiss and depositing her at the T station. Although he looked slightly off-kilter, a trace of wistfulness diminishing the strength of his smile, the night was apparently still young for him. Swaying a bit, Toni jabbed the key at the lock until it finally stopped spinning and made contact. Exhausted by the effort, she collapsed against the heavy door, nearly falling to her knees as it swung wide.

It took her a few seconds to realize that something was wrong. It was almost as if she were standing outside her body, watching herself in slow motion, as she surveyed the shambles of her suite. All around her was chaos. Bookcases were overturned; her stack of reporter's notebooks lay gutted on the bed; broken computer disks littered the floor. Her dresser had been emptied, her clothing tossed around the room. On the desk, the computer hummed blue, left on by some unknown hand; window after window was open on the screen, as if someone had been searching all her files.

Toni rushed to the desk and pawed through the wreckage. She yanked open the bottom drawer and rifled through her accordion files. The photo of Tara had been taken—along with all the others.

Toni leaped up and tore into Chelo's room. It, too, had clearly been searched, but not nearly so violently. There was no sign of Chelo herself. She was probably still at the library, trying to make up for taking the afternoon off to visit Austen Riggs.

She couldn't stay here. Snatching up her bag and a few articles of clothing, Toni fled. Sober now, her heart pounding in her ears, she ran down the stairs and out of the building. She paced up Plympton Street, trying to regain her composure. She needed to warn Chelo that their room had been burglarized. She needed to sit down and figure out what to do. She needed to be somewhere safe, with someone she could trust.

She jogged down Mass. Avenue, sweating in the icy night, until she reached the line of pay phones near the entrance to the T station. Cabot answered on the second ring.

"Cabot, it's Toni. Our room got broken into—I'm really scared and . . . and I need a place to stay tonight."

Quickly, her voice trembling, she made arrangements to meet Cabot at Phillips Brooks House, rejecting his worried urging to wait for him at the newsstand.

After leaving a series of urgent messages for Chelo at her favorite libraries, she pushed another coin into the dirty slot. She didn't even have to think about the number; seeing it once in the business school phone directory had burned it into her memory.

It took ten rings to get Dora to answer, but just hearing her voice was enough to unleash Toni's memories of that night at the Cromwell.

"It's me," she tried to say, but no sound came out. Her throat was sealed.

"Hello?" Dora repeated, annoyed. "Okay, I'm hanging up."

Toni beat her to it, slamming down the receiver. She was exhausted, dizzy; a wave of drunkenness suddenly roiled her.

Cabot would no doubt be preparing the right elixir of reason and affection to calm her down. But something in her resisted calm. Instead, she stared in the opposite direction, down John F. Kennedy Street. Toward the lighted window she imagined across the river, where Dora was reading her cases or entertaining her clients or studying the loot she had snatched from Toni's dorm. Toni's legs started moving, her feet smacking hard against the frosted pavement. She ran toward the business school, pain jabbing at her sides as if she had bruised her lungs. She couldn't detach herself from Dora.

/ / /

Hearing a dull thump against her window, Dora Givens glanced up to see a scattering of dirt and ice on the pane. In the background, the headlights of passing cars danced on Storrow Drive, their tires whooshing in the ground-up salt and melted snow.

Dora turned back to a four-part case on Intel that would be discussed Monday morning. It was a struggle to pull any strategic lessons from the thicket of nerdy techno jargon. Who gave a damn about MIPS, anyway? Six months from now all the acronyms would be different.

She thought she heard the crunch of crusted old snow. Then, a sudden *crack* on the glass in front of her. She looked up to see a big gob of mud sliding down the window. Great—some nut was getting off by throwing snowballs.

She stood up, ready to give whoever it was a piece of her mind, and came face to face with Toni Isaacs. Eyes wild, Toni glared at Dora through the glass and then bent down, clawing at the snow and mud on the ground for something to hurl at the window. It was hard to look at Toni, in a way. She looked dumpy and vulnerable. She was really letting herself go.

Dora peered out the window. No security officers anywhere.

Toni opened her mouth and yelled something. Her invective was lifted away by the sounds of wind and traffic. Still, Dora didn't have to be an expert on lip-reading to get the point.

She observed Toni with the blank, controlled look she had perfected working with those pigs at MTV three years ago. Toni was crazy, certifiable. Of course, Dora *had* gotten her arrested. Identifying herself as the catering manager when she called the police had done the trick. Unfortunately, Toni hadn't learned the key lesson: everything would be fine if she just minded her own damned business.

Toni grinned, almost maniacally, and pawed a sprinkling of small rocks. Was she going to try to break the window now?

Enough was enough.

Dora grasped the bronze handles on the bottom of the window frame and yanked hard. Squealing, the window rolled up all the way. A rush of cold air filled the room.

"What the *hell* are you doing?" Dora demanded. She tried to speak in a low, authoritative tone, but her words were clipped by the wind; she heard her voice fade in and out like someone on a poor telephone connection.

"A lot less than you did!" Toni screamed back.

"I don't know what you're talking about." It was freezing out there.

"Oh, that's rich!" Toni shouted back over the din behind her. "My room is ransacked and you have nothing to do with it?"

"I'm closing this window," Dora said. "You're delusional. Get some help." She was troubled by what she heard. A break-in? What kind of third-string amateur was she working with?

"I *am* getting help," Toni snapped back. "Self-help. I know you're behind the prostitution ring, I've seen what your recruiting methods have done to people, and now you've committed a felony. Two of them." She flung the rocks to the ground. "Breaking and entering and kidnapping! You think the police aren't going to be after you for Mantini? You're going to jail, sugar."

"Do you really—" Dora began. Then she stopped in mid-sentence, forcing herself to think matters through. The pause was effective, giving the impression that Toni's charges did not justify the breath required to answer them.

Dora leveled a contemptuous gaze directly at her enemy. "You'll embarrass yourself worse than before, hon." *Give her the right hook.* "So let me give you a word of advice, woman to woman: Look closer to home. The longer you obsess about me, the more problems you're going to have. And I'm not talking about bullshit like your little academic disciplinary proceedings. Real, serious shit."

Dora slammed the window down and dropped the shades with a quick snap. Seconds later she flicked off the lights and slipped out the front door. No matter how fast Toni moved, Dora Givens would stay one step ahead.

/ / /

At eight-thirty the next morning, Toni called Detective Rivera. The ancient Phillips Brooks House radiator was clanking its morning fanfare against the wall behind her. Though she had slept only a few hours, she wanted to get everything done before Pat, the PBH administrator, showed up to demand her office and desk.

Toni had little memory of the slow walk back to Harvard Yard the night before. Cabot had met her at the door of PBH with a hug and a worried look but did not press for an explanation. In one of the small upstairs rooms he had built a nest for her—two worn blue wool blankets and a pillow neatly laid out on a red leather couch. A sagging bookcase behind her provided a sense of security. After washing her face, she relaxed on the sofa, Cabot keeping guard from a nearby chair. The next time she looked up, the first rays of dawn were streaming in the window, crosshatching Cabot's sleeping form. Mouth open and arm wrapped around his head, he breathed in short, audible bursts like a frightened child.

As Toni waited for her call to be transferred to Rivera, her mind wandered to Didi Carón. They had finally spoken a week after the Mardi Gras Ball; though friendly and flirtatious, they'd avoided setting up a subsequent date. She liked Didi and knew that he liked her . . . but she didn't think they were meant to be. Like most of her classmates, Toni hadn't yet given up the idea that at some point in college she would find her true soulmate. Apparently, she and Didi had connected briefly, assessed their mutual prospects, and whirled their way out of each other's lives.

Just as Rivera picked up the line, a cup of hot chocolate crowned with miniature marshmallows appeared before her. With a shy grin, Cabot plopped down in front of the desk and rubbed his sleepy eyes with the back of his hand. He listened carefully as Toni informed Rivera of the break-in. As she spoke, she realized that she had no intention of going down to file a report. Whoever broke in would have been clever enough to leave no trace.

"Besides," she explained, "I guess it's really more a matter for Harvard than for you guys." She took a sip of cocoa and recounted her call to HUPD. "They were characteristically lame. Get this—they seem to think it's a *house* matter. So I suppose I have to report it to my buddy Dean Kwok. Oh, joy."

"Dean Kwok?" Rivera sounded startled.

"Yeah. He's house master at Adams. Though he'll probably think I did it myself, to distract attention from my Ad Board case," she muttered bitterly.

"Hmm." Rivera's tone was odd.

"What?" Toni demanded. "What's going on?"

"Nothing, really."

"Do you know something?" she pressed, the hysteria of last night's confrontation with Dora fresh in her mind. "Does it have to do with the break-in?" She felt Cabot's warm hand on hers, and let their fingers intertwine.

"No, no," Rivera hastened to reassure her. "It's not that. It's just that . . . There's something I think you should know."

"What?"

"I shouldn't be telling you this, but you're a good kid . . ."

Toni winced at the word "kid."

"Someone in the department obtained your phone records for Dean Kwok."

Toni stiffened. "My what?"

"The record of all calls you made or received over the past three months. You and another student—a Tara Sheridan."

"Me and Tara?" Toni's shock turned to confusion. "Why?" Cabot leaned forward and tugged on her sleeve. "What?" he mouthed. She shook her head.

Kwok hadn't revealed why he wanted the records, just claimed official university business, and one of Rivera's colleagues had obliged. "I found out about it after the fact. Thought you should know," Rivera repeated, sounding regretful, "since this guy's supposed to be responsible for your safety." After giving her some advice on how to ensure it was safe to return to her room and urging her several times to be careful, he hung up.

Not quite sure whether to be frightened or angry, Toni put down the receiver and turned around to find her roommate being brought up to date by Cabot. Luckily, Chelo didn't ask many questions, since Toni didn't have many answers, and didn't seem to blame her for their room getting trashed. She reported cheerfully that she had already started cleaning up.

Toni filled Chelo and Cabot in on the call. Both were suitably shocked; in fact, the whole thing seemed to bother Cabot even more than it did the roommates.

"Why would Kwok want your phone records?" he asked.

"I have no idea, but I'm going to find out."

"What do you mean? You can't tell him that detective told you."

"I don't intend to." Toni rolled a mini marshmallow around her tongue. "But I can do a little detective work of my own."

Cabot frowned. "I don't think that's such a good idea. You just had someone break into your room—"

"—looking for something." Toni finished. That gave her an idea. "That's the only way to find out the truth around here. Going through the proper channels certainly doesn't get me anywhere."

Cabot gripped her arm, his fingers digging in hard. "Promise me you won't do anything illegal."

Toni smiled and pried herself out of his grasp. His concern was touching, if a little painful. "It's kind of late for that."

"I'm serious."

"So am I." She pulled out a new reporter's pad, eager to forget what had happened and get back to work. "You know Kwok pretty well. Where do you suppose he keeps his secrets?"

Cabot blanched and shut her pad. "Don't even ask. It'll only cause trouble."

A little of the protective-male thing, Toni was discovering, went a long way. She reopened the pad and flashed Cabot a warning look. "I think I can handle it."

"I don't think so," Cabot said, "or you wouldn't be hiding out here."

"Thanks a lot for rubbing that in." Exhausted from the night before and jittery at this newfound intimacy, Toni lashed out. "So you spend your days saving the world, but I shouldn't fight back when I'm being personally attacked?" Cabot opened his mouth, but she cut him off. "This is *my* investigation, and I can investigate whatever and whomever I want, you know. If you won't help me, I'm sure someone else, like"—she cast about for a name—"like Lucius would be happy to."

Cabot flushed. "What the hell does your ex have to do with this?"

"Nothing," she declared defiantly. "Only that he understands I have to do things for myself. He doesn't assume he can always fix or control things."

"That's such a crock."

"Really?" Hurt, Toni cocked her brow. "I guess *our* point of view is something a Winthrop couldn't understand." As soon as the words were out of her mouth, she regretted them. Cabot flinched as if she had slapped him. They stared at each other for a long moment. Toni didn't know which was more confusing—how she had gotten herself into this mess, or how she was going to get out.

Before she could say anything, Cabot was at the door, pulling on his jacket. "You're tired," he said. "I'll give you some privacy." And with that he was gone.

16

Dayton Moore fastened his wrist brace, gave his racket a few test swings, and headed down the dank hall toward the squash courts. At this hour, the subterranean world of Harvard's racket-sports facility was almost deserted; hardwood floors gleamed brightly where court doors had been left open. His step quickened as he approached the squash pro's desk. He was ready for a tough game, the kind of challenge that would leave him on top of his form for the rest of the day.

"Ah, Professor Moore," Alastair Campbell greeted him. Dayton was surprised to see the other man dressed in a jacket and tie, rather than his usual Harvard-insignia polo shirt and shorts.

"I left you a message," Campbell continued. He spoke with a gentle Scots burr; Dayton wondered, not for the first time, how much it helped him professionally. Sometimes he thought that the principal exports of Scotland—lagging only slightly behind whisky and kilts—were golf, tennis, and racket pros.

"I must attend a funeral service, you see," the pro continued. "A friend of mine from Strathclyde. Heart attack. He was only forty-three." Dayton nodded in understanding and turned to head back to the locker room.

"Professor Moore!" Campbell called after him. "I knew you wouldn't want to miss your game, so I took the liberty of finding you a partner. Another of my excellent students"—Campbell flashed a smile—"and a good match for you, if he tries hard enough."

"Fair enough," Dayton said. "Thanks very much. Where do I find him?"

"Court Three," Campbell answered, pulling on a dark overcoat. "You may know him: Sterling Kwok."

Dayton slowed a step. "Yes, we've met," he said. "Thanks for arranging things, Alastair. Sorry to hear about your friend."

The door of Court Three was already ajar, and inside was Sterling Kwok, natty in crisp white tennis shirt and shorts, a pair of protective goggles already in place.

"Sterling," Dayton said.

"Hello, Dayton," the other man responded. His tone was cool, and Dayton surmised that he had learned the identity of the day's partner when it was too late to back out. Too late to back out, that is, without being rude or churlish, and neither was within Kwok's range.

The two men moved silently into position. "Volley for serve, Sterling?" Dayton asked, hitting a soft shot against the back wall.

Dayton had never particularly liked Sterling Kwok. His affected mannerisms, his Anglophilic persona, and above all his readiness to uphold the status quo—all had grated on Dayton each time they met. But when he heard that Kwok had opposed his being granted tenure—had even tried to organize a group of senior faculty in a vote to overturn the Sociology Department's decision in Dayton's favor—annoyance had turned to dislike. Since then, their interests had clashed repeatedly at faculty meetings and Ad Board sessions. Dayton scorned Kwok for being the epitome of Harvard's past—and Kwok clearly despised Dayton for being part of a Harvard future he dreaded was coming all too quickly.

A stray shot caromed off the side, catching Dayton in the shin. He rubbed the sting for a second, then took up his racket, fiercely determined to beat Kwok.

Grudgingly, he admired the older man's fitness and stamina as he returned shot after shot. A light sheen of perspiration filmed Kwok's face, but the dean was barely breathing hard. Dayton redoubled his efforts, hitting the ball with a focused topspin. The force of each blow sent shock waves rippling from the racket and up his forearm, settling in his shoulder joint with an almost satisfying pain.

The court echoed with the impact of ball against wall, a hypnotic rhythm counterpointed by the half-voiced grunts of the two men and the squeak of their sneakers on the polished floor. Each time the rhythm was broken and a point won, the score was announced unceremoniously and the next serve launched almost at once. Both men were intent, their faces masks of controlled aggression.

Dayton smiled to himself. It was primitive, really, a battle between two alpha males. Though nothing concrete was at stake here, all the fighting instincts, thousands of years old, that had driven war and conquest, pillage and slaughter, were coming into play in this tiny underground room. The flimsy cotton that covered their keen bodies might just as well be chain mail, and these rackets could be scimitars. Dayton supposed that this was one of the advances of civilization: a duel whose effects could be washed away with only a hot shower.

He intended to win.

/ / /

"Hey, Toni." The speaker approached the dining room table, where, inspired by Van's childhood tale, Toni had attempted to create her own homework factory. A carafe of the diesel fuel the dining hall called coffee stood ready, next to assorted mini boxes of cereal and stacks of textbooks. "Not up for your room or the library, huh?"

Toni glanced up to see a fellow junior. The woman was African American, light-skinned, with pale eyes and masses of frizzy golden hair. Her uniform identified her as a common Adams House type: the dancer. Bits and pieces of striped knit clothing from the 1970s complemented a fist-size embroidered Burmese backpack and a nose ring.

"Hey, Simone," Toni answered. "Let's just say I prefer wide-open spaces, huh?" She didn't exactly relish the thought of going back to her room alone. "What's up?"

"Oh, um, I have four papers due at the end of the semester, but I've done *nothing*." Simone giggled and then gave a self-conscious shrug. "I'm assistant-directing the Caribbean Club's production of

Death of a Salesman. You're Bajan, right? So you *know* how apropos it is. The whole subordinated group success thing."

"Right," Toni replied. "I'll pencil it in."

"Oh!" Simone gave a spacey, apologetic smile. "I forgot to tell you—there's, like, some social worker and two underprivileged kids waiting for you in the foyer. I didn't know you did PBH!"

"Huh?" It took Toni a moment to understand what Simone might be talking about.

She sprinted to the entrance, catching Mrs. Mantini and her two grandchildren just as they were about to leave. She grinned at Mrs. Mantini, who smiled tightly in return. The woman's unexpected appearance mystified Toni—why would Blanche Mantini drive all the way from Revere without checking to see whether Toni was going to be in?—but she wasn't about to send them away. Obviously Mrs. Mantini didn't want to discuss her son in public. "Maybe it would be better if we talked in—"

"Your room would be fine," Mrs. Mantini said. "Unless you don't want to, with the kids here and all. It might be too much trouble."

"Of course it's no trouble," Toni said. "We can have some tea. It's four flights up, though—and I have to warn you that my room is really a mess." It would take days to get the place into real order. On the other hand, if Mrs. Mantini saw the wreck, she might be more inclined to help with information about Dave.

As the group made its way through the tunnels from the dining hall to B-Entry and then up the sweeping staircase to her fourth-floor suite, Toni noticed the way Mrs. Mantini and her two grandchildren ogled the gold walls and ornate candelabra. The children couldn't close their mouths. "What is this?" the older woman asked. "Some kind of castle? You kids really have it good."

Toni inserted her key into the lock and, cracking an apologetic smile, slowly swung open the door. She followed her guests' eyes into the room and gasped, feeling even more shock than the night before.

The suite was spotless. Overturned furniture had been righted, papers organized, clothes folded and put into drawers. A mop leaned drying against the wall to the bathroom, next to a half-used bottle of Murphy's Oil Soap. In a basket were various orphan shoes, old magazines, and an old hairbrush. Toni read the note placed on top: "Didn't know where these went. C."

Toni thanked God—not for the first time—that Chelo was her roommate.

Blanche sank into the black-and-gold Harvard chair Toni offered, and rested her handbag on the floor next to her. The kids resisted Toni's invitation to join her on the futon sofa, instead standing shyly next to their grandmother.

Toni cast about in her mind for some object to occupy them. There was nothing appropriate for kids in the entire suite. While the hotpot was boiling water for their tea, she noticed them giggling and pointing at the computer on her desk. "Hey," she said, "do you two know how to play computer games?"

The little girl nodded eagerly and took a step forward. "We play Tetris at school," she said.

"Galactic Invaders!" the boy shouted. He stuck his fist in front of his mouth and giggled.

Toni laughed. "Come over here, then," she said. With the help of Chelo's thick physics textbook and an old, unread copy of *Democracy in America,* she set them up on chairs at her desk and, relieved, turned her attention to Blanche Mantini.

"Are you sure you want them playing with your computer?" Mrs. Mantini asked, taking the mug of tea from Toni and inspecting the Radcliffe logo with interest. "It looks expensive; they could break something."

"Oh, Mrs. Mantini, they'll be fine. The thing is indestructible." Toni handed her guest milk and sugar; she regularly pilfered these from the dining hall, and now she congratulated herself on her forethought.

"Thanks, dear." Mrs. Mantini still looked worried. "That's real nice of you." She took a sip of milky tea and closed her eyes with a sigh. Her worn face looked suddenly tired and old, and Toni realized how exhausted she must be despite her spunky demeanor. Even apart from her son's disappearance, she must have been through a lot: she appeared to be in her late fifties, and clearly there was no Mr. Mantini to help raise the two young grandchildren.

"It's really good to see you again, Mrs. Mantini," Toni said. "I hope I can help in some way."

Blanche opened her eyes and blinked a bit before focusing on Toni. She took another sip of tea and looked around for a place to put the mug. Toni dragged the wooden coffee table closer, and Mrs. Mantini set the tea gingerly on a magazine. She dug around in her handbag for a tissue to slip under the mug.

"Well," she said, her voice businesslike, "I really appreciated the story you did about Dave—and you kept your word about sending me a copy. Only took a day to get to me. That note you wrote meant a lot, too."

Toni lowered her eyes. The article wasn't her best; she'd written it in a hurry.

Mrs. Mantini nodded. "You kept your word. The photo of him looked real nice, and you said some things the other reporters couldn't be bothered to say. I can see you're out to find some answers."

Toni smiled, and Mrs. Mantini continued. "You want to get to the truth, and you're not afraid of the Biotecnica Company. And I doubt you're afraid of a place like Harvard, no matter how fancy it is." Blanche said "Harvard" just the way people did in jokes, with no "r"s, though she seemed to attach random "r"s to the end of words that didn't need them, like "idea." She paused and regarded Toni. "I suppose that's why you took those garbage bags."

Toni choked on the sip of hot tea she had just taken. "Mrs. Mantini," she managed to gasp, "I am so, so sorry. You've been so kind, so trusting—and I never intended to disrespect you. I'm *so* sorry." In the background, the computer beeped and the kids squealed.

"Well," Mrs. Mantini said, "you should be. I doubt your mother raised you to go through other people's trash bins."

"No," Toni said, "she definitely did not."

"Well, now I know how the Kennedys must feel," Mrs. Mantini said cheerfully. Toni looked up in dismay, and Blanche gave her a severe look. "I can't say I approve of what you did," she said, "but I can see that you're honestly sorry and I don't believe you meant to hurt us."

"Oh, no, I didn't want to at all, Mrs. Mantini, and I'm sorry I did." Toni leaned forward to grasp the wooden arm of Blanche's chair. "I was trying to find out what Dave wanted to tell me, and I got so caught up with thinking I was this hotshot reporter and . . ." How would she put this? "And I thought you didn't want to discuss some of the things Dave was into."

Blanche eyed her silently. Finally she nodded. "Well, you've got a point there, and that's why I came over. You know, I just wanted to get rid of all that crazy stuff that might have gotten him into trouble. See, he told me about you before—"

"He did?"

"Well, not in detail. Only that he'd met a reporter who knew what she was doing. Said he had decided to go public with a big story, even though . . ."

"Even though what?" Toni asked, though she knew the answer.

"Even though it would be dangerous," the older woman finished. "Like I told him all along. I said, 'Just keep your nose to the grindstone, do your job, don't mind other people's problems.' "

The little boy ran over and whispered something. She shook her head. "We'll be leaving in a minute." His face was transformed into a mask of distress and he clutched the crotch of his Garanimal jeans. "Grams, I *have* to!"

"It's okay, Mrs. Mantini," Toni said. Before Blanche could object, she led the boy to the bathroom. The two women exchanged artificial smiles as they waited for the tinkling to end. It was followed by a grown-up sigh of relief.

When the boy was back at the computer, Mrs. Mantini leaned forward and lowered her voice. "David didn't go into a lot of details with me about his, uh, situation at work. The reason he was so upset. But he told me one thing I think you should know. He says—" Mrs. Mantini looked around the room, as if casing the joint for bugs. "He says the problem—whatever it is, Harvard is part of it."

"I heard about his adviser—" Toni offered cautiously.

"God rest that poor woman," Mrs. Mantini said with a helpless gesture. "But it's not that. It's something different."

"I'm not sure I know what you mean. What Dave meant," Toni said.

"Well, you're the reporter, not me," Mrs. Mantini said casually, smoothing her dress. "I just thought you should know that." She spoke lightly, as if she had delivered a message and was now free. "Anyway," she said, raising her finger, "I'm counting on you to do the right thing and clear my son's name."

/ / /

Toni skipped dinner and instead just rested on her bed, her hands folded behind her head. Despite the events of the past day, a half-smile played upon her mouth. That had been pretty weird, to stand outside Dora's room pelting her window with mud.

"Look closer to home," Dora had instructed her. Dora had such chilling self-control; she was a terrific liar. Toni wondered what her colleagues—or employees—thought of her. She was sure Dora would turn on them in a minute if push came to shove.

Well, what if Dora already *had* turned on them? Did that mean she was telling Toni the truth now?

And Cabot . . . It was hard enough to admit to someone you liked him, or to react appropriately when he indicated (bumbling, stumbling, testily but kind of sweetly) that he liked you, without the conversation turning into a symposium on interracial dating. Although she had debated the subject with Val long into the night, she had no idea how to talk about it with white guys.

And what about Dean Kwok's strange trick of obtaining copies of her and Tara's phone records? What did Dean Kwok think—that she was really a prostitute? Who did he think *he* was? Nixon? Talk about your obsessive bureaucrats.

She got up and pulled the telephone from her desk to her bed. After checking the number in the student directory—she'd managed to avoid calling him for a few months—she sat cross-legged and dialed her ex.

"Hi. It's me, Toni," she said.

"I know it's you," Lucius answered. "Am I back in your good graces? On your dance card for the next cotillion?"

"I'm afraid I wouldn't pass the paper bag test." The old black bourgeoisie, supposedly, had limited their social set to those whose skin was lighter than a brown paper bag. During their two years together, Toni had razzed Lucius plenty about his high-yellow origins. "Anyway, I wanted to ask you something. Seeing as how you know the inside of this place a lot better than I do."

There was a guarded pause on the other end. "I guess I'll take that as a compliment."

"Oh, come on," she said, "I'm just kidding. But seriously, I need your help. What do you say?"

Within minutes, Toni had filled three pages with notes. How

Dean Kwok fit within the constellation of powers at Harvard. His transformation from student radical to guardian of tradition, as perceived a generation later. His faculty friends and enemies.

"He's fundamentally suspicious," Lucius said. "Or maybe the word is 'territorial.' He doesn't trust the staff at University Hall, especially his secretary, Mrs. Hale. He thinks she's a plant, working for his enemies. He calls his Adams House office his refuge from the world." Toni mechanically took all this down; the idea she'd been toying with since her conversation with Rivera was solidifying into a plan.

"Hey," Lucius asked, "what are you planning to do, anyway?"

"Ad Board, remember? Gotta get prepared—and information is power," she lied. She was about to do something either incredibly useful or colossally stupid. There was no point in giving anyone a chance to talk her out of it.

17

As Toni slipped the key into the lock, she wondered what the punishment was for breaking into a house master's office. Could she be jailed? Expelled? What about the dreaded *expungement*—in which all records of an offender's presence at the university were destroyed? She shook her head. Only Harvard would devise the ostrichlike punishment of pretending that an offending student had never existed in the first place.

Lost in the shadows that lined the Adams House hallway, Toni braced herself to run in case the door squeaked loudly. She needn't have worried; the heavy slab of wood swung open without a sound. She peered into the darkened room, making sure that her baseball cap was firmly in place, then adjusted her oversize dark sweats.

Stepping inside, she felt a twinge of guilt square off against the adrenaline stiffening her muscles. A few hours earlier, she had duped Joe O'Callahan, the house super. She'd been in luck: tonight was the Celtics' game against the Detroit Pistons, and Joe was a diehard backer of the beloved home team.

She waited until the Celtics and Pistons were tied in the third quarter, 88 to 88, and then burst into his office, claiming to have locked herself out of her room. Joe looked up reluctantly from the tiny black-and-white set perched on the desk, clearly torn between the game and his duties as super, just as Toni had hoped.

"Uh, sure . . ." he said, stalling for time. "I'll be right with you." Moving like molasses, he got up and took the heavy ring of keys from the nail on the wall, keeping his eyes on the grainy screen the entire time. When a Pistons player stole the ball from the Celtics forward, Joe lunged at the screen. "God almighty!"

"Hey, Joe," Toni said, trying to sound concerned. "I don't want to bother you. Here . . ." She stretched out her hand casually, palm up-ward. "Let me do it."

"Uh . . ." Joe looked around, distracted. "If you can wait a sec. . . . I shouldn't . . ."

"Oh, c'mon," Toni urged as she gestured for him to throw her the keys. "Don't worry, I'll bring them right back." She tried a new tac-tic, crossing her arms to evoke a worried mood. "It's probably not good for me to delay taking my medication." She coughed raspily.

She was pushing it, but the ruse seemed to work. Joe turned away from the television and looked at her. The star forward was just get-ting up and the yellow-jacketed sports commentators babbled on. "Oh, medication," he said. "No, you don't wanna miss that." He fin-gered the keys and then tossed them onto the counter. "Just don't go nowhere with them master keys. Bring 'em back straight away." His voice trailed off as he turned his focus back to the television.

Toni grabbed the keys before a commercial came on or Joe changed his mind. The locksmith was on the next block; she'd have just enough time to get the master copied. As she ran, a heavy sense of discomfort collected in the pit of her stomach.

/ / /

Keeping the light off, Toni felt her way around the reception area to the door leading to Kwok's private inner office. It, too, was locked, but her copy of the master key worked again. She switched on one of the green-shaded reading lamps. The clock above the fireplace solemnly emitted three rich peals: three A.M. Like most Harvard buildings, the room was rich, heavy, and masculine, with dark, gleam-ing wood, plush oriental rugs, and heavy crimson-leather chairs. Anemic-looking, gilt-framed house masters from decades past lined the walls. Kwok's huge desk, beautifully handmade of cherrywood and burnished to a lustrous gloss, commanded attention from its place in the center of the room. Toni approached it and carefully pulled open the drawers, one by one. Her search yielded nothing of interest, but the bottom drawer was locked.

A collection of lacquered Chinese knickknack boxes sat on the desktop. Toni gave each a quick shake until she heard a faint jingle. She triumphantly took out a ring with two tiny gold keys.

The first one was slightly too big for the desk lock, but the second fit. Toni rifled hurriedly through Kwok's confidential files. Inside were Administrative Board records of disciplinary action against various students in the House, notes from committee meetings on tenure decisions, and nomination letters for the Adams House Senior Common Room. Nothing related to prostitution or Dora Givens or Dave Mantini, or even to her own upcoming Ad Board case. No secrets at all. Maybe Lucius didn't know what he was talking about. It wouldn't be the first time.

Toni put away the files and got up to check the rest of the room. There was nothing hidden in or behind the bookshelves. Nor did the musty closet contain anything sinister. The other file cabinets housed uninteresting yellow files. Not one thing in the entire office implicated the university in criminal activity or explained Kwok's interest in her phone records.

The only place left to look was the cabinet that housed Kwok's large-screen TV and VCR. Toni tugged at the door. Finding it locked, she scrambled to her feet and retrieved the tiny key ring from the desk. Sure enough, the larger key fit.

The cabinet was neatly lined with videotapes in black plastic cases. Toni scanned the typewritten labels, a litany of Sterling Kwok, Media Hound: "S. Kwok: Induction Ceremony." "S. Kwok: Faculty Club Speech." "S. Kwok: Asian Update Interview." "S. Kwok: Kowloon Bay Rotary Club Speech." "S. Kwok: Boston Today Interview." "S. Kwok: Manhattan Harvard Club Sesquicentennial Honorary Speech." Impatient, Toni rooted deeper in the shelf. The cabinet door must have been locked for a reason.

"Gotcha!" she exclaimed. All the way in back were several videotapes in unmarked cases. She pulled out the tapes and opened one. The label on the cassette itself was hand-lettered, "Scene 1," but the handwriting wasn't Kwok's. She popped open the second box. It read: "Scene 2." The third read, predictably, "Scene 3."

Standing up, Toni flipped on the television and nearly swallowed her tongue as sound blasted out. She punched the volume control frantically and inserted the first tape into the VCR. Remote in hand, she retreated to Kwok's deep leather chair and sat on the edge, her feet firmly on the floor. She quelled the urge to kick back and put her feet up on that five-thousand-dollar desk.

A thought occurred to her. In the movies, criminals were always taping huge wads of cash beneath drawers. She groped the underside of the desk. Finding nothing, she pulled open the center drawer, stuck her hand in, and felt along the roof. Her fingers touched metal: it felt like a ring embedded inside. She pulled it, and a hidden door at the back of the drawer sprang open with a click. A colored glass vial tumbled out. Aghast, Toni looked down at the desk, then up at the screen. At that moment, she couldn't decide which was more shocking: the drug paraphernalia spilling out of the secret compartment in Dean Kwok's desk, or the on-screen image of Dean Kwok penetrating Tara Sheridan on a king-size bed.

Toni turned the cheap glass vial over and over in her hand, inspecting the resinous crystals within. She felt around inside the drawer and found a pipe. Fashioned from brass inlaid with mother-of-pearl, it was clogged with the same substance. Putting it to her nose, she sniffed. It smelled foul. She was no drug expert, but years of celebrity exposés in *People* magazine and on ABC after-school specials had taught her enough to know what she had discovered. *Kwok kept crack in his office.*

It was mindboggling that a man in Kwok's position would take such huge risks. All the administrators Toni knew were exceedingly cautious, spending their careers gingerly stepping through the mine fields of faculty politics and student sensitivities; simple survival was their greatest achievement. But then again, why shouldn't Kwok be an addict? Hadn't that been the message of antidrug campaigns since Betty Ford? That anyone could be an addict? And, contrary to popular belief, crack and heroin—the so-called drugs of the masses—were making a strong comeback among the rich and educated, weary of airy designer drugs like cocaine.

Toni turned her attention to the lurid scene on the television screen. It was a surreal silent movie, the grunts and conversation inaudible. A fragile-looking Tara was now crouching on all fours as Kwok rolled on a new condom. The room was modern and plush but characterless, like the set of a soap opera. Clothes were strewn about the floor and on a reproduction Queen Anne writing desk. The scene appeared to take place in a standard business hotel.

Tara kept her head down, her face half hidden by hair, so Toni couldn't read her expression. On his knees, Kwok entered her from behind, an expression of obscene pleasure on his slack face. With each wild thrust, Tara's breasts quivered erratically. From the dean's wild, glazed eyes, Toni could see that he was clearly high. She imagined what the rest of the story would be. She pointed the remote control at the television and clicked it off.

She put the vial and pipe back in their secret place. Just before squeezing the trapdoor shut, she felt around the entire compartment once more. Taped to the top of the drawer was a three-by-five card. She removed it and read the lines: "1 rock—'van requisition.' 1 pure g.—'fund-raising meeting.' " She flipped over the card. On the back was a five-digit telephone number beginning with a university prefix. Her heart began to pound. She knew the number. It belonged to the president's office at Phillips Brooks House. Cabot's number.

Toni considered Cabot's behavior over the past few weeks: His disappearance from the police station. His anger on the trip back from Blanche Mantini's. His opposition to investigating Kwok. She had to admit that he'd always had a mysterious aspect. He was unnaturally reticent about his high-toned Boston family. And, come to think of it, she always saw him at PBH or at the *Crimson* or in some public place—never in his room.

She felt her stomach drop as the implication of her unwelcome discovery sank in. Toni had never thought Cabot capable of this. She glanced down at the code words on the card: "Van requisition." "Fund-raising meeting." She searched her mind for their meanings but came up empty. As president of PBH, Cabot was responsible for overseeing both the vans and all fund-raising efforts. It was the perfect excuse for the dean of students to contact him, the perfect cover to fill a drug order.

A moment later, Toni heard the unmistakable sound of a key in the outer office door. She slid the drawer shut and stuffed the card in her pocket, then rushed to eject the cassette from the VCR. After giving the room a quick glance, she flicked off the desk lamp and leaped behind the door.

It swung open and someone hovered in the doorway. Toni stood on her toes and flattened herself against the wall, holding her breath. After what seemed like an eternity, the man strode across the room to the desk and yanked open the top drawer. She stood trembling, fingers crossed. *Oh, God.* Her mind raced. Here she was, alone, in the dark, having told no one where she was going, and in possession of information that could destroy two men's careers.

The figure bent over the desk, reaching deep inside the drawer. Toni heard a click as the latch of the secret compartment released. He was going for the crack. She couldn't swallow. He put the vial in his pocket. Her heart was pounding so hard that it roared in her ears. He was sure to hear it. She felt dizzy. She had to get out.

She slipped from behind the door and inched her way toward the exit. Immediately the man looked up and saw her silhouette. They both froze. He cursed softly, and Toni let out an involuntary moan of fear. Panicked, she sped out the door, throwing the coatrack behind her to trip him up. As it clattered to the floor, she tore open the outer door and fled into the hall. Making a frantic split-second decision, she headed for the tunnels. Administrators rarely ventured into this subterranean maze, which underlay all the houses and led to Harvard's central kitchen. The tunnels were student and dining hall worker territory. She would have a better chance of escaping Kwok here.

Toni bolted down the steps to the basement, moving so fast that she almost tripped over her feet and fell down the stairs. Behind her she could hear her pursuer's ragged breaths. He was moving surprisingly quickly for a man over forty. At the bottom of the stairs she paused to pull open the heavy metal door leading to the tunnels. Bright light poured out, momentarily blinding her. She covered her eyes and stepped in, peering wildly in both directions; then she chose the main tunnel. Although Kwok was probably more familiar with it, the chances were also greater that people might still be up.

She sped along halls covered with titillating graffiti, the videotape clutched in her left hand. The only sounds in the echoing corridor were her staccato footsteps and the heavier pounding of her pursuer. She passed empty weight rooms, squash courts, the pool table that sat under the stairs in a wide spot in the tunnel. It was an exhausting course; sections of the floor were on different levels, and no sooner had Toni run down one flight of steps than she had to run up another.

Panting, she paused to catch her breath. The hiss from the steam pipes above her reawakened her to the danger she was in. She looked frantically about her. Adams was a nocturnal house. People always stayed up talking into the early morning. Someone should be around. *But where?* She heard a noise in the laundry room. Gasping with relief, she ducked under the pipes and ran toward the sound. She flung herself into the room. It was empty. Laundry lay abandoned on silent machines, while in the corner the soda machine whirred and purred to itself.

She fled back into the hall and toward the experimental theater space. Here bold psychedelic murals stretched on either side. Gaudy, cast-off props littered the corridor. She popped her head into a room painted entirely black—walls, ceiling, floor. The stale smell of pot and cigarette smoke hung heavily on the air. *No one.*

By now Toni was gasping so hard for breath that she couldn't hear her pursuer anymore. She threw a quick glance over her shoulder. He was still there: a blurry masculine figure dressed in black. Right behind her.

"Stop!" the man croaked, advancing toward her with an arm outstretched.

"Get away!" She spun around and ducked down a narrow passageway. Its stark white walls and gradually inclining floor indicated that it was one of the dining hall tunnels. She was hundreds of yards away from the House now and didn't know her way around.

"Toni, stop!" the man shouted. The sound echoed, bouncing off the walls, attacking her over and over. She hesitated, then gulped for air and tried to run faster.

The tunnel widened, and a vast blank space opened up before them, gleaming coolly fluorescent. They were approaching the kitchens. The slap of their feet resounded hollowly on the bare cement. The corridor grew colder and colder as it neared the river.

Toni's labored breath rasped in her ears. Exhausted and not quite sure why she was running anymore, she reached the end of the corridor and tried to open the door that loomed in front of her. It was locked. Dead end.

In an instant the man was on her, clutching her shoulders. Toni screamed and thrashed in his grasp, clawing at his hands. But he held tight, and she was too tired, too frightened: she couldn't escape. She went limp.

Slowly she became aware of his voice, repeating her name over and over. "Toni, calm down. Toni, you're hysterical. Toni, calm down."

She stared at him and understood for the first time that the stranger who had pursued her was not Sterling Kwok. It was Cabot Winthrop.

After a moment of disbelief, she erupted. "How can I calm down?" She was hoarse with fury and fear. "I thought I was running for my life!"

"Toni," he insisted gently, "you're hysterical. You know I could never hurt anyone." He smiled tentatively. "*Especially* you."

Behind his gold-rimmed spectacles, Cabot's eyes beseeched her.

She laughed, a humorless bark. "You don't know how reassuring that is, Cabot." She struggled to get free of his grasp. "And quit saying I'm hysterical. What if I am? *You're* a dealer and a pimp!"

Cabot recoiled and a deep flush slowly covered his neck and face. "Toni—" he choked out. "You don't understand." He actually looked hurt.

Toni folded her arms in front of her and challenged him. "What? Have I insulted you or something?"

Aware that already she was having trouble believing everything she had learned about him, Toni found herself hoping it was all a huge misunderstanding. She dug her nails into her arms, trying to keep herself angry. "I saw you with my own eyes in Kwok's office. I know you're his drug connection."

Cabot stared at her. His face was red and he was clenching his fists. She could hear his rapid, shallow breathing, and she began to be afraid again. Shaking his head, Cabot took one step toward her and stopped. He raised his hand and began to cry.

/　/　/

Toni listened as Cabot haltingly explained himself. Huddled with his head in his hands, he admitted to being Kwok's drug connection, but claimed the dean had pressured him into it. Cabot had ready access to crack: he did much of his volunteer work in drug-infested neighborhoods. He hated dealing, but Kwok feared the risks involved in finding a new connection and insisted that he continue.

"I knew it was all going to blow up in both our faces eventually," Cabot finished, "especially once you came up with the idea of investigating Kwok. I shouldn't have tried to talk you out of it, but I didn't know what else to do, except remove the evidence myself. I didn't want to be found out—and by you, of all people."

He looked lost. "I don't know how to get out. He has too much on me."

Toni pondered this bizarre remark. To be president of Harvard's largest student organization, Cabot couldn't be intimidated by anyone: not recalcitrant city officials, not antagonistic peers, not housing-project toughs. There was no one more in control of his own actions than Cabot Winthrop III.

"How exactly was Kwok able to force you to be a drug runner?" she asked coldly. "And does he force you to pimp for him, too?"

He frowned. "You've called me a pimp twice. Why?"

"Answer my question!" Toni yelled.

Cabot swallowed hard and took a deep breath. "Look, I can guess what you're thinking, that I'm not the person you thought I was. . . . And you're right. I'm a fraud. What Kwok has on me is this: I'm not . . . I'm not actually a student at Harvard."

He looked at Toni but got no reaction. She had no idea what he was talking about.

He ran his fingers through his hair, almost yanking at it. "I never got accepted. I don't live in a house. I'm not one of you guys."

Toni gaped at him. "You had to get in. I've seen you in classes. You run PBH. There are buildings on campus named after your family!"

"Exactly!" he spat out bitterly, clenching and unclenching his fists. "My parents and my grandparents and my great-grandfather all studied at Harvard or Radcliffe, and even with all those millions in donations *I didn't get in!* Do you know how stupid you have to be to come from a family like mine and not be accepted?"

Cabot raced on, emotions flickering across his face. "The crazy thing is, I really love this school. This is the only place I ever wanted to come.

"So maybe you can imagine this ambitious seventeen-year-old who got one of those *skinny* envelopes in the mail on April fifteenth. I felt like my life had ended before it even began. I concocted this wild plan: I figured I would just pretend to be a student—I'd live off campus, get a fake ID, go to classes, and just not take exams. And it was just crazy enough to work.

"I knew something would go wrong eventually, someone would have to find out. But I never thought it would be the dean of students—he's so removed from actual students." Cabot's voice quivered. "And I never thought I could be so weak, to allow someone to blackmail me into . . ." He turned his face away.

"Into becoming a dealer?" Toni supplied. He cringed but did not contradict her. "Then . . . you actually need the money?" It was hard to believe.

He nodded. "It's not even enough, to tell you the truth. It just pays for food and clothes and books."

Despite her desire to keep her distance from him, Toni leaned forward, placing her hand lightly on his arm. "But where—?"

"Mainly I stay at PBH," he answered. "I use that room on the second floor. Or I crash at friends' places. I pretend it's too late to walk home. I shower at the gym." He grinned. "If you gotta be homeless, Harvard's a great place to be. And when I turn twenty-one, I'll have access to my trust fund, so I'll finally be able to live more normally."

"But what about your parents?" Toni asked. "Don't they expect to get invited to parents' weekends, or to get tuition bills?"

Cabot grimaced. "They couldn't care less," he admitted. "They think the trust fund is paying my tuition."

Toni shook her head. "I guess I just don't get it—I mean, what's the big deal about going to Harvard? It impresses people who don't go here, but it's not the end of the world if you don't get in."

Cabot looked directly at her. "This is my *life*. In spite of everything, until this Kwok thing started, I was *happy*. That's probably hard for you to believe, but it's true. I didn't care about the credential—I just wanted the life."

"Prostituting yourself for a prostitution ring," Toni mused aloud. "You and Dora have more in common than I would have expected."

Cabot frowned. "What are you talking about? What's all this about pimping and prostitution? And who's Dora? You think I go to prostitutes? Is every guy from a rich family automatically depraved?"

Was it possible that Cabot had nothing to do with Class Ring? For the first time it occurred to Toni that Kwok's drug use and his involvement in prostitution might not be directly connected.

"When I was in Kwok's office," she explained, "I found a videotape of him having sex with a student who used to live in Eliot House and work as a prostitute." Seeing Cabot's incredulous expression, she continued, informing him of the latest developments in her investigation.

"Toni, you have to believe that I didn't know anything about this," he insisted.

"Yeah, well, it takes time to sink in." Toni felt dizzy. Cabot was a drug dealer. He was *not* a student. He was homeless. He was *not* a pimp connected with Dora and Class Ring. "Now I see why you ran for your life when Kwok showed up at the police station. And why you've never invited me to your room." She faltered, suddenly shy. "But why did you chase me?"

"I'm sorry," he apologized. "I never meant to frighten you. I didn't even know it was you. I just wanted to plead with whoever it was not to narc on me.

"C'mon," he coaxed, pulling her to her feet. "Let's go back where it's warmer."

Toni nodded numbly and tried to relax. Though it had turned up more than she wanted to know, the raid was a success. She now had evidence to implicate Kwok in the prostitution ring. Once the true story came out, the Ad Board proceeding should slip away. Her account of that night at the Cromwell would finally be legitimated. This time, the police would be on her side.

Provided she acted fast.

18

By nine A.M., the Cambridge police station was already hopping. Angry motorists argued about their impounded vehicles; street vendors protested their licensing fees. Sitting on an orange Naugahyde chair, waiting for Carlos Rivera to arrive, Toni felt surprisingly safe. If you weren't in handcuffs, the police station wasn't such a bad place to be.

Though not nearly as exhausted as she might have expected after her sleepless night, she felt a vague dissatisfaction. She wondered if she would ever know half the reasons for Dora's and Dean Kwok's behavior.

She heard footsteps behind her and saw one of the desk sergeants gesture toward her. Turning around, she spotted Detective Rivera.

He smiled. "Somehow I'm not surprised to see you here."

She felt awkward at his amiability, the events of the night they met still fresh in her mind. "Well, thank you for taking the time to meet with me."

"Is this top secret?"

She couldn't tell if he was being serious or making fun of her. "It's confidential." She swallowed hard.

Toni had already seen the video several times, including one screening with Chelo. It was good to have a confidante who, even at five in the morning, was sensible and efficient.

Now she studied Rivera as he silently watched the tape. There was not a sound in the room except for the hum of the VCR. His jaw tightened, and she knew he believed her. Finally. The tape went black and he turned off the set.

"That's Tara Sheridan," Toni explained. "I'm sure you recognize the name. She's a Harvard student who's taken some time off from school; I suppose it's obvious why. My roommate is going out to get a statement from her today."

"That won't have any legal effect."

"Then I'll use it for my article," she countered.

Rivera pursed his lips and nodded. Toni gave a carefully edited version of the raid, eliminating all references to Cabot and the house superintendent.

Rivera leaned forward and balanced his elbows on the table, hands folded together. "That's a pretty serious act," he said. "I certainly wish you hadn't trespassed on private property and stolen the video. If the police had done that, the tape would be inadmissible as evidence."

"All right," Toni conceded, shifting in her seat, "I know it was wrong. But I had to find out what was going on. To protect myself, if nothing else. They're trying to kick me out of school." She hurriedly pulled another large envelope from her bag and set it before him. It contained supporting materials that Chelo recommended she provide to buttress her credibility: her first article about prostitution; summaries of her conversations with Tara, Dora, and the johns; and a description of the drug paraphernalia she'd found in Dean Kwok's office. The police could take it from there.

Rivera's fingers closed over the envelope. "I'll have the sergeant bring you a release form. Now, you're certain you found drugs in the dean's desk?"

"Well, it looked like drugs to me. There was a vial, a pipe with a nasty-smelling residue. I'm no expert."

"But to the best of your knowledge. To the best of your knowledge, the substance you saw in the dean's desk was crack cocaine. Isn't that correct?"

Toni could see where he was going with this. "Yes. To the best of my knowledge."

"All right." Rivera thought for a moment. As he leaned back, his chair squeaked noisily. "There's a judge who owes me a couple. I'll see if I can get a search warrant and send a car over. There's no law against sleeping with students. Not yet, anyway. Though that video-tape should be enough for anyone. But drugs—that'll make it easier. Drugs are the hot button these days."

Toni felt a great sense of relief, mixed with profound skepticism that it could really be this easy. "So what should I do?"

"Go home. Get some sleep, have breakfast, go to class. Whatever you usually do." He looked at her for a moment, then smiled. "Though I guess you usually spend your time working, like me. We'll give you a call if something happens. Don't worry, you'll get your story."

Rivera was trying to be friendly, but Toni felt disquieted as she shook hands with him and headed back down the hall. Was that his view of her—as a scheming journalist chasing her big story?

She walked down Western Avenue to Putnam and into the Square. The giant digital clock atop the Cambridge Savings Bank read 9:02. Maybe she could look in on "Early Modern Europe" for a change.

Toni entered the Yard, passing the statue of John Harvard. A Crimson Key member maneuvered a group of uniformed Korean schoolgirls on a campus tour. "This is called the statue of three lies," the Keyster droned while the schoolgirls giggled and slapped each other with their Hello Kitty bookbags. *Three lies*, Toni thought. *"These are the best and the brightest." "These are the best years of your lives." And "This is all worth twenty thousand dollars a year."* She turned into Sever Hall and took a seat at the back of the classroom.

On the blackboard, the professor was diagramming the family re-lationships of the Medici while the students carefully noted every long-dead uncle and cousin. Some of this, after all, might be on the test.

Toni tried to follow the lecture and keep up with the note-taking, but eventually resigned herself to the fact that she was getting noth-ing out of it. She closed her notebook and sat quietly, feeling the ache of tiredness in every muscle. After what seemed like years, the professor concluded her discussion and answered a few questions, and the class stood up to go.

Toni walked with the crowd through the Yard and headed back to Adams House. Back in their suite, she glanced at some mail—bills and credit card offers, mostly—then took a quick shower. On her way out of the bathroom she paused at the answering machine and contemplated the rapidly blinking message light. The stack of pink "While You Were Out" notes from Chelo was daunting. She picked them up with a groan. She could have written them herself: The secretary of the Black Students Association reminding her about the important upcoming meeting. Assorted friends checking to see if she was alive. Cabot apologizing again. Her parents wondering why she hadn't returned any of their calls and what in the world was going on. Oh God, her parents. Hearing that their only daughter had been arrested for prostitution would be a shock to Harlan and Matilda Isaacs; Toni was not looking forward to that call. She backed away from the blinking phone machine. Around noon she dropped onto her bed for a nap and instantly fell into a heavy, dreamless sleep.

/   /   /

"Toni knows that Dean Kwok was involved in the"—Chelo paused, searching for a euphemism for "prostitution ring"—"in the escort operation."

Tara took a drag of her cigarette and flicked her eyebrows, torpedoing Chelo's effort at subtlety. Oh, well, she hadn't expected this to be easy.

Chelo had emerged from the long bus ride to Austen Riggs only to find Tara packing up. Her treatment program completed, she was flying the next morning to Santa Fe to stay with an aunt for a few months—a compromise between her desire to go off on her own somewhere and her parents' wish to have her home in Darien. Chelo wondered what the Sheridans knew about their daughter's activities at Harvard.

Watching her friend carefully out of the corner of her eye, and trying to keep her tone neutral, Chelo informed Tara of the discovery of Dean Kwok's office video cache. Surely Tara didn't want anyone to know about her relationship with Kwok; not mentioning him during their previous visit was a pretty glaring omission. Chelo was confident that Tara knew a lot more, too, though it would be perfectly understandable if she told her and Toni to get lost permanently. Tara had never asked anyone to investigate and publicize her life. Clearly, though, Tara needed saving from something.

It was eerie, this meeting with her friend the student prostitute. Tara spoke freely, casually describing that first night with the dean in the Mark and Sextant Hotel. Kwok had been alive with curiosity about who "Phoebe Hilton" really was. He hadn't recognized her as one of the sixty-four hundred Harvard undergrads he supervised, and apparently hadn't expected truth in advertising. While she consumed the forty-dollar sushi sampler sent up by room service, he barraged her with questions. Nervousness melted into skepticism, which ultimately became grudging belief; a faux Harvard student couldn't possibly have known the school in such detail. He'd said he should leave; but, unable to contain his eagerness to fulfill his fantasy, he'd stayed.

Kwok's emotions intensified over time. He was both anxious and excited every time they met. Tara was afraid he was developing a thing for her, but later, after getting similar reactions from other clients, she concluded that he was just excited about the sex and the sinfulness of it all.

Kwok and Tara talked a lot during their weekly sessions. He gossiped about the faculty—who was having affairs with whom, who wasn't going to get tenure. He told her how, when he was in college, everyone claimed interest in exploring their "erotic potential." Back then, *The Joy of Sex* and *The Sensuous Woman* were sold in every bookstore.

Sex with clients was different from sex with Harvard students, and not necessarily inferior. The clients appreciated the encounters more than Harvard boys did. Once past the small talk and foreplay, once they donned a condom, they'd get *really* excited. Kwok's forehead would sweat, Tara said; his eyes would gleam; he'd lick her body everywhere.

"Did they ever object to using condoms?" It was a question of great personal interest. Chelo's fear—the fear of everyone in her generation—was that sex could kill.

"No." Tara shook her head. She searched through her bag, pulled out a handful of shiny foil packets, and tossed them to Chelo. "I can't believe I didn't throw them away. The clients always used them."

Chelo examined the prophylactics. Each was labeled "Veritas." The escorts were required to use them, Tara explained, and Class Ring had a detailed system to make sure they did. Each condom was numbered; in the customer service reports they filled out after each session, escorts noted which ones had been used. Dora—Tara agreed that she had to be the same woman as Dominique—warned that if an escort didn't insist the man use a glove, she was out, no matter what the client said. Dora said that the comparative advantage of the service was in providing a safe fantasy. The Veritas label on each condom reinforced the Harvard identity of the prostitutes. Branding was everything.

Had Tara known about the videotapes?

Not immediately. She learned of them only when Kwok, terrified, had accused her of trying to blackmail him.

Tara realized instantly where the video must have been shot: at the incall location the service used, an executive hotel suite in downtown Boston. Someone—Dora, most probably—must have installed the camera. This incall facility was sort of a frequent-john perk, like being elevated to "club level" at a hotel. The clients liked it because it minimized fuss and, furthermore, had an air of exclusivity: only repeat customers who filled out customer-service cards were entitled to this first-class privilege.

"Isn't that kind of formal for an escort service?" Chelo asked.

Apparently not. Dora was into all sorts of cutting-edge marketing practices. The cards asked simple questions: Height, weight, age of client. Length of the sex act; types of foreplay; degree of satisfaction. Clients received a twenty-dollar discount each time they filled it out; of course, everyone did. Dora claimed that people loved giving their opinions. They'd tell anyone what they thought, as long as they didn't have to substantiate their opinions with actual facts.

Once the video turned up, Tara began to get antsy. Dora told her not to worry, that the video was just a product idea. Like shopping malls that took your kid's picture with Santa Claus whether you wanted one or not. Parents always ended up buying the photo in the end, as a keepsake of a special day. The videos would be used the same way. People might be too embarrassed to ask for a video themselves, but would gladly purchase them, turned on by their own nastiness.

Tara knew this was a lie. She'd heard shock and fear in Kwok's voice; he wanted no video memento of their time together. Yet Dora seemed utterly convinced of the truth of her weird assertions. When Tara insisted that the idea was a bad one, Dora suggested she take a breather.

"That was when I started thinking I had to get out," Tara admitted. "She sounded crazy." When, two weeks later, one of her johns went into cardiac arrest, she made her decision.

A porter knocked on the door to the suite, tipped his cap respectfully, and started collecting her bags. Tara sprang up, located her purse, and extracted a ten.

"I'm at a B-and-B in town until my flight tomorrow," she explained. "Can't stay here a night longer than the program. I'm not really bulimic, you know. I just needed a safe, private place to stay until things got sorted out."

Chelo didn't know what to say. Tara had said her piece and left it behind. Along with Chelo. She searched for some statement that would provide closure to Tara's story, but the words escaped her. They weren't really friends anymore. They had little in common now, and what they did share—this story—was precisely what would prevent them from enjoying any long-lasting bonds of affection. Chelo accompanied Tara down the hall, trailing the porter and the bags; when Tara climbed into the taxi, she leaned through the open window and kissed her on both cheeks.

She realized only afterward that she had finally appropriated one of Tara's worldly gestures for herself.

19

Four hours after Toni had dropped off to sleep, the telephone rang. She sat up with a start and, instantly awake, heard herself agreeing to meet Carlos Rivera in Dean Kwok's office.

She scrambled for notebook, schoolbag, and keys. Locking the door carefully behind her, she hurried down the stone staircase, through the underground corridors, and up the stairs to the master's office. She smoothed her hair and knocked.

"Come in," Rivera called through the door.

She turned the heavy brass knob and stepped into the room. It looked different by day. The gleaming desk, its drawers pulled out, was the center of a group of men who stood pawing through stacks of paper. Two wore gloves. One was bent over the desk, reaching into the drawer she remembered very well.

"There's a secret compartment in there!" she blurted out. All heads turned to look at her, except for the man at the desk, who released the latch of the secret drawer, then straightened and faced her. It was Sterling Kwok.

"Thank you, Ms. Isaacs," Kwok said. "I am well aware of my

desk's unique qualities. As you can see, gentlemen," he went on, stepping away from the glistening cherrywood, "the so-called secret compartment is empty. Quite empty." One of the white-gloved technicians verified the assertion.

"But last night—" Toni was shocked, confused. "He had a pipe. I saw it. And what looked like crack. Are you sure you're looking in the right compartment?"

"There's only one compartment, Ms. Isaacs. And it's clean." Rivera's voice was flat.

"The video, then. What about the video?"

Rivera's face colored as a discreet cough sounded from one of the armchairs by the window. Toni turned and saw a man with gray hair and a patrician profile. He looked like a university president, though she knew he wasn't. He must be one of the muckety-mucks from the Portfolio.

"An indiscretion, shall we say?" he asked, apparently addressing the other men in the room. His voice rustled softly but the attention it commanded was complete. "Most unfortunate. Dean Kwok has told me all about it. Sad, really. I understand that the young lady involved had some sort of breakdown when Sterling brought the relationship to an end."

"Relationship?" Toni was horrified.

"Indeed." The gray-haired man swiveled in the chair and rested his eyes on her. They were curious, appraising, and cool. "And, Miss Isaacs, I hardly think it is in the best interests of your young friend for you to publicize her error in judgment. No, the best course is to respect the privacy of those involved, don't you agree?" The smooth voice now contained a note of steel. "I'm sure your own past experiences have made you aware of the value of privacy concerning one's personal activities."

Toni turned to Rivera in a panic. "Can't you see what they're doing? This is a cover-up! Last night in here, I saw—"

The man in the armchair interrupted. "Breaking and entering. Now, Detective Rivera, I haven't practiced law for some years, but it seems to me that that's a felonious offense in Massachusetts."

Toni searched Rivera's face for some sign of sympathy.

"Excuse me, gentlemen," he said briskly. "I'd like to have a moment with Ms. Isaacs alone." He looked at Toni and stuck his thumb in the direction of the door.

Toni stepped outside. Rivera followed, shutting the heavy walnut door behind him.

"Listen to me," he said in an angry whisper. "These men are doing you a favor. If you walk away from this now, they won't press charges. All you have to do is keep your mouth shut about what you thought you saw last night—and maybe a few other things."

She sucked her teeth, an involuntary gesture of disapproval lifted from her mother. "But I *did* see those things! And Sterling Kwok and Tara weren't having an affair. It was part of the prostitution service!" She looked at his scowling face. "You read the notes I gave you. Don't you believe me?"

He exhaled sharply. "This isn't about whether I believe you or not, Toni. This is about evidence, and I don't have any. I know something's wrong here—that Kwok character is about two steps away from a padded cell at McLean. But there's no case here. Not one I can make stick. And I know there isn't anybody down at the precinct, or in the district attorney's office, who's willing to take on all of this"—he gestured around at the time-worn elegance of the surroundings—"without some goddamned evidence."

"What about investigating?" she pleaded. "Don't you ever follow leads, question witnesses, search for the truth?"

He stared intently at her, and she could see regret in his eyes. "I wish I could help you. My advice is just to forget it and stay out of their way. Concentrate on taking care of yourself—on not getting expelled." He held her gaze for a second, then went back inside.

Toni turned to walk away, feeling the heat of tears in her eyes. She was *trying* not to get expelled. The door opened behind her, and she heard footsteps on the flagstones of the hall.

"Ms. Isaacs." A voice that made her skin crawl sounded from the doorway and echoed down the corridor. "Clearly, you have not understood the gravity of your situation."

It was Dean Kwok. She stared at the chestnut tiles at her feet.

"You have compounded your troubles and those of the university with your unlawful acts of last night." His voice was controlled; was she the only one who could hear the fury? Now two other men had joined them; she felt their eyes on her back. They were all watching her, the big loser.

"This episode will be added to your docket at the Ad Board session," Kwok pronounced.

"Well, I'll try to make it," she mumbled.

"I'm sure your parents would appreciate your attending. They are quite concerned."

She spun around and glared at him. "You can't speak for my parents."

"No, I cannot, Ms. Isaacs," he replied, fixing a baleful gaze on her. "But I can speak *to* them, which I have. And, although they were understandably dismayed to learn of your run-ins with the police last month and this morning, they expressed gratitude that the university had taken the liberty of informing them."

Toni gawked at Dean Kwok, at the university men next to him, at Detective Rivera behind them. Her parents would kill her—if they didn't have heart attacks first. Everything she did ended in disaster.

"Your parents have accepted my suggestion that we discuss your situation before your Administrative Board appearance." Kwok nodded in response to her shocked expression. "I have responsibilities to parents and to the students themselves, Ms. Isaacs," he concluded without a hint of irony. "There are certain matters that we cannot, in good conscience, keep private."

Without a word, Toni turned around and raced across the foyer, pounding down the stairs two at a time.

/ / /

In the early hours of the morning, Toni flicked off the microfiche machine, which hummed into silence, and rubbed her eyes. She'd spent the past several hours at the *Crimson,* scanning through forgotten events chronicled in the back issues.

Her discoveries had made Kwok her enemy, which was too bad, since from what Chelo told her after dinner, the dean was just a client, not the ringleader. She had turned over a rock, and he was the first bug to crawl out. That Dora or someone else had sent him tapes of himself having sex with a student—presumably to blackmail him—explained his sensitivity to her investigation. Now his animosity had shifted to her. It was one of the laws of the jungle: you attacked whom you could. He had no power over the university or the Class Ring escort service, but he had a lot of power over Antonia Isaacs.

What puzzled her was the presence of the other man in Kwok's office. A quick check had verified her guess that he was Philip van Rensselaer, a member of the Portfolio. She'd assumed that Kwok had called him in that afternoon to help nail her, but after spending half the night reviewing Harvard's administrative history, she wasn't so sure.

Like most students, Toni had only the vaguest notion what the Harvard Investment Portfolio Committee was, or did. The Portfolio was just part of the university; it was just *there*.

In fact, she'd just learned, the Portfolio was relatively young, having been created to oversee the university's endowment only four years before Toni entered Harvard. The microfiched *Crimson* articles from years past told of cutbacks in government research grants, low returns on university-owned securities, alumni fund-raising efforts that fell short, capital campaigns that needed financing. That Harvard, with its endowment of more than five billion dollars, needed more money seemed implausible to Toni. But, like most Americans', the university's desires outstripped its resources.

There was much controversy, it seemed, as to why Harvard's return on its endowment was lower than desired. Toni had found stories describing ad hoc budget committees, accompanied by pie charts of expenses and revenues and the occasional "open letter" signed by concerned faculty members—in short, the kind of story that she would normally skip, in favor of something more interesting. Yet the participants in those debates had been as emotional and convinced of the importance of their struggle as any contemporary student advocating the cause du jour.

E. Fenton Merrill '41 opined in one letter to the editor that Harvard had no business investing in anything but blue chips, Treasury bills, and land. Going on to rail against the Core Curriculum and "androgyne" students, he concluded with an untranslated remark in Latin.

Voices like Mr. Merrill's, however, seemed to have been drowned out convincingly by more gung-ho, entrepreneurial, risk-taking types.

One letter from a group of MBA candidates addressed the issue bluntly:

Instead of depending on writing grants, kissing up to alumni, raising tuition, and watching the markets leave us behind, Harvard should start making big bucks doing what we do best: being smart. In particular, the University needs to get involved more on the equity side, in start-up ventures using its own human capital and technology. . . .

In the end, the Portfolio was created and, like so many other heated political struggles at Harvard, the investment controversy was promptly forgotten. Toni wrote down the names of the students whose names appeared most frequently in stories about the Portfolio and who might be able to tell her more. Still, they were unlikely to know why Count Dracula van Rensselaer was so interested in her.

Reading these old newspapers was disheartening. She realized that in a few years, nothing of the present—no matter how assiduously chronicled—would be remembered. Kwok must know that. He could be confident that the daily routine would envelop his sins as surely as water closes over a sinking stone.

The sudden slamming of a door ended her rumination. Toni froze. A shoe squeaked on the linoleum floor.

She got up to see who it was. At this hour, it was probably a comper, mowing herself into the ground. "Who's there?" she called, trying to sound brisk and businesslike.

"Aren't you a little senior to be hanging out in the middle of the night?" a voice queried dryly.

Toni breathed a sigh of relief. "Lucius! What the hell are you doing here?"

He waved a folder. "Redoing my résumé. It's interview season, haven't you heard?" He was in rare casual dress, his jeans snug against his muscled form.

She tried to smile, but the effort yielded little success; her mouth quivered. Damn, she wasn't going to lose it in front of Lucius. "I've had a really shitty week," she mumbled.

He stepped forward and held out his broad arms with the self-assurance of a symphony conductor. She stiffened, then leaned toward him, the remembered security of his embrace too comforting to resist completely. He smelled clean, with a note of pine.

"It's okay," he murmured, and she closed her eyes, resting her face against his soft cashmere sweater and letting herself relax for the first time in days. After a few moments, they stepped apart and she told him everything, ending with a review of that upcoming disaster, her Ad Board appearance. He listened without once finishing a sentence for her. She couldn't help but notice how much more grown-up he seemed these days. He was a large, handsome man. He would knock them out in interviews.

"Looks like you've taken on all the powers that be at the same time," he commented.

"It wasn't intentional, I can assure you," she replied, then described what she'd been learning about the Portfolio.

"It was really controversial, you know," he said after she finished. "Kwok claimed it would steal the soul of the university."

Toni zeroed in on the name. "Kwok was involved?"

"Yes, but he *opposed* the creation of the Portfolio. He said that the university had to focus on education, not making money. 'No man shall have two masters,' that kind of thing. He was just a junior dean at that point, but ended up being the chief spokesman for a lot of more traditional faculty members—especially the ones who weren't in sciences and had no salable skills. He said there would be long-term drawbacks that no one could predict."

"But he lost."

"His faction was told to deal with reality—that if Harvard didn't run itself more like a business it would be left behind. So basically the Board of Overseers and the Corporation handed over all this power to the Portfolio."

"And that's who I ran into?"

Lucius nodded. "But van Rensselaer isn't even the chairman. There are three members. The chairman, the guy who orchestrates everything, is Gustavus Mims."

She said the first thing that struck her. "That's a strange name for—"

Lucius curled his lip mischievously. "For a white guy? Well, that's because he's black. Haven't you ever heard of Mims's Finest Hair Straightening Creme?"

Toni was surprised. "Him?"

Lucius nodded. "His great-grandmother invented it and invested wisely. You can bet *he* passes the paper bag test." Toni flushed. Lucius's family might be bourgie, but they were bush league compared to millionaires like Mims.

Lucius continued. "That episode pretty much ended Dean Kwok's advancement, you know. He hasn't been a power player for years. I'm surprised van Rensselaer bothered to show up."

A realization dawned on her. They—whoever "they" were—didn't care about Kwok at all. They must be after her. A story about Harvard students prostituting themselves was too big to get out. It would threaten the biggest asset of all: the Harvard name itself. "They're going to expunge me," she said bleakly.

Lucius shook his head. "You've got to look at it another way: if they feel threatened enough to Ad Board you, then they're taking you seriously. You've got some kind of power over them."

It sure didn't feel like it. "You think I should keep on going?" Toni asked, keeping her eyes on the desk. Five months ago she'd declared that his approval meant nothing to her anymore.

He smiled and, in a delicate, unhurried gesture, touched her hair. "Why do you think I was so crazy about you? The fighting was the part I liked best."

Toni looked up, and Lucius leaned down to kiss her. At the last moment she shifted, diverting his action into an awkward hug. This wasn't the time for kissing ex-boyfriends—a questionable idea under the best of circumstances. Her life was a mess; besides, there might be someone else now. She thought hard. She needed to discuss something with Chelo right away: a contingency plan. Dora, Kwok, the Portfolio—they had all been two steps ahead of her at every turn. Now she needed insurance against them.

20

Toni was the first to show up for the appointment at University Hall late Friday afternoon. Her parents, originally scheduled to arrive that morning, had been delayed by Detroit's evil weather vortex and were going directly from the airport to the meeting. Toni sat in Kwok's outer office, wishing that the snowstorm had enveloped the East Coast and closed Logan Airport as well. If she wasn't going to be able to see her parents before the meeting, would it be too much to ask for just one more snow day in her life?

It was only natural that Matilda Isaacs, pillar of the AME Church and president of Greenlake Parents for Better Schools, was outraged to hear that her daughter had been arrested. "Like any common woman of the town!" she had wailed on the telephone when Toni finally summoned the courage to call. Matilda Isaacs's upbringing in Barbados had instilled in her both a strong sense of pride and a sensitivity to humiliation that few who had grown up in the anonymity of American cities would likely appreciate. What Toni did fault her mother for was her unwillingness to listen.

Genteel whispering from Kwok's inner sanctum brought her

out of her musings. A young woman—a university attorney, Toni guessed—was being briefed on Toni's crimes. Riffling through one of the magazines piled on the coffee table, Toni looked idly at the shining pictures: happy consumers, movie stars roughing it on their twenty-room ranches in Jackson Hole. They failed to distract her.

The outer door opened suddenly, and Toni's mother swept in, wearing a tailored red suit. Her smooth, coffee-colored face was impassive; only the lines on her forehead and around her broad, elegant nose betrayed her mood. She looked coolly at Dean Kwok's secretary, who was efficiently moving small pieces of paper around the desk, and then crossed the room to her daughter.

Bestowing a tiny, dry kiss on Toni, she said, "Your father is using the men's room, girl." Toni heard the foreignness in her mother's voice, which only registered on her when strangers were present. Mrs. Isaacs dropped her voice. "We'll talk about this whole thing later over dinner."

Toni's heart sank. Her mother's impeccable grooming and dignified, icy bearing spoke volumes, though perhaps in a language only Toni understood. Matilda Isaacs was going to support her daughter valiantly in front of those who dared threaten her flesh and blood—Toni had never had a second's doubt about that—but she was already well into the role of Tragedy Queen. Toni felt like crying.

Kwok came out of his inner office and invited them both inside. Toni watched the two greet each other warily and with the utmost formality. "Perhaps you'd like coffee, Mrs. Isaacs?" he offered politely; just as politely, Mrs. Isaacs declined. He proffered a chair. "I'd like to wait for Mr. Isaacs before we begin our discussion, but we can get acquainted in the meantime." He waved a hand. "This is Ms. Anne Elliot, one of the university's able legal counsel." The woman smiled and inclined her head. "Anne is here," Kwok continued, "to ensure that everyone's interests are protected. I hope you have no objection?"

The question hung in the air. It was clear to Toni that the lawyer's job was to cover the university's ass, but none of these impeccably polite people was going to say that.

Toni heard the voice of Kwok's secretary float in from the anteroom, followed by her father's gruff thanks. Harlan Isaacs entered the

office in a gray pinstriped suit and fraternity tie and shook hands
with Kwok and Elliot. Before taking a seat, he gave Toni a quick hug
and a kiss on the top of her head. Her mood brightened instantly.

"Good. Now that you are here, Mr. Isaacs," said Kwok, "I believe
we can begin."

"Yes," said Matilda. "You can understand that we are vexed indeed by the charges made against our daughter." Her tone allowed no
room for confusion.

Battle of the British Accents, Toni thought. *Hong Kong versus Barbados in the center ring.*

"Dr. Kwok." Toni's father leaned forward and smiled. "I'm sure
there has been some kind of mistake. Toni's a good girl. Even if her
behavior was rash, I can't believe that she was involved in anything
criminal." She glanced from one man to another. Her father seemed
to be slowly melting the frosted personality in front of him. *Go, Dad!*

The dean sighed apologetically, avoiding eye contact with Toni. "I
only wish you were correct, Mr. Isaacs." He gestured to the young attorney, who handed him a thick folder. "As I told you, your daughter
was arrested and charged with prostitution."

"Criminal solicitation, actually," Anne Elliot clarified.

"Those charges were dropped!" said Toni. Her too-loud voice
rang painfully in her own ears.

"Yes. Your daughter," Kwok said, "seems to have found a sympathetic ear in the police department. However, the university has some
very strict guidelines for student behavior. The question of whether
this is conduct unbecoming to a Harvard student will be decided internally, by the university's system of justice."

"Do you mean she may be expelled?" Matilda looked aghast. Her
daughter's Ivy League education was one of the triumphs of her life.
Her own education had been acquired piecemeal over many long
years of study: first in Barbados; then in London, in a nursing school
affiliated with a charity hospital; then, finally, in the United States.
Toni remembered her junior high school years, when her mother
worked late each night on her master's degree in hospital administration. Even now that she was a university professor of nursing,
Matilda felt that she could have accomplished more. She had vowed
that Toni would have all the opportunities she never had.

"That is one possibility," Kwok allowed.

"Antonia!" Mrs. Isaacs could scarcely contain herself. "Please explain to Dr. Kwok why that is impossible."

Toni glanced at her father. His brow was furrowed, but he managed an encouraging smile. "Well, I certainly don't want to be expelled," she said. "My education is the most important part of my life." She waited a second to see if they bought this.

"Of course it is!" Matilda chimed in righteously.

Slightly more confident, Toni continued. "As I told you, Dean Kwok, I was researching a story for the *Crimson*. Perhaps my decision to pose as a call girl wasn't the best, but my motives were good." Though it was the truth, it sounded ridiculous and smarmy.

"That may be so," Kwok said. He made a little steeple with his fingers and leaned back in his chair. "But there is also the matter of your breaking into my Adams House office."

She waited for him to continue.

"Of course," he said in a flat tone, "nothing was taken."

Toni smiled tightly. She had a feeling he'd play it like this.

"Well, of course not!" Harlan Isaacs exclaimed with relief. He chuckled, exchanging glances with all three of them. "Toni's no thief. She probably just wanted to be Woodward and Bernstein—didn't you, honey?" He looked from Toni to the dean. "How about that, Dr. Kwok?" He laughed jovially.

Toni nodded, but felt a prick of embarrassment, not at what her father said, but at his whole posture before Dean Kwok—the Negro supplicant making light of problems, coaxing a smile out of the boss, overlooking every humiliation because a thick skin was the first requirement for survival. Kwok wasn't white, but it was the same tired scene. A wave of fierce, angry love for her father passed over her.

"The Administrative Board may be willing to put it down to a student prank," Kwok concluded. "Some disciplinary action would be necessary, but expulsion seems, shall we say, a tad extreme?"

Toni glanced at the smooth face of the university attorney; she clearly knew nothing. Obviously Kwok didn't want his own indiscretions trumpeted far and wide.

"Toni," the dean went on, "much depends on your attitude now. If you're willing to admit your wrongdoing and face up to the consequences—" He paused, then continued with a light staccato emphasis that only she would understand: "To bring this chapter to a close,

I can foresee a happy continuation of your Harvard career. Otherwise—" He shrugged his shoulders.

"You are very fair, Dean Kwok," Matilda was saying.

"Yes, I'm sure that Toni will take the high road," Harlan added.
"I know that she doesn't want to be expelled, and I'm sure that she's
sorry for the inconvenience she's caused."

Toni's thoughts accelerated. If she took a stand now, the Ad
Board would expel her. She wasn't eager to manage a Radio Shack or
a Wendy's like the other college dropouts she knew from high school.
If she let Kwok think he'd had his way, it would at least buy her some
time. She could continue her investigation—very discreetly—and
find a way to vindicate herself.

She hated to cave in but, as her father always said, sometimes
you had to take the harder right. "Yes," she said, hearing her voice fal-
ter. "I see what you mean. I hope the Administrative Board will be as
understanding as you've been, Dean Kwok. I'm going to concentrate
on my studies from here on in." Had that been too fake?

Kwok's beaming face, and the nods and smiles from Anne Elliot,
assured her that it had not. "Excellent, excellent," he said. "No hard
feelings, then." He rose from his desk, twinkling cordiality at the
Isaacs family. Anyone would have thought Toni had won a Rhodes
Scholarship, rather than almost being booted out of college.

The Isaacses stood up along with the dean. "So everything is settled, then?" Matilda asked.

"Not entirely," Kwok admitted. "The Administrative Board will
meet formally to decide your daughter's case. And, I must warn you,
her behavior had better be impeccable between now and then. But"—
he made a deprecating gesture—"I believe I have some influence in
that quarter."

"With the right attitude, one can achieve any altitude," Matilda
recited from her litany of peppy, up-by-your-own-bootstraps affirma-
tions. Toni cringed in spite of herself. Still, this was a far happier ending than she had anticipated.

"Yes, exactly," Kwok said. He ushered the family to the door. "I'm
so glad we were able to iron this out as friends." He took Toni's arm
in what looked like a kindly fashion; only she was aware of the tight-
ness of his grip. "I know your daughter won't disappoint us. Isn't that
right, Toni?"

"I'll try not to, Dean Kwok," she said. "I know how much it means to you to enjoy your relationships with students."

/ / /

Toni might have spent the rest of the day nursing her depressed, self-pitying mood—she could square off against crackhead deans and crazy B-school madams when required, but parental disapproval enfeebled her—except for an unexpected event. Chelo was waiting for her at Adams House, flourishing a thick stack of computer printouts and brimming with excitement and optimism, moods that had grown scarcer in their little dorm room over the past few weeks.

Chelo had made great strides in collecting information about Dr. Waxman's research. Toni had nearly forgotten about Dave Mantini's deceased former employer, so remote did Waxman now seem from her current troubles. Chelo explained how, with the aid of house tutor Carl Christianson, she had managed to hack into the university invoicing system. She had constructed an elaborate excuse about wanting a lab-assistant job in the biochem labs, and needing to know what sorts of materials they ordered on a regular basis so that she would seem familiar with the terminology during the interview. To avoid suspicion, she asked Carl for printouts from three or four years ago, around the time Waxman's last article was published. The purchases were predictable—except for eighteen cases of a material called DMSO.

"Secret Agent Chelo!" Impressed, Toni allowed a spark of excitement to ignite within her. "But tell me in English, please," she begged.

"Dimethyl sulfoxide. It's a topical penetration agent."

"Okay, tell me in Spanish, then."

Chelo laughed. "It's a chemical that penetrates the skin really rapidly. You could use it in an ointment. I've never heard of anyone using it in a lab—it's mostly for sports medicine. You know, when you strain a muscle and you rub that deep-heating stuff in."

Toni nodded.

"You can put any kind of medicine in it; then the medicine can be absorbed quickly. Through the skin." Chelo reminded her that Waxman's research on hormones had contributed to the treatment of an array of gynecological problems. Estrogen cream was an innovative, though expensive, therapy for menopausal symptoms. DMSO was important because the ointment worked faster than pills. Given that Waxman's last article discussed the application of her research to men, Chelo hypothesized that the penetrating agent could be used as an additive to a drug to treat prostate problems. "It would be lucrative," she reflected. "Proscar is one of the biggest pharmaceutical moneymakers of all time."

Toni knew what she might be getting at: perhaps Dave Mantini had been working on this with Waxman. And maybe this kind of drug was the product his and Dora's company, Biotecnica, was preparing to market.

"But what's the connection to the escort service?" Toni asked.

"Maybe there's some kind of internal political or scientific battle," Chelo answered. "Dave could have found out about Dora's other job, and used the evidence to discredit her at work. Maybe that's why he contacted you."

Toni thought back to her conversation with the two biochem grad students. "Maybe he's just another disgruntled worker who's obsessed with the success of his colleagues. A conspiracy theorist. Or maybe he's just plain crazy."

"Crazy but smart," Chelo amended, presenting Toni with some abstracts about estrogen therapy and developments in prostate research, all of which were neatly marked with a yellow highlighter. "He's a real scientist, Toni. He's done cutting-edge research." She stretched, tossed her braid from side to side, and sat down at the desk, preparing to go back to work.

"The other grad students said he sold out," Toni mused from her seat on Chelo's bed. "Maybe they were just jealous that he got a good job."

"Nothing wrong with earning a living," Chelo remarked, as she opened her physics text and started the week's problem set.

/ / /

"There's nothing wrong with earning a livin'," Van's date told him that evening. "If you've got something other people want, why not make a dollar on it?" Emma ("Call me Em!") McChesney was a buyer for Neiman Marcus, in town from Dallas for the fashion designers' annual show. In the morning, she would be flying out to New York and the Seventh Avenue scene, but tonight, she wanted to unwind.

"So I called the number my friend Diane gave me, and I guess this was my lucky day!" Her slender face creased into a good-natured smile. Emma looked to be in her late thirties—which meant, of course, that she might be anywhere between twenty-eight and sixty. Her pastel suit and four-inch heels stood out in the dining room of the Mark and Sextant, though they would have passed unnoticed at a business lunch in Dallas.

"Don't you like your fish?" She gestured toward the grilled tuna Van had left untouched.

"Thank you, it's fine." He forced a smile. "I had a bite earlier. I guess I wasn't really fixing to eat. I'm sorry."

"No need to apologize, friend. And I hope you don't mind my questions. I'm just naturally curious. I'm sure that's no surprise to you, a fellow Texan."

He laughed, feeling himself ease into a better mood. He tended to lapse into old speech patterns when he was around Texans. "Of course I don't mind," he said.

She looked at him kindly, and he caught a flash of understanding in her alert green eyes. "Laugh while you can, right? Seize the day, that's my motto." Emma signaled to the waiter, who glided over with the check. "Speaking of which," she went on in a slightly lowered voice, "you and I have some business to get on with upstairs." She signed for the dinner, and the two headed for the elevators.

As the gilded glass cage climbed toward the twenty-seventh floor, Emma pulled an Hermès wallet out of her bag. "I suppose you want cash, honey." She drew a cream-colored envelope from the wallet and offered it to Van.

"Cash is always good." He started to put the envelope in his jacket pocket, then, with a hurried gesture, handed it back. "On second thought, you keep it."

"You're not going to bow out of our little arrangement?" Emma looked disappointed. The elevator chimed and the doors opened.

"No, no." Van's white teeth flashed in the first real smile of the evening as he extended his arm to hold the door for her. "Certainly not. It's on the house. Consider it my going-out-of-business sale."

The woman laughed. "I should be playing poker on a night like this." Van touched her arm lightly, enjoying the moment of friendly companionship.

Inside her suite, she offered him a drink. "Sure you don't want anything?" she called from the mini-bar. "I'm having a gin and tonic."

"No, thanks," he answered. He sat on the edge of the king-size bed to take off his shoes.

"No drink? That's unusual for a college man, I reckon. Particularly a Texan."

"I'm kind of in a 'body-as-temple' phase right now."

"Good for you! I must say, you have quite a temple there to protect. But what's this about going out of business?" Em called to him from the mini-bar, her voice carrying over the clink of ice in her drink. "Why, business must come to you like station wagons to a Wal-Mart. Such outstanding features—and the blond hair's an interesting look. Different, but it works for you."

"Thanks," answered Van. "I dyed it last night. I'm still not entirely sure why. Anyway, in answer to your question, all good things must come to an end."

Emma came into the bedroom, glass in hand. "Aren't you the busy bee?" she commented, gesturing at the condoms and lubricants Van had set out. "And you don't fool me for a second. Something's wrong. Good things don't have to come to an end. Not at your age." She looked at him appraisingly. "Doesn't your sweetie like what you do for a living?"

Van stared at her for a moment. "I'm not sure that I have a sweetie. Not anymore." He stood up and walked abruptly to the window.

"Broken heart, darlin'? I thought only you were allowed to do that." Emma set her glass on the table, switched out the light, and crossed to the window to join him.

After a moment of silence, she spoke. "It's beautiful, isn't it?"

Below them, the city sparkled. Cars raced one after another down the expressway, headlights glimmering.

"The first time I ever saw a city," said Emma, "I was fourteen years old. I couldn't believe anything could be so big. I got off the bus and started to cry like a baby; I just couldn't help myself. It seemed wonderful, that all these people could work together to make something so grand." She ran the pleat of the moiré curtain through her hand. "I still feel that way. Especially at night, when I'm flying over a city, and I see the lights down below me. All of those people, safe in their houses. Not thinking about me, or caring about me, but ready to go to sleep and get up in the morning. And maybe make something for me to buy or sell or eat or wear or read or listen to. Or not. But safe in their houses, all the same." After a moment of silence, she touched his arm lightly and walked toward the bed. "Know what I mean?"

Van stood at the window, the city lights blurring through his tears. This stranger was right. People depended on one another, and there had to be a way for them to work together. Especially people who loved each other. He was going to try again.

Emma's voice startled Van from his reverie. "Come lie down with me, friend," she said, patting the candlewick bedspread. "Your turn to tell me a bedtime story."

21

Toni exited the Harvard T stop and slunk along the street, praying she wouldn't run into anyone she knew. After a nightmare dinner with her parents at a fancy waterfront restaurant, she was two steps away from needing scream therapy. Against her will, the evening's events replayed themselves in her mind. Bouncing her nylon-clad legs against the overstuffed armchair as she waited for her parents in the hotel lobby, Toni had felt approximately six years old.

When the senior Isaacses turned up, the torture continued. Though relieved at the outcome of the meeting with Kwok, they were understandably disappointed in her. Matilda was her usual disapproving self, while Harlan offered an affecting performance as peacemaker. It would have been a lot easier, Toni imagined, if they had just locked her in a room and programmed her to become a good Stepford daughter. Luckily, tomorrow Harlan and Matilda were off to New York to visit an old frat buddy of Harlan's, and Toni could return to the safety of communicating with them via letters and phone calls.

Toni glanced up, narrowly missing a white punk with a spike of blue hair and a metal post through his tongue. "Watch where you're going, Martha Stewart," he lisped. Self-consciously, she checked her outfit. She was wearing the navy blue dress, conservative flats, and tiny pearl earrings she saved for fancy outings with them. Nerd clothes. She stifled a laugh. Dissed by a mall rat!

Just then she caught sight of a familiar Carhartt jacket and work boots crossing Mass. Ave. "Cabot!" she called, running after him. He must be heading back to Phillips Brooks House. For a second, she felt a rush of sympathy, and then affection. His situation made her parent problems look like a Sunday brunch.

He turned around and smiled brilliantly. "Hey, Toni!" She felt a strange closeness to him, the closeness from having confided so much in each other, the strangeness from having skipped several key steps in their friendship.

"Do you have time?" she asked. "I mean, to talk?"

"Sure." He gestured for her to walk with him to PBH.

They strolled in companionable silence across the frozen Yard. *"Mi casa es su casa,"* he said as he unlocked the door to PBH. "Well, it's not really *mi casa,* right? But I think I can find some coffee." He led her into the small room she had spent the night in previously. Calmer now, she noticed the details for the first time. The large leather sofa she'd slept on filled most of one wall; ancient velvet drapes covered the windows, shutting out all light.

"Welcome back to my lair," he said. He went over to a built-in cupboard and unlocked a drawer. Taking out a can of instant coffee, he turned to her with a flourish.

"All the comforts of home," Cabot joked. "Decaf okay?"

"Sure," she said. He went off in search of hot water, and Toni checked out the room. It really was like the secret hideout of every child's fantasy; the high ceilings and dentiled moldings made it seem like a room in a castle. She and Cabot could have been the only two people in the world.

She ran her fingers along the bookshelves in the corner, examining the titles he collected. Italo Calvino, Jane Austen, Chinua Achebe, Gabriel García Márquez, volume after volume of *Doonesbury,* a book of Hokusai prints. The perfect reading matter for a hermitage. Quite a difference from Lucius's collection, with his obligatory copy of *The*

Souls of Black Folk coexisting uneasily with *Thriving on Chaos* and *Getting to Yes*. Why did someone with such an agile mind fail to get in to Harvard? She looked up as Cabot returned, a steaming mug in each hand.

"There's a bag of Pepperidge Farm cookies on the mantel," he said. "Broken cookies from the outlet store. Still, just as good."

"Thanks, I'm full. The coffee will be fine." Actually, it was bitter and dusty tasting, but she sipped gratefully.

"Have a seat," Cabot invited, gesturing at the roomy couch. Toni curled up in a corner, slipping off her shoes.

"What's the trouble?" he asked.

She stretched her arms out and leaned back against the warm leather. "Dinner with my parents."

"Ow!" Cabot sat in the center of the couch and winced. "I bet they're not too happy with you just now."

She snuggled further into the couch, nestling her head against its arm. Cabot glanced over at her but then sat forward, his elbows on his knees. He nodded seriously.

"It's more the feeling that I'm alone," she explained. "Like I have nobody to turn to. They just don't understand what I'm going through; they can't, really. And I could never tell them."

"That must be rough," Cabot said. "I was never close enough to my parents to feel that I could turn to them. It must be hard for you to have that, then lose it."

She considered his answer. "I'm sorry."

He made a face. "Can't miss what you never had," he said.

She wasn't sure how to respond. She waited a moment. "It's obvious to them what I should do—protect the things that are really important: security, reputation, family . . ." She reached over and touched his shoulder. He gave a slight start. "I'm not so confident about this story, you know. 'Prostitution thrives at Harvard.' I'm not exactly making the world a better place by writing *that*. Maybe I've just put so much into it, I can't admit that I'm wrong."

"Or maybe you want to do the right thing, and most people have forgotten that there *is* a right thing to do," Cabot suggested, relaxing into the couch. He brought his hand up and gripped hers, which still rested on his shoulder. "You understand that instinct, but like most of us, you don't have enough experience to believe it's right."

Toni closed her eyes and let his words sink in. When she opened them, she found him gazing at her. "Can I impose on your hospitality a little more?" she asked.

"Anything."

The huskiness in his voice gave her pause, and she suddenly found herself wondering what she really wanted to ask.

Apparently speech was unnecessary. Cabot slid across the couch to her. She felt his arms wrap around her, at first gingerly, then firmly. She leaned into the warmth of his embrace, feeling the muscles of his back through his threadbare cotton sweatshirt. His hair had a light, sweet smell. The room was utterly still, their breathing the only sound.

They clung together for a moment; then he broke away. She looked at him questioningly. "Whatever you want, Toni," he murmured. She nodded, and he reached up and slipped off his glasses, folding them and setting them on the table beside her. She gave a tiny sigh as she leaned back for his kiss.

Their mouths met, sweetly at first, then more passionately. They kissed for a long time. It was like high school, the first time she realized a kiss could be pleasurable, a mutual exploration that could go on for hours.

But she wasn't in high school anymore, and a kiss, while wonderful in itself, was a prelude to other urgent matters. A moan caught in her throat as Cabot's hand slid into the neckline of her dress. His finger first brushed against her nipple, a deliberate accident, then touched it again, teasing. She gave herself over to his touch and then, her body warming quickly from the fast current of desire, she fumbled with the straps of her dress, eager to feel his hands and lips on her body.

He lowered his mouth to her neck and breasts, Toni arching her back in reaction. Ten, twenty minutes passed. At one point he looked up at her, smiled widely, lifted his body higher and kissed her deeply on the mouth.

"You realize this is—it's like a dream come true," he whispered. "I've—I've imagined this before." He paused. "More than once."

Tenderness and desire coursed through Toni's body. "Really?" she whispered, moving her fingers through his hair.

Trembling, his cool hands moved over her smooth, warm flesh. She fumbled at his zipper, but he set her hand aside. "Just lie back," he whispered. "Let me take care of you."

Toni pressed her face against Cabot's shoulder, holding on to his neck with one arm. She felt her dress move up her legs, his hands on the back of her thighs, then grasping her buttocks through a lining of cotton. A moment later her panties were on the floor.

She felt herself tremble as he spread her legs apart with hands that were surprisingly firm. She closed her eyes but at the same time imagined him looking down at her. A moment later he was kneeling on the floor, his tongue exploring her smooth thighs, moving steadily, unstoppably toward its target.

Tears formed in Toni's eyes and dripped onto his shirt as his mouth connected with her body. She felt his tongue move inside her and she clutched his shoulders hard, holding on for ballast while at the same time controlling his body to ensure that he wouldn't stop. She heard soft, ragged moans which, after a moment, she recognized as her own. As she approached the breaking point, she lost sense of where she was, though never of the man whose body was wrapped around her own.

A moment later, Cabot's face was next to hers. He whispered something in her ear that made her smile. She pulled on his shoulders and he covered the back of her neck with small kisses.

/ / /

In the still-dark early hours of the morning, Toni walked through the frosted Yard toward Adams House, her breath trailing behind her in an elongated, vaporous spiral. The last few hours had been remarkably exhilarating. She did have a romantic side, and it was already trumpeting the news of the bright, exciting future. That was just as well; soon enough, her cynical, practical side would weigh in with the observation that she had never had a white boyfriend before, and while they were on the subject, why had she picked the whitest man in the world to romance? Her mouth felt a little bruised from Cabot's kisses, and her tongue dry, still tasting of his terrible coffee. She let herself in the entry door and headed down into the tunnels to get a soda from the laundry-room machine.

As she passed the entrance to the pool, she noticed a puddle of thick, dark red liquid collecting at the edge of the tunnel's concrete floor. She gasped, but then the vinegary smell reached her nostrils: it was wine. Soft music and the rhythmic lapping of water came from the pool—some late-night partiers, no doubt. She started to move on down the hallway but came to a halt, overtaken by uneasiness.

She pushed open the heavy door to the pool and stood for a moment to get her bearings. The room was clouded with chlorine and humidity. A skin of moisture covered the tiled walls; air bubbles collected at the pool's deep end. "Hey," she called, "anyone still here?" The classical music coming from a small boom box in a dark window niche was the only response. She moved closer to the pool, hearing her steps resound in the room.

As she reached the edge of the pool, she saw something floating in the water and stepped back, startled. She leaned forward to take a closer look. The object came into clear view, and Toni screamed, the noise reverberating against the tile walls and boomeranging back at her. The lapping noise she had heard was the sound of a body bobbing over and over against the side of the pool. It floated as men do, back and buttocks visible, legs hanging below the greenish surface.

Panic rising in her, Toni drew closer to the floating body, forcing herself into action. The pale amber flesh was slightly discolored and contrasted strangely with the platinum-blond hair; she couldn't tell if the man was alive or dead. She squatted down and slid her hands into the warm water under his arms and grasped his smooth skin, quelling the urge to vomit. One of her hands lost its grip and the body slid back under water. Torquing under the force of her other hand, the body turned slowly onto its back. Rivulets of water flowed from the pectoral muscles back into the pool. The narrow hips and long, muscular legs began to sink again. The head bobbed on its side.

Dry heaves started rising in Toni's throat. This time no sound would come from her trembling mouth. The body in the water was Van's.

/ / /

Without thinking, Toni pulled off her shoes and stepped down into the pool. Water soaked through her pantyhose and weighed down the bottom of her dress. She waded through the heavy water toward Van and grasped him from underneath, locking her hands behind his neck and keeping his head out of the water. Blinking to clear the tears from her eyes, she dragged Van to the edge of the pool. She lifted his head and one of his shoulders to the side, heard the scraping noise as his skin touched the concrete lips of the pool and an awful knock as his head hit the floor. Getting him out would be awkward but not impossible; the water made his body buoyant. Toni took a deep breath and ducked all the way under the surface. The sleeves of her dress ballooned with air and the chlorinated water stung her eyes when she opened them to get her bearings. She placed a hand under the small of Van's back and between his shoulder blades and pushed as hard as she could. She let out a strangled sob; a big air bubble gurgled up to the surface. Starting to choke, she coiled her legs once more and then pushed as hard as she could.

Toni's head broke the surface. Hacking out the water she'd ingested, she coughed for air, grabbing the side of the pool for balance. Van's body rested precariously at the water's edge. "Don't move!" she implored as she pulled herself out of the pool. There was blood on her knee.

She straightened Van's body and, slipping her forearm under his neck, tipped his head to the side. The act was rewarded by a cascade of water from the side of his mouth. Was he still alive? He had to be. He *had* to be.

She worked two fingers into his mouth, brushing past his swollen, unnaturally white lips. His tongue felt like sandpaper against her fingers. How long had he been in the water? There was nothing trapped in his mouth, but he didn't seem to be breathing.

She looked from his mouth to his chest, uncertain exactly what she was supposed to do. Placing one palm over his chest, she pressed down with the other with powerful, short pumps. One, two, three, four, five, six. She waited several seconds. One, two, three, four, five, six. She turned to his mouth and righted his head.

Taking a deep breath, she fastened her lips to his and exhaled into his mouth until her lungs were empty. She repeated the action, ignoring the sandpapery feel of his white lips. Nothing. She returned to the heart massage. As she pumped his chest, her panic grew. She had never been trained in CPR or emergency assistance; she didn't know what she was doing. You could kill someone by not doing it right. She ran from the room, her wet garments chafing her skin, in search of anyone who could help.

22

The ambulance barreled out of Oxford Street and skittered onto Cambridge Street, sirens blaring, lights flashing red and blue. Inside, Toni was nearly thrown against the door. She tightened her bloodless grip on the safety strap and pulled herself back onto the bench. Back at Adams, when they were loading Van into the ambulance, the paramedics had warned her about the ride. They hadn't wanted her to come, but something in her face had made them relent. The younger one had shrugged. "Well, c'mon, then," he said in a thick Jamaican accent, motioning toward the open door. "Hop on up and hold tight."

Despite the jolting, Toni kept her eyes trained on Van's motionless form. His skin, a distressing shade of grayish blue, looked waxy and unreal. She couldn't tell if he was breathing. Occasionally she forgot to breathe herself, as if in sympathy, and the air would finally burst out of her in a loud, ragged gasp.

The paramedics crouched less than a foot away from her. The Jamaican sang out codes into a crackling radio, while both maneuvered smoothly above Van, as if engaged in some elaborate synchronized-swimming routine. They were performing CPR, of course: methodically pumping his heart and breathing into his lungs, a far cry from her own desperate, clunky efforts. She wondered again how long Van had been under. Weren't accident victims these days surviving longer and longer periods without breathing? Toni concentrated on their progress to the hospital. They passed Cambridge Rindge and Latin, the city's only public high school, where several youths in hooded sweatshirts practiced early-morning skateboarding off the cement ramps, and then the public library. Cambridge was a small city, for Christ's sake; why was it taking so damned long to get to the hospital?

As soon as the ambulance pulled into the circular driveway of Cambridge City Hospital, the doors flew open and the paramedics shot Van's stretcher to the back, shouting codes and figures at the knot of ER staff awaiting their arrival. Toni flattened herself against the ambulance wall, straining to catch any sign of life in the gray body that flew past her. Two aides caught the stretcher in midair, and the wheels dropped, hitting the asphalt with a thud.

"We're in cardiac arrest!" one of the paramedics shouted.

"Okay, folks." A young South Asian woman signaled the two aides to head in and ran alongside the stretcher, barking out commands. "Code blue. Let's go. *Stat!*"

In seconds Toni found herself alone on the wet pavement in front of the emergency room entrance. She stood silent, somewhat dazed but unexpectedly pleased by the feel of the cold rain against her face. She let out a deep sigh. They had made it to the hospital, and Van would be all right. He was Van, after all. He had survived war and hardship in Vietnam, the long trek to the sea, encounters with Thai pirates, months in a refugee camp, and God knew what else. A siren sounded in the distance. Toni blinked and looked around the parking lot. The rain was coming down hard. Van was certainly not going to end his life in an indoor swimming pool at Harvard. She shook her head and headed for the emergency room. Not here, not now. Not Van.

/ / /

The ER staffer on duty pointed the first police officer on the scene in Toni's direction.

"Excuse me, miss, but I'll need to ask you some questions

about—" The officer stopped, pencil poised over his pad, and regarded her. Hunched over in her chair, Toni continued to stare at the
floor. The officer cleared his throat. "Miss Isaacs?" he asked. "Adams
House, Harvard College?"

Toni nodded, tossing him an indifferent glance. "Ms.," she corrected. He looked vaguely familiar. She turned away.

"You were present at the scene of the accident with Mr.
N'Gooyen Van Men?"

Puzzled, she shook her head, but then realized he was trying to
say "Nguyen Van Minh," Van's full name. Stifling a smile, she recalled the first time they'd met, back when he was still Nguyen Van
Minh. It had been the spring of her freshman year. She had gone to
a party in the Quad, sponsored by the Black Students Association.
Most of the partygoers were black, but the person who seemed most
at ease—most joyful, really—was an attractive Asian guy. He was doing some version of the hustle with a senior woman, and he didn't
just dance—he radiated energy. Later, they had talked, and Toni was
surprised to discover that this *presence* was a freshman just like her. He
was a resident of Canaday Hall and a member of the "dorm crew"
that cleaned freshman bathrooms. "Canaday's like a prison," he had
said. "Can't wait till I get to Adams next year. You should try for
Adams, too." Toni had nodded dumbly, and taken his advice.

The policeman repeated his question, jarring Toni back to the
present. "Well, no," she explained. "I wasn't there. I found him afterward. I was the one who called the ambulance this morning."

"You get around, don't you?"

"Huh?" Toni looked up, startled. The policeman gave her a sour,
knowing look. Now she understood why he looked familiar. It was
Dobbs, her tormentor from the Cromwell Hotel incident. And he
couldn't resist reminding her.

Just then the attending surgeon emerged from the ER, her face
carefully arranged to project neutral concern. Toni could read the
news as clearly as if Dr. Lalita Mukherjee had been wearing a black
robe and carrying a scythe. She groped for the seat behind her. Dr.
Mukherjee caught her arm and gently guided her down.

"I'm very sorry," she said, sounding as if she really meant it. She
sat down next to Toni. In her pale green scrubs and cap, she didn't

look much older than Toni herself. "Your friend didn't make it." Her voice, with its singsong Bengali lilt, made the news sound strangely hopeful.

Toni squinted, trying to make sense of the words. "Didn't make it." The paramedics and ER staff had acted so quickly, so purposefully. Surely that meant something. It didn't seem to make sense that they would rush Van to the hospital and work on him so hard if there had never been any hope of saving him.

She doubled over, the urge to vomit welling up again. Dr. Mukherjee placed one hand on her lower back and the other on her forehead. "Breathe slowly," she said. Toni took a few quavery gulps of air and let them out raggedly. *In—out. In—out.* Her head felt as if it might float right off her body. Gradually the pounding of her heart began to slow. "That's it," the doctor coaxed, "slow, deep breaths."

Several sets of footsteps clattered down the hospital corridor and stopped at the front desk. Toni heard the crackle of the police radio, then Dobbs murmuring something. The footsteps resumed, growing louder against the bare linoleum.

"Why did he die?" she managed to choke out. "I mean, what did Van die of?" Could she have averted Van's drowning in some way?

Dr. Mukherjee cleared her throat, but before she could reply, a man's voice cut her off. "That is none of your concern," he instructed Toni. "I'll take it from here." His tone was like the closing of a book.

Toni winced. She'd have known that voice anywhere. She looked up into the icy face of Sterling Kwok.

Kwok turned to the surgeon. "Why, hello, Lalita," he said, his mild smile exactly appropriate for the circumstances. "How's your dear mother?" It turned out he had been the doctor's freshman adviser.

With a squeeze of her shoulder, Dr. Mukherjee left Toni to join Kwok and several other men in the center of the lobby. Toni strained to catch what the doctor was saying to the cluster of men, but she spoke rapidly, her voice low, her head close to Kwok's ear.

Toni got up and took a step forward. What the hell. She was past caring what Kwok could do to her. Compared to Van's death, her college career seemed trivial. She could hear Dobbs reading his notes back to the doctor, droning on like the voice-over in a poorly dubbed foreign film. "The immediate cause of death appears to have been drowning. The body was unclothed at the time of discovery." Dr. Mukherjee nodded, and Dobbs continued. "We're in the process of asking some questions about the decedent's recent history. . . ."

Kwok noticed Toni and shot her a look that would have stunned an elephant. Dobbs glanced up and waved her forward. "No, it's okay. In fact, we would like to speak to you, Miss, er, Ms. Isaacs. You may be in a position to assist us."

Folding her arms tightly, Toni joined the group. Dr. Mukherjee asked if she could leave. "I really need to get back to the ER."

"Of course." Dobbs nodded. "Thank you, Doctor."

Dr. Mukherjee pressed Kwok's hand and then gave Toni a quick backward glance before hurrying down the corridor. Toni had never felt more alone.

As soon as the doctor was out of earshot, Kwok turned on Toni. "Well, Ms. Isaacs," he began, "it appears that Mr. Nguyen may have consumed significant quantities of drugs and alcohol prior to his death. Did he seem suicidal to you? Or was he simply irresponsible?"

Toni's mouth dropped. "What—" she sputtered. "Are you *serious*?" She looked from Kwok to Dobbs and then back again to Kwok. They certainly looked serious. No one said anything.

She tried a new tack. Turning to Dobbs, she adopted a conversational tone. *Let's pretend that you and Dean Kwok don't already think I'm a criminal and a loser.* "Could you tell me what happened, Officer Dobbs? Why do you believe that Van—that my friend was using drugs and alcohol?" She could see the lines of tension around Kwok's mouth, but he held his peace. He had to be feeling the heat: a student dead, on his watch. He, too, would find this situation horrific.

Toni found it difficult to concentrate. Her mind kept wandering back to Van. Had he been present, he would have lit up a cigarette and blown smoke into Kwok's pinched face. "Lighten up, Sterling," he would have taunted. "Any Vietnamese can tell you that tragedy is an inescapable part of life." He enjoyed the thought that others considered him a nihilist; he encouraged the belief. But what had Van really felt? Toni recalled his appearance that night at the Mardi Gras

Ball, his costume in disarray and his face almost haunted. His references over sake bombs to being in charge of his family.

Kwok broke in. "I'd appreciate an answer to my question, Ms. Isaacs. What do you know about Mr. Nguyen's drug habit?" He was pushing as hard as he dared, she imagined.

"He didn't have one," Toni said definitively. "Everyone knew that. He rarely even drank."

"I see," Kwok intoned. He turned to Dobbs. "Let's be sure to advise the medical examiner of this news."

Toni sucked her teeth. "You asked, I answered."

Dobbs assessed the situation, glancing from Kwok to Toni and rapidly calculating his own position. Kwok's mouth hardened in annoyance. Just then another uniform appeared at Dobbs's elbow and whispered something. Raising a brow, Dobbs turned to Toni. "Why don't you tell us who else was in the pool last night, Ms. Isaacs?"

"What?" Toni and Kwok blurted in unison.

Dobbs nodded. "We have reason to believe that the deceased wasn't alone."

"How?" Again Toni and Kwok spoke in concert.

"I'm not at liberty to say."

Of course, Toni thought. There was spilled wine—but no wine bottle. Someone must have taken it. Kwok regarded her as if examining a specimen. She met his gaze and held it. "I wasn't there until later," she said evenly, answering his unspoken question. "I didn't see anyone else."

"I think you're a bit confused about our roles here, Ms. Isaacs," Kwok said. He would have hit her if he could: so his expression told her, try as he might to control it. "We are trying to understand how a Harvard undergraduate managed to drown in his house pool."

"Well, so am I," Toni retorted. She had to get out of here. "If you believe that I'm trying to interfere with the investigation, then perhaps I should continue this discussion with the help of an attorney." She opened her bag and pulled out her thin reporter's notebook. "Let me start by making a few notes about this meeting." It surprised her to hear her own voice. Though a bit shaky, her tone was cool and polite. She felt like a third party, observing the scene from above.

Dobbs looked nervously at Kwok. Toni had found Van's body; she was a source for the police, and if she became hostile, it would be Dobbs's problem, not the university's. He clapped his hands together and made packing-up motions. "Ms. Isaacs is right, Dean Kwok. More questions now won't make much difference."

23

Chelo ripped down the notice from the fourth-floor wall and threw it on the floor. The husky policeman who had puffed his way up the stairs behind her watched silently and smiled sympathetically at the kid in the CalTech sweatshirt who accompanied her. The slender Asian boy stared back, his face closed and expressionless.

Chelo frowned as the officer cut through the yellow police tape that criss-crossed the door and removed the padlock placed there the morning Van died. DO NOT CROSS. POLICE LI read the tape, twisted on the dirty tile floor. She mouthed the words silently.

She had not been entirely surprised to be summoned to Kwok's office Sunday morning. The dean asked Chelo if, as chairperson of the Adams House Social Committee, she could meet Van's parents and his brother, Andy, at the airport and help them pack up his belongings. Chelo nodded silently. She waited for some words of concern from Kwok, but they didn't come.

Though Van had been here only thirty-six hours ago, Chelo felt they were opening a time capsule. Like many student living quarters, the room was moderately messy and moderately clean; neatly stacked books cheek by jowl with casually strewn-about clothes. The midafternoon sunlight flowed through the cupola window, giving life to swirling dust motes. Warhol and Wallys Chen posters from the Coop adorned the walls; a mini-fridge stood ready near the bed. A hooded Macintosh computer sat on the clean desk, waiting to be turned on and brought back to life. All in all, Van's room was somewhat spare in contrast to his sybaritic public persona. This did not surprise Chelo. Though he had projected perfectly a Eurotrash image—casual weekends in New York; summers spent painting in France—Chelo had already guessed that his income, like hers, was limited.

Chelo told the policeman she'd let him know when they were done packing. "Maybe we should put together all the boxes first," she suggested to Andy, wondering if she sounded inappropriately anal. Who gave a damn, really, what order they worked in? Van would probably have told them just to torch the place anyway. But Andy quietly began folding and taping.

Watching Andy, Chelo experienced the unsettling sensation of watching Van himself. That morning, when she'd met Van's parents and brother at Logan, she understood at once how vast the chasm was between his previous life and college. Mr. and Mrs. Nguyen, dressed in neat but shabby clothes, were tiny and frail. As they left the plane and stepped into the gate, they seemed lost, the way that immigrant parents so often did in public among powerful, bulky Americans. And behind them, sullenly dragging his feet to show his embarrassment at belonging to these pathetic foreign people, was a much taller and highly impatient teenager, Van's younger brother. In jeans and a sweatshirt, Andy Nguyen looked fully as American as his parents looked foreign.

Of course he seemed American, Chelo thought. He must have been only a little kid when his family escaped from Vietnam.

The couple leaned over to their son—their only son now? Chelo wondered—and whispered something in Vietnamese. "I don't know!" he retorted in English, scowling in irritation. "What are you asking me for?" Chelo realized they were looking for her, the Harvard person who was to meet them at the airport. She scurried over, gritting her teeth in recognition at the boy's contemptuous tone; she used it with her own mother at Safeway or Pic N' Save.

Crowded into the back of a cab, the four of them were silent through most of the ride to Cambridge. Chelo, not much of a talker in new social situations, attempted a few innocuous questions about the flight, the weather, how old Andy was. He was eighteen, a freshman at CalTech, two years younger than Van. Had they been to Boston before? They hadn't, of course, just as Chelo's mother had never been. Travel was expensive.

Andy, who was drinking in the sights from the Charles River as they rushed along Storrow Drive, piped up unexpectedly to say he'd been thinking about coming to Harvard this summer. "Minh . . . I mean, my brother told me I should come to summer school. He said I'd like it, and it would help me if I wanted to transfer from CalTech. He was going to check on a scholarship. Of course he never did." He was silent for a moment and then remembered something. "We were going to share an apartment." His mouth tightened and he looked back out the window.

Chelo felt a pang and concentrated on the road ahead. She hadn't even known Van had a brother.

Mrs. Nguyen picked through her coin purse as soon as the dilapidated and undoubtedly overpriced Harvard Square hotel came into sight. Chelo quickly grabbed a twenty from her pocket and pushed it through the plastic device that was the only means of human contact with the driver in front. There were protests in Vietnamese.

"It's okay, it's okay," Chelo insisted. "Andy, please explain to them that the school gave me the cab fare." Andy automatically translated.

Chelo discerned relief on Mrs. Nguyen's face. The older woman looked exhausted.

Chelo couldn't bear the thought of the Nguyens having to pack up and catalogue a university life they had known nothing about. Better for them simply to receive the relics of Van's life and decide for themselves in what context they should be remembered. "And tell your parents that I'm going to pack everything up," she instructed Andy. "So they should just rest, okay?"

Van's family exchanged many sentences in Vietnamese. Mr. Nguyen nodded calmly, took a breath, and said, "Thank you," in a heavy accent, bowing his head slightly. Like his wife, he had dark rings under his eyes.

"I told them I would go help you carry things." Andy cast an embarrassed but determined look at Chelo.

She was grateful; she realized that he knew, of course, that Harvard had not given her money for the cab ride.

It took hours to fill the boxes, methodically separating the accumulation of Van's life into piles of either memorabilia or garbage. Andy rarely spoke, except to make occasional comments about the items he was packing. "Man, how many clothes did Van *have*?" Chelo heard him say from the closet. She was clearing the desk and found herself lingering over papers, envelopes, assignments, anything with Van's all-too-human script on it. She pulled a soft, leather-covered folio from one of the drawers.

"What's this supposed to be for? Um . . . Chelo?" Chelo looked up, startled. Before her stood Van, ready for the winter formal. But of course it was Andy, holding up the white silk brocade jacket Van had bought for thirty-five dollars at Keezer's.

"I think that would look really good on you," she said idiotically. But it was true. Andy even stood at a tilt, the way Van had. But he smirked and rolled his eyes as if there were no point in even answering, and Chelo remembered he was just eighteen.

She looked down at the first page of the bound book in her hands. In Van's quick but elegant European penmanship were a quote in Vietnamese and one in French. And then a simple sentence in English: "For my one and only."

She turned the page and felt her pulse quicken; she had seen something like this before.

It was Van's diary. Not the one for Professor Moore's class. This was his own.

6/21   Thank God I got a job in Cambridge this summer.
       Classes ended a few weeks ago and, much as I hate to admit it, I'm in the habit of writing this journal now. Stuck, I guess. Funny that everything I wrote before was in first person, since it seems everything I write ought to be intended for you. And everything I do, and everything I am.
       Don't worry, my dear one—I'll still respect your privacy and use utmost discretion, even as I want to shout from the rooftops. We all have our little quirks, no? No one has to know about us, except us, right?
       Someday, not far off, I'll give this to you and watch your face as you read about yourself. My little gift to you, X.
       And in the meantime, I'll do my best in other ways. Your friend, your lover, your partner in crime. I'd be your slave if that were the price of watching you breathe while you sleep.

Chelo flipped through the pages. There were scores of entries.
"Clothes are done," Andy announced, shutting the closet door. "I'll do the bookshelf by the bed now."
Chelo casually closed the diary and reached for another handful of material from the drawer. She waited until his back was turned, then slid the diary into her lap. Leaning down, she fumbled with her bookbag as if searching for something and slipped the journal into the bag.
She wondered what was coming over her. She was relieved when Andy turned on the boom box in the corner and picked a tape from Van's collection. "Tell me if you like this," he said. "My parents listen to this stuff all the time. It's French songs that were popular in Vietnam."
"It's beautiful," she said as the tape began to play. Andy, too, was dawdling, looking at books, turning them over in his hands. He opened a scrapbook. She looked away, not wanting him to feel self-conscious. The desk was finished. There were now just a few odds and ends.
As she stood up, she realized she hadn't heard a sound from Andy

in several moments, just the music. He sat on the bed, reading a blue plastic–covered essay he must have found on one of Van's shelves. Chelo hesitated a moment, then joined him on the bed, and Andy handed it over: "Mangoes in Summertime." Van must have written it for his freshman expository writing class. Chelo hesitantly paged through the essay, not sure if she was supposed to read it.

"It's all about Vietnam," Andy mused, wistfully. "Minh loved mangoes. He always complained that you couldn't find the right kind in the States." He shrugged, as if to dismiss the topic. "I don't know anything about that."

"It must have been very sad for him to leave Vietnam."

Andy snorted lightly at this, though his expression was sweet and almost indulgent. "Actually, he wanted to leave, even though he was only eleven at the time. It was tough for him there. That's what he wrote about in the essay." He laid a finger against the plastic folder on her lap and held it there for a moment before jerking it away.

The music filling the room was soft but compelling, with overrich harmony. *"Je veux qu'il revienne, car c'est lui qui j'aime,"* a woman sang.

"We're all mixed blood, you know," Andy explained, turning to look at her. "My mom's dad was French. But Minh is the only one who really looked like he wasn't all Vietnamese. His features are kind of unusual, you know?"

Chelo nodded, suspecting that she and the rest of Harvard saw Van in a different light than his family and compatriots.

"Van got razzed a lot growing up in Saigon," Andy continued. "People made fun of him, insulted him. Over there, if you're 'Amerasian' "—he made exaggerated quotation gestures with his fingers—"everyone assumes your mother was a prostitute or something, disloyal to the country."

Andy stopped suddenly and reddened, conscious that Chelo was sitting next to him on the twin bed. He grabbed the blue folder and quickly flipped to the last page. "Here," he instructed. "Read this part."

Chelo read from the point Andy indicated.

That day Minh walked home from school at dusk. He enjoyed the feel of the late-afternoon breeze against the backs of his arms and

legs. Halfway into this daily journey, he heard a shout somewhere
behind him and almost instantly experienced a quick thud of pain
on his neck; something warm and wet oozed down his shoulder. It
was a mango skin, half rotted from the sun. He saw a couple of
young hoodlum types laughing over in an alley. "Half-breed," they
shouted as they ran away into the darkness. "American father,
Vietnamese used goods."

Chelo swallowed. Andy nodded, and she continued to read.

Minh had never felt the hatred of others in such a sharp way. He
was confused and wanted to explain to these miscreants that he
didn't have an American father, he was all Vietnamese. But he
could see as plain as day that his explanations would make no
difference.

His shoulders were shaking, so he squatted down in the dust
for a few moments and put his face in his hands, shutting his
eyes tightly. In the shadows further down the street a beggar child
of about the same age, dressed in rags, stood watching Minh.
Minh opened his eyes and saw this other boy looking at him. The
other boy was frail and extremely thin; his chest was slightly
concave, underdeveloped because of inadequate nutrition. The boy
looked at Minh innocently, eye to eye, in understanding. He was
definitely a half-breed, too. For a few painful seconds, Minh was
transfixed, for he saw himself in that beggar child.

He jumped to his feet and ran as fast as he could, his face
caked with dust and tears. That night, no matter how hard he
washed, Minh could not remove from himself the sickly
fragrance of mangoes. It stuck to him like the inescapable summer
heat.

Chelo was at a loss for words.

"I remember that day," Andy told her, staring in front of him, his
eyes out of focus. "My parents punished him really hard, because he
wouldn't tell them what happened."

"It sounds like he didn't have much of a childhood in Vietnam,"
Chelo said.

"Not here, neither," Andy replied, in his unexpected Texas twang. "When we came to Texas, Minh was responsible for the rest of us, even though he was only thirteen. We were in refugee camps for a couple of years. And when I started college this year, he sent me money for books. Told me not to bother our parents."

Chelo nodded, wondering how in the world Van had managed that.

"It just makes me feel so"—he fumbled for the right word—"so *stupid,* you know? That there are things about my own brother, this guy I shared a room with practically my whole life, that I don't even know. He never talked about any problems, and I never asked if he had any." Andy dropped his head into his hands.

"He'd stay up late every night studying, way past anyone else," Andy continued. "Not just schoolwork, but other things. Novels, dictionaries, magazines. I'd hear him in the bathroom practicing speaking with a Texas accent. He tried out for sports. He even got on the debate team. Did you know he was elected homecoming king? Do you know how unusual that is in Texas, for a Vietnamese guy to be homecoming king?" He searched her face for understanding. "People said he had become the perfect American.

"When he got into Harvard, he was so psyched. It was such a big relief for him. He said, 'Well, I showed them.' My family thought he meant the Americans. But he meant that he had showed the other Vietnamese—that they could never stop him from being happy."

Andy abruptly clammed up and busied himself with one of Van's scrapbooks. On the first page was a picture on a yellowing piece of newsprint, an old *Crimson* article that showed one of Harvard's new freshman tennis stars. Nguyen Van Minh, his tanned face sparkling and happy, stood in his tennis whites with his arms around team members.

Chelo looked up and saw that Andy's eyes were shut tight. His jaw was clenched and his chin quivered.

"Oh, God, Andy, I'm so sorry," she said, reaching an arm around his shaking shoulders. His body stiffened under the contact but did not move away. "I'm sorry. I'm sorry."

His eyes still closed, Andy tried to speak. "I have this picture at home." His voice cracked. "Minh sent it to me two years ago." Tears made their way down his cheeks as he stabbed toward the bookcase with his finger. "I have it right there, right next to my bed."

Suddenly, Andy broke into a loud, convulsive sob, doubling forward with the exertion. His crying was throaty and violent. It didn't match his soft hair and skin.

"I'm sorry," Chelo murmured again, but the sobbing boy didn't seem to hear her. She hugged him closer and leaned back until they were lying together on Van's bed. She could hear the catch in Andy's throat as he tried to master his tears. Finally, he managed to raise his head and look her full in the face. His breath was hot on her cheek. She knew what he was thinking: *Why? Why my brother?*

As if to answer his unspoken question, she bent down and kissed him on the lips. He froze, and then leaned suddenly into her, meeting her mouth and tongue.

Later, she tried to remember the exact sequence of events. Once the inhibition of touch fell, the rest followed quickly. As she might have expected, a jar of condoms sat on the lowest bookshelf next to the bed. She recalled the taste of Andy's mouth, his sweet-smelling hair, the feel of her hands against his smooth chest, the softness of his belly against hers. Contrary to popular belief, she wasn't a virgin—Johnny Espinosa had seen to that in eleventh grade—but she doubted she could ever be carefree about sex. Not until she finished med school, at least.

They lay quietly, Andy's head pillowed against her shoulder, until the sounds of students passing by Van's door brought them back to reality. Chelo was the first to break the silence.

"Maybe you want to be alone in your brother's room, Andy," she said. "I should get some work done, and you could finish up in here."

He looked sad, but also relieved. "Thank you, Chelo. I mean, not just for this"—he made a self-conscious gesture—"but for everything. You know, with my parents earlier. And thank you for being a good friend to Minh."

She kissed his forehead and left him lying on the bed, surrounded by the souvenirs of his brother's life. Outside the door, she pulled her blouse straight and paused for a minute. Then she headed down the stairs.

/ / /

"I realize that this is irregular," Aimee Milvain said to the man in front of her. "But it's absolutely essential that it be done before his family sees him." Still reeling from Van's death, she did not feel up to this kind of intrigue. But she knew she had to act quickly.

The mortician looked at the earnest girl in front of him, pondering the odd request. It was rare that any of his clients made requests at all.

"Well, miss," he began, "it's like this. While we do always make the effort to dress and groom the deceased in an appropriate manner, especially seeing as how there'll be an open viewing, trying to change the hair color could be overstepping the lines—"

"Please, let me explain," Aimee insisted, afraid her absurd scheme would fail. "He only recently dyed his hair blond anyway—it was just a joke!" She leaned forward and lowered her voice. "Listen, he was the pride and joy of his family. You can imagine how that is." She glanced up to assess his expression. "Let them see him as they remember him. If they see their son, their Vietnamese son, with blond hair, they'll think they'd lost him already. I know it's stupid, but surely you know these things mean a lot."

She handed him an envelope containing five hundred-dollar bills from her parents' account. Before he could protest, she thanked him. "For your trouble, please." Her parents would probably think she'd become a cokehead. It didn't matter.

"Well, I could get into big trouble, miss," he began in a dubious tone. "But . . ." He appeared to waver. "There's nothing wrong with trying to minimize the family's grief at a time like this. That's my job, after all." Aimee flashed him a grateful smile and headed for the door before he could change his mind. "And I guess his girlfriend might know best in a matter like this."

At the door she stopped. She considered letting the remark stand, but thought better of it. She said softly, "I wasn't actually his girlfriend. Just a friend who loved him very much."

"Well, maybe this is the right thing to do," the man said diplomatically, more to himself than to her.

Outside on the curb Aimee waited for the Watertown bus to take her back to Harvard Square. *I did the right thing,* she thought. *For once.*

24

The *Crimson*'s first in-depth coverage of Van's death appeared in a piece headlined "Drowning Death Ends Life Lived 'On the Edge.'" Published in the Tuesday edition of the paper, Milt Bach's article portrayed Van as an unstable young man destroyed by his own excesses:

> The late, great Andy Warhol never had the pleasure of meeting the late, great Nguyen Van Minh, but the pop artist might have been able to provide some valuable insights into the mysterious death of our campus's own pop hero. As a mere freshman, Van made it into the pages of *People* magazine (with a color photo to boot). He played on the tennis team here at Harvard, and—like the mighty Warhol—managed to surround himself with a seemingly inexhaustible supply of Beautiful People. But in interviews conducted with dozens of students and faculty members, one impression of the late student became unmistakably clear: in the days preceding his death, Nguyen Van Minh appeared increasingly erratic, impulsive, and desperate for attention of any kind.

The writer combined half-baked opinions from a dozen different students who barely knew Van to create a picture of a consummate hedonist, a pleasure seeker with mysterious sources of income and a taste for drugs and wild parties. University administrators were quoted on the need for troubled students to ask for help. Milt even threw in an obligatory banality by a peer counselor about how high levels of pressure could lead to substance abuse.

Perched upon her desk at the *Crimson,* Toni crumpled the page in her hand. Caught up in her own grief, she hadn't tuned in to the behind-the-scenes politicking that got Milt assigned the story. "Jesus!" she muttered, glowering. For a minute or so she savored the pure heat of her anger; after the past few days of numbness, it was unexpectedly revitalizing to feel anything.

She considered tracking Milt down and beating him to death with a shovel; she settled on writing a refutation instead. Smoothing out the crumpled article, she scissored it into one-line strips and taped them onto a sheet of notebook paper. Under each line she jotted one or two key words. She frowned. Ever since Dr. Mukherjee had broken the news outside the ER, a thought had been nagging at her. Not even a thought, really—just a feeling that something wasn't right. The autopsy had revealed the presence of a huge quantity of prescription barbiturates in Van's system, and that didn't fit the Van she had known.

Toni drummed her pencil against the desk. The more she thought about it, the more the feeling grew into suspicion. What if Van's death wasn't drug related at all? What if the drugs were a plant to make the police believe it was an accident? It was possible. After all, someone else had been at the pool.

/ / /

Chelo listened to her roommate's suspicions with a sense of dawning dread. "I'll be right back." She hurried into her room and closed the door. After a few deep breaths, she picked up her backpack and pulled out Van's diary. Her heart skipped a beat. She had been carrying the diary around with her for the two days since that afternoon with Andy, but hadn't opened it again. Why? She'd had no problem racing through the sex diaries she'd purloined from her boss's office. But

Van was dead, and half the campus seemed to be engaged in a revisionist campaign of character assassination. Staying away from his diary, she'd imagined, was a way of respecting his memory.

But maybe that wasn't the real reason, she admitted now, as she turned the volume in her hands and traced the gold lettering on the cover with her index finger. What, exactly, had she been protecting—the purity of Van's memory or the insulated world she'd created for herself at college?

Opening the door, she marched out to the common room and dropped the volume in Toni's lap. Toni looked surprised. "Open it," Chelo instructed. Toni obeyed, turning to the first page and reading the inscription penned in Van's neat, European-style lettering: "To my one and only. June 14." She whistled. "This—this is Van's?"

Chelo nodded. "Don't ask, just read." She pulled up a stool and crouched next to her. Toni regarded her silently and then took her hand. Chelo returned the pressure, feeling a burden beginning to lift. Together they turned to the second page.

"X is his lover," Chelo explained a little awkwardly. "A man—Van didn't want to use his name or even his real initial." Toni nodded, not asking how Chelo knew. They read on, gradually, irresistibly falling into Van's interior world.

7/4   X told me the other day that he was "infatuated by my aliveness and my willingness to reach for the limits of human experience." Well, I have to say I never exactly thought of my life that way, but it's kind of true. So many people live scared little lives. As he probably knows, there is a great advantage to coming from a Third World country—you see how arbitrary all concepts of social roles are in America, this place of wild hopes.

Then he asked me what I saw in him. I laughed and said his face and body. That sort of annoyed him, I guess, so I said I wasn't really sure. This is actually quite true. I don't know if I ever thought about it analytically before, since I've been so overwhelmed by the toxic cloud of infatuation. But here it is: I don't think that I care for him because he's exceptionally intelligent, even though he is, or because he's urbane and interesting, even though he is, or because he has a good body, even though he does. And let's face it, as far as sex goes, although he's an eager learner he's not the most skilled of lovers (though that will come in time, I'm sure).

The real reason I've fallen for X is that he sees into me. He knows who I am and who I'm not. I feel exposed when he looks at me with those intense eyes. I can't con him or impress him. But at the same time I know he sees into the part of me that is important. And I guess that's something I've always looked for.

7/28   Leticia just got back from her semester in Madrid and wanted to get together. I had an idea of what this might mean, so I thought I should mention it to X. You never really know if someone is the jealous type, and we hadn't directly addressed this delicate area of commitment. So I said to X that my friend Leticia, whom I'd slept with more than once the year before, was back in town and wanted to see me, presumably with friendly but ulterior motives. He seemed kind of amused by this statement. We were semi-secretly reconnoitering at Café Pamplona and under the table he took hold of my fingers and said, "Minh, what we have is between us. What either of us does with anyone else shouldn't affect our attachment. You're young and should experience what life offers. So catch up with your friend Leticia."

Did I mention that he's started calling me Minh? He says that I don't need to cover up my Vietnamese soul with an Anglicized nickname.

"Why do you think their relationship was secret?" Toni mused.
"I don't know," Chelo replied slowly. "I wondered."
"Well, what are the possibilities?" Toni ticked them off on her fingers. "He's married, or in the closet, or he's a tutor, professor, or administrator."

8/14   Aimee once told me that unhappy people write a lot because happy people always have something better to do than write. I guess I know why I haven't written much this summer. I can tell I'm pretty far gone. This afternoon I was in the basement of Thayer Hall, making some extra money proofreading one of the

"Let's Go" travel books. I was listening to the radio and I thought to myself, "Wow, Madonna is so deep. She really knows what love is like." This is probably not a good sign.

8/23   X has a decidedly kinky side, which took me some time to discover but which suits him in a certain way. I don't think he's had much experience with guys before, if any, but now that he has one available he's endlessly fascinated. The other day he asked me a series of questions, most of which I answered in the affirmative. (I'm embarrassed to say that I was embarrassed by my answers.) How old was I when I lost my virginity with a girl? Sixteen, I answered, at the Texas State Speech and Debate Tournament. How old was I when I lost my virginity with a guy? (Could you be more specific? I asked, and then he blushed and asked another question. I love the fact that I can make him blush.) Do I like anal sex? Well, it's kind of an acquired taste. Do I prefer top, bottom, active, passive? I hate those words, I said. What's the point of being a social pariah if you can't be free from restrictive labels? If you care about someone, you try to make each other happy when you make love. That's it. Had I ever been in a ménage à trois? Yes. With women or with other men? Um, both—I mean, all three possible combinations. Had I ever had sex with someone while someone else watched, the way they describe it in *Penthouse Forum*? No. Why not? Guess I never had the opportunity. But I have no philosophical objection.

X is so funny. It's interesting to watch him try to free himself, more or less successfully, from all the social conventions he's grown up with.

Chelo did a rapid mental calculation. All three possible combinations? She shifted in her seat, beginning to feel a little self-conscious. Knowing that someone was bisexual or gay was a bit different from reading about their sex life in intimate detail. Van was so honest about his sexuality, so . . . human, really. She went back to reading.

9/15   Oops. Checked my finances, and I seem to have spent more than I planned to this summer. What else is new. Looks like once

again I'll be red-dotted at registration. I can't imagine going
directly to grad school after graduating—I'm so sick of being short
of money all the time.

10/2   Yesterday I had an interesting conversation with Dora.

"Dora?" Toni almost shouted. "Do you think it could be the same
Dora?" It wasn't a common name, outside of Victorian novels.
"Did you ever see them together?" Chelo asked.
"No," Toni admitted. "But clearly there was a lot about Van I
didn't know."

It started out annoying. "Rumor has it you're involved, Van. How
come you don't tell anything to your best friend, Dora?" "I don't
kiss and tell," I told her, not mentioning the fact that she's far
from my (or anyone's) best friend. Anyway, unsuccessful in getting
any details out of me, she moved on to her current fave subject:
her sugar daddy, Pierre. Pierre is allegedly very rich and very
handsome. I believe the first (she's been flashing some rather
pricey-looking jewelry) but am somewhat skeptical of the second.
Dora's new bell-bottom look may be a fashion statement, but it
seems to limit her market potential for demi-prostitution. "Market
potential," ugh. I guess some of her B-school vocabulary is rubbing
off.

"It must be the same Dora," said Toni. "I knew there was more
to her involvement in this thing. What the hell was she doing with
Van?" She flipped the page.

10/4   I got a phone call from a woman who introduced herself as
"Mrs. Robinson." Ha, ha. She said that she'd heard from a friend
of mine, Dora, that I was a nice boy to get to know and would I
like to swing by the Cromwell Hotel that evening? She added she
was very generous. Total *weirdness*. But I have to say I was
intrigued, since as it happened at that very moment I was
balancing my checkbook and discovering how little money I
actually had. At the same time, I wondered what Dora has been
saying about me to the world.

10/7   Finally got hold of Dora to ask why she was pimping for
me with Mrs. Robinson or whoever. She was blasé. "Van, why do
you make your life unnecessarily difficult? Why throw away a
good opportunity?" And then she explained how this woman was a
wealthy Ukrainian-American cosmetics CEO with a taste for young
men. I told her the rumors were true about me being involved
with someone. Besides, it wasn't my style.

10/11   I've been thinking a bit about Mrs. Robinson's offer. I
finally remembered where I'd heard about her before—a squib in
Vanity Fair. She seemed a pleasant enough tycooness in the
interview, and her photo didn't look especially retouched. If I met
her socially and she had a pleasant disposition, I wouldn't rule out
sleeping with her. So if I would sleep with someone for free with
barely a second thought, why not do it for money?
     Life is full of little ironies. I went to get my mail after writing
the above comments. My only letter was one of those awful cheap
computer printout notices informing me I'd bounced not one, but
five checks, and there's a $13 service fee for each one.
     Damn.

10/21   I just reread these entries. What are you thinking, Van?
Thinking about hiring yourself out is one thing while you're single,
but am I not, after all, "in like" (or maybe more) with someone?
     Maybe I'm afraid of commitment (or afraid someone else is
not really committed to me), so I'm toying with these ideas to
sabotage the whole thing. I dunno. . . .

Toni and Chelo exchanged glances. "Dora, pimping again," Toni
said bitterly.
     "He's not going to do it," Chelo said, shaking her head. "He may
be broke, but he's not like Tara. He's strong."
     Toni shrugged. "Maybe."

11/2   Either the magic is over, or I've graduated to a higher level
of infatuation for X. I don't constantly fantasize about him
(anymore), I don't invent pretexts to call him, and I don't take

certain routes across campus in the hope of accidentally bumping into him.

But I feel comfortable, happy even. Is this security? Last night we had a late dinner in the city. When I woke up this morning I listened to the birds sing. Swear to God. That is scary.

When was the last time I spoke so effortlessly with someone? It feels like everything has come together for me. I can't quite believe it.

11/8   "For a man to gain material advantage from his sexuality is a form of social rebellion."

This is what X actually said to me. I was floored. Could someone be more in touch with his own sexuality than I? I've hardly thought so.

Here's the scenario. We were at his weekend place, reading the Sunday paper. So I rather gingerly broached the subject of Mrs. Robinson in a "Ha, ha, can you believe this?" way. He responded, "Well, why not, Minh, as long as you're safe?"

Then he added, "If you're expecting me to be jealous, I'm not. I already told you I can't be completely attached to you because of my other obligations and my image in the university, so I don't expect the same from you."

I didn't know if he expected me to be grateful or annoyed. But then he dusted his fingers across the back of my neck and said, "I'm crazy about you. You know that, don't you?"

And I forgot whatever I was going to say.

"Wow," Chelo said, "you were right. X was definitely someone on campus."

"Great," Toni said. "That narrows it down to any one of ten thousand people."

11/13   Friday I had the bad idea of staying in and studying when everyone was going out to Dada. I went to squeaky-floored Lamont and tried to absorb Heidegger, along with the other non–life forms studying there. But I found myself spending most of the evening staring at decade-old graffiti ("Free the Bound Periodicals" was my favorite).

Came home around ten and played through my messages, all the trivial people I know and love. Then the phone rang. I let the machine answer it. "Van," it began, "I'm in town again and your friend Dora insisted I call again." I grabbed the phone.

"Yes?" I said. I knew it was Mrs. Robinson.

"Oh, I thought you were out, Van!" She seemed startled but excited. "I-I just finished my last meeting and assumed you'd be out doing whatever you do, but thought I'd try my luck . . ."

And just like that I agreed to meet her at the Cromwell an hour later.

The rest was oddly simple and rather predictable, as if I were following a script written by someone else. I showered, changed into a dinner jacket and bow tie (might as well have some professional pride, I thought), and then knocked sharply at the door of her suite.

An attractive woman answered the door. She wore a Chanel suit and apparently had just reapplied makeup. Younger than I expected, about 36 or 37.

"I'm Diane," she said, giving me a firm, businesslike handshake, as if closing a deal.

"No need to be so formal, Diane," I said as I leaned over to kiss her cheek.

Honestly, I don't know what came over me. Guess I've seen *Breakfast at Tiffany's* too many times.

She giggled for a second, but then closed her eyes and wrapped her arms around my neck and nestled her face against mine.

We talked a little bit but it didn't take us too long to end up on her bed. (She thoughtfully wiped off her lipstick before we kissed much—always a sign of a considerate woman.) "I hope you don't think I do this often," she said. "Really, I almost never do. There are some men who are interested in dating me, but I tell you, dating in my situation is so difficult."

I was leaning on my elbow next to her, tracing my fingers across her breasts. I leaned over and swirled my tongue around each nipple and let my other hand move down her side, letting my fingernails graze her skin. Then I climbed on top of her and pressed down against her hips with my body and held her face between my hands. She started to moan softly and tried to kiss me. For a moment, I wouldn't let her. "You're a beautiful woman, Diane." And I meant it.

Her face lit up. Radiant. Then she pulled my face down to her lips. It's weird that a mere compliment allows one to wield such power over another.

We made love slowly and rather tenderly. I kept wondering if I was proficient enough. But judging from her sighs and the flush that broke out across her chest when she came, my workmanlike effort was sufficient.

We stood at the door and kissed shyly but happily, as if we were fifteen years old and on our first date. Then I picked up the envelope and left.

I thought I would feel sordid. But instead I feel exactly as I did before, only $400 richer. It reminds me of the way I felt when I lost my virginity. I was glad to have done it, but I wondered, *What's the big deal? Why did I feel this would change my life?*

"But it did," Chelo whispered. She felt like crying. How could Van write about this as if it were just a pleasant experience? How could two of her friends—and how many others—have secretly been prostitutes? What was going on?

11/15   Told X about Mrs. Robinson, half-expecting him to blow up.

"Wasn't she in *Vanity Fair?*" was all he said.

I felt cross. "You could at least be jealous."

All of a sudden he was on me. "Did she do this?" he said, rubbing his hands on my chest. "Did you kiss her like this?" he asked, licking the lobe of my ear.

I laughed gratefully and rolled over onto the floor with him.

12/1   Since I met Mrs. Robinson, Dora has been giving me evil, knowing smiles. It's annoying. Thank God she's going far, far away for Christmas break.

12/12   My reputation is spreading, I assume as a result of the enthusiasm of friendly Diane. On a return trip to the Cromwell, she gave me an antique Chinese lighter. "Not that I approve of smoking," she said as she lit a Camel, "but you might as well do it in style." Then she said she had a friend who might be interested in meeting me.

"Whatever," I said with fake nonchalance, unsure how to answer.

Anyway, yesterday I got a call from another Diane, this one a brilliant and rather chatty young book editor from California staying at the Ritz Carlton.

I was surprised at how young this Diane was. Couldn't be more than 31 or so. She had good skin and perfect breasts and a nice ass and was very, very skilled in bed.

I wasn't sure if it was my role to say anything, but I asked, "Um, don't you have a regular boyfriend or something?"

She sighed and said, "Oh, Van, there are far more progressive and interesting women my age than progressive and interesting men. And the good ones have no time to invest in a relationship. I'd love a perfect romance, but in the meantime, if I may be crass, a lay like this will keep me going for a month."

12/15   Contrary to what I would have imagined, my life as a working boy more closely approximates being a shrink than a gigolo.

Last night I had a call from a certain "Frederick," an investment banker. X was in New Haven at some conference but said he promises to make up for his absence this weekend. "We'll do something to remember over Christmas break," he assured me.

Anyway, Frederick was your basic handsome yuppie but had unsure, darting eyes. He used to be married. He said that when he divorced his wife he thought he was in love with another woman, whom he planned to marry. Only after getting divorced did he realize he didn't much care for the second woman at all. What he was in love with was the thought of freedom. He said it didn't occur to him he was gay until he was 32.

"You've got to be kidding," I commented.

"No, really," he said. "Growing up I thought I was different but I never thought I was attracted to men."

Well, it takes all kinds, I guess. To me sexuality seems so overwhelming I don't see how you just couldn't notice something.

I felt sad for him, though. He says he doesn't know how to meet men. He grew attached to the long-term commitment aspect of marriage (even though he cheated) and is afraid he won't be able to find it.

I told him, "You'll find it, but the difficulty of being a sexual minority is that you won't find any clear role models. If you look for approval from others, you're bound to get screwed up. But if you trust yourself, you'll probably be fine. You seem like good husband material, regardless of the gender of your chosen one."

His eyes brimmed over with gratitude.

By virtue of tricking for money, I seem to be finding an incredibly intimate window into people's lives. It's a kind of responsibility.

"Uh, Toni, maybe we should stop," Chelo suggested. "I feel really weird reading about all this personal stuff. I don't think it's doing any—"

Toni held up her hand, her eyes still intent on the page. "No, wait, I think we're on to something here." She turned the page. "Yes, we are." She jabbed her finger at the entry dated January 11. "Take a look."

Out of the blue Dora came up to me and said, "Van, it would be a lot easier if your clients paid you the full amount and you just gave me the 30% agency fee."

"And what agency fee might you be referring to?" I asked, floored by her implication.

She laughed in her artificial way and said, "Come off it, Van—you're handsome, but connections like this don't just happen. There's overhead! Telephone charges! Marketing!"

I didn't know what to say. Of course, it seemed eminently logical that I would be part of some organized effort, some sort of service. It's unlikely that Dora would have so many horny, rich female friends. Most women don't even like her.

Told all this to X. He laughed. I wish he would be jealous. I'm tempted to push myself over the edge just to get a reaction from him.

2/6   As I was handing Dora her $120 cut, I grilled her about the structure of our little organization. She was closed-mouthed. At a certain point I realized she actually doesn't know. She just fields calls from a semi-friend of hers who tells her about clients. "For legal reasons" she won't give me the name.

"Dora was in it up to her neck," Toni said, her eyes blazing. "She may have fooled Van, but she doesn't fool me."

2/9   Had a big argument with my parents about my not moving back home after college. God, they're so dependent! It's time for them to get a grip on being in this country. Of course, I was consumed with shame afterwards. Related my traumatic story to X. Good to have a shoulder to cry on. This is why everyone wants a relationship—to have someone you can trust completely, someone with whom you can let go.

2/20   The goddamn lying bastard!!!
    Why is it you never know how much you care about someone until they fuck you over?
    Jesus, I'm so angry I can barely write. I was clenching the first pen so hard it broke and spurted blue ink all over my hand.
    Is this how you treat a lover?!! But I guess the word "lover" is a bit strong for you, because clearly I'm no more than a piece of flesh.
    You bastard.

2/23   Three days later. I'm really falling apart but I want to write down what's been happening. Historical value, whatever.
    I was having coffee with X in Back Bay last week. He seemed alternately distracted and lightly amused, as if waiting for the conversation to be through. Then we talked about other stupid things and somehow we got to the subject of this library book I said I'd return for him, and he said I had been irresponsible and not returned it on time, and I said yes I did, I turned it in on the evening of the sixteenth when it was due, right before I went to the Brattle, and he said I was lying because I didn't even go to the

Brattle that night, I went to Boston, to the Ritz no less, and I told
him he didn't know what he was talking about, and I was
wondering again what his problem was, that he always has to have
the last word about everything.

Then suddenly it hit me. "How do you know I went to the
Ritz that night?" I asked him. I'd never told him.

"Oh, well, I just determined, through logical means, that . . ."
Unable to finish his thought, he looked at me with a stupid little
smile, the kind a child has when he's caught in a lie and doesn't
know what to say. "I ran into that friend of yours, Dora, and she
told me."

I felt sick. It was one of those moments when you feel you're
about to topple over a cliff of unpleasant discovery. An awful
feeling.

"You *did* know I went there," I whispered. "And you know
what I did there." As soon as I spoke I knew it had to be true. All
the pieces fell together. "You know Dora, and you know that Dora
was the one who connected me with clients. And Dora knew I
might be available because . . ." I didn't want to finish but I had
to. "You didn't just *allow* me to sleep with strangers. You *arranged*
the whole thing. All along, that's what you were doing."

I was whispering, more out of astonishment than anything
else, astonishment that this was happening to me. *To me!*

He turned on the charm, but I could tell he was nervous.
"Minh, don't be angry, don't blow things out of proportion.
Remember, our relationship isn't about anyone or anything else.
Don't let conventional morality get in the way—"

I stood up from the table. Tears clogged my eyes and I could
barely see him. My throat was convulsing.

"Just know that I had my reasons," he insisted.

There was nothing else I wanted to know. I left.

2/24 Avoiding everyone. Felt really dysfunctional at the ball. Ran
into Didi, who tried to cheer me up. Didn't help much. Thought
about talking to Toni, who's been poking around on her own, but
what good would it do to involve yet another person in this mess?
I'll deal with it myself.

"Hey." Chelo put her arm around her roommate's shoulders and dabbed at her face with a tissue. Toni had begun to cry, the tears quivering dangerously over the pages of the diary. "It wasn't your fault. You couldn't have known. He didn't want you to know. People only saw what Van wanted them to see."

"But he should have been able to trust me." Toni shook her head. "He helped me; I should have been able to help him."

3/3   Found Dora at the B-school and tried to talk to her.

"Later, much," she said, and breezed right by.

I grabbed her arm. "We need to talk *now*, Dora," I said. I was pretty out there. I insisted we go to her room. I think she was afraid I was going to kill her. After about ten hours of grilling, she finally gave it up and spilled the beans.

I was right about X, the ring, everything.

3/4   Not talking to anyone.

He has his reasons. There are no reasons for what he's done. No reasons that could erase the past few weeks.

Not answering my phone. He's called several times. I can't talk to him.

3/5   God, someone tell me what to do. I don't know.

He came by yesterday. I was sitting at my desk staring at the wall when he knocked. Somehow I knew it was him. He'd never been to my room before. Privacy considerations and all.

I opened the door slightly.

"Yes?" I felt more tired than anything else.

"Can I come in? Minh, I need to speak with you."

A thousand rejoinders passed through my head. I noticed him shift from one leg to the other and realized I'd stared at him for 30 or 40 seconds without saying anything. I let him in.

He spoke nervously and quickly. His forehead was sweaty. It didn't become him. "I don't want to talk about how I got started in all this. Suffice it to say I have a limited income and enemies I need protection against. This service is a means of doing this."

Fuck you, I thought. *I don't care about your enemies or your friends, either. Your service has ripped out my heart.* But all I said was, "I don't want you to call me Minh anymore. Call me Van, like the rest of the world."

Funny, this made him shut up. His eyes seemed wounded. I watched the floor, so as not to look at him.

Then he said it.

"Minh . . . Minh, I love you. I love you and can't bear not to be with you."

This, he had never said before. These were the words I most feared and was always most desperate to hear. But still? Even now?

I was jolted, my effort to stay cool a failure. My chest filled with something—joy?—and I hated myself for feeling it. *Am I so easily bought?* I asked myself. I resisted looking up at those eyes, which could trap me forever.

He stepped forward and embraced my body. My arms hung at my sides, leaden. *Go away,* I thought. *Go away and take our past with you.* But I said nothing.

"I promise I'll make it right between us. I promise! But do you love me, Minh? Did you love me before? Could you love me again?"

I leaned my forehead hopelessly against his shoulder and he tightened his grip.

"Do you even have to ask?" I whispered.

3/6   I spend a great many hours developing different theories about how X and I can still have a relationship despite, essentially, our whole history together. In my manic moments, the most I can come up with is this: (1) X really loves me, something I didn't know before; and (2) our bond is unique and can't be compared with others. Sex between us is different from sex with other people. I thought it was okay that I was sleeping with other people, and sleeping with them for money, so the fact that he also had a role in it is not highly significant.

This, at least, is what I tell myself in my manic moments. I remind myself how happy one is to be loved, in whatever form.

Of course, most of the time I don't really believe this. What does love really mean in his strange mind? I love him; I've known that for a long time. But what does it mean?

A couple of clients who remember my number have called. I don't bother to answer the phone. The appeal of being a sexual counselor has worn off. The "agency," apparently, is no longer sending people to me. I guess that's the value of being close to management.

I find myself remarkably uninterested in the workings of this apparent prostitution ring, which for all I know may still be operating. I suppose there are other little sex workers who report to Dora, people who entered for businesslike reasons. She's not the type to mess around with a small-scale enterprise.

Toni's been working on a story about student prostitution and is causing a little bit of a problem with it. How brutally ironic, no? I told him not to worry, that I wouldn't inform her about his activities. And he doesn't have to worry about any more be-ins, or other embarrassments caused by me. Exposing him would make me lose the one thing of value I have.

Him.

3/8　Things are getting marginally better. I can't say I've forgiven him. But I don't think about it much anymore. I can live with that.

Didi Carón came by. He wanted advice, and a kiss goodnight. "I want to be like you," he told me. "You *don't* want to be like me." I started laughing, then saw I was hurting his feelings. "Baby, don't worry. Just go slow, and never forget who you are. You won't have to turn into a stereotype. I promise."

Chelo looked up anxiously at her roommate. "Was Didi involved with Van?" she asked, too quickly.

"Let's just keep going," Toni replied.

3/9　"Why haven't you been calling me?" I asked him, late last night. He turned away from me.

"What the hell is wrong with you?" I insisted. "A new beginning takes effort, you know."

He looked at me, almost indifferently. Then he spoke.

"We should see each other a bit less." This from the man who days before urged me to take him back.

I walked up to him until I stood over him in his chair. I held his chin with my hand. "You've really got a problem, you know that? You can't stand to be close to someone. Or maybe you just can't stand being close to me. To another man. Is that it?"

In that moment his eyes flashed with a look of pure hate.

"What is it about love?" I asked. "Do you like it? Do you hate it? Are you afraid of it?"

I was gripping his face hard. Suddenly I felt the wind go out of me. He had jumped out of the chair and pushed me up against the wall. My head throbbed with pain. His face was red and his breath labored, but still he did not talk.

"Do you feel better now?" I whispered. His eyes narrowed in anger again. "You do, I know. Pushing me means you're in control of something that's out of control. Why don't you just hit me again?" I saw excitement mix with his anger. Then I felt a hard, painful slap.

But before I left he held my face between his hands and kissed me tenderly.

3/10   It's all so transparent, I now see.

X cannot really accept loving me. This is a fundamental truth. Part of this is his inability to accept that he can love a man deeply, no matter what his pseudo-liberal public beliefs may be. And part of it is that he probably cannot accept loving anyone. Too much of a loss of control. As long as I was tricking with strangers (as long as I was a whore, in other words) he was in control.

It's only a matter of time before this affair ends. But I'm just as clueless now as I was a month ago about what I will do afterward. My life will end in some way when my relationship with him ends. My future is vacant. I see nothing ahead. There's just been no one else like him. I'll never feel this way for anyone else.

Too bad that the person who loves me is the same person who can never love me.

3/11   Talked to Didi again last night. He was concerned he'd led Toni on. Don't worry, I told him. She's been preoccupied with other matters.

Dyed my hair blond. Looks like shit.

Can barely read my handwriting. This is a mess.

Is this what a breakdown is like? I had a new thought today, thought that I would phone up all my

Chelo and Toni could not decipher the remaining sentences. The last few entries, undated, were written in a barely legible scrawl. The ink ran and sentences trailed unevenly up and down the sides of the pages.

After they managed to stop crying, Toni went to wash her face, and Chelo boiled water for tea. By the time Toni returned from the bathroom, she was all journalist. Snapping open her reporter's notebook, she plopped down on the sofa and reached for a pencil. "So," she said crisply. "Let's think. What do we know?"

Chelo handed her a mug and marveled at the transformation. "Well, we know that Van knew who ran the prostitution service."

"Yes, and that it was a university figure, suave and intelligent, with a reputation to maintain." Toni took a sip of tea. "That's probably why he killed him."

Chelo jumped, spilling milk on herself. "Killed? You're saying Van's lover *killed* him? Van's heart was broken, Toni. He was falling apart. It's possible that he committed—"

"*No he didn't!*" Toni bellowed, startling them both. "Van didn't commit suicide. He was murdered. And who else but his lover would do it?" Toni put down the mug and scribbled furiously. "X wanted to end the relationship and Van didn't. He knew Van could go to the police, and he needed him out of the way. He must have—I don't know—lured him into using drugs that night, the way he lured Van and Tara and God knows how many others into prostitution. You saw how Van felt—he was still in love, willing to do anything to keep the relationship alive."

Chelo nodded. "Maybe he loaded Van's drink. Or made it seem like they were both doing drugs."

"Right," Toni followed Chelo's line of thought, "and then he urged Van to go swimming—"

"—and left him to drown when he lost control."

"Bastard." Toni threw the notebook down on top of the diary. She took another sip of tea and then turned to Chelo. "So, who do you think it is?"

"I don't really know," Chelo said.

"You don't?" Toni asked. "Are you sure?"

"How could I know?" her roommate responded uneasily. "There's no clue, nothing specific, except for—" She shook her head. "No, Toni, it can't be—"

"It is, Chelo," Toni insisted. Chelo opened her mouth to protest, but Toni held up her hand. "Look at this entry," she said, proffering the diary. "He gave it away at the end. Think. It's got to be him."

25

Toni shaded her eyes with one hand as she scanned the rapidly filling lecture hall for an empty seat. Students in Professor Moore's Core class were, for the most part, aspiring yuppie bohemians who cut a dash in their charcoal turtlenecks and Italian leather jackets. Toni felt unkempt and slightly scruffy in comparison.

She spotted a vacant chair in the next-to-last row and moved toward it. Clutching her schoolbag tightly, she squeezed past the students already uncapping their Mont Blancs and checking the sound levels on their microcassette recorders.

Toni wedged herself into a splintery wooden seat just as the bells of Memorial Church tolled the hour. A wiry woman with frizzy hair—one of Moore's T.A.s, Toni guessed—stood at the front of the room unloading a carton of photocopies and lining them up neatly on the table. Other graduate students stood by, sipping coffee self-importantly, ready to hand out Moore's pearls of wisdom.

"Did you get the articles from last week?" Toni turned in the direction of the question and saw an eager freshman in an oversize sweater, her hair pulled back in tiny plastic barrettes.

"No, I wasn't here last week," said Toni. "How do you like the class?" The girl looked as out of place here as Toni felt.

"It's good." The young woman thought for a moment, then blurted out, "I don't understand a lot of the readings. I mean, what is deconstruction, anyway? And then people get up and ask these questions . . . it's like they're speaking some kind of secret code, and I don't know what they're talking about."

"They don't know what they're talking about, either," Toni said. "That's the secret."

The woman gave her a hesitant smile, and was about to reply when a hush fell over the room. Toni turned her attention to the front of the hall, where a confident, clean-cut Dayton Moore was striding to the lectern, coffee mug in hand.

"Stigmatization!" His rich voice rippled through the crowded room. "One of society's favorite means of control. Call me a name. Why not? It's easier than confronting me directly. I'm just a stupid broad—a damned queer—a cheap whore."

Moore surveyed the upturned faces before him, then took a perfectly timed sip of coffee. "Why are variations of the sexual norm stigmatized in our society? How does the social order reinforce our negative perceptions of people who are 'different'? If you recall the readings for this week"—he gestured for the first of his transparencies to appear on the screen overhead—"we have some rather different theories to consider."

Toni settled back, and listened with half an ear to Moore's well-crafted lecture. He had the students in the palm of his hand; she could hear the pre-meds clicking their four-color pens in unison as they tried to capture his major and supporting arguments in red and green. Other students—even the tragically hip, who almost never made an appearance on campus before noon—were poised in concentration. You had to admit, the man had charisma.

Forty minutes sped by. Toni found herself captivated by his words in spite of herself. She forced herself to remember her task. Why had she come, anyway? She had thought to confront Moore, to bring him down by revealing what she knew—with plenty of witnesses looking on.

Now it didn't seem like such a good idea. But she saw no alternative. There was no way she could go to the police with her theories; Kwok had seen to it that her credibility in that quarter was completely quashed.

Moore, having finished his lecture, stepped to the front of the stage and smiled. "Any questions?"

Hands shot into the air.

A petite redhead stood up and began a scarcely audible diatribe concerning Thomas Szasz. Toni waited impatiently. As soon as Moore had responded, she leaped to her feet.

"Professor Moore!" she shouted. Heads turned, and she was the target of dozens of looks. Another student, caught in mid-question, grumbled and sat down.

"Yes?" Moore took a few steps forward and peered up at his questioner.

"I'm interested in relating what you've just said to some hypothetical cases." Toni shivered as she realized what she was doing. At least she would be safe here, surrounded by two or three hundred of her peers.

"Let's say that someone was involved in a relationship," she went on, "but that he was uncomfortable with it. Perhaps it was a relationship that was socially stigmatized"—there, she had related it, at least peripherally, to the class—"maybe a same-sex relationship." She paused. "Or a relationship with someone from a different race or culture."

Moore smiled. "Ah, Ms. Isaacs of the *Crimson*," he said genially. Someone groaned loudly at the mention of the student paper. "So glad you could join us. You were saying?"

He didn't seem rattled, but Toni went on. "Someone who was involved in that kind of relationship would go to any length to cover it up, wouldn't they? I mean, that kind of stigmatized relationship." Toni was drawing some puzzled and disgruntled stares from her "classmates." Maybe this was a stupid plan, after all. It wasn't having any visible effect on Moore.

"Not *any* length, Ms. Isaacs."

"Oh, I think you'd be surprised, Professor Moore," said Toni. The other students were beginning to make their impatience audible; she clearly heard someone hissing at her from the back row. "I have some documents—some personal documents—which clearly indicate that this kind of thing is more than possible." More groans.

Moore took a quick step back, sloshing coffee into the lap of one of his grad students. "I know you're an able reporter and no doubt have a remarkable facility for finding personal documents, Ms. Isaacs." A flurry of whispers rose from the class; there were wry utterances of the phrase "Ad Board." A thin smile of triumph creased Moore's handsome features. "But I think we'd better move along for now."

Toni reluctantly sat back down. Her plan had been a total failure; she had revealed too much and had gotten nothing in return.

Moore took a few more perfunctory questions, then dismissed the class with a joke and a gesture. He was instantly obscured from Toni's view by the dozens of admirers who flocked around him. She took the opportunity to gather her things together and beat a hasty retreat. Trying not to catch the disapproving eyes of her fellow students, she walked quickly through the halls of Sever and out into the frozen Yard.

She was just trudging up the Widener steps when she heard Moore call her name.

Heads turned to watch the popular young professor sprinting down the asphalt walks. He took the steps two at a time and caught up to Toni.

"I want you to know that I got the point of your little demonstration just now," he said. Toni knew that this scene looked, to the casual passerby, like a charming student-teacher interaction; only the rage in his eyes betrayed his real emotions.

"I'm afraid I don't know what you're talking about, Professor," Toni answered.

He brought his face close to hers; she could see the warm cloud of his breath in the wintry air. "Don't fuck with me. Do you understand?"

"You don't frighten me," Toni lied. "I've got evidence. You'd better turn yourself in. I know you were having an affair with Nguyen Van Minh. And I know you were there when he died."

Moore reached out to grab her, then stopped as a group of students walked by. He moved closer, spitting angry words through a grotesque parody of a smile. "You don't know half the story. And who would believe you, anyway? You're in a lot of trouble. Need I remind you that I am a voting member of the Ad Board? Though that's the least of your problems." Unexpectedly, his hand brushed her cheek, lingering for a moment. "You'd better take care of yourself, my friend. And keep out of the grown-ups' business." He dropped his hand and started to walk down the steps.

"That's what you told Van, isn't it?" Toni improvised. "I read about it in his diary."

Moore stopped for a second, then turned and walked swiftly back. "You're bluffing, aren't you?" He studied her. "No, I don't believe you are. So Minh kept a diary? Give it to me."

Toni shrugged. "I don't have it on me."

"Don't play games."

She thought briefly. The outlines of her plan were becoming clearer. "I want something in return, Professor Moore."

Moore calculated this new information. "Fair enough," he said.

"Tell me what you know about the Class Ring escort service. About Dave Mantini, Dean Kwok, and all the rest. And don't *you* play games," she said, cutting off his protestations of ignorance. She hurried down the steps and joined the pack of students heading toward the river houses. "I'll be in touch," she hollered over her shoulder.

/ / /

Dayton Moore watched Toni Isaacs walk away. She imagined she was in control—well, in just a little while, nothing she could say would make any difference. This scenario had only one possible outcome: it would end with him as the winner.

He began the walk back to William James Hall, feeling that everything was finally in place. Once he had Van's diary, he would wrap up all the loose ends. Toni Isaacs wouldn't be a problem. Plenty of people had an interest in keeping her silent.

Back in his office, he closed the door, took his phone off the hook, and stared into space. He remembered the first day he had noticed Nguyen Van Minh. The young Vietnamese man had stood out even among the Eurochic throngs that filled his classroom.

When he read the first installment of the sex diaries—of course, he had sworn to the students that they were confidential, but he'd in-

structed his teaching assistants to code them so they could be identified in the event "counseling" was required—he had been flattered
and amused by Van's confession of a crush, and by his speculations
concerning Dayton's sexuality. The balance of power had shifted,
however, when Van came by his office one afternoon.

"Office hours are over," Dayton had said without looking up from
his desk. "Catch me next Tuesday at three."

"I was hoping to catch you now," answered a slightly raw baritone. Moore's gaze traveled upward, over a lithe cashmere-clad torso,
into a smiling face and deep brown eyes.

He felt slightly ill at ease, yet strangely excited. "Well, it seems
you've caught me. Now what are you going to do with me?"

"I thought coffee, for a start," the young man said. The professor
hesitated, but then closed his files and headed out the door with his
student.

That first afternoon had been magic. "Sometimes the first time
you meet somebody can be just like finding an old friend," Van had
said, lifting his eyes to Dayton's over the steaming froth of his cappuccino. "Don't you agree?"

"I guess I don't have much of a talent for friendship." He felt the
heat of Van's gaze and—he couldn't deny it—a strong attraction as
well.

"Oh, I think you do," the younger man said. He set his cup carefully in the saucer, then picked up his companion's hand and traced
a line in his palm. "See, right here. You have a very strong talent for
friendship."

"Anything else I need to know?" Dayton joked, dizzy with the
feeling of Van's hand in his.

"I think you've already guessed," Van said, softly.

The next morning, he had woken and hardly dared to breathe,
watching the golden body sleeping next to him. He thought back now
to the wild joy he had felt, the dawning hope that he had finally
found the love of his life—and the fear that had come with it.

/ / /

Peppy Tejano chords echoed in the stairwell outside their suite. Chelo
was at home. Though Toni hated to admit it, she was a little disap-

pointed. After her encounter with Moore, she needed some time to herself.

Chelo was sitting on the floor of their common room, surrounded by stacks of books. She looked up and waved a pad covered with penciled notes. "Toni, I think I've figured it out!"

"What do you mean?" she asked, hearing the tiredness in her voice.

For once, Chelo didn't notice her mood. "I was looking through the citations to Waxman's article again, and I came across this." Chelo shoved over a photocopied clipping in the elegant Palatino of a highbrow journal of politics and the arts. Toni scanned it quickly. A famous novelist, discussing his treatment for what was coyly referred to as a men's condition, graphically described some of the unanticipated side effects of his medications—including vastly increased sexual drive.

"I was like an animal," confessed the novelist. "Forty years slipped off my biological clock, and I was back to being the stud of Brighton Beach."

"I read some articles about these prostate treatments," Chelo explained. "They often had the 'unexpected benefit' of curing impotence, sometimes in men who hadn't been able to have any kind of sexual relations in years. Look at this article from the *New England Journal of Medicine.* The patient complained that he ended up with priapism"—Chelo giggled—"meaning that he had an erection all the time."

Toni smiled. "I'm sure it worked wonders for his professional life."

"Yes, especially since he was a Catholic priest."

They burst into peals of laughter. Chelo was the first to recover. "We shouldn't laugh, you know. I mean, after all, he must have felt terrible."

"I guess. But this guy"—Toni pointed to the magazine—"felt *goo-ood.*" She made a face.

"You see what I'm saying," Chelo said. "If this stuff can make enough of a difference in sick men that they write an article about it, or complain to their doctors—"

"Then healthy men would be willing to pay big money for it,"

Toni guessed. "That's gotta be it, then," she said excitedly. "Biotecnica's not researching prostate treatments. They're developing a sexual enhancement drug. Does that make sense?"

"There's no way to know, really, without seeing the product. But I'd guess Waxman's research paved the way to that kind of compound," Chelo said. "Did you read the rest of the description?" She held the photocopy away from her as if it smelled slightly putrid. " 'I became frenzied, like a boar in rut, snorting as the sweat poured off my body.' "

"That's not inconsistent with the Dean Kwok we saw on the video," Toni said. "If Biotecnica has a real sex drug, they'll be shoveling money into the bank."

"But how would Kwok get the Biotecnica drug? Or maybe it's a coincidence, and he has one of those conditions. . . ." Chelo trailed off. It didn't seem very likely that a healthy man of Kwok's age would need medication of that kind.

"From Dora, somehow." Toni thought for a minute. "Maybe she gave it to Class Ring's loyal customers, as an incentive." Dora was a madam, and Kwok was one of her customers; she worked at the company developing the sex drug, he acted like someone taking it. It couldn't be a coincidence.

"They must have given Kwok a free sample," she said.

"And a lot of other people, too," added Chelo.

"It's a great marketing idea, isn't it?" Toni observed. "Give the guys a pill that turns them into seventeen-year-olds again, they'll keep coming back for more." She shook her head.

"No, not a pill," said Chelo. "It's topical, a cream, a lubricant."

Toni clapped her hands. "The Veritas condoms!"

"What do you mean?"

"They're the drug delivery system," Toni said. "They must be."

"Wait!" Chelo raced to her bag and, for once, began digging through it recklessly, tossing items onto the floor. "Tara gave me these. She said they had to use them every time. These condoms, and no others. She got in trouble once for buying a box of Trojans when she ran out of these. Dora was really strict about it—Tara thought it was just concern about safer sex, you know." Triumphantly, Chelo held up a shining foil packet.

Toni crossed the room to look more closely. In its wrapper, the condom looked like any other upmarket prophylactic. The Veritas shield and serial number were the only identifying marks.

"Is this the only one you have?" asked Toni.

"No, she gave me a bunch of them." Chelo spread a sheet of white paper on her desk, then carefully tore open the condom packet and slipped its contents onto the pristine surface. The latex disc shimmered in a clear gel, which left a translucent stain on the paper. "Lubricant, I guess," said Chelo, nudging the condom with the end of a pen. "It could be in there. . . . The DMSO would help it absorb faster."

Toni looked at the shiny circle. "Is there any way we could find out if there's anything special here? Discreetly, I mean. Some way we could get the thing tested and not have everybody know our business."

"Maybe." Chelo thought for a second. "Maybe I could ask Carl Christianson."

Toni smiled. "Ah, the power of love. His, I mean. Seriously, though, ask him—and make sure the answer is yes."

/   /   /

Later that evening, Chelo led Toni down a series of hallways, through scuffed metal doors, and past blaze-orange biohazard stickers to Carl's lab, in a deserted corner of the science complex. "He dropped everything to do this," Chelo told Toni. "I said you were doing a special story about industrial espionage."

"I guess I am," said Toni. "I hadn't thought about it that way."

Chelo rapped at a door adorned with yellowing newspaper cartoons and clippings. "Carl?"

"Come in," said a faint voice. They pushed the door open and found themselves in a gray room lined with slate-topped lab benches holding a shiny array of unfamiliar equipment. There was a strong, bitter smell in the air. Carl set a pair of tweezers down carefully on a lab tray, extinguished a bunsen burner with a metal snuffer, took off his mask, and crossed the room toward them.

"Hey, Chelo. How's it going, Toni?" The women murmured their greetings.

"I've got your results," Carl went on. He gestured toward a stack of printouts and graph-paper pads on a nearby table. "Pull up a stool."

Toni and Chelo joined him around the table. "What is it?" Chelo asked.

"A hormone cocktail," said Carl, referring to his notes. "It's 5-alpha-androstenol, to be exact, with a dash of pure testosterone. It's combined with a synthetic yohimbine, and the whole mess is suspended in some kind of super-DMSO, which means it's absorbed almost on contact. I've never seen anything like it." He looked at their blank faces and went on. "It must be a sex drug. Definitely worth a little industrial espionage."

"Does it work?" Toni blurted.

"Who knows? You'd have to test it. But it seems to have amazing potential."

This had to be what Biotecnica was producing. "Would a company make a lot of money on something like this?" asked Toni.

"It depends what you mean by 'a lot,'" Carl answered. "Of course, almost every guy would want a boost like this. But you'd have to do a lot of testing to be sure it was safe. A *lot*. Let me show you something." He stood up and beckoned them to follow.

As they made their way down the darkened corridors, Carl hummed softly. He stopped in front of a door marked "Leon Kurtz" and pulled a huge, jangling ring of keys from his pocket. "Kurtz won't mind if I show you his office." He ushered the two women inside a small room crammed floor to ceiling with books, papers, and molecular models. "Take a look at this wall." Carl gestured at a rank of shelves that contained row after row of thick black binders, identical except for the neatly typed labels on the spines.

"U.S. Patent Office," Chelo read aloud. "Are all these Dr. Kurtz's drug patents?"

"Back-up data for the ones he filed before he came here," said Carl. "When he was working as an independent researcher. Once you're a member of the Harvard faculty, you have to go through the Office of Sponsored Research, and Harvard takes a cut. But Kurtz was pretty busy in the years he was working indy, as you can see."

"If he's patented all these drugs, why does he need a job as a professor?" Toni looked around the office. Compared to the postmodern splendors of the Biotecnica building, this was a dump. "I thought there was a lot of money involved."

"*If* the drug is marketable." Carl took a seat and gestured for them to do the same. "Kurtz has never been able to sell a patent to a major drug company, and there's no way he could bring something onto the market himself. It's not a simple process at all. There are endless clinical trials before the FDA even considers giving approval. It's an investment of millions and millions of dollars, and it's hard to get people to take a chance with that kind of money."

"What about start-up companies?" Chelo asked. "There seem to be dozens of them in Cambridge alone."

"Start-up and shut-down. You need a lucky break to make it in the pharmaceutical industry."

"So is every new drug company running on the edge?" Toni asked.

"Absolutely," Carl said. "There's a limited amount of venture capital available, and companies often compete for the same pool of funds. Several companies or university labs often try simultaneously to create the same product. They have to come up with positive results pretty quickly, or investors will move on to something else. Or worse—the company will have a product almost ready to launch, only to discover that a competitor has beaten them to it."

"So how can you tell if a company is about to make a big splash, or if it's years away from making its first dollar?" Toni asked.

"You can't," Carl replied. "That's all inside information. Unless there have been leaks to the financial press, you could only find out from someone who worked there."

Toni thought for a moment. She knew whom to ask what Biotecnica was really up to. The problem was finding him.

26

"He threatened to kill me, you know," Dave Mantini whispered, sliding into the booth next to his mother and snatching off his cap. "That's why I never showed up." As his shadow fell across the table, blocking the little light given off by the netted candle, the Harvard reporter glanced up and dropped her fork; it clattered against the plate.

"Shh!" he cautioned, glancing around the dim restaurant at the other dinner patrons. His mother looked worried.

"Sorry," Toni Isaacs stammered. "I had no idea you were coming. I hardly recognized you."

Good. Cutting his hair and shaving off his beard and mustache had been a smart idea. With the baseball cap, he must look like the other Italian men in the North End.

Toni had called his mother the night before, as she had several times in previous weeks, to keep her abreast of the investigation. Perhaps she suspected that his mother knew his whereabouts. Blanche held out the receiver so he could listen. This time the reporter claimed to have information about Professor Dayton Moore. Dave had listened hard, and when Toni asked to meet with Blanche, he nodded at her to accept. If Toni Isaacs was willing to publicize the illegal activities taking place at Biotecnica, it might finally be safe to come out of hiding. His nearly three weeks underground had worn him out.

"Who?" she was asking him. "Who tried to kill you?"

"That professor, Dayton Moore. He's a friend of Dora Givens."

Toni's eyes widened. He could see her making the connection. She stared at him, examining the cut next to his eye.

"He caught me by surprise at home," he explained, fingering the welt. "I wouldn't have thought he was that strong."

He'd been humiliated that day. Moore had laughed at him, told him he fought back just like a girl. It was clear that Moore had gotten off on slamming Dave against the wall.

"He must have been the one who broke into my room," Toni muttered. "He stole the photos I found in your mother's trash." She cast an embarrassed glance at Blanche, who was busying herself with her salad.

"Those were from Dora's desk," he said. "Maybe you should tell me what you know."

She took a sip of wine and then told him the whole story: a prostitution ring of Harvard students that used special condoms with some kind of sexual potency compound.

He clapped his hand against his head. "Jesus Christ!"

"Of course," she allowed, "you already knew a lot of this. You asked Professor Moore that question about prostitution at the movie screening."

"Huh?" Dave was confused. "My question to Moore was metaphorical. I meant that the university was prostituting itself. Selling its soul for financial gain. I didn't know the people in those photos were hookers."

"Oh." She appeared momentarily taken aback. "Well, I need your help to understand this, Dave. I feel so alone—except for my roommate, who never asked to be involved. These people know who I am, and they're trying to kick me out of school."

So he told her what he knew.

Biotecnica, Dave explained, was rushing a new product to market—something they'd been working on for years. He'd been in charge of one of the test protocols. "Then I found out that the data for the test protocols were being changed," he said, still angry.

"Why?"

"We knew the product worked in lab experiments," Dave said. "But something was wrong with the human trials. When the first round failed, there weren't any usable results to submit for FDA approval. Everyone was afraid we would never get to the point of selling the product. Then, about nine months ago, things started getting better. The data started to say what we hoped they'd say. Only, I figured out that the data were being corrupted."

"You mean they were false?" Toni asked.

He hunched forward. "Not false, exactly. Foreign. You could say they'd been imported from a different testing environment—not from our regimes. It's fake science." He was still outraged. "You can't just cobble together data from different studies. That proves nothing—no safety, no efficacy, no double-blind protocols. And it's illegal. I was ashamed to be associated with such people. I wanted to find out what was really going on.

"I figured out that it must be this Dora Givens who was substituting data. There was no reason for her to be hanging around the Floor at night—she had no understanding of science. All these business types care about is how much faster we can do it than the competition.

"It certainly never occurred to me that they'd use prostitutes." He stared at the beads of water collecting on the side of Toni's glass. "I assumed that they were testing the product overseas somewhere, maybe in the Third World, where you can pay the subjects less. Still, I knew that would be hard because of demographic differences—race, height and weight, smoking. Somehow they must have set up a testing regime with these clients of prostitutes. Maybe the clients didn't know."

"They had videos," Toni explained. "And customer-service forms for frequent clients. Height, weight, date of birth. They used numbered condoms."

"It's not a stupid plan," Dave admitted. "It couldn't prove anything verifiable, but it could give them a good idea of what worked. Then they could replicate those formulae in the rest of the study. It was a huge shortcut."

"Wouldn't it be dangerous?" she asked.

"Of course!" he answered. "All drugs are dangerous—that's why you need testing under controlled circumstances. Yohimbine is a vasodilator; in conjunction with testosterone compounds, it can put users at risk of stroke and heart attack."

"I'm lost," Toni said. "So Biotecnica invented something that included testosterone and yohim—"

"Biotecnica didn't invent anything!" he interrupted. "They based everything on Dr. Waxman's research! She was the first one to successfully synthesize supertestosterone. Before she died, Biotecnica and a lot of other private companies wooed her. But she always refused to join them, no matter how much money they offered. She loved the academic life. She was made for it. After Grinfast tanked, Biotecnica took her research and just added one thing: a sublimating agent they had discovered. It was more powerful than DMSO. They added it to the 5-alpha androstenol that Waxman developed, and came up with a sex drug."

Excited, he slapped the table; his mother shot him a warning look. "The thing I don't understand is why Dora hooked up with Moore. I saw them together outside the firm a couple of times and found out he had stock options. She must have brought him in, but why? Maybe they were old friends, and she wanted to cut him in for the initial public offering."

Now it was Toni's turn to get excited. She shook her head and gave a bitter laugh. "I know why," she said. "The sex diaries."

/ / /

Chelo sprang into action as a faraway church bell struck eight, signaling to the Biotecnica guard that it was time to open the doors for the night cleaning crew. Head down, she joined the last members of the group as they entered the building.

"*¡Híjole, hace tanto frío, apenas se puede creerlo!*" she exclaimed to one of the women. Instead of responding to Chelo's attempt to be one of the gang, the woman regarded her suspiciously. Though she looked about the same age as Chelo, she stood a good six inches shorter—and, tuning in to the chatter of the others, Chelo immediately realized her error. They were all Central American—Salvadoran and Guatemalan, probably—and her Mexican idioms had already set her apart as a stranger. They might now turn her in to the guard, who was muttering about hurrying up and not letting all the cold in.

"*¿Sabes qué?*" Chelo asked the woman, who'd turned away from her. "If I'd known it would be this cold tonight"—she continued in Spanish—"I never would have agreed to substitute for my cousin María. She hasn't been here very long, and my aunt wanted to make sure she didn't get fired." She stamped her feet and pretended great cold.

"*No te preocupes,*" the other woman responded. "No one's been here more than a few months. Just say you're her cousin. A lot of the girls work under other names, anyway."

"Oh, right," Chelo answered. Her own mother had done the same thing for a number of years before normalizing her immigrant status. "*¿Y cómo es?*" she asked. "And how is it?"

The woman shrugged. "It's work. You can wear *un Walkman* if you want."

Chelo followed the workers past the night receptionist, who took no notice of them, and down a set of concrete stairs to the basement. The women scurried over to a large metal board that held a number of time cards. Chelo was getting more nervous, but there was no way out now. The last two or three women pulled their time cards from the slot on the metal board, and as luck would have it, there were three left. Chelo quickly grabbed one and punched it, reminded of her part-time high school job as a checker at the Kmart on Olympic Boulevard. Before sticking it on the Out board, she checked the name: "Víctor Echeverría."

While the other women were busy selecting their equipment for the evening's work, Chelo took the opportunity to slip away to the rest room. After twenty minutes, she peeked out. The corridor was empty. She selected a cart and put on her Walkman, though she didn't press Play. Aimee Milvain had once told her that pretending to listen to music was a great way to prevent weirdos from trying to talk to you.

Chelo maneuvered her cart into a service elevator and pressed the button for the fifth floor, the highest. She'd work her way down.

/   /   /

Within forty minutes, Chelo was down to the second floor. At the first secretarial station she'd stopped at, ostensibly to empty the trash, she'd discovered an office directory. She hid it among the rolls of toilet paper at the end of the cart. Two departments seemed promising: the testing lab, on the fourth floor, and the strategy department, on two.

The testing lab was brightly lit and filled with people still working. She watched two of the other Latinas stand outside and wait to be buzzed through a series of interlocks by a security guard. This area was a no-go. She'd have to try Strategy.

Although the floors were still lit, their emptiness made them seem sinister, the fluorescent lights a poor counter to the blackness outside. Chelo rolled her cart down the wide hallways between the cubicles, looking straight ahead and smiling and nodding whenever she passed a human. The silence was broken by a few pockets of noise from people apparently oblivious to the fact that she was listening to them: two young analyst types playing Risk on a computer screen; a night secretary ordering a product from the Home Shopping Network; a man in his thirties furiously typing what appeared to be a screenplay.

Toward the rear of the room, a woman sat in her swivel chair and looked directly at Chelo from her cubicle. "What is this shit? What are you trying to pull, anyway?"

Chelo stepped back in alarm. The woman stood up and strode over to her, her face irate. Then Chelo saw that her eyes were elsewhere and a cord trailed down from her head: she was wearing a hands-free telephone headset and talking to someone else entirely. Reaching around her, the woman took a box of tissue from the cleaning cart and returned to her desk.

"You're saying you don't have the *resources* to deal with my feelings now? *Fuck* your resources."

Chelo licked her dry lips, the Spanish phrases she had intended to mumble if questioned long forgotten. She had been banking on the fact that most Americans expected little—good or bad—from non-English-speakers; she hadn't realized that the job itself would make her invisible. She backed away from the open door, not quite sure whether to feel relieved or insulted.

/ / /

The center of each floor was open, divided into prefab cubicles. The only actual offices were against the walls. Chelo explored the corridor of offices, reading the names on the doors. "Carl Mihaly, Vice President." "Stu Chang, Vice President." She checked the office directory.

This was it: they were both in Strategy. Light poured out of the next office. "Dora Givens, Vice President." Her knees turned to jelly; it was good she had a cart to push.

The office was empty, but a steaming cup sat on the desk, and the computer was running. Too dangerous. Dora might be back any second, and if anyone found Chelo out, it would be the suspicious, self-serving Ms. Givens. Chelo kept rolling.

She had worked in enough part-time jobs to know that paper accumulated. The only question was where. If Dora was at the epicenter of Biotecnica's scam operation, she must be near the source of the paper flow, too.

In the first of a set of conference rooms Chelo found nothing consequential. She picked up a few stray papers and tossed them into her recycling bin. They made her feel very credible. She began to hum.

She opened the door to the next conference room and was nearly knocked over by the stench emanating from several cartons of greasy Chinese food. *"Perdón,"* she whispered to the man sitting there. He didn't move, and she realized he had fallen asleep sitting up, his right hand still on his HP12C calculator. A pool of orange pectin sauce was leaking steadily from one of the cartons, eddying toward the man's flannel shirt. She shut the door in relief.

There were several more conference rooms. One had a white-board with various boxes connected by lines and arrows under the caption "Bacchus Roll-Out," but there was nothing more revealing than that.

She was beginning to think she had come up with a really stupid idea. Still, it was too early to give up. She continued humming and emptying trash cans. *"¿Basura?"* she called out as she rolled forward. "Gar-badch?" Twice, late-night workers ran up to her with friendly smiles, their green recycling bins in hand, and poured their paper in themselves. She smiled back. They were like a cheerful ad about the beauty of the multicultural workplace.

Chelo checked a storage room. There were office supplies; stacks of files; whiteboard easels with lots of markers; brochures about Biotecnica; a mini-refrigerator. She picked up a brochure. "Bacchus!" it said in fiery red letters. Chelo had read once that red stimulated the libido. She guessed the brochure's designer had read the same article. Although the phrase "prerelease mock-up" was emblazoned across the top, the brochure was expensively printed. She opened it and began reading.

> Bacchus, in Rome, and Dionysus, in Greece, were the gods of energy, power, passion. For generations, they served as symbols of the unexplored potential that the ancients knew could be summoned from every man. And today, Bacchus is no longer just a symbol.
> BACCHUS. The key to unlocking your full male virility.

Chelo's hand trembled. This was it. It had to be. Glancing over to make sure the door was still shut, she continued to read.

> BACCHUS condoms are the boldest breakthrough in medical science, biotechnology, and—dare we say—art that the world has seen in decades. BACCHUS is the first prophylactic that does not reduce sexual pleasure but actually *enhances* it!
> Some things must be experienced, rather than described.
> Consider these actual comments from those who have experienced BACCHUS:
> *"Euphoria." "Zest." "Beyond my wildest dreams."*
> *"Sensational! Adds a magnificent new dimension to lust."*
> BACCHUS. Unlock your potential, now.
> Available at pharmacies and drugstores.

Chelo began rifling through the rest of the boxes. "Diligence documents," one was labeled. Another consisted of hundreds of pages of computer printouts. "Trials," the label read. These had to be the data Mantini had told Toni about. She flipped through the printouts but could make no sense of them.

Finding a carousel projector, Chelo extracted a slide and held it against the ceiling light: some kind of bar chart. She yanked the whole wheel off the projector's moorings and set it on the bottom of the trash can, covering it with a litter of papers and soft-drink cans.

One of the display easels contained a flip chart; she riffled through it, and the first page sent an electric charge up her spine: " 'Sextasy' Presentation, 2/21." That must be what they called the sex drug internally, Sextasy. To the rest of the world, it would be Bacchus.

She read the captions on the rest of the pages: "Investor Relations." "Road Show." "FDA Approval." "Timeline." As far as she could tell, they were still in the testing period. The road show, whatever that was, was happening soon. But "Market Launch" was still three or four years away.

Chelo pulled off several pages and stuffed them in with her trash. For good measure, she added the contents of several more small trash cans. Coffee dribbled out of one. No matter; she'd blow-dry every page if she needed to.

/ / /

Back in the basement prep area, Chelo checked to make sure nobody was watching, then transferred the papers she had stolen into a plastic grocery bag. Three or more of these seemed essential for the well-accoutred cleaning lady.

Straightening up, she turned to go. As she approached the steel door leading outside, she was brought up short by a red-faced guard.

"What the hell do you think you're doing?" he challenged her.

Chelo checked behind her. No luck this time, he was talking to her. She stared at him for a moment, trying to figure out what answer she was supposed to give.

"Come on," the guard said. "Don't think I don't know what you're trying to pull."

Chelo felt her knees weaken. "I . . . I . . ."

"Hey, she new," someone responded from behind her. "She no know the rules." It was the short woman she had spoken with earlier. "Are you okay?" the woman asked in Spanish. "It's all right if you have to leave early. This *pendejo* is only trying to give you a hard time. You just need to punch out."

"*Gracias,*" Chelo said, noting the contrast between the woman's broken English and her fluid, confident Spanish. "*Hasta luego.*"

She grabbed Víctor Echeverría's time card and punched him out. She hoped he would be pleased with the four hours she had put in during his absence. Shielding her bags and their precious cargo from the guard's angry glare, Chelo walked out the door.

/ / /

This chick never sleeps, Toni thought as she watched Dora Givens across the carpeted expanse of the business school cafeteria. Toni wore jeans, a sweatshirt, and a baseball cap. Dora, on the other hand, looked ready for a job interview with the House of Dior.

Dora stood up, leaving her *Wall Street Journal* and a half-finished scone on the table; Toni rose from her own table and followed her toward the exit.

Dora clicked smartly down the hallway. "Great presentation today, Dor!" an overeager man with a receding hairline called out.

"Thanks," she answered flatly, neither stopping nor making eye contact with her admirer. She moved quickly and, without pausing, pivoted right and pushed through a door. Toni rushed down the hall and ducked in after her.

The ladies' room, clouded with perfume and anxiety, was filled with women putting on their faces and their accompanying interview attitudes. Dora wasn't among them. Toni walked into a stall, grabbed some tissue, and pretended to blow her nose. Out of the corner of her eye, she watched a woman in a blue suit trying to fix a huge white bow on her chest. The woman's shoulder-length hair and early-eighties look were a far cry from the Armani'd and DKNY'd matchsticks next to her who aimed eyeliner pencils at themselves and coldly evaluated their stark profiles in the mirror.

Toni exited the booth and busied herself washing her hands. The woman was on the verge of tears as she tugged her bow back and forth with no noticeable improvement. Wordlessly, one of her classmates buried a long fingernail in the center of the wide ribbon, undid it, and retied it.

"I can't do this," the bow-adorned one whispered. "I can't do another consulting interview."

"Who do you have?" DKNY asked.

"Booz."

"Don't sweat it," she said. "They gave forty-four offers last year."

"But I'm an engineer!" the woman wailed.

The other career waif shrugged. "Stick to Porter's five forces. You'll do fine."

With a grievous deep breath, the sad woman left the room, followed by the cool, thin success stories.

Toni squatted down and confirmed that she and Dora were now alone. She stood up and pulled an ancient pack of cigarettes from her bag. She located some matches and lit up. The cigarette was vile, but the illicit feeling was delicious: bad-girl-acting-cool. "I've got an extra if you want one, Dora."

The door to the closed stall banged open, and Dora emerged. "Smoking isn't p.c." She leaned over to scrub her hands. "Haven't you heard?"

"I don't care at this point," Toni replied. "My college experience may end pretty soon."

Dora yanked paper towels out of the wall dispenser. "Well, a Harvard education isn't for everyone." She reached to pull the door open.

Toni tossed her cigarette into the sink. "Don't be hasty, Dora. It's worth your while to hear me out. Professor Moore gave a good interview. Seems like the same old story to me: you do all the work, and he gets all the credit."

"Oh, really?" Dora asked casually. "He does like to hear himself talk. Still, I'll bet you're making it up."

"Making what up?" Toni asked. "The part about the prostitution ring, or the part about the doctored drug tests at Biotecnica?" Dora stiffened. "Or the part about murdering Van Nguyen? That's the subject I'm most interested in now."

Dora spun around and glared at her. "Then you listen to me, bitch." She spat the word. "I have never killed anyone, or had anything to do with that kind of shit."

Toni kept her mouth tightly locked. She forced herself not to move.

"You have nothing on me," Dora continued. "So I called the cops on you that night at the Cromwell. Who cares? Your conspiracy theories are as ridiculous as Dave Mantini's—and look what happened to him. His career is over."

"I had dinner with Dave Mantini last night." Toni watched Dora carefully for signs of surprise. "I guess you and Professor Moore did manage to scare him for a while. Still, he found a way to do the right thing." *He told me all about you.*

Her words did not have their intended effect. Instead of looking alarmed, Dora laughed. "That's great, Toni," she said, folding her arms comfortably in front of her. "You think Dave's done 'the right thing' and I've done 'the wrong thing.' You know, I keep forgetting you're an undergrad."

Toni hastened to regain the upper hand. "You don't seem to care that you've destroyed your company's integrity."

Dora stared at her, puzzled, and then laughed silently, shaking her head in condescension. "Integrity? Let me tell you about integrity. When I started working at Biotecnica, the company was on death row. Their first product had died and they'd given up on the second—Bacchus. It had maybe six months of life left to trickle away. Of course, no one bothered to tell me when I interviewed that the company was about to be sold in a fire sale to some stupid pharmaceutical giant like Merck or Squibb or Glaxo."

She ran her fingers through her bangs and triumphantly locked eyes with Toni. "You see, Toni, the founders had been given six years by the limited partners to produce positive cash flow. They failed, and Mark Tansen, our esteemed founder, couldn't handle it. So Jerry Frost and I did. I made the best of things, did what I had to, and saved the company. *That's* integrity." With a final appraising look in the mirror, Dora shouldered her Coach bag and left the room.

27

Despite her West Coast origins, Toni Isaacs had a keen appreciation for irony. She hung up the telephone, still digesting what Lucius Cornell had told her. It was ironic, indeed, that his ambitious corporate side—a source of tension in their relationship, particularly last year, when she was not above using phrases like "evil corporate fascists"—was exactly why he was proving so helpful to her investigation. Like many liberal arts majors, Toni had never tried to understand the world of commerce, preferring to imagine it as an alternate reality inhabited by pod people in blue suits who spoke a secret language. She was certainly grateful for Lucius's knowledge now.

She glanced at the stack of recent *Wall Street Journal*s she'd "borrowed" from Lamont Library, the scattered printouts from several electronic searches on the pharmaceutical industry, the copies of documents Chelo had filched from Biotecnica. Four days before, the *Journal* had reported that Biotecnica was going public, even though it might be years before any of the company's products hit the market.

That brought up the second great irony of this investigation. According to Lucius, the true interest of Biotecnica's owners—including Dora, who must have stock options—was to make money, whether or not that included actually making Bacchus/Sextasy. They could sell the company without selling the product. All they had to do was convince investors of the potential for great returns. Those investors, in turn, might sell off the stock if its price rose, dumping it on subsequent investors who were banking on future returns, and so forth. The sixty-second MBA Lucius had provided taught Toni that rational investors didn't buy stock on the basis of what companies were doing now, but on the basis of what they thought the companies would do in the future. Fortunes could be won or lost years before a company actually produced anything.

But most ironic of all, the public offering that would make them all rich (and "rich," Lucius had made clear, meant far more than the piddling five or ten million dollars Toni had imagined) was going to take place within days—maybe hours—of her own Ad Board hearing. Small world.

/ / /

Sterling Kwok's late-night brooding was interrupted by an unannounced visitor to University Hall.

"I thought you might be here, Sterling," Dayton Moore said as he entered the private inner office. "I'm glad I stopped in."

I, on the other hand, am not, thought Kwok. "How can I help you?" he asked with icy politeness.

"Actually, I thought *I* could be of assistance to *you*," Moore answered offhandedly, his eyes flickering over the dean's luxurious furnishings. "It seems we have a mutual acquaintance."

Kwok kept silent.

"Toni Isaacs."

Kwok's heart skipped a beat, but he forced himself to stay calm. So Dayton Moore was going to be the first person waving from the peanut gallery to cheer his fall. He was well aware that university powers would exact retribution for his disgraceful slide into drugs and coeds. No doubt he would be moved to a smaller office in some half-forgotten hall, his administrative status substantially downgraded. He smiled. The one bright spot in all that would be the probable reassignment of Mrs. Hale.

If the students knew what he had done, they would surely be horrified; no doubt they'd favor a more draconian punishment to fit the crime. But Kwok was determined that they not find out. The faculty, on the other hand, knew how to read the tea leaves. They could infer a beheading from a change in parking privileges. What was Kissinger's maxim? That in academia the battles are so fierce because the stakes are so petty.

"What's on your mind, Dayton?" he asked.

"Apparently, our student friend has got a big story ready to go, about scandal in the university." Moore draped himself over a chair and set his briefcase on the floor next to him. "I don't think she plans to say much about the drugs. I think she'll focus more on the call-girl aspect, which she thinks is connected with some biotech company in Cambridge."

"Please," the dean said dryly, "*do* sit down."

Moore smiled, a cloud of smugness enveloping him like expensive cologne. He hoisted up the briefcase and snapped it open. "A lot of names will be named," he warned. "That doesn't seem to be in anyone's best interest." He pulled a large padded mailing envelope out of his briefcase and tossed it onto the desk between them. "Here are the three final installments in the series, in case you're collecting the whole set to mix and match with your friends."

Kwok struggled to keep his face impassive and his body in his chair. *Jesus!* Moore had been sending those sex tapes? "Get out of my office," he whispered.

"No, I don't believe I will." Moore was cheerful. "It's time for you to think about yourself. And about the university."

"I'm sure you'll understand if I don't choose to take advice from you," Kwok replied. He'd been fucked. He'd been duped by this intellectual cream puff.

Moore ignored this. The upholstered wing chair creaked slightly as he leaned back and began to talk. He mentioned a start-up company of which Harvard was the largest single owner and explained what would happen when the media got wind of illegal drug tests using Harvard student prostitutes.

"Harvard's name will be muddied from here to the Ganges," Moore summed up. "And the school will be eighty million dollars poorer. That's a lot of financial aid." He stroked the dean's glossy desk. "Not to mention some nice office furniture."

Scandal at Harvard was always newsworthy; the story would play worldwide. It could bring down the administration. God, it might destroy the Portfolio. As for Dayton Moore . . .

He eyed the other man, realizing exactly what Moore expected of him. Clearly, everything Antonia Isaacs was going to write and publish was true, including everything she might say about Dayton Moore. And Moore was expecting Sterling Kwok to save *his* ass, in order to save the university's.

/ / /

Toni climbed the granite steps to the Fogg Museum. Earlier that morning, someone had delivered a handwritten note from Dean Kwok requesting an audience with her there. Despite the cold wind outside, she felt a little feverish; for two people with little in common, she and Kwok knew far too much about each other.

Inside the oak doors, she unwrapped her scarf and took in the cool, tranquil atmosphere of the galleries. She'd never been to the Fogg before and was surprised at how authentically classical it looked. Tourists passed through alabaster arches to a large central interior space, gazing in awe at the Renaissance statues and portraits, while students hurried up the stairs for art history discussion sections.

"I take it you're not familiar with the Fogg?" As if out of nowhere, Kwok appeared next to her.

She shook her head.

"It's a wonderful resource," he told her. "Though not nearly large enough to do justice to the university's collection. Only a tenth of the holdings can be displayed at one time."

Toni nodded, falling into the role of pupil with docent, and followed Kwok, unsure of his intentions.

He led her to a second-floor gallery that housed sculpture and paintings by twentieth-century Americans and Europeans. They moved in the slow pavane of the educated laity, glancing at works and reading the informational cards next to them. Time ticked by. Toni waited for the big bomb but was too exhausted to hasten its detonation.

She glanced up from a sculpture called *Unique Forms in Space* and met Kwok's eyes. "Of course you wonder why I've asked to meet you," he said.

"I do." Her throat was tight.

He looked at the Brancusi and his face softened slightly. "More than half my life has been spent in this community. And each day I'm reminded of my own ignorance."

They moved into the next room. The works grew more abstract. Everything was rectangular or circular, in black and white or unfriendly primary colors. A target, an American flag, a row of gray boxes.

"You've become aware of many things in a short time," Kwok continued. "The question I'd pose is whether you see them in perspective. Whether you see the context behind the truth. The context that *creates* truth."

"I don't understand," she answered. "Is that an elaborate way of saying I don't know what I'm talking about? Or did you ask me here to give me your side of the story?"

Color rose in his cheeks. "My actions play a very small role in this drama, Antonia."

"That's not what I saw on the—"

"Forget about the video!" he whispered furiously. "That's not the important thing here."

"Then what is?" she snapped back in frustration. And in anger. *My friend died last week.*

"It's everything around you." He looked at her. Was it sympathy she saw? "It's the art in this room and the minds in this building. It's our collective commitment to learning. Antonia," he lectured, "the dream of Harvard has always been to create a bastion of learning where knowledge is pursued for its own sake. If I'm not mistaken, that has been your objective, as well."

"You are mistaken," she answered back. She was just supposed to take this bullshit? "Funny, Dean Kwok, but from my perspective the dream looks more like a nightmare every day. Then again, I'm not surprised you'd get it wrong. Whose Harvard dream were you thinking of, anyway? Robert McNamara's, perhaps? Were the napalmed children part of that one? How about the Unabomber? There's a dreamer for you, a real idealist. Forgive me if I find it hard to view them as role models."

Kwok shook his head. "Then what about Robert Frost? Or Gertrude Stein? Or W.E.B. Du Bois?"

"You left out Ralph Waldo Emerson, I think," said Toni. "Oh, and

William James." She could play this game, too. She'd picked up a thing or two in her three years on campus. "Don't you see that the world passed this place by long ago?" She took a step closer to him. "This isn't the center of the universe. It's just a pretty good place to go to college."

"Isn't that enough?" Kwok gestured around him. "Isn't it enough that this is a place for learning? For asking questions?"

"Maybe," she admitted. "But what does that have to do with my story?"

He held her gaze for a long moment. "Let me say that I hope you truly believe in what you are doing. Don't fool yourself into thinking that the rest of the world will understand your words."

"What's that supposed to mean?" she asked.

"Subtleties will escape the public. Free will, choice, integrity . . . no one will ask about those. What they'll remember will be juicier: 'Prostitution ring.' 'Secret drug testing.' 'Ill-gotten gains'—there's a perpetual crowd-pleaser, Antonia. I'll tell you the message they'll hear: Harvard students are arrogant, self-destructive, spoiled brats. Harvard University is a loathsome Gomorrah of decadence and elitism. It became involved in something it shouldn't have become involved in. It didn't stop something it should have stopped. They won't care about your intentions; they'll hear only what confirms their own plebeian prejudices. Everyone with a pet peeve, a political quarrel, a festering vendetta against the university or anyone in it will have new ammunition for their battles." He relaxed slightly and tipped up his chin in seeming contemplation. "The whole strategy and existence of the Portfolio will be called into question."

Kwok fell silent. His words popped in her head like fireworks. Harvard would collapse, and it would be *her* fault? To judge by what Lucius had told her, the Portfolio wasn't about to fall apart.

"So if I tell my story I'll be thrown out of school, or worse. The same deal you made before, right?"

He smiled ruefully. "No, that's not what I'm saying. I'm asking you to think about what you really want, and why. If you want to make this a better place, consider how you would do it. Put yourself in the position of the dwellers in the city, not just the rebels battering against the city walls."

They drifted in front of a painting of three bright rectangles, stacked vertically. "Do you like Rothko?" he asked, indicating the painting.

"What's not to like?" she said. The advice session appeared to be concluded.

"One of our professors has a theory about this series. She traces Rothko's evolution as an artist from his early paintings of the Pietà, the dying Jesus cradled by the Virgin Mary. The middle shape is the Christ, and the top and bottom shapes are the torso and lap of his mother. I'm inclined to agree with her, if only because I find these abstractions oddly human, and quite moving."

"It's possible," she said.

He sighed. "I can tell you're not convinced of Professor Yule's theory. An artist who is too subtle may find that his true meaning is lost. But if he is too obvious, he achieves nothing."

/   /   /

Toni bolted down the Fogg steps and wandered aimlessly through the Square, hoping the crassness and energy of Harvard's commercial strip would clear her head. What did Kwok really want? Was it as simple as keeping her mouth shut? For that matter, what did any of them want?

She decided to find Cabot. For days she'd been ignoring the pleading messages he left on her answering machine. Her memories of their night together were bound up with the discovery of Van's body. But he could help her now: He knew the university, its players and its politics. He would know how to read Kwok. She needed him.

She sprinted to PBH and yanked open the large wooden doors. There in the cavernous foyer, as if by magic, Cabot stood talking to the bookkeeper. He turned, forgetting his conversation in mid-sentence. The bookkeeper discreetly disappeared, and Cabot silently led Toni into his office, where he embraced her hard.

They fit together perfectly, and while he held her, she could almost forget everything that had happened. But eventually she broke away and filled Cabot in on the past few days, repeating nearly word-for-word her conversation with Kwok.

Eyes wide, he leaned forward, as intent as a child watching Barney. "I can't believe it!"

"Join the club."

"I mean, what Kwok was saying," he responded eagerly. "It really sounds like he's offering you a deal. Or saying that you could get one from the higher-ups. They know how much you can damage the school. I mean," he added hurriedly, "they *think* you can damage the school."

She shook her head. "As if single-handedly I'm going to destroy Harvard's reputation."

"It's not just the reputation, Toni. They must be thinking financially. The whole investment strategy could be questioned. The Portfolio must have its enemies in the school. He was telling you how much it's worth to them for you to cooperate."

She would have laughed if it weren't so absurd. It was a little late for her to become an obedient subject.

Cabot blinked. "Don't you see? You have *power* over them. You've become a *player.* You're not on the outside anymore—I mean, you don't have to be on the outside if you don't want to be."

Toni was perplexed. She was hardly going to ask for a seat on the Board of Overseers. This was about her survival as a student. And as a human being.

"But that's not my job, to be on the inside."

Cabot squeezed her hand. "You can make it your job. Telling all is the easy way out, don't you see?"

He was wrong on that score—telling all wasn't a bit easy. The easy thing would be to drop everything, to leave Harvard. To give up. "I don't follow you." Her voice sounded weary to her.

"Toni, what do you think is important? Do you think there should be more funding at Harvard for public service? Should the university be a socially conscious investor? Should it allow its workers to unionize?"

"I—I don't know," she answered. "What I think is irrelevant. I'm just a reporter—ex-reporter, maybe—for the *Crimson.* That's it." She didn't want any more responsibility.

"What you think *is* relevant." Cabot's eyes shone. "They'll listen to you. They'd have to; you've got them by the balls." He slapped his palm against his forehead. "God, it's so obvious now. You hold all the cards. You've got more influence than any student in a generation. In generations!"

"I don't want to have influence!" It all sounded so farfetched.

"But you have to think about the impact of what you do," he urged.

"I *have* thought about that," she said heatedly. She stood up. "You sound just like them."

"C'mon, Toni, you know I'm not like that."

She went on: "Maybe all this bullshit has happened because no one was willing to listen to the obvious truth about right and wrong. The prostitution, the recruiting, the testing. Van's death. Your drug peddling. Wouldn't you still be doing that if I hadn't found out?"

"You have no right to say that! It's not the same. You have no right to judge—"

"That's the thing, Cabot," she insisted. "It *is* the same. We're all willing to make any compromise, invent any justification, to get what we want. And it's not just our generation; it's always been that way."

"I don't know what you're talking about."

"I don't want to make any more compromises," Toni continued. "I want to act on my principles. Unfortunately, I don't even know what they are anymore." She pulled on her coat and took a step toward the door. "I don't know why I'm writing this damned story. Maybe I don't really give a shit about what happens to real people."

"I care about you."

She stared at him. If she stayed with him another second, rested her face against his warmth . . .

"I have to go, Cabot," she said apologetically. "I have to figure this out myself."

/   /   /

At 2:30 A.M. one of the outside lawyers, a Joel Someone, knocked on Dora's office door, giving her an excuse to hang up on the market analysts.

"What?" she demanded. There was no point in being nice. It made her crazy to think of Biotecnica paying for each unproductive hour of these inexperienced junior associates' time.

"Hi, Dora, I'm sorry to bother you again. It's just that the underwriters need to double-check the backup on the Stage Three animal protocols." He gazed in trepidation at her desk, where her lunch and dinner sat cold and untouched.

"Sanjay has it." She kept her eyes focused on the computer,

where she was rerunning a spreadsheet. Eight months into his job, the young lawyer was already burnt out. If she gave him two seconds of eye contact he'd be begging her to review his résumé.

"It's just that their industry people told me to make sure—"

Like a robot she repeated, "Call Sanjay."

If Dave Mantini were still here, he'd be having a field day, informing the lawyers and underwriters of stuff they didn't need to know. Scaring that loser off the track was the single useful thing Dayton Moore had done. But she never should have negotiated so many stock options for him. Jesus Christ, what had Moore been thinking that night with Van Nguyen? She didn't even want to know what exactly Moore had done with or to Van; no doubt he'd have some self-serving excuse for it. What a messed-up closet case. She felt sickened to have been so close to such a disgusting psychopath. She'd take a john anytime over an egomaniac like Dayton Moore. *Beaux and Eros* indeed.

She brought up another file on the computer screen. In the reflection on her monitor she saw Joel hesitate a moment, then leave. It didn't really matter whether he found whatever it was he wanted to double-check. Nothing short of a meteorite crashing through the roof was going to stop this train from leaving the station. As long as they kept the initial offering price conservative and didn't get too greedy, the promise of Bacchus would be snapped up by the investing public, and everyone would get rich. It mattered to no one whether the stuff was actually produced.

She checked her watch. Time to head over to the financial printers for the final read-through of the prospectus.

/ / /

Harvard had a thousand faces, Sterling Kwok reflected as he sat silently in the unmarked building on Francis Avenue. Unfortunate that he should be stuck contemplating *these* three aged countenances from the other end of the long mahogany table. Twenty years after dreaming of changing the world, he was just another supplicant before the powers that be. He could predict how they were going to respond. But he had a duty to say his piece, nonetheless, for the sake of the university.

Sterling knew that Antonia Isaacs would never understand this side of him. He was surprised how much her good opinion had come to matter to him.

Gustavus Mims moved rapidly through business in his characteristic soft bass. His jowls quivered ever so slightly. He was in his sixties and gray-haired, but he looked healthy; he was aging gracefully. Philip van Rensselaer, on the other hand, was a modern-day Cotton Mather, frothing with fire and brimstone. His skin was pulled tight across his skull; his blue-veined hands were covered with liver spots. And Lloyd Buckley seemed a nonentity. He was a soft man with watery blue eyes, his nose perpetually flared by allergens. But he was a brilliant player in university politics. Funny that Mims had ended up with so much power. Score a point for the progress of people of color, if you could call elevating the grandson of a millionaire to Harvard's most powerful position an act of progress.

Sterling waited for the signal to speak, as if he were a first-former at prep school again.

"Dean Kwok has indicated he would like to say a word," van Rensselaer intoned.

Sterling rose automatically, lightheaded and uncertain, just the way he was supposed to feel. He tried to make eye contact with each of his superiors, without great success.

"Gentlemen," he began, "I thank you for allowing me to attend today's session. It goes almost without stating that the concerns which impel me to address you are serious and urgent. I have prepared a short memorandum which describes the issue that the university faces, but I have a strong desire to speak on the matter."

Van Rensselaer's face had contracted into an unconscious sneer. Mims nodded amiably, no doubt anticipating what Sterling was going to say.

"There has been discussion in other university committees and, I imagine, in this one, about the probable publication in the *Crimson* of a story about students working as prostitutes." Sterling's words rang out like bullets.

"Unfortunately, it appears that the story goes much deeper and, furthermore, that it is not merely a figment of this student's imagination. I must admit that the details are still somewhat sketchy to me; they concern the testing of a sexual enhancement drug on unsuspecting . . . clients." Kwok's throat was parched; he was choking on his words. He knew what he was: a man tying his own noose. There was no doubt as to the Portfolio's information-gathering abilities. These three knew everything they needed to know. He paused and took a sip of water from the glass in front of him.

Mims coughed lightly.

Sterling felt his shoulders slump. They weren't even going to let him finish.

"Dean Kwok," Mims began, "we are aware of the allegations regarding product testing at the Biotecnica Company. Is that the crux of your concern?"

Sterling nodded, mute.

"Have you counseled her?" Mims asked.

"I have," Sterling replied.

"What is her attitude?"

Did he even know? Did she? "Unhelpful," he answered.

Mims made a note. "Please continue," he said with a gentle wave.

Sterling swallowed again and forced himself to move his vocal chords. "The university has a financial interest in the company under discussion. We are represented on the board of directors and therefore have certain liabilities."

Van Rensselaer fixed his permanently bloodshot eyes on Kwok. "And if the allegations regarding falsified data are true," he interjected, "and the company goes forward with a public offering of shares, then the university will be liable for a material misstatement under the securities laws, if not outright fraud.

"Despite the fact that we have no involvement in these spurious allegations, we will be on the hook for millions!" he added gleefully. "Any investor who loses money will be able to sue us."

"Yes," Sterling mumbled. He wasn't a lawyer; he never should have mentioned legal matters while talking with van Rensselaer.

Silence ensued.

"For these reasons, the public offering should be stopped," Sterling concluded. "Surely it can be delayed. At least until these issues are resolved."

The members of the Portfolio barely glanced at one another. Apparently they communicated by telepathy.

Mims spoke. "The problem I foresee, Dean Kwok, is that things will likely never be fully 'resolved,' " he drawled elegantly. "You know as well as I do how scandals molder and fester. They never quite die away. . . . No, there are times we have to march forward, armed with the knowledge that we are right."

"With all due respect, the allegations of this particular student—"

"Are just that—allegations!" van Rensselaer spat out. "What evidence is there to support them? What have we seen in print, even in the *Crimson*? Nothing! If we quashed every deal blemished with a last-minute crisis, nothing would ever get done. And your alma mater would be that much closer to bankruptcy. There's a far easier way to solve this problem, Dean Kwok, and it is partly your responsibility to implement it. Get her to stop. Save our lawyers a lot of trouble. And keep your own face out of the paper."

Buckley wheezed in agreement.

"Philip," Mims interjected smoothly, "I daresay Dean Kwok has his hands full without being the full-time guardian of a college junior." He obliged Sterling with a cool smile. "You just do what you can, and we will do the same. Perhaps we will have a conversation with her pursuant to her upcoming Administrative Board appearance."

"Thank you for your attention and patience, gentlemen," Kwok said. He picked up his valise and coat and left the room.

They were so intransigent. So ensconced in the trappings of power that nothing but a disaster of the most enormous proportions could make them see reality. There was a glaring lack of intelligence behind their position. *Quem deus vult perdere prius dementat,* Sterling silently mouthed. Whom God wishes to destroy, He first makes mad.

28

Toni set the cordless phone down on the toilet and turned on the water in the bathtub. As the old-fashioned tub began to fill up, she found herself missing Chelo. She knew she'd been right to insist that Chelo go stay with friends in Lowell House after the confrontation with Moore, but the place seemed so empty now. She snatched up Chelo's bottle of Mr. Bubble and, smiling, poured several capfuls of blue goo into the rising water. For once, the hot-water gods were on her side; clouds of steam began to fill the room.

Toni stepped into the tub and gradually eased herself into the steaming water. The heat climbed over her back, and the muscles in her legs and thighs began to uncoil. Sighing deeply, she turned off the water and slid farther down, the bubbles covering her belly and breasts and shoulders. The hot water felt like a massage. After a few minutes, she sat up and reached for the new issue of *Essence* on the sink. Now her relaxation therapy was complete.

A noise out in the suite startled her to attention.

Unmistakable, it came again—footsteps on the worn parquet that were too heavy to be Chelo's. This was the moment she knew would come, and she was naked and vulnerable.

As silently as possible, one limb at a time, she climbed out of the tub, then hunched over shivering on the bath mat. Her heart was throbbing so loudly she couldn't hear anything from the other room. Whispering to herself to stay calm, she tugged savagely at her sweatshirt and jeans, trying to get them on her wet body. Reaching into her jeans pocket, she checked for the can of pepper spray her father had insisted she bring with her for protection in the city, that September a million years ago when she started her freshman year.

She listened intently to the sounds from the other room. Rustling. Drawers being opened and quickly rattled closed. Muted swearing, then the heavy steps again. The bathroom was getting more and more humid, like the orchid house she had visited on a family trip to Hawaii. Time to make her move, before she lost the advantage of surprise.

She threw open the bathroom door, banging it as loud as she could against the hallway wall, and strode into her bedroom. Dayton Moore whirled at the sound, dropping a heavy volume he had taken from the bookshelf. They both stood silent for a minute, staring at the textbook sprawling open on the floor.

He was the first to recover his equanimity. "Don't want to break the binding," he joked, bending over to pick up the book. He straightened up to find Toni standing closer to him, spray can pointed straight at him, a look of determination on her face.

"Mace?"

"Something like that." There was another long moment of silence.

"I take it you were expecting me, then," said Moore. "Or do you greet all your guests like this?" Toni only raised an eyebrow in response.

"Still, it wasn't very bright of you," he went on. "What if I'd had a gun?"

"You don't," Toni pointed out. "That would be too obvious." She had taken a chance there, but she knew Moore thought of himself as a winner—someone who'd get through this ordeal unscathed. Winners didn't have to shoot people. He expected to defeat her with his usual weapon: his mind.

Moore smiled, more out of habit than anything else. "I suppose you're intending some trade of information? That seems fair. May I sit down?" he said. Toni nodded and, after a second, returned the canister of pepper spray to her pocket. She perched on the end of her bed, away from him and close to the door. He sat in a black Harvard chair opposite her.

She breathed deeply, trying to think of this as just another interview. *Start with a softball question.*

"What's your motivation, Professor Moore, for setting up a prostitution ring?"

"That's quite an allegation," he responded. "I'm just a teacher and scholar." He flashed the winning smile she'd seen before, but the ends of his mouth twitched, as if admitting the artificiality of any emotion between them.

She pressed on. "I guess the word for you is 'pimp,' isn't it? Or would you prefer 'matchmaker'? You connected the prostitutes with the clients, that much is clear." Her voice was barely above a whisper.

"I advise you to check with your paper's lawyers before you print anything like that."

"Dora was your partner, but that doesn't mean she's still on your side." Look closer to home, she remembered Dora advising through her dorm window. Toni made herself speak louder. "You used the sex diaries from your class to recruit the students most likely to participate. My guess is that you identified the candidates and she recruited them." She sat forward, keeping her knees slightly bent, ready to jump if she had to. "I don't know exactly how you got the clients— friends of friends, word of mouth, personal ads?—but I'm sure you disguised your own involvement all along. It wouldn't be hard to set up a ring, I've learned that much—even a service offering the Harvard name." She paused to watch his reaction.

"Is that all?" Moore asked.

"You know it's not," she snapped. "You set up the ring for the purpose of testing Biotecnica's sex drug."

Moore was silent.

"You know," she goaded him, "Dora's told me quite a lot about you. I suppose my story is rather one-sided, since you haven't told me about her. I'm sure you have insights that the world would benefit from."

This was her lure. It hadn't been entirely successful with Dora, but Moore had a different temperament.

He crossed his legs, settling back into the wooden chair. Toni grudgingly admired his poise. "Solely for the purposes of our little trade, and without admitting any of your allegations," he began, "let me correct some of your misapprehensions. I met Dora several years back, when she was an undergrad at NYU. I wrote a paper on her; had you done a full search of my writings you might have come across it. 'Sweat Equity,' I called it.

"Dora is something of an expert on prostitution," he continued. "In college she turned tricks on the side to support her nightclub habit. She saw herself as an arbitrageur, someone making a premium off market transactions that others were unwilling or unable to perform. She lacked the vocabulary at the time to describe her work that way, but that's the gist of it."

"That was years ago," Toni pointed out.

"True enough," Moore agreed. "A couple years ago she developed an interest in venture capital. She wanted to be part of those exciting start-ups. Get in on the ground floor. But you know"—he waved his hand airily—"Dora's like the rest of those private-sector types: technically competent but utterly lacking in creativity."

"Really?" Toni rejoined, louder. "I thought she managed the whole setup and you just assisted her. She referred to you as—what's the term they use?—oh yeah, the 'back-office guy.' "

"Well, Toni," he said, a bit too precisely, "you've spoken with Dora and you've spoken with me—whom do you believe?" Ever the professor, he didn't wait for a reply. "Dora presented a *problem,* and I presented a *solution.* And don't get too excited by what I say. Keep in mind that it's your word against mine. You have no real evidence of anything."

"The solution you proposed," Toni interrupted, keeping him on track, "was to test an illegal drug on innocent people—"

"Oh, you've seen yourself they're not so innocent." He laughed. "Anyway, why would I go to all that trouble?"

She knew, suddenly. She knew that he had no grand scheme at all, that he did everything for the most simple reason. "For money," she answered. *Like any other schmuck.*

"I'm well compensated. I don't need money."

"But you want it," she said. "No matter how much you have, it's never enough, is it?"

"Meaning?"

"It's not enough to be a tenured professor, to be a published scholar, to have the respect of students, to have a lover—" His face tightened. "You're like everyone you criticize in my generation: you want it all! You want as much money as your friends on Wall Street, as much power as your classmates in government, as much *achievement* as anyone could possibly have."

He started to say something, but she kept going. She had the answer she'd been waiting for. "The Biotecnica IPO is going off tomorrow. It's what you've been working for. It'll provide you with the millions you think will finally make you complete."

"Are you finished with your speculations?" Moore asked irritably. He stood up and brushed down his camel coat, ready to go. "Obviously your next step will be to thwart my unjust enrichment by preventing the offering before it happens. Let me give you some unsolicited advice: Don't. And you can save your scowls for your real enemies."

"I have only one enemy, Professor Moore," she countered. "You."

"Wrong again, Toni," Moore answered adamantly. "You're clever, but you're no Machiavelli. Permit me a short lecture: The university protects its self-interest. That self-interest is determined by the Portfolio. End of lecture. You think they're going to thank you for your tabloid journalism? The Portfolio owns part of Biotecnica. How much is it worth to them to keep you quiet, through whatever means are necessary?"

Moore had homed in on what Toni feared—that she was truly alone. "You threatened Dave Mantini." But she was just talking now, as lost as a student writing an essay with no thesis.

"Oh, who cares, Toni? Who really cares?" Moore asked, exasperated. "Dave is the most minor footnote in this long, boring treatise. A wretched little whistle-blower. Read *Dilbert;* everyone thinks his job is fucked up. Let me ask you a question: What result do you predict for your breakthrough exposé, assuming that any newspaper will publish it? Do you think that Tara Sheridan's parents will be excited about that story? Smacks of exploitation to me, and I'm sure you're against that kind of thing."

"I wasn't planning to mention the names of the students," she lied.

"You weren't? Then maybe I will, in a follow-up piece." He leaned forward, towering over her. "You're not after truth, Toni, not when it's painful or complicated. Let's face it, you don't know what you're after.

"I, on the other hand, do know." He held out his hand and wiggled the fingers impatiently. "Time to pay up."

Toni ducked into the common room and retrieved a foil-wrapped package from the minifridge. She unwrapped the layers to reveal Van's diary, which she handed over. "I assume you've kept a copy of this as 'evidence' against me," Moore said. "Of course, no court in America will admit it." His voice trailed off as he began to thumb through the book, touching the pages gently. His eyes raced across the entries, and Toni noticed that a vein pulsed on his neck. In the midst of turning a page, he froze and blinked hard.

So he was capable of human feeling after all.

Now, she instructed herself.

"Was it hard to murder him?" she asked in as normal a tone as she could muster.

"What?" He looked at her, his eyes blank.

"I mean," she said dispassionately, "was it difficult? You know, grabbing his hair, holding his face underwater—" She made a rough gesture. "He was a pretty strong guy."

"You've got matters quite confused," he said, the image she'd called to life dancing in front of them. "It didn't happen—Van didn't die that way."

"He tried to protect you," Toni said generously. "He referred to you as 'X,' you know. But he gave it away at the end when he mentioned the 'be-in' after the *Deep Throat* screening. Funny, I thought that was just another Van performance. Turns out it was for an audience of one. Just like the last night you were together."

"It didn't happen like that!"

The sudden anguished force of Moore's voice rattled her, but she pushed further. "Of course it happened like that, Professor Moore. I'm sure you don't think of yourself as a murderer, but guess what? You are."

"You're wrong!" he insisted angrily. "It wasn't like that." He reached behind him for the chair and sat down. "I'll tell you a few things, and then you'll see that you're wrong." He spoke, and she understood why he was finally willing to answer her questions. Because he, too, had a truth he needed to preserve.

/ / /

How easily that night came back to him. Replaying itself in full color.

He had been reading in bed when the phone rang; it was long after midnight. He had picked up, even though he knew who it would be. It was Van, calling from some hotel pay phone in Boston. After only a few words Van had started sobbing. He needed to see him. They had to talk. Dayton always hated the manipulativeness of tears. I thought you were too cool to make such a big scene, he'd said.

"I love you," Van had said, choking out his words.

Dayton had been silent, not knowing how to respond anymore. For the last weeks he had been guided by a more powerful sensation: the feeling that if he weren't freed of this smothering intimacy, he would suffocate.

I've moved on, he had told Van. Maybe you should, too.

Silence. When Van spoke again, his voice was stronger, and angry. He had pretty clear ideas about how the mastermind behind Class Ring operated. He wasn't impelled to tell the world, but he would if he needed to. Shunting him aside wasn't really an *option*.

What do you want? Dayton had asked.

Van didn't answer at first. Then: "You're going to meet me in half an hour. My terrain, not yours: the Adams House pool. We'll talk as long as it takes to fix things."

Dayton clutched the receiver long after Van clicked off.

He wasn't very familiar with Adams House; he and Van had spent most of their nights together at Dayton's brownstone in Back Bay. On the way over, he took care to avoid running into students who might know him.

Inside the pool room Van stood in his overcoat. Every time a few days passed in which he didn't see Van, Dayton was amazed at how attractive he was. Even the bleached-blond hair—his newest, most bizarre affectation—couldn't conceal his beauty.

Dayton pulled the door closed behind him and walked slowly to the other side of the pool. He knew his task: keep Van unruffled and silent for the next two weeks. After that, he would have better options.

As he watched Dayton approach, Van lifted a wine bottle and took a swig, tilting back his head and closing his eyes. Surprised to see Van drinking, Dayton put his hand on the bottle and pulled it away. There was a moment of tension as he feared Van would fall into his arms. But he didn't.

"Have a drink," Van offered.

Dayton shook his head—the last thing either of them needed was alcohol—but changed his mind. What the hell. He put his lips around the head of the bottle and drank, detecting the scent of the Merlot and the taste of Van's mouth on the bottle at the same time. He felt Van's eyes assessing him, lingering over his face and neck, moving down his body, as if memorizing details.

"It's almost our anniversary," Van said in a friendly, matter-of-fact tone. "Of the first time we spoke, I mean. I came to your office almost exactly a year ago."

Dayton set the bottle on the ground and touched Van's wrist. "Listen, Minh—"

Van jerked away. "Doesn't that mean anything to you?" he shouted.

"Calm down!" Dayton took two steps forward and accidentally kicked over the bottle. A thin, bloody trail of red liquid dribbled toward the pool.

"Who are you to tell me to be calm?" Van retorted. "Who the *fuck* are you?"

"Just take it easy," Dayton said. He fumbled in his coat pocket and found the pill bottle. He drew it out and quickly twisted it open, emptying the contents into his cupped hand.

"Having an anxiety attack?" Van asked. "I thought you were above all that."

Without warning Dayton stepped forward and pushed a tablet against Van's mouth. Surprised, Van pursed his lips and spat hard. Dayton retracted his hand as if bitten.

Van glowered. "You think you can solve this by tranquilizing me? Make me into a Stepford Boyfriend who only thinks happy thoughts?"

"It's Xanax, Minh. It'll help you think more clearly—"

"I have thought clearly," Van replied contemptuously. "That's the whole problem. I see clearly what my life would be like without you."

Dayton blushed. "Don't be ridiculous," he said more softly. "You'll find someone." Van *was* being ridiculous. Dayton had seen how everyone fell head over heels for Nguyen Van Minh; he himself was Exhibit A. "You can have your pick."

Van stared at him. "I don't want just anyone; I want you." He laughed. "God, I sound pathetic. You said it yourself, Dayton: everyone has only one true other half, one person who makes them complete. I can't be complete without you."

Had he said that? They'd both said a lot of things, late at night, in the lazy way that lovers talk. Anyway, Dayton had more important things to resolve. "Look," he said calmly, "that's not what we're here to talk about."

"Oh, you kill me, sweetheart." Van laughed again, with a genuineness that was eerie under the circumstances. Then his voice turned abruptly harsh. "Do you think I care about your whoring operation now, in comparison to everything else?" He shook his head, smiling faintly. "You didn't think I'd figure things out? About the condoms you had the girls—but not me—use every time? About the videotapes and the questionnaires and the 'debriefings'? C'mon, I'm not that dumb. I go to Harvard, remember?"

"No one's going to believe you," Dayton warned.

Van grabbed his arm, the one still holding the pills. "Cut the crap." Dayton felt Van's warm breath on his face, smelled his hair and the Merlot. "No one has to believe it. They just have to *talk* about it to derail your marvelous life plans." Suddenly Van dug his fingers into Dayton's hand, grabbing the cache of pills. He jumped back and rocked unsteadily.

"You think you're through with me? Maybe you are, baby." Van tossed two pills into his throat and swallowed them, dry. He leaned over and deftly swept up the bottle of wine. "You want to walk away, keep me silent forever?" He dropped three more pills into his mouth and took an angry swig. "Here's your chance. I'll do the hard part for you."

"That's enough, now," Dayton cautioned, sounding like someone's dad. His heart hammered out an alarm. The pills weren't the common yuppie tranquilizer Xanax. They were Neuprodil, a potent

sedative he had once taken for pain after a skiing injury. Dayton's
fallback plan was to keep Van quiet for a few days, so he could easily
be monitored. One tablet would have knocked him out for twelve
hours. Five tablets mixed with a bottle of wine—

"Take a stand, Dayton. Decide what you want from life," Van ha-
rangued him. "You either take me, with all the complications—that's
what love's about, isn't it?—or . . . or you take responsibility for the
alternative." He pushed the rest of the pills into his mouth, making
a face as they slid past his tongue. He tipped the bottle, sloshing liquid into his throat, and then, with a terrible discipline, swallowed.

Dayton knew what he should do: run over, plunge his fingers
deep into Van's mouth, trigger his gag reflex, force him to vomit.
There had been twenty or thirty pills in that bottle.

"It's your responsibility now." Van's speech was slurring. "You
don't have the option anymore of pushing me away, of pushing me
away . . . Why are you so afraid of loving me? You can lecture about
it, talk about repression and transgression and the social construction
of sexuality, but when it comes down to it, when it comes right down
to it, you can't see yourself as the kind of man who loves another
man. That's it, isn't it?"

Dayton needed to get help, to call an ambulance. Then he could
explain how this undergraduate came close to death in his presence.
Then Van could scream out whatever images came to his hallucinat-
ing mind as they brought him back from the edge. And in a few days
the whole goddamned struggle would start again.

"Fuck you!" Van yelled thickly. His shoulders slumped forward,
as if his head were too heavy to lift. "How can you just stand there?"
He looked around, dazed. "What are these things, anyway?"

"Maybe you should sit down," Dayton suggested.

"I don't wanna sit," Van responded. His voice was empty of in-
flection. He struggled out of his coat in slow motion and dropped it
at his side. He started to pull off his shirt. "I want to be clean of you,"
he said. "You soil me. I wish I had never met you."

Dayton watched silently.

Van removed his trousers and carefully set his socks inside his
shoes. He shivered next to the edge of the pool in a pair of drawstring
boxers.

"Don't do this, Minh," Dayton told him. He was always making a big show of things. Even this striptease—he'd done it before, at the *Deep Throat* screening.

Van appraised him through drooping, sedated eyes. "I loved you," he said plaintively.

He loosened the drawstring awkwardly and dropped the boxers to the ground. He waited a moment for a response that did not come, and then dove into the pool.

It wasn't a dive, really; more a fall. Warm water splashed up against Dayton's coat as Van broke the even surface.

Van twisted and contorted under the water, as if he didn't know which way was up. After an eternity that could only have been five or ten seconds, he reared his head in a tremendous whoosh of expelled air and water. He coughed thickly, water flying from his mouth, and kept coughing, trying to catch his breath. Treading water awkwardly, he finally found the bottom, then jerked his head around until he finally saw Dayton. "Sweetheart, I can't feel my legs, please—"

Then Van lost his balance and went under again.

Dayton carefully paced the circumference of the pool and checked the depth markers. Van was only in five feet of water. He had escaped from Vietnam by boat when he was eleven. He and his siblings had survived an attack by Thai pirates, for God's sake. He would be fine.

Van was under for ten seconds. Fifteen seconds. Twenty sec—

He broke through again, got his mouth above the surface. His eyes stayed closed and his arms flailed under the water, fighting some otherworldly foe. A low wail suddenly pierced the lush, muggy air of the pool room. Some word—it sounded Vietnamese. Almost as if Van had forgotten Dayton was even there. The wail was followed by an awful gagging sound drawn from deep in his throat.

Dayton couldn't take this anymore. Out of the corner of his eye, he saw Van sink again. He grabbed the pile of discarded clothes, the wine bottle; he fumbled on his hands and knees for the pill Van had spat out. It took at least four minutes to drown, didn't it? Someone would come in any second and fish Van out. All the more reason for Dayton to leave. He would asphyxiate if he didn't get out fast.

As he pushed open the door to the tunnel, he glanced backward one last time. Van floated on his chest, his wet back and buttocks reflecting the soft pool light.

Nausea rose up within Dayton, making his throat buckle. He ran through the tunnel to the staircase leading out of the house and burst out onto the street. He braced himself against a lamppost, stopping only for the moment it took to steady himself. Then he picked up the bundle, which smelled of wine and his beloved, stashed it under his arm, and ran to his car, parked six blocks away.

29

The room was hushed as Moore's voice died away. Toni cleared her throat, uncertain how to respond to this confession of moral failure. He had made his choice. It was the wrong one.

"I'm sorry," she said, and was surprised to realize she meant it. Moore looked at her for a moment, shook his head, then bolted from the room. The door slammed behind him.

Toni locked the door and sat down carefully on her bed. She wasn't quite sure what to do next. Moore was right about proof: it was his word against hers, and the value of hers had been sharply discounted in recent weeks. The newspaper story seemed like the most logical next step. The only step, really. It wouldn't take long to write the final version; she'd put together a decent draft the night before and talked it over with Chelo. Toni quickly fluffed out her curls with her fingers, got her things together, pulled a coat on, and left.

Out on the darkening street, she finally felt the physical after-effects of the last hour. She leaned shakily against an icy black iron railing. She needed hot liquids and sugar. Bypassing the *Crimson* for now, she headed up Plympton Street and down Massachusetts Avenue toward Store 24. At the lights in the center of Harvard Square, she waited for a break in traffic and then dashed from Out-of-Town News across the street toward the Coop. As soon as her feet hit the sidewalk she heard a siren. She turned to see where the ambulance was going and found the flashing blue-and-red lights of a police cruiser easing toward her. It pulled to a stop and a Cambridge cop got out, straightening his police cap.

He'd come to get her.

She considered walking briskly away, but already a small crowd had formed a semicircle near her, hemming her in.

"You know you were jaywalking back there, miss, don't ya?" the cop asked.

"I crossed the street, if that's what you're asking—" She stopped herself from saying "Officer." Politeness hadn't gotten her very far at the Cromwell Hotel. This time she would be more savvy.

"I'll need to see some ID, please," the cop said in a bored voice.

"Oh, all right," she answered as she fumbled for her wallet. Both of them knew he had no probable cause. She picked out her driver's license and, for good measure, her Harvard student ID and slapped them into his palm. "And I'd like your badge number, please."

"Right on the badge," he said, turning his shoulder so that she could see. "Back in a sec." He strolled nonchalantly to his car and picked up the radio.

The crowd was in no hurry to disperse. Where were the protesters against police harassment when she needed them? Student activism was way overstated. Conservative media and politicians regularly asserted that Harvard was under the grip of p.c. orthodoxy; if so, it was a highly secretive regime.

The cop finally put down his handset and stepped out of the car. She held her hand out to retrieve her ID cards and unleashed her pent-up rage. "The next time you pull over a black student, it'll result in a complaint to the Massachusetts Commission Against Discrimination, the state human rights commission, and the student committee on—"

Instead of handing back her identification, the officer grabbed Toni's wrist with one hand and with the other slapped on a handcuff. The metal was cold against her skin.

"What the hell are you doing?" she shouted, pulling back. It was a mistake; he had a firm grip on the other cuff, and the metal bit into the bone of her wrist.

"There is a warrant out for your arrest," he explained flatly.

"What are you talking about? He's crazy!" she shouted to the crowd, as it inched backward.

"Felony breaking and entering," the police officer was saying. Her raid on Kwok's office. He pulled out a laminated card and started reading. "You have the right to remain silent—"

Suddenly she saw a familiar face. Horace Glover, in his green Timberland jacket, was walking in her direction, expounding loudly to an attractive light-skinned woman at his side.

"Horace!" she shouted. He looked up to see who was calling him, his face already arranged into a welcoming smile. When he saw Toni, the smile froze and his eyes widened.

"Horace! Please, get over here! I need your help!" she yelled, beyond any kind of embarrassment.

The president of the Black Students Association looked from Toni, to the police car, to Toni again, and then pursed his mouth. He would see this as another episode of police brutality; it wouldn't hurt that the incident would appeal to his political instincts.

He picked up his clip toward Toni as the policeman hustled her into the backseat of the car, carefully keeping her from bumping into the metal divider. As Horace approached her, he put an arm over his friend's shoulder and pulled her close. He spoke to the other woman loud enough for Toni to hear: "Some people just want to keep pulling us down."

Without a glance at Toni he walked on, rounded the corner, and disappeared. Toni was speechless. The policeman tossed her bag on the floor in front of her, closed Toni's door, walked around to the driver's seat, and started the engine. She leaned forward, and large, messy tears began to fall.

They'd done it. It didn't matter anymore who "they" were. They'd made her powerless.

/ / /

For the second time in a month she was booked at the Cambridge jail. No one showed the least surprise at seeing her again.

"You'll have a hearing before a magistrate tomorrow morning," the desk officer told her. "You can make one phone call."

She heard a soft, deliberate cough behind her. She twisted around and saw Carlos Rivera, who looked as if he'd rather be anywhere else—dead, even—than here. She stared at him, uncomprehending.

"Joey, let me have a word, okay?"

The desk sergeant shrugged and idled over to the coffee stand against the wall. "Somebody missed their turn to make coffee!" he sang out.

Toni didn't move, so Carlos came up to her.

"Look, I'm sorry about this, Toni—"

"There was never any charge," she said, beyond tears. "Not for breaking and entering. It was all resolved, remember?"

He lifted his hand as if to comfort her, but then let it drop awkwardly to his side.

He bit his thumbnail. "One of the university's attorneys swore out an affidavit yesterday about the break-in, and the magistrate served the warrant today."

She was slumped over, her shoulders aching with fatigue and defeat.

"Joey, let me have the keys for these handcuffs, will ya?" Carlos shouted across the office. The other officer tossed him a key ring, which the detective caught with one hand. He unlocked her and she rubbed her reddened wrists.

He put an arm around her shoulder and froze for a second. Then he pulled her closer. His touch was warm and strong. "If I could do something, I would, Toni. I hope you understand that. Don't make too much of this, you'll be out tomorrow morning."

She looked directly at him. "That's too late. The IPO goes off tomorrow. Everything will be over and done with by ten in the morning. They've won." She barely choked out the words.

He didn't try to argue. For a moment they shared a sad, intimate silence. Then she heard Desk Sergeant Joey jangle over.

"Look," Carlos said, "if you need to contact anyone, let me know. Don't worry about this one-phone-call thing."

"Just call my roommate," Toni answered. "Call Chelo and tell her to turn in my homework for me." She told him the number where Chelo had been staying.

"Done," he said. "Listen, I'll stop by to see you later." She nodded as he walked down the hall to his office.

"You gonna make your call now?" the desk sergeant asked lazily. He seemed to be searching in the top drawer for the keys to her cell.

"No," she answered. "There's nothing left for me to say."

/ / /

The next morning, Dora Givens kept her ears tuned to the CNBC business report on TV as she examined the room she had lived in since September. Considering how aggressive most business school students were, it was pretty amazing that they put up with such tiny accommodations. Not that it really mattered. The future held plenty of glamorous places to live.

She glanced again at the television screen, waiting to see the rest of the world's take on the IPO. There were so few biotech offerings these days that the sale of the company's stock this morning was guaranteed to make news. She'd tendered fifty percent of her shares—the maximum she was allowed to sell for six months under the lock-up arrangements—two hours before.

It hadn't been easy to hand over the stock; she was pretty sure it would continue its climb. Oh, well. There was value in security, especially after the mess of the past few weeks. Money in her hand was real; anything else wasn't.

She dumped a box of Bacchus prospectuses into the trash. She'd already done the heavy cleaning the night before, shredding the research files on the twenty-two student vectors who had carried out the product testing and purging the secret data room at work. For their kitsch value, she had considered keeping some of the Veritas condoms she and Dayton had had manufactured, but she avoided the temptation. What were they but clutter, anyway? She'd done the job she needed to do, and now it was time to move on. Continue evolving, as the bumper sticker said.

The difference between herself and Toni Isaacs, her engaging would-be nemesis, was that Dora was not really a risk taker. Toni was. She still couldn't believe how easy it had been to hoodwink Toni into showing up at the Cromwell Hotel. Dora never went into anything without knowing exactly how it would turn out.

Impatiently, she pushed back her bangs and flicked the remote. CNN ran the same stories as CNBC. Apparently there wasn't *that* much news in the world. She put the TV on mute, picked up the telephone, and dialed a number she'd memorized over the past couple of days.

"Pet World," a middle-aged man answered.

"Hi, this is Dora Givens calling again. Look, I've finally made my decision. I'll take both of the corgis, the eight-week ones. I can pay by phone, right? Good. I'll need them shipped."

She worked out the details and a few minutes later, merely by paying sixteen hundred dollars, was the proud owner of the two cutest puppies she'd ever seen.

For the first time she felt how rich she had become. Four million bucks was a lot of money. And it was liquid.

One more loose end and she'd call it a day. There were some things she needed to work out with her lawyer.

/ / /

Every light burned at Biotecnica, and for once the cavernous building seemed homey and friendly; every employee had brought a friend or two to the festivities. Judy Gallagher smiled and patted her short white hair as a tuxedoed young waiter refilled her champagne glass without even being asked. You could just feel the energy ripple through the building. It was an exciting time to be part of an exciting enterprise, even for a part-time receptionist "of a certain age" like herself.

Judy took another sip of the bubbly drink. She stole a glance at the handsome waiter and saw that he was smiling at her. She blushed but then smiled right back at him.

They all had a right to be happy, after all. Who said there was no American dream anymore? It had occurred here, right before her eyes.

/ / /

Standing perfectly straight in his office in William James Hall, Dayton Moore rolled his head, noting with a certain perverse satisfaction the cracking noises of stored-up stress being released. He could really use a good massage. He pinched at his waistline where, to his great dismay, a small but detectable roll had recently formed. Starting next week he'd be back at the gym every morning. Now that he was in his thirties, any deviation from a strict regimen of exercise and diet was fatal, at least to the ego. Half his male classmates from Swarthmore were already bald and pudgy.

He did a few more stretches and then sat down in his leather swivel chair. He leaned back and slowly twirled around, inspecting the place he'd labored in for several years already. This office was impossibly small. And shabby. The carpet was pulling away from the walls, revealing the concrete beneath; you could bet it wouldn't be replaced for years. And the thousands of books, carefully organized on the shelves he had installed himself when he was still an assistant professor . . . many were in foreign languages, including Italian, French, German, and Spanish. Dayton cringed. French he knew well, but he had long forgotten his introductory courses in the others. Giving the impression of being multilingual had been sexy in his youth; now it seemed like yet another affectation.

The most unpleasant thing about Harvard was its affectations. With a few exceptions, the students and faculty were quite smart and generally hardworking. A few were brilliant. But, God, they were so annoying in their need to call attention to themselves, to tell everyone *I matter, so listen up!* They could be raising their hands in class, putting up posters for some boring Asian music festival, or talking behind you at the Brattle Theater about their sex lives. Everyone had a schtick; everyone had an identity to hawk. Toni Isaacs seemed to think she was some kind of exception to the norm at Harvard, when in fact she epitomized it. Namely, she seemed to think that she had some unique insight into life that demanded the attention of the rest of humanity. But she wasn't unique. No one was.

Scratch that. No one except Van.

Compared to Van, everyone and everything else was stale. Tired and tiresome. They observed, while Van lived.

There was no way to describe Van that was not trite, perhaps because all the good adjectives were wasted on anyone else. Brilliant.

Handsome. Brilliantly handsome. Sensitive. He had experienced a lot of life. He was sexy. Pick your cliché: he was a walking personal ad, a knight in shining armor, a pearl among swine, a dreamboat. But the dreamboat had sunk, and he, and everyone else, should get over it. Sometimes things just didn't work out.

30

Toni walked out into the bright day, feeling little sense of relief. She didn't believe she'd had a complete thought in the previous twelve hours. Every muscle in her body ached, and her eyes burned as if she'd spent a double all-nighter at the *Crimson*. Her release was anticlimactic. A policeman unlocked her cell shortly after nine, muttering, almost as an afterthought, that the charges had been dropped; a clerk handed over her keys and wallet.

It had occurred to Toni during the night that she knew nothing about law or criminal procedure; the information provided by television had not proved particularly useful. She had received no helpful advice or consolation from any streetwise hooker with a heart of gold; on the other hand, she hadn't been tortured by beefy, sadistic prison matrons, so that was pretty much a wash.

Her imprisonment seemed vaguely unconstitutional, and certainly un-American, but there wasn't much for her to do at this point. Everything was done already, the Portfolio had seen to that. The IPO had been launched. There was nothing to do but wait.

/   /   /

Back in the room that no longer felt like home, Toni telephoned Chelo and then took a long, hot shower. Changing into a wool suit, she sat on her desk and absentmindedly examined the spines of the textbooks. *Prolegomena to Any Future Metaphysics; Man, the State and War; The Autobiography of Alice B. Toklas.* It would have been fun to read them.

She heard footsteps in the hallway outside and then a knock on the door. The chair grated shrilly against the wood floor as she pushed it back and got up to greet her caller.

He was a blond man in his early thirties. At her blank stare, he reminded her that he was the Adams House senior tutor, the person who had allegedly been responsible for her education since the beginning of sophomore year.

"Are you feeling okay? You shouldn't be nervous," he assured her placidly as they headed down the stairs of B-Entry.

She strode ahead of him. Up the path between Lehman and Boylston Halls, past the stone monument donated to Harvard decades before by Chinese graduates of the university, the duo of administrator and student approached University Hall. She gazed at snow-covered Harvard Yard, panning all the way from Grays Hall to Thayer; it was proving to be a long winter.

"Well, here we are," the senior tutor said, pushing open the door to University Hall. "The committee is already inside. Yours is the only case today. As you know, I'll serve as both your advocate and the university's representative." Toni didn't pay attention to the details of the kangaroo court. She focused on a squirrel running around. Apparently squirrels almost never remembered where they hid their nuts, instead finding them through luck alone. Much as she had unraveled this mystery, she reflected.

The senior tutor coughed. "So, I just wanted to ask you, Toni . . . why?" He looked at her and then at the ground.

She shrugged and headed up the granite stairs. "Does it matter now?" she asked him over her shoulder.

/ / /

Sterling Kwok's attention began to wander after just twenty minutes of the elaborate bureaucratic minuet. The student's senior tutor had done a credible job of explaining the most obvious facts of her case without providing any of the more prurient or sensationalistic details. Andrew Onderdyck and the other members of the Ad Board made notes from time to time, as if recording information they did not already know from their briefings beforehand. They were slightly nervous, though. At the end of the table sat Philip van Rensselaer and, next to him, Gustavus Mims himself.

Sterling stole periodic glances at Antonia Isaacs. She sat behind a small cherrywood table in a black Harvard chair, her hands folded in her lap, staring straight ahead. She had dressed appropriately and didn't seem scared. In fact, she wasn't displaying any emotion, which was a bad sign; it seemed proof that she had given up.

He hadn't expected to feel sympathy for Antonia Isaacs. She had basically ruined his life. Or rather, he had ruined his own life and she had informed the rest of the world of that fact. It had been years since he had respected himself, and he knew well enough that his moral decline had started long before he starting screwing coeds and messing around with controlled substances. His self-loathing, however, didn't create his sympathy for Antonia.

No, his sympathy had a more direct source: his simple, knee-jerk support for the underdog, the fundamental characteristic of all sincere liberals. She was the underdog today. With Gustavus Mims and his blue-blood sidekick in attendance, Antonia Isaacs was more heavily outgunned than she could possibly imagine. The truth—a kind of truth, anyway—was on her side, but truth was an unreliable ally.

The nature of Sterling's position at the university guaranteed that he would be widely misunderstood. He wished he could have a few minutes alone with Antonia Isaacs to explain something about who he really was, although he suspected she would never believe him. Perhaps she feared she would turn into her caricature of him: a sellout, an Uncle Tom, part of the problem, not part of the solution. Dayton Moore—who, ironically, was a member of the Ad Board, although he hadn't bothered to show up today—had been far more clever than Sterling had ever imagined. The video blackmail—he'd walked right into that one. This was the danger of university life, he had learned over the years: forgetting that everyone else was just as smart as oneself, and just as keen to protect his own interests.

He saw Antonia check her watch, as if she were at a dull lecture extending into lunchtime.

The senior tutor finished his presentation and sat down next to her. One of the professors on the panel asked a clarifying question, which the senior tutor answered, and the room lapsed into silence.

Gustavus Mims cleared his throat.

"Miss Isaacs," he began quietly but clearly. Everyone around the table leaned in slightly.

"I realize that these proceedings must be highly distressing for you and your family. You must know that neither I, nor the members of the Administrative Board, nor the university, has any vendetta against you."

Antonia's eyes flicked over to him, as if examining him for the first time.

"Nevertheless, we cannot shirk our duty to preserve the decorum and integrity of the university community. You do understand that, don't you?"

"Yes," she said quietly.

At least a dozen snide comebacks must be zipping through her mind, Sterling thought.

"We need not even broach the issue of your first arrest at the Cromwell Hotel. The university has neither the capacity nor the desire to regulate behavior outside the perimeter of the school. But breaking and entering is a felony in this state. Furthermore, you violated the privacy of your fellow students by examining confidential administrative files. Keep in mind that Harvard is bound by federal privacy law. These breaches cannot be tolerated and will not be repeated, by you or anyone.

"We must also consider more inchoate matters," he continued. "The standards and credibility of the school. Our 'image.' "

Mims paused, took a sip of ice water, and resumed speaking.

"Earlier today, a local company made a public offering of stock in the financial markets. Such events occur regularly, particularly among companies headquartered in Cambridge or along Route 128. It is not unusual that Harvard University, a major institutional investor, owned a minority interest in the company. It is well known that we own shares or partnership interests in many companies. Some are successful; others are not. This is one of the ways that we make it possible for students to study at the university."

Antonia seemed to mumble something and Mims looked up in

blank surprise. The senior tutor would be frantic: the grand summation was not the time for students to speak their mind.

"Excuse me, did you have a comment, Miss Isaacs?"

"Yes," she said, quickly clearing her throat. "Mr. Mims, you said, 'We make it possible.' I just wanted to know—when you say 'we,' you mean the Portfolio, not Harvard in general, don't you?"

There was total silence at this breach of protocol. Mims looked at his neighbors one by one around the table and then moved his mouth into a broad, engulfing smile.

"I meant Harvard as a whole, Miss Isaacs. 'The Portfolio,' as you refer to it, is but one of the many bodies that make up this university. We all do our part for the institution." He consulted a folder in front of him. "You yourself received grants of financial aid totaling several thousand dollars during your freshman and sophomore years. Where do you suppose that money comes from?"

Shrinking in her chair, Antonia returned to silence.

"Continuing, then," Mims said. "You may even have wished to prevent this particular stock offering. There's no point in getting into the reasons for your interest at this point. I cannot read your mind, Miss Isaacs, so I cannot anticipate your plans after today's session. Nor can I know whether your colleagues at the *Crimson* share your enthusiasm for the subject. Whenever possible, the university steers clear from interfering in student extracurricular activities."

Now Sterling felt embarrassed. He had expected more sophistication from the Portfolio Goliaths.

"In fact, the public offering has been completed. The Biotecnica firm will market its products, or perhaps not—one never knows with start-ups. One can only sell what the market will bear." He paused. "Do you have anything to add?"

She shook her head. She was smart, Sterling observed, not to get herself in deeper. But he had always known that Antonia had brains.

"What's past is past, Miss Isaacs. This committee will discuss your case and issue a recommendation within a few days. You are free to do or say what you wish. It is clear, however, that the matters you have previously discussed with various parties are neither factually correct nor particularly newsworthy. The choice is yours." He paused. "What, then, is your choice?"

The message was obvious to everyone: Keep quiet and we may

show some leniency in helping you to salvage something from this mess. Make a fuss and watch us smash you.

The only question, in Sterling's mind, was whether Antonia Isaacs felt she had anything left to salvage.

/   /   /

"The sequined harlot who services senators nightly in plush Washington hotel rooms . . . the hit man hired by the jealous suburban housewife to assassinate her philandering husband . . . the Haitian immigrant who flees oppression in the developing world and winds up carting away your trash . . .

"These three individuals, separated as they are by geography, occupation, and class, have one quality in common:"

Dayton Moore paused before delivering the punch line, thinking of his telephone spending spree in the hour before the lecture. A Jaguar, for Christ's sake. The orgy of consumerism went against every middle-class precept of thrift his parents had taught him in Cherry Hill, New Jersey. Those ideas had made sense for the Moores, who weren't rich. But now he was.

"Each performs our dirty work," Moore continued, his voice deepening. "Today we will examine, in a cross-cultural analysis, the systems society has established to ensure that our collective dirty work is accomplished smoothly, efficiently, and—most important— silently. My lecture is about the sale, barter, and exchange of a commodity that is generally considered the exclusive domain of psychologists: shame. Join me, if you will, in dissecting the economy of shame."

The predictable undercurrent of excitement swept through the room. The undergrad guide published by the Committee on Undergraduate Education called Moore's class "Pop Culture Meets Heidegger," though he doubted whether the guide's editors knew the first thing about Heidegger. There was a lot of fakery "in the house." As if illustrating his thought, a hiply dressed and coiffed young woman smiled at him from the front row. He met her lascivious gaze. Why the hell not? Either you were a Nietzschean superman or you weren't. You had to have guts to succeed in this institution, that was for sure. Otherwise you'd end up as a doormat, like Sterling Kwok, still slavishly devoted to the university that now scorned him.

He sneaked a glance at his watch. Just forty more minutes and he'd be done for the week. And then it was time to begin really living.

Dayton Moore returned his thoughts to his lecture, and to the unconcealed admiration of students thirsting for knowledge.

31

Dora trundled her carry-on through the sterile neon glare of Logan Airport. Her ticket and passport had already been scrutinized and her luggage checked, giving her plenty of time to enjoy a Diet Coke and the current *Vanity Fair* before her flight was called for boarding.

She selected a seat near her gate, with a clear view of the entrance and the exit. Nothing would go wrong at this point, but it was best not to take any chances.

The tourists around her were all of a kind: healthy, well-cared-for men and women in early middle age, fussing with their Louis Vuitton overnighters and their Dooney and Bourke duffels. Gros' Anges Island was known for catering to the needs of the BMW set; the tropical paradise offered coral reefs, snorkeling and scuba, windsurfing in calm waters, and lethal rum punches.

Gros' Anges also offered some of the world's most sophisticated offshore banking facilities, established in 1945 by some Prussian aristocrats who had suddenly found it convenient to leave Nuremberg for the sunny Caribbean. The Deutschesbank im Fremdenschaft held its own with the famous gnomes of Zurich. Dora's profits from the Biotecnica IPO had already made their way into an ultra-secret "dark" account, which only she (or somebody whose fingerprints, voiceprint, and retinal patterns matched hers exactly) could access. Once a month, for as long as she needed, a soft-spoken German in an exquisitely tailored suit would present her with a briefcase filled with traveler's checks; the rest was up to the DIF.

She thought again—this would be the last time—of the fifty percent of her stock she would never profit from. The venture capitalists who'd provided Biotecnica with its money in the difficult early years were savvy enough to know the temptation the key players would face to cash out after the IPO. So, by contract, half those options wouldn't vest until they worked six more months. She knew that the other managers and scientists would stay with the company during that time, scared of losing a single cent, even as the walls came crashing down around them.

Dora wasn't waiting for anything. As far as she was concerned, Biotecnica was a sunk cost, a completed case study. She didn't have as much money as she'd planned, but she had enough. She smiled to herself. She had almost reached critical mass, the dream of every business school student: enough money so that you could invest it and live on the income, retiring while young enough to enjoy your profits. Four million wasn't quite it, but every business venture was different. You had to thrive on chaos.

That was the part that Dayton had never understood. For him, the whole deal had been about ego. She had listened with every appearance of acceptance to his rants and rages about the "prostitution of the best and the brightest," the "trading on the Harvard name," but inwardly she had judged him and found him fatally lacking in cool.

Falling in love with Van had been his worst mistake—that, and killing him. Dora felt only contempt for Moore's weakness.

"Will the first-class passengers on Flight 467 to San Juan, Puerto Rico, and Gros' Anges Island please board at Gate 17?" The mellifluous voice of the stewardess cut short Dora's reverie. She gathered up her bags and headed out the door to freedom.

/ / /

In the paneled boardroom, the Administrative Board meeting was drawing to a close. "Miss Isaacs!" Gustavus Mims had grown impatient. "We have other matters to attend to this morning. We would greatly appreciate the courtesy of an answer."

Toni looked at him, her expression all polite curiosity. "I just feel that I don't understand the situation. If the university has done nothing wrong, why is it so important that I stay quiet?"

Mims scrutinized her closely, then began, with wary impatience, to explain. "The world of finance is a sensitive one, Miss Isaacs, and the power of rumor and innuendo is not to be underestimated. And"—he shrugged—"who can promise that our friends at Biotecnica are completely above reproach?"

"The important thing is damage control," interrupted Philip van Rensselaer. He gripped the edge of the heavy oak table, his knuckles bloodless and white.

"Mr. van Rensselaer is nothing if not discreet," Mims said with a humorless chuckle. "There are certain financial-disclosure issues. No one would go to jail, and the financial liability would be minuscule compared to the university's holdings." His gesture encompassed the boardroom, its fine art, its priceless antiques. "But our responsibility is a more abstract one. Harvard cannot afford a scandal of this kind. We have more than three centuries of prestige at stake, and we will not lose that because of your misguided passions." Mims sat absolutely still, his eyes fixed on Toni's.

"I'm beginning to see what you mean," she said, and took a sip of water.

/   /   /

Dayton Moore was less than thrilled by the reception he was getting for what was usually a surefire lecture. "The Economy of Shame" was one of his best, but it just wasn't up to par today. He raised his voice a little, tried to make more eye contact with the students, but he could sense that he was losing their attention. He glanced again at his watch: twenty-eight minutes to go. Maybe he should just let them out early.

"The French novelist Jean Genet called them 'the subterranean people.' People like himself—a thief, a homosexual, a prostitute, and a police informer. People society would sooner bury and forget about." Moore lost his thread for a second, as the door to the lecture hall opened and two men walked in.

They came down the aisle toward him, and he saw they wore the navy blue uniforms of the Cambridge Police Department. An icy fist clenched in his chest. Something had gone very, very wrong.

"The French novelist Jen John—I mean, John John—I mean, Jean Genet . . ." Moore spluttered to a halt. What *did* he mean? The police officers continued to advance, and his words were drowned in the buzz of excitement that rose from the students.

"It must be some kind of role-playing thing," he heard a young woman inform her friend. "They did something like that in my roommate's Core class last year." Students across the auditorium were standing up for a better look, as the two men neared the lectern. Moore covered the microphone with his hand.

"We'd like you to come with us, Professor," said the taller of the two. Moore nodded, then uncovered the microphone and spoke into it for the last time. "I seem to have an appointment with these gentlemen," he said, with an ironic smile. His voice was easy, humorous; it charmed the students into instant silence. "I look forward to seeing you all very soon. Enjoy your"—he checked his watch—"twenty-six minutes of unexpected freedom!" With a graceful gesture, he stretched out his wrists for the policemen to handcuff, and walked with them up the aisle as they recited the litany of his rights.

The doors closed on a roar of talk from the packed auditorium; just as he was being led out of the building, Dayton Moore laughed to hear a familiar sound: his students were applauding.

/ / /

"What is your answer, Miss Isaacs?" Van Rensselaer's impatience had passed the limits of endurance.

Toni folded and refolded her hands. When she spoke, she formed each word with care. "Well . . . first of all, I want to thank you gentlemen for taking the time to explain the situation so clearly. I must admit, I hadn't understood how much Harvard had to lose in this matter." She looked around the table, and noticed a self-satisfied smile on each face—except for Sterling Kwok's. "And I want you to know that what you've told me has made me even more convinced that I did the right thing."

"That you *will* do the right thing," murmured Gustavus Mims.

"No, Mr. Mims; I chose my words carefully." Toni leaned back in her chair. Choice did exist. She was making one. "I'm sorry to have wasted your time, gentlemen, but I think you should know that I have already shared a full dossier of information on Biotecnica and its illegal activities, on the involvement of a faculty member in the death of a student, and on the university's knowledge of and collusion in some serious criminal activities."

"Shared information?" Van Rensselaer turned a dusky burgundy as he momentarily forgot to breathe. "You couldn't have. You've been under surveillance." Mims scowled at his colleague.

"Oh, I'm well aware of that, Mr. van Rensselaer. But you underestimated me. I'm sure the Federal Express clerks at the Government Center office will remember a young woman bringing in a number of packages shortly before closing time last night—packages addressed to *The Wall Street Journal, The New York Times,* the U.S. Food and Drug Administration, the office of the U.S. Attorney ... Do I need to go on?" Toni silently thanked Chelo for responding perfectly to Rivera's cryptic request that she turn in her roommate's "homework." The contingency plan she had dreamed up the night she was researching the Portfolio had worked. Later, she would thank Chelo in person. For being the smartest, most loving person she knew.

The room erupted in angry shouts. Toni stole a glance at Sterling Kwok, who was nodding at her in approval. He had never underestimated her. He had been so indirect in expressing his true intentions—but by now she had learned how certain games had to be played. It would be Kwok's victory, in part, when the Portfolio fell.

"Do you have any idea what you've done, young lady?" asked Gustavus Mims.

"I hope so," she answered, standing up and carefully smoothing her skirt. Before he could continue, the door burst open, and an anxious Mrs. Hale ran in.

"The office is full of reporters! Television cameras! I don't know what to do." Mims stood and made for the door, but was stopped by van Rensselaer.

"I'll handle this, Gustavus," he said, straightening his tie as he reapplied his patrician cool for the press. "I believe you have a letter of resignation to write." Accompanied by his Brooks Brothers hangers-on, the elderly Brahmin swept out of the room.

Mims turned to Toni in a fury. "I hope you realize what you've done, Antonia Isaacs. You'll regret this when you're older."

Toni stood her ground. "I guess it's a good thing I'm not older, then." With a slight wave to Sterling Kwok, who was doing his best to calm his hyperventilating secretary, she took her leave.

Outside the room, she watched for a moment in fascination as crowds of reporters swarmed around van Rensselaer. His face was a mask of correctness and concern as he answered their questions with vague platitudes and evasions. She shrugged and swung open one of the heavy glass doors, sandblasted with the university shield and motto: Veritas. The men in that room had forgotten what they once surely had understood: that the truth had its own power, made its own rules. It was not for her or for anyone else to control.

Toni blinked for a minute in the bright sunshine, then saw the reporters—not as many as surrounded van Rensselaer, but enough to block her way. Broadcast networks were rolling vans onto the carefully preserved turf of the Yard; parka-clad field producers swilled coffee and barked orders into cell phones.

"Is it true that Harvard was involved in secret drug testing?" Someone stuck a microphone in her face, and she waved it away.

"What about your own arrest for prostitution, and the rumors that Harvard students have been part of a campus-wide sex ring?" She stared blankly at the eager young reporter, shook her head, and pushed on past.

"What are you going to do now?" an older woman called after her.

Toni paused, considering the question. "Go to the library," she answered. "Maybe I can learn something." She swung her bookbag onto her shoulder and continued walking under the barren elms, past the unchanging brick and ivy of Harvard Yard.

ACKNOWLEDGMENTS

Our deepest gratitude goes to our editor, Jon Karp, who saw our destination and showed us how to get there. Every author, collective or otherwise, should be so fortunate.

Special thanks to Lynne Turner and Paul Singer, who lent us their Illinois farmhouse one wintry week in 1992 and gave all of us—related or not—parental support.

Holly Adiele, Jason Mazzone ('93), and Rachel Singer Sullivan carefully read the manuscript in many versions, providing us with both much-needed criticism and kudos.

Aya de Leon ('87) made many thoughtful suggestions, as did Polly Arenberg, Bob Bergman, Eirene Chen, Lynn Chrisman, Joel Derfner ('95), David Deschamps, Lawrence Eaton, Celeste Gobeille, Rob Goff, Gail Gorman, Kristiana Helmick, Joy Henry Hinton ('84), Roma Kusznir (M.B.A. '93), Yan Liu, Tom Madden, Nicole Martel, Jocelyn Melcher ('92), Teresa Melcher, Cam Peters, Henry Robles, Steven Saylor, Laura Serna (M. Div. '97), Adrienne Su ('89), Jerry Sullivan, Deborah Thompson, Linda Tognetti, Holley Vantrease, Diane Wachtell ('83), Sharon Whitt ('88), Rob Wood, Catherine Wuenschel, and Nan Zabala ('91).

Discussions with Davida McDonald ('92) and John Kole were invaluable in working out certain details of the plot. Many thanks to our focus-group participants: Kate Anderson ('84), Mridu Gulati ('93), Emmeline Kim Owyang ('93), Steve Rohde, and Damon Silvers ('86); and to Tom Haroldson ('88) for Grinfast and Diep Vuong ('87) for a last-minute save.

We are indebted to Ellen Reeves ('83) and Jeffrey Goldberg for pointing us in Jon Karp's direction. Our appreciation also to Professor Catherine Clinton ('73), who has always given good advice and continues to do so.

Like a thoughtful college counselor, our agent, Liz Fowler ('84), found us before we had reached our potential and helped us put our best foot forward. Thanks to Nancy Kates ('84) for making the introduction. And, of course, we are grateful to everyone at Palmer and Dodge.

For most of our lives, we had little awareness of the tremendous service that talented copy editors provide to society. Now we know better. Thank you, Jolanta Benal. And finally, our gratitude to Benjamin Dreyer, who shepherded *The Student Body* through the production process with unflappable patience and professionalism.

ABOUT JANE HARVARD

JANE HARVARD is four authors who graduated from Harvard College in 1986, the school's 350th year. Before attending Harvard, the four were educated in public schools.

FAITH ADIELE serves as the Christa McAuliffe Chair/Visiting Professor in English at Framingham State College. A former fellow at the MacDowell Colony and Ragdale Foundation, she has published in *Ploughshares, Ms.,* and anthologies from Norton, Beacon, Doubleday, and Routledge presses. Adiele lives in Somerville, Massachusetts, where she is at work on a memoir about growing up Nigerian/Scandinavian in Washington State.

MICHAEL FRANCISCO MELCHER is a securities lawyer in New York City. Raised in Orange County, California, he earned JD and MBA degrees at Stanford University, where he wrote, produced, and directed several musical parodies of law-school life. Along with another business-school classmate, Melcher created and edited the *Stephanopouletter*, a political fanzine. Before practicing law, he was a foreign service officer with the U.S. Information Agency in India and Taiwan.

BENNETT SINGER has served as producer or associate producer on a number of nationally broadcast PBS documentary series, including *Eyes on the Prize: America at the Racial Crossroads* and *With God on Our Side: The Rise of the Religious Right in America.* He is the editor of the award-winning *Growing Up Gay/Growing Up Lesbian: A Literary Anthology* and an editor of *Voices of Freedom: An Oral History of the Civil Rights*

Movement. At Harvard, he was executive editor of the *Independent,* a campus weekly. A Chicago native, Singer lives in Brooklyn, New York, and currently works as executive editor of *Time* magazine's education program.

JULIA SULLIVAN has been a freelance writer, translator, and editor for the past ten years. She has taught American literature, medieval studies, and science fiction at Rutgers University; her work as a playwright and librettist has been read and staged throughout the Northeast and in England. A native of Massachusetts, Sullivan is currently employed as director of communications at Cambridge College, and is the editor of the forthcoming *incandescence: an online magazine of the arts.*